Praise for *A Cou*

"Power's deep knowledge of Indigenou[...] [...]gh in keen depictions of the Indian schools, [...] she illuminates the characters' struggles with generational trauma, which arise as they try to sustain their connections to the past. This story of survival shines brightly."

—*Publishers Weekly* (starred review)

"*A Council of Dolls* reached out, grabbed me, and did not let go. Power's ability to make language sing, cry, scream, and laugh illuminates this heart-stopper of a book that shines a light into the dark corners of America's history. I wanted the generational journey I was taking with these unforgettable characters—and their dolls—to never end. Read it—and be healed."

—Marie Myung-Ok Lee, author of *The Evening Hero*

"*A Council of Dolls* absorbs through the skin, enters the bone, and disperses through the psyche—it perfectly captures the internal roots of the Native experience. Through the lives of three Dakota women, we grapple with the emotional, psychological, and spiritual toll on Indigenous peoples enduring an often brutal system and, moreover, how strength, healing, and love reverberate down each passing generation to dispense hope and resiliency. I cannot more highly recommend Power's newest masterpiece."

—Oscar Hokeah, PEN/Hemingway Award–winning author of *Calling for a Blanket Dance*

"Moving. . . . Hypnotic."

—*Star Tribune* (Minneapolis)

"Mona Susan Power's new novel is an honor song to the love and strength of Native families and our stories, to our brilliant selves.

I couldn't have known how much I needed the wisdom and offerings of these pages."

—Kelli Jo Ford, author of *Crooked Hallelujah*

"This tender and magical novel will stay with me for a long time. Mona Susan Power writes with dazzling empathy. The result is a heartrending and many-layered narrative, a captivating story which is also a thrilling testimonial to the power of stories."

—Margot Livesey, author of *The Boy in the Field*

"A resplendent novel about the spirited lives of three inspiring women who endure significant change and hardship. Each story [was] so deeply compelling I wanted to read quickly, but was magnetized by the transformative power of each voice. A mighty, dazzling whirlwind of storytelling. These stories lift from the page. Prepare to stay up all night. *A Council of Dolls* is mesmerizing. Take a deep breath! Mona Susan Power can peer into darkness and transform it."

—Debra Magpie Earling, author of *The Lost Journals of Sacajewea*

"A work of exquisite beauty and courageous truth-telling, and an unforgettable homage to ancestral suffering and strength."

—Sheila O'Connor, author of *Evidence of V*

A Council of Dolls

A Council of Dolls

A Novel

Mona Susan Power

MARINER BOOKS

New York Boston

A COUNCIL OF DOLLS. Copyright © 2023 by Mona Susan Power. All rights reserved. Printed in the United States of America. No part of this book may be used or reproduced in any manner whatsoever without written permission except in the case of brief quotations embodied in critical articles and reviews. For information, address HarperCollins Publishers, 195 Broadway, New York, NY 10007.

HarperCollins books may be purchased for educational, business, or sales promotional use. For information, please email the Special Markets Department at SPsales@harpercollins.com.

A hardcover edition of this book was published in 2023 by Mariner Books.

FIRST MARINER BOOKS PAPERBACK EDITION PUBLISHED 2024.

Designed by Lucy Albanese

The Library of Congress has catalogued a previous edition as follows:

Names: Power, Susan, 1961- author.
Title: A council of dolls : a novel / Mona Susa Power.
Description: First edition. | New York : Mariner an imprint of
   HarperCollins Publishers, 2023.
Identifiers: LCCN 2022031117 | ISBN 9780063281097 (hardcover) | ISBN
   9780063281110 (ebook)
Subjects: LCGFT: Novels.
Classification: LCC PS3566.O83578 C68 2023 | DDC 813/.54—dc23/
   eng/20220808
LC record available at https://lccn.loc.gov/2022031117

ISBN 978-0-06-328110-3 (pbk.)

24 25 26 27 28 LBC 5 4 3 2 1

For my ancestors

Contents

PART 1

Naming Ceremony

Sissy ~ 1960s

It's the spring of 1969 here in Chicago, and Mama says Old Mayor Daley has his big fists wrapped around our necks. She says he doesn't care about brown people like us. "If this city had a proper name, it would be 'Prejudiced, Illinois,'" Mama tells me while she braids my hair. I'm in the second grade at school, so I know what that word is all about. It's a mean word that says we can't eat in just any restaurant, even if my parents have enough money, and we can't move to just any neighborhood. If I got to name our city, I'd call it "Sweetland," because sometimes you have to be nice to people and places and dolls if you want them to be nice back. Though it doesn't always work.

I almost forget what *my* real name is. I have so many names. When Mama's in a good mood, she calls me Sissy or Prunella— after one of Cinderella's wicked stepsisters. I think she's the sister whose knee cracks. Mine doesn't. They play the Cinderella show on TV every year, and one year Mama promised we were gonna watch it together. "It's a big musical," she said. "You'll love it!" She forgot I'd already seen it and knew all the songs by heart. But when I spilled a glass of milk at the dinner table—my hand knocked it over since I can be clumsy like that—Mama said, "No TV!" She said I had to learn to be more careful but changed her mind later when Dad asked her to let me watch. I only missed a little bit, the opening number.

I feel funny when I hear new songs, almost like I forget to breathe. Can you walk inside a song? I think I do.

Mama says I have a "Christian name," though we left the church in a huff a few months back, when Mama shared in confession that she never felt the presence of anything sacred except at the Sun Dance we go to in North Dakota at summer solstice—the one Mama says is "private" because it's illegal. Dad said she was looking for trouble to say such things to old Father Weasel (his name isn't really Weasel). Mama gave him a look, and he went quiet. I know what he was trying to say. Sometimes Mama's in a mood she can't keep all to herself; she has to spread it around. She'll pick a fight with anyone, and it's no use tiptoeing, being sweet and well-behaved, because she'll get you on that, ask why everyone walks on eggshells near her like she's a crazy person. Then you're in the doghouse.

She spread her mood on Father Weasel during her last confession. She even pushed up the sleeve of her nice gray going-to-church dress to show the priest her scars from a flesh sacrifice, though he probably couldn't see much through the screen that separates him from us. And when Father Weasel told her the Sun Dance is Devil's work, she said if Jesus had made his own Sun Dance at the end, maybe we'd be in better shape. Father Weasel lost his head and told Mama she was beyond penance. I heard him, since I was in a nearby pew saying five Hail Marys and two Our Fathers for confessing that I was sometimes angry with Mama in my thoughts. Mama grabbed my arm and dragged me out of church, and I never finished saying penance, so I guess I'm still carrying around that sin of anger inside me, with nowhere to let it out.

Mama reminds me that I have a Dakhóta name, too, on top of the Christian one. She says Grandma gave it to me in a ceremony the year she lived with us. I wish she was still here, with her soft hands and smiles and nice back rubs when I couldn't fall asleep right away at bedtime. I miss her stories about the day Sitting Bull was killed, how she was three years old, yet she remembered *everything*. But Grandma didn't like it in Chicago; she said all that noise hurt her head. So she went back to North Dakota, back to what she calls "buffalo country," though I've never seen any buffalo there. Only one I ever saw is stuffed and dead at the Field Museum. He doesn't look so happy. I should give him a name the next time I see him.

As much as I love Grandma, I'm different from her when it comes to how I see our city. I like falling asleep to the noise of honking cars and sirens, grown-ups laughing as they walk down the street. Noise makes me feel safe, reminds me that there are people all around and I'm not alone. North Dakota scares me at night when the indoor lights go out and the stars switch on—a million more of them than I ever see in Chicago. The hills and towns where my relatives live get quiet, so quiet all you hear is your breath as you try to sleep. I start to imagine there's nothing outside but ghosts watching my every move. Even by day North Dakota feels strange to me because there aren't as many people, and all the ones I've seen are either white or Indian. If they're white, they'll most likely stare at you as you walk into a store or a diner, as if you're part bug. I begin to miss our neighborhood in Old Town Gardens, where we have friends who are Black, white, and Indian, or have family from Japan or the Philippines or Mexico. They have names I've never heard before that take practice before I can say them right. Mama says it's important to "pronounce them correctly" because we don't want to be like the ones who change people's names when they think they're too hard.

I don't understand why Mama can be superpolite to friends, only using the name they want, while she has all kinds of bad names for Dad. Some of them I can't say because they're not nice and I'd get punished. When she calls him those names, her eyes are so red it looks like the whites are bleeding. She stomps around and throws things. One time she cracked the wall with a heavy pot. Another time she cracked my father's head, and he had to go to the hospital. I helped her clean the mess. I almost threw up. But when you're real scared, sometimes you can control that.

Now, when Mama's eyes get bright red, I crawl under my bed, a trick I learned when I was small. Dad and Mama were watching the news, and I could hear it, though I was playing with the Black doll I begged Dad to get me for Christmas since she looks more like us—closer to Indian than white dolls. She wriggles just the same as them when you pull the string on her back, and wears the same clothes. But I can tell the difference. I call her Ethel, after one of Mama's friends I think is nice. I was brushing Ethel's hair the way she likes when my parents went super quiet. Dad put down the book he's always reading and leaned in as if he couldn't believe his ears. My dad's favorite anchorman, the one who puts his glasses on when things get serious, was talking about a guy named Speck. Which is one of Mama's choice words when she's cleaning the floors, going to war against those specks. Every time they mentioned his name, I saw a black spot in my mind, a dark smudge on the wall there. He'd killed eight student nurses right here in our city, but another survived because she made herself real small under the bed.

Dad noticed I was listening and motioned to me. But Mama said, "She's only four. She won't remember any of this." So they kept watching the news and I kept brushing Ethel's slick hair, thinking all the time about smudges on the wall and hiding somewhere so death can't find you.

Dad has a long name I didn't used to say right: Cornelius. If someone asked me, "Who is your father?" I'd have said, "Corny," because the rest was too big to get past baby teeth. For as long as I can remember, I've gotten strange ideas in my head. One of my strange ideas is to picture Dad's name backward, as Kneeling Corn. Sometimes I see it as the corn kneeling, yellow cob almost cracked in half as it bows to itself. Other times I see my dad kneeling on corn, which must be painful. But he stays down there because it's safer than standing up and facing Mama.

Both my parents are tall, my father Lakȟóta tall from South Dakota, my mother Dakhóta tall from North Dakota. Dad was in the Korean War, fought near a place called the Yalu River. Mama wrote the name down for me, along with the name of Dad's medals and his marine unit. She said I should be proud of him, as if I wasn't. She said he was so tough, being an Indian from the Dakotas, that he could stand the cold better than most troops, and he wasn't too fussy to eat anything. No one thought he'd come home alive, but he did. His older brother died over there, the one Mama was supposed to marry. The one she said should have been my father. She said it real quiet when she thought I was asleep. But I heard her. I wonder who I would be if my uncle had been my dad. Maybe I wouldn't be Sissy, who dreams herself into songs, who spills her milk at dinner, who makes Mama so angry. I have a bunch of secret thoughts, and one of them is that I'm glad Dad is my father, even if it means I have to be Sissy and not the better version Mama wishes I'd be.

Dad lets me sit on his lap sometimes when he's reading, and now I can read along, but he used to let me pretend, when I was too little to figure out the words. He doesn't mind when I latch an arm around his neck and rest on him like he's my pillow. I like to look over at Mama, sitting on the couch. She's reading, too. And I pretend she's the one I'm hugging. I try to love them both the same. But with Mama, I have to picture what it looks like in my head because it's the only place she lets me show her. She doesn't like to be touched.

If I was allowed, I'd run my finger across Mama's face the way I do with Christmas bulbs to feel their shine. I bet Dad would like that, too, since he says she's more beautiful than any actress in Hollywood. She sticks her tongue out when he says that and waves her hand like she's shooing flies. I don't know why she doesn't see what we do when she looks in the mirror: how her long face Dad calls a "perfect oval" is smooth as dark cream with a dimple in her chin that gives it fight. She has black hair shiny as crow feathers, and long eyelashes that brush down her cheeks when she's sleeping. Watching Mama makes me miserable sometimes because I don't think I'll ever look like her. Everyone says I'm cute, like Grandma, with a heart face and brown eyes that crinkle when I smile. People say both me and Grandma are "sincere," even in our looks. Which I guess means we try hard.

Mama calls me her shadow, so that's another name. She says I'm always underfoot, but I can't help it when she takes me everywhere. She doesn't like to be alone. She tells stories about what she was like at my age, when she was seven years old. How she went to Indian boarding school with her sisters, but they were older, so they slept on a different floor. How she cried and cried until some Ree girls almost smothered her with a pillow. She always stops the story there and says to be careful around Arikaras, the ones she calls Rees, because they used to be our enemies. I nod and tell her I'll remember. There was a nun who was mean to her because she didn't like that Mama was smart and that she'd taught herself to read before she ever went to school. The nun locked her up in a dark closet when she knew all the answers, because she was supposed to be dumb. She told her the Devil was in there with her, and Mama sassed back that she didn't care.

"But I did," she admits. "I was scared of the Devil. I held perfectly still for however many hours I was locked in there. And sometimes, I swear I could feel his hot breath going up my neck, and my skin would burn, like it touched fire." She tells me I'm lucky to have teachers who *want* me to learn, instead of nuns who want to keep me down. But I can't imagine anyone keeping Mama down, not even Dad, a marine with medals. She's the only person I know who grows when she gets mad, gets bigger and bigger until it's like she fills the whole room, and there's no air left to breathe.

Mama likes spooky movies. Not Dad. He says he's seen enough to scare him for the rest of his life. So, I watch them with her. We have an old TV that flickers and makes everyone in the film look shaky. Mama lets me hold Ethel while we watch, though I keep her turned away from the screen because I don't want her to be scared. We see movies about ghosts and about angry men who kill people and try to get away with it. We see movies about monsters with sharp teeth, mummies wrapped in what looks like toilet paper, and creatures called zombies that are alive and dead at the same time. You don't want them to bite you. Even though Mama doesn't say so, I remind myself to be careful of zombies. I guess they must worry me because I had a nightmare after that show. The dream started out fine. I was walking in the park that's hidden in the center of our building complex, and it was a shiny day, the sun nice and warm so I could wear my favorite dress that has what Mama calls "spaghetti straps" instead of sleeves. I was walking by myself, something she would never let me do when I'm awake. There weren't any people around, but then I saw a puppy on the path ahead, a tiny, curly-haired poodle the color of Mama's gray going-to-church dress. It had a funny fur-do on its head, a little puff like a cloud, held together with a red ribbon. I named it even though it didn't belong to me. I called it Judy. Judy stared like she heard me think up the name for her. She grinned at me with tiny puppy teeth. She was the cutest puppy I've ever seen. She picked up something in her mouth and tried to run with it, but it was too big and kept tripping her. So I went over to save her all the work. When I got close, she dropped the thing in her mouth as if she was giving me a present. I started to reach for it until I saw it was a long finger still wearing a turquoise ring like the one my dad gave my mother. Judy grinned at me again, and I saw there was something wrong with her. She was a zombie poodle with bloodstained fur, and if I wasn't careful, she would bite me! What I did surprised me, but it worked like magic. I started singing my favorite song, "Over the Rainbow." And Judy sat as if I'd trained her and stopped chewing on the finger. When I got to the last line of the song, the one that ends with a question nobody ever answers, I woke up.

I don't tell Mama about my nightmares. She doesn't like to hear what bothers me. So nightmares get piled up next to my angry thoughts, which don't get cleared away by penance anymore. I didn't think I'd miss confession or receiving the Host on my tongue, which the big kids had scared me would taste like raw liver, though it really tasted like nothing but old crackers. I'd just had my First Holy Communion two months before we left the church in a huff, and during the time we were still there, it was a relief to share those angry thoughts with someone outside my head. I especially wish I could sort them out with Father Weasel after I see the scariest movie of all, one Mama has me stay up late to watch with her. She even makes me nap earlier in the day, so I'll be wide awake past my bedtime. Dad is asleep when the movie starts. She has me read the title aloud, the list of actors' names as they come on the screen, so I can practice my reading skills. Pretty soon, the names are going by too quickly and I can't keep up, and Mama laughs and laughs because she says I sound like I'm speed-talking. But then we get quiet because the story is all about a mother and her daughter, a little girl named Rhoda. At first, I think the little girl is perfect, the kind of kid my mother wants; she never spills things or dances at the wrong time. But after a while I figure out she's like the zombie poodle in my dream: if you get close enough you see there's something wrong, and you'd better look out. Rhoda doesn't think twice about hurting people to get what she wants. She's scarier than ghosts or monsters, because at least you can see them coming. I get a new name after Mama and I watch that movie. She starts calling me "Bad Seed." You wouldn't think I'd like that, but she smiles when she uses the name and even swipes my nose with the end of one of my braids like we're playing.

Mama's teaching me to do housework because she says she kept Grandma's cabin clean back when she was a kid. It was all on her shoulders, since her brothers and sisters didn't want to waste the day trying to clear out the "damn flies" and keep the place free of all the dirt raining on them since they lived in the Dust Bowl. Mama does the floors, and I do the dusting with old rags that were clothes until Mama couldn't patch them anymore. I dust everything I can reach and stand on a chair when I can't. Mama laughs at how I look, wrapped up in one of her aprons that's too big. She says I'm a hausfrau, like one of those German wives she saw living on her reservation, the ones who'd spent a long time living in Russia, so people got confused and called them "Rooshians." "Hausfrau" is my cleaning name.

I'm careful when I'm dusting, try not to walk into a song in my head, try to be graceful like my favorite ballerina, Maria Tallchief, and not a clumsy mess. But I'm not perfect like Rhoda. One day I slip when I'm reaching up to replace a Hopi pottery bird Dad bought Mama at a powwow. The bird is one of my favorite things, a dark baked red with black designs on her open wings. Her back forms a dish, though we never put anything in it; that would cover the squiggles of art. Since I don't know any Hopi names, I call the bird "Julie Andrews," imagine her flying through that song

"Climb Every Mountain," carrying me with her. I'm probably humming that tune in my head when I fall off the chair and take the bird with me. It flies out of my hand and crashes on the hard linoleum floor that Mama keeps so shiny, without specks. Julie Andrews cracks into two big pieces. *I* don't crack in half, but some part of me wishes I had. Mama comes running when she hears the noise, and now she calls me the name she never uses, the Christian one we walked away from in a huff. The name sounds angry, like it's a pair of flying scissors that will shear off my hair or even cut my arms like a flesh sacrifice. Mama is howling over the pieces of Julie Andrews, and when she looks up at me, her eyes are red. For the first time, I put together that story about the Devil keeping her company in the school closet with the color of her eyes when she's mad. Maybe the Devil drops in again when I make mistakes. Maybe he wants me to be perfect, the way Mama does. But I thought it was God who wanted that, not the Devil. I tell myself to shut up because Mama is moving toward me now. I run to my bedroom that is small as a dark closet and zoom under the bed, crouch in the back corner away from Mama's hands. It's a heavy old bed that somebody left when they moved out because it was too hard to carry away. Even Mama and the power of her red eyes can't lift that bed, though she tries to thwack at me with a broom. I just push it away when the bristles attack. I don't come out from under the bed until Mama gives up and has been quiet for a long time. By then she's glued Julie Andrews back together. And every time I look at her, I feel bad for breaking her back. You can see the crack that runs straight through her.

Dad shows me his name in the paper when a big article of his gets published. He writes at a newspaper for a living. Mama says I should be proud of him for being the first person in his family to go to college, the first Indian to work for a major Chicago rag. As if I'm not proud of him. He doesn't get too many big stories in the paper, so we don't make much money. But that never bothers me the way it does Mama. She hates living over a drugstore that has a small diner in the back. She hates the constant smell of chicken noodle soup that comes up through the floors. But I like the sound of the machine that whips up ice cream malts. It's a friendly noise that makes my mouth water. And the druggist who owns the shop is always nice to me, gives me a gold foil–wrapped toffee when no one is looking. I keep the wrappers in my secret hiding place, and every now and then I take them out and count them. Today there are twenty-four. I pretend they're worth a million dollars each and then fall over laughing because I can't imagine that much money in the world when every penny in our family is so important. Mama checks on me to see what's so funny, and I have to sit on the wrappers quick, to keep her from noticing them. I give her a polite smile and shake of the head, just like that perfect girl, Rhoda. Mama shrugs and goes back to whatever she was doing.

She must be cooking something with hamburger because I can smell the meat. I hold Ethel up to sniff the air. We're both hungry. Mama calls me into the kitchen. Today I'm Prunella instead of Sissy.

"Prunella, you're big enough to set the table," she says, and she nods at a pile of dishes and silverware, and my father's favorite coffee cup. One by one I carry each piece as carefully as I can, pretending I'm as perfect as Rhoda was before she went mean. I'm so scared of messing up, I hold my breath the way Dad taught me when he showed me how to swim. Mama says I'm too slow, but I don't care. And when a tune goes off in my head, the sad one from *Carousel* about walking through storms, I tell it to go away. Dinner is about ready by the time I finish my job, and I've held my breath so hard for so long, I feel stuffed with air. I'm not hungry anymore. Ethel tells me to eat, and it's a surprise. I'm supposed to be *her* mama, not the other way around.

Dad says Mama and I are glued together, but he's teasing. Dad and I aren't alone much, so I'm excited when Mama says we're on our own for dinner because she's got a meeting. We're not really on our own, though. Mama's got some vegetables and chipped beef for us to heat up when we're hungry. Dad tries to hug Mama as she grabs her purse and heads out the door, but she ducks under his arm so quick he's left standing there, holding nothing. He sees me watching and smiles.

"Your mom's off rabble-rousing," he says. One of his arms is still open, so I slide into it. He scoops me up. I'm so high in the air against his chest that I almost drop Ethel. Dad carries us to his reading chair, and all three of us sit down, one on top of the other. Ethel makes a face at me like she's sick, and I make a *sorry* face back at her. She doesn't like being swooped around.

"I shouldn't have said that." Dad pushes my hair behind my ears. "Your mama is great at fighting for us, fighting for our community. Sometimes people take their anger and use it in a good way."

Yes, I agree with my father in my head. *Mama is a good fighter.* Though I don't tell him what I'm thinking since I don't want to bring up a subject that makes him tired. Mama wins most arguments in our family, but every now and then she battles with Dad over the one she lost when I was born. She longs to leave for work every day just like he does, and when Dad points out everything she does at home to keep us afloat, including taking in typing assignments for a friend during tax time, she makes a disgusted sound with her teeth. One of her favorite comments is: "You and your darned socks! You think they mean anything in the grand scheme of things?!" Mama isn't cussing when she says this; she has a darning egg made of wood that she uses to mend the holes in Dad's old socks. He wears them down from being on his feet so much, rushing after important stories.

Mama gets wound up and argues like she's giving a speech. I've learned a lot from her angry shouts about the mayor, the president, and our whole stinking government—how Indians are lured to big cities to turn us into white people and make sure we lose what's left of our land. "That's something worthy of my time," she says, "striking a blow against injustice!" Sometimes Dad's voice is so quiet it's hard for me to hear everything he's saying to calm her down. I only catch bits and pieces, and usually the words make me sad because Dad says *I'm* the reason she should stay at home, *I* should have the guidance and safety they never had, taken away to Indian boarding schools when they were so young. There's a word he uses that I don't understand because I miss too much of what he says around it: "indoctrination." He wants Mama to keep me away from those kinds of doctors or teachers who will do worse than take my land: they'll steal my spirit. Mama must love me very much to let Dad win this fight; she must want to protect some part of me that I can't even see.

With all those angry memories banging around my head, I don't feel like talking. I just listen. I lean against Dad's chest and like how my head goes up and down with his breathing. I hold Ethel the same way. Her head goes up and down, too. Dad asks me something he never asked before: "Is Mama nice to you when I'm not around?"

His question scares me, so I close my eyes.

"You know she loves you?"

I'm a dead rock. I don't move.

"She had it so hard growing up. Saw some awful things. A student died in that school she talks about."

Where the Devil sat with her in the closet? I almost speak what I'm thinking but can feel Ethel pinch my hand like she's trying to warn me. Mama might not like me telling Dad one of her stories. I didn't know someone died there. I wonder if Sister Frances had anything to do with it. Mama still hates Sister Frances the most, even though she's supposedly been dead a long time. That nun would sniff at Mama right after she stepped out of the shower and tell her, "You stink. Wash yourself again." She tripped Mama once when she was going down the stairs, then looked away like it was just Mama being clumsy. Mama chipped her tooth, and she said she looked like a wolf on that side of her mouth until someone filed it down for her. Sister Frances is always the boogeyman in Mama's school stories, which makes me wonder if some part of her is still alive, chasing old students like a monster that never gets tired. One thing I've learned from scary movies is that monsters might be slow, but they never give up until you kill them.

Dad asks me again, "Is Mama good to you?" And my head is filled with so many pictures. Mama brushing my hair and teaching me to bake oatmeal cookies. Mama chasing me under the bed with her red eyes, her mean words. Mama surprising me one night when I'm sick, so sick I wonder if I'm making it all up? No. I see her sitting in the dark with me, singing a song that begins, "Go to sleep, my little owlet." I don't know what an owlet is, but it sounds nice. Her voice is so different, my eyes are crying. But when she sees the tears, she gets mad and says, "I can't do *anything* right!" And she slams out of my room. Then I really cry because Mama took it wrong. She thought I was upset when it was just all this love for her pouring out of my eyes.

So I tell Dad, "Yes." And I can feel Ethel nod her head yes, too, though after Dad puts us to bed, she whispers that she crossed her fingers because it was a lie.

◆ ◆ ◆

Mama has a new friend. We visit him during the day when Dad is at work and Mama's sick of "playing housewife." She likes to say, "I'm not Myrtle from the suburbs," though I can't think of any Myrtles we know. Her friend, Ben, is a photographer who lives one entry over in our Old Town Gardens complex that covers a whole city block of connected apartment buildings. He has a daughter named Brooke who is a year older than me. She doesn't look like she belongs to him—his hair is gray and curly while hers is long and silvery blond like a princess's. We play in her room while Mama and Ben visit in his.

"You must be rich," I told Brooke the first time I saw her room, filled with books in a bookcase, and a dollhouse as tall as I am.

"Nah, my parents are divorced," she said, as if that was an answer. "All this is loot."

I didn't understand but let it go to be polite.

Today Mama and I go over to Ben's place earlier than usual, even before we've straightened the apartment. We leave the breakfast dishes in the sink, which never happens, because Mama says it's a sin.

Ben doesn't look at me as he ushers us through the door—his eyes are full of Mama, who is a great beauty according to everyone, including me.

"Well, look at you," he says, and bows and offers his hand, spins her into the hallway as if they're going to dance. Mama puts a stop to that, but she smiles at Ben as she sidesteps his footwork.

Brooke peeks out of her room and beckons me over. I've brought Ethel this time because I like Brooke and don't think she'll be mean to Ethel. Sometimes Ethel gets funny looks from people, which makes me angry. She's a beautiful doll, a small baby with chubby cheeks and wide, curious brown eyes. Mama said she's so small because she's just a "preemie." When I asked her what that meant she said a baby who is born too soon, so they're not fully developed. But I think Ethel is developed just fine. And I like it that she isn't smiling, which shows what a thinker she is.

Ethel and I perch on Brooke's bed while she tiptoes to her closet and pulls out a small trunk. She's acting like whatever she's going to show me is top secret, which makes me super curious. Just as she's about to open the trunk, which looks brand-new, like it's never been opened before, Brooke notices Ethel.

"Who is this?" Brooke steps over to us and tips her head to one side as if she's trying to judge whether she and Ethel will get along.

"This is Ethel," I say proudly.

Brooke holds out her hand and, before I can react, she shakes Ethel's in a careful, delicate way because their hands are such different sizes.

I can feel Ethel sit up straighter, like she's preening on the inside.

"Ethel likes you," I tell Brooke. I surprise myself by adding, "She doesn't like everyone." I never thought about it before, how picky Ethel is when it comes to the people in my life. She either loves or hates them—no in-between. Maybe dolls don't have room for complicated feelings. "I'm very pleased to meet you," Brooke says. "Welcome to my humble abode."

I help Ethel bend over in a little bow, and quick as that, we're all good friends.

"What's that?" I can't help the curiosity rising in me as I stare at the small blue trunk, just large enough to contain a pair of girls' tap shoes.

"This is my birthday gift that I'm not supposed to know about yet." Brooke smiles. She has the most beautiful teeth. I never thought teeth could be pretty but hers are, like a good witch turned regular ones into pearls. "My mother sent this since she's abroad right now and I won't get to see her. Dad didn't even try to hide it—he tucked it behind coats in the front closet. It's exactly what I asked for." Brooke goes to the door and opens it a crack. Sticks her head out.

"All is quiet." She wrinkles her nose. "Well, not a hundred percent quiet, but only the sound of them doing their thing."

I don't ask what she means by this mysterious remark since I'm dying to see what's in the trunk.

"Voilà!" Brooke opens the trunk and sets it up so I can see the contents. On one side is a Mary Poppins doll—I recognize her immediately because she's wearing her black hat and blue coat and she has an umbrella in her hand. On the other side are the dresses she wore in the movie. I can't help but gasp. I didn't know little girls could own such perfect things. Then I feel bad for Ethel. She has only one dress and it's plain, a drab green like dusty leaves; no ruffles or ribbons sewn to look like flowers. I don't want her to see all she's missing, so I set her beside me where my body will block the view. Ethel grumbles under her breath but doesn't want to cause a fuss.

"I'd let you play with her, but I have to keep her brand-new until Dad officially presents her—that'll be another week. Then we can play with her all the time."

There is something serious about Brooke, something grown-up and exciting. I have the feeling she knows a lot of secrets about the adult world, things Ethel and I can only guess. I nod my head in wonder as Brooke stows away the incredible doll.

As if to conjure magic of my own I tell Brooke, "My dad took me to see that movie." I don't say that I was too little to remember much except that he let me eat Milk Duds, which Mama would never have allowed.

Brooke nods. "I almost peed during the laughing scene. When

the tea party gets stuck on the ceiling. Made me laugh and laugh. My parents were still together then." Brooke plucks a piece of fluff off her dress. "Why'd you go with your dad?" she asks. "Doesn't your mom like movies?"

"She loves movies, but only the scary ones, or the ones where someone dies, and everyone is crying at the end." I didn't say that when kid movies come to town, she makes Dad take me, says he doesn't spend enough time with me and it's our chance to get to know each other—as if we don't.

It's like Brooke can read my mind. "Yeah, your mom doesn't seem the type to do stuff she doesn't care about. She's a boss. At least, that's what Dad says."

Ethel is on alert—I can feel her straighten up with nerves. I could pinch myself for saying as much as I did. Mama might not like it. I'm not sure. I don't always know what will make her mad, and what will be just fine. Sometimes I expect her to toss a bomb and blow me up, though she ends up smiling. Other times I'll chatter some story and not realize until it's too late that she's gone really quiet. The kind of quiet where a fire is starting, and you don't yet smell the smoke.

Ethel whispers that I should change the subject, so I do.

I ask Brooke if her father has other friends that come over during the day, and when does he do his work?

Brooke wrinkles her nose again. "He works different times, there's no set schedule. He goes on assignment, which can be a day, an hour, and once it was a week. Right now, your mom is his main friend." She opens her mouth to say more, then shuts it quickly. It's like her mouth decided for her. She looks at me and I can feel a warmth there—her eyes are usually sharp blue, but they've gone a softer color, blue that has worn down to gray.

"I've always wanted a sister," she says.

Ethel makes a noisy swallowing sound. Ethel understands

something ahead of me and I'm angry that she should be as quick as Brooke. That makes me the slow one in the room. Or maybe I'm just the cautious one who doesn't want to open any door before I know what's behind it.

I nod because I don't want to be rude, but right now I don't want a sister because that would mean something's up with Ben and his daughter and my mother, something I'm not sure I'd like.

"My dad *really* likes your mom," Brooke says. Ethel coughs and I can interpret—it's one of her danger signals. I'm thinking we should go back to our apartment, me and Mom and Ethel, and see about those breakfast dishes. I'm beginning to understand why I didn't take to Ben even though he's never done anything wrong to me. I don't like the wart on his neck that reminds me of the bolts that stick out of Frankenstein's. I don't like the way he watches my mother as if she's an ice cream cone he wants to gobble in three bites—not caring if he gets a headache from the cold. I didn't want to say it before, because I like his daughter so much, but Ben gives me the creeps.

Turns out there is nothing to fear. Just as I'm thinking that Ben is *not* someone who should be Mama's friend, I hear a shout. The next few minutes are a bit crazy and to calm myself down I pretend we've fallen into a movie—not a fun one like *Mary Poppins* where penguins dance in a park, but a scarier one where Mama is calling my name in that voice that means: *jump!* So I do. I grab Ethel and I'm out of Brooke's room so fast I almost trip on the hall carpet. Mama's nice, ironed shirt is rumpled and not all the way tucked into her skirt and there's a splotch of blood running down the front. She's motioning me to hurry up, we're going to leave, but then Ben staggers out of his bedroom, pants off and something pink and wobbly hanging between his legs.

"You bith me!" he shouts. His mouth is bleeding pretty bad, and I can see part of his lower lip hanging off. There's so much blood in his mouth it's hard to understand what he's saying, but I think it's a lot of curses. Brooke doesn't seem too upset. She just turns around and goes back in her room, shuts her door on the racket.

Mama is angry. Her eyes are as red as the blood on her shirt. "I told you not to kiss my mouth!" she shouts at Ben. "I don't do that!" Then she grabs my arm and it's a good thing I have a decent grip on Ethel because Mama yanks the two of us out the door. We leave Ben and his broken mouth.

As soon as we get back to our place Mama whirls on me and shakes me by the shoulders, which means Ethel gets shaken, too. "Stop staring at me!" she orders, and I look down. There's a new scuff on one of my penny loafers. I wasn't even looking at her when she exploded, but I know better than to "contradict," one of Mama's favorite words when I try to explain myself.

"Stop being so nosy!" Another shake. I might not understand all that happened with Mama and her friend, but I know it's one of her mysteries I'm meant to leave alone. So, I take Ethel into our room and comb her hair. She's as nervous as Mama, jittery. Her baby teeth are chattering. I whisper a word to her that Grandma crooned when I was little and couldn't fall asleep: "Ábu." I draw it out slowly, over and over, like chanting a magic spell. It works. I can hear Mama moving around the bathroom, taking a shower, but Ethel has closed up and gone to sleep. She snores softly, like a baby, and never lets go of my finger.

In coming days Brooke and I wave when we see each other in the park behind the building. But Mama and I don't visit her again, so I never get to play with Mary Poppins. Even though I like Brooke, I feel sick to my stomach when I remember the way her father looked when he shouted at Mama as we ran out of his apartment, how the blood dripped off him. I'm just fine with losing out on making friends with the new doll. I ask Ethel if she's sad about that and she says no. She says that some situations are just more trouble than they're worth and, besides, Mary Poppins looks boring. Ethel seems to know more about grown-up matters than I do, so I ask her what Mama was doing with Ben in the first place. Mama doesn't like people touching her, it's the very first thing she taught me when I was still small enough to be held while she fed me with a bottle. I must've yanked her hair and poked her chest because she pushed me back with an angry look and said, "Don't touch Mama here, or here, or here." She pointed to her hair, her face, and what she called her "bosom."

"Why'd she let Ben touch her when he's nowhere near as good as Dad?" I ask Ethel. Dad is smart and kind, and so handsome with his black hair slicked back, though one curl always escapes by the end of the day and covers his forehead. He looks like a Lakȟóta Superman.

She tips her head to the side, thinking, her cute baby face squinched to show this is a tough one to answer. Just when I bet she doesn't know either, she says, "She feeds him grief."

That only confuses me more, but I don't tell Ethel. I'm supposed to be her mother and not her student.

Mama isn't able to wash the bloodstains out of her pretty white shirt. She works on it for some time in the kitchen sink. But Dad never pays attention to things like clothes, so we move on like Ben never existed and Mama never chewed off his mouth.

Ethel and I know how to tell time. We peek at the kitchen clock because our stomachs are rumbling with hunger, and we want to check when Mama will start dinner. Not for an hour. Ethel sighs. I promise her we'll survive, and for a second there I sound like my mother since that's something she likes to tell me: "Get over it, you'll survive." The phone rings while we're still in the kitchen doorway, and we both jump.

Mama swoops into the room and grabs the phone. "Yes?" Mama sounds suspicious, like she doesn't trust whoever's calling, which is different from Dad, who says, "Hello!" in a cheerful way when he answers the phone. Dad acts like only friends would call us.

Usually, Mama brightens once she hears who's on the other end of the line, but today she drops into a kitchen chair like her legs don't work. Ethel tugs on my hand, urging me to leave Mama to her conversation, but I linger in the doorway, nervous and nosy.

"She doesn't like a snoop," Ethel whispers. But for once I ignore her.

Whoever's on the line does all the talking. Mama just sits there, listening, her face so blank I think of chalkboards at school when they're wiped clean. I strain to hear what she does and can just make out the voice of a man. That's all. I hope it isn't Ben, his anger gone and mouth recovered. I glance at the clock. Mama sits with the phone stuck to her ear for five whole minutes without saying a peep. Then her lips mash together—she stands and hangs up the phone. Ethel and I look at each other, confused.

"Come *on*," Ethel urges, and this time I listen. I creep back to my bedroom and climb under the bed like I'm in trouble. Ethel doesn't ask why. She must want to hide, too.

Mama never does start dinner. Ethel and I stay under the bed until we hear Dad's key unlock the front door. He calls out, "Where is everybody? Why's it so dark in here?" He must turn on the light because my own doorway brightens.

"Sissy?" Dad jangles his keys as he peeks into my room. I can hear the worry in his voice. I scooch out from under the bed, dragging Ethel behind me. There's dust in her hair.

"Are you okay?" Dad hugs me and checks my face.

"Yes. But Mama got a phone call. I think she's upset."

Dad heads into the kitchen and I trail behind. Mama is sitting at the kitchen table, staring at her folded hands. It's like she's not in her body anymore. Today seemed ordinary, and now it reminds me of one of the spooky movies Mama likes so much.

Dad turns on the overhead light and Mama finally moves.

"What's happening?" Dad sits down across from her and reaches for her hands. But she tucks them away in her lap.

"I lost track of time. I'll heat up some leftovers in a minute."

"We can have dinner downstairs, maybe some burgers? I know Sissy would love a malt." Dad's voice is gentle. Maybe that's what makes Mama finally look at him, remembering he's someone safe.

"Jack called." I can barely hear my mother's words. It looks like she's chewing the inside of her mouth.

"Jack?"

"My father."

"Oh."

My parents fall into that "oh" like it's a deep hole. I've never heard mention of my grandfather, so I guess I fall into that "oh," too.

"I thought he was dead," she whispers. "I hoped he was."

"What did he say?"

"He's old, sick. He wants to make amends now that his insides are shot. He's married to a third woman. They never had kids. He's living in Minneapolis and wants to wire me money for a train ticket to go see him before he dies." Mama says all this in a flat drone, reminding me of someone under a spell. Like they're words that don't mean anything at all.

"Do you want to go?" Dad asks. Mama wakes up even more; she looks surprised.

"Do I want to see him after all these years?! Absolutely not!" Mama jumps out of her chair and begins pacing back and forth. I'm glad the table is between her and us. She reminds me of a mother lion in the Lincoln Park Zoo who growled at us when we walked by, even though we don't really like zoos and wish all the animals would be allowed to go home.

"Did I ever tell you *when* it was he ran off to Rosebud, where he met his second wife and had his next set of kids? Though God knows if he even divorced Iná. I never had the heart to ask her. It would be just like him to be a bigamist. Or is there such a thing as a trigamist?" Mama's laugh is mean.

"I don't know. I'd have to look it up." Dad is still speaking carefully, the way you do when there's an injured cat who needs rescuing, but you don't want it to claw your eyes out before you can help.

"When did he leave?"

Mama's hands flutter over her heart. She has large hands that I don't think of as gentle. Strong, but not graceful like Maria Tall-chief's. Though tonight they drift together to form a butterfly lighting on her chest.

"The last time I saw him was at the memorial for Blanche. He showed up drunk, of course. Iná was already beside herself with grief and there he was, making everything harder. Shaming us. He was there at the start, and by the time we sat down for the feed, he was nowhere to be found. Someone said they'd seen him walking off with one of his good-time buddies." Mama is stone again. She looks like someone who has never cried a single tear.

"I didn't know. I'm sorry." Dad shakes his head, and his face shows the pain that Mama's can't.

"He sent postcards now and then. No mázaska to help out, not even once. That's when the boys started doing hard work for a rancher, even though they were so little." Mama looks at her hands and snatches them off her chest, like they've betrayed her. "I never want to see him again."

"Then you won't." Dad rises and tells us we're going down to the drugstore for dinner, that we all deserve a treat now and then. Mama seems relieved, her face suddenly falling in a way that makes her look young. Like she's Dad's little girl and not his wife.

"Here's to now, and our life in Chicago. Here's to burgers and malts!" Dad tickles me and makes me laugh so hard Ethel does, too. Once we've all washed up and are walking down the stairs, Ethel tells me we've got a lot to chew on.

"You mean burgers?"

She pinches me for being slow. "No. I mean the bombshell your mother dropped."

I'm sure she knows I'm playing dumb, pretending not to understand. There are some stories I don't want to be mine, or Mama's—some stories I'd rather be like fairy tales, which have scary parts where you don't think the hero will win or even survive, but then magic comes to the rescue and brings a happy ending. I don't want to have a grandfather named Jack unless he's the one who climbed a beanstalk into the sky and bested a giant, making off with the goose who laid golden eggs.

Dad surprises Mama with the idea of a vacation. He says he's never taken a sick day at work, and he has a week coming to him. Over dinner he says, "Call me nuts, but I miss my mother-in-law. How many husbands would ever say that?" Mama smiles, which makes him puffier. Mama's sunny weather can make Dad taller with happiness. "Why don't we take a road trip to North Dakota and see your mother?"

Mama leaps out of her chair; she doesn't usually move that fast unless she's angry. She goes behind Dad and wraps her arms around him while he's still leaning over his pork chop. Dad jumps in shock but then wipes his hands with a paper napkin and pats her on the arm. Ethel can't see them from my lap, and for once that's fine. I like this moment where it's just the three of us—me watching my parents look happy. All of us smiling. Dad winks at me so I'm not left out.

Days later we're all packed up and Ethel and I have taken over the entire back seat of the car. Dad always buys Fords that Mama says are on their last legs. We do a lot of praying and cajoling to keep this latest one alive. Dad gives her a pep talk before we head to the Kennedy Expressway. We're up earlier than usual—the sky on fire with morning, the light beginning to climb buildings. Each of us has a job: Mama is in charge of the Texaco maps, I'm the delivery person for snacks Mama packed in a cooler, Ethel has to keep me company and not slide off the seat to the floor, and Dad is supposed to get us all to Grandma's place in one piece.

Mama's the boss at home but Dad is the boss in the car. He even seems bigger when he's sitting behind the wheel, doing his final check to make sure the mirrors are lined up right. I know we're about to take off when Dad flexes his hands and cracks his knuckles. Then he strokes the steering wheel and talks in his gentlest voice, the one he uses when I'm sick with a fever: "Well, ma'am, we've got a long trip ahead of us, nine hundred miles. I know we're asking a lot of you to travel that far and back. You must feel you've been carting people all over creation without getting much in the way of thanks. But we are grateful. And we put our faith in you. We know you can do it. We're heading out to see a very special lady—you'll like her. So, let's get this show on the road and ride safely."

As if answering, the car snorts to life, coughing like Grandma does in the mornings to clear her pipes. "Well, there you go," Dad says, patting the steering wheel, and he sets us in motion.

Ethel cheers, but I'm the only one who can hear her over

the noise of the car. She's perched on our old blue quilt that has patches on patches. She looks excited and I realize she's never been to North Dakota before, so this is a real treat. On other trips Mama said I could bring only one toy with me, and I was littler then, so I brought my Conrad Bear because if I didn't, he would get upset and glare at me for days. Now I'm too old for teddy bears and Conrad is used to Ethel taking over.

"Can we stop at Stuckey's and get some cinnamon-pecan rolls?" I ask Dad. He knows how much I love them.

"If we don't get held up by anything and we're making good time," he says.

"You don't need the sugar." Mama shakes her head at how Dad spoils me.

"Aw, it's a pretty rare treat," he says. And because he's the boss of the car and he's bringing Mama somewhere she wants to go, I know she'll let him buy me the rolls and maybe even some taffy.

Ethel is smiling, happier than the expression painted on her face. She breaks into a laugh, and I can't help but laugh with her. We love Chicago and our place on Blackhawk Street but when I think of home, I see clouds taking over the sky, dark green angry clouds like the kind the Wicked Witch of the West brings with her wherever she goes. It's nice to travel somewhere the storms can't find us, where Grandma will chase them away with her broom. I take Ethel's hand and squeeze it. We can't stop grinning at each other, and when Dad starts singing "King of the Road," we both join him at the top of our lungs, and Mama doesn't even complain.

Mama says the idea of North Dakota is better than the real thing. Once she's actually standing in Grandma's small house, with two chairs and a table and one foldout cot because Grandma gave the rest of her furniture to a family who lost everything in a fire,

Mama curves in on herself and shrinks smaller than I've ever seen her. Grandma has some bread and butter in the kitchen, a small jar of chokecherry jam, and a braid of thíŋpsila. One egg.

Mama is pacing the dirt yard, stomping through a garden she says looks scraggly and úŋšika. She wrinkles her nose when she passes the outhouse.

"Look at how she lives!" Mama cries. Dad is following in her footsteps, like he doesn't want to make an extra set of tracks. He reaches out and holds her arms, says, "We'll help her. Don't worry. She has a big heart and can't help giving everything away. It's how she was taught."

"My brothers should do more!"

Word gets out that Mama is home, so relatives and longtime friends start coming over to visit. They bring coffee and donuts, powwow chairs, and one elder brings a coffee can full of wasná, which is enough to make Mama calm down and smile. Grandma offers me a pinch and Mama tells her not to waste it on me, that I won't think it's sweet enough. But Grandma pops it into my mouth like I'm her baby bird. I would like pretty much anything she fed me.

"Look at that." An older man who Mama calls Uncle John points at Ethel with his lips. He reaches for her, and I slowly hand her over, worried that he'll say something to upset her. Her eyes are big with everything that's new. Uncle John runs a finger down her soft hair and then her cheek. His finger is the same color as her face. He smiles at Ethel and lifts her in the air like she's his grandbaby. He brings her to the crook of his arm and begins a slow two-step through Grandma's kitchen.

"Uncle John likes your baby," Grandma says. "She looks like one of us."

Later she tells me that Uncle John lost his grandchild years before. Mama whispers something so Grandma can't hear: "He's never been the same since the accident, poor thing. He was always good to us kids." It sounds like a sad story I don't want to hear. All I know is that Ethel trusts Uncle John enough to fall asleep in his arms. She stays there all afternoon while he listens to my parents visit with folks. She wakes up when he feeds her a piece of donut, which leaves a trace of sugar powder on her lips. She licks it off and goes back to sleep.

We're staying at a cousin's place not far from Grandma's house. We tried to sleep on Grandma's floor, on the bed Mama put together with blankets and pillows from home. None of us is fussy. But Mama sleepwalked that first night and Dad found her crying in the yard, clawing through dirt. I saw her myself because the noise woke me up. Ethel told me not to go outside but I did. Grandma didn't wake up that whole night. Her hearing isn't so good anymore, so she didn't hear Mama wailing.

Dad put his arms around her and for once she let him hold her. That's when I knew she must be sleeping. Dad held Mama and rocked her right there in Grandma's garden. And in a voice so soft it was almost like a dream song, I heard Dad sing "Íŋkpata," a Lakȟóta lullaby his mother probably sang to him. He kissed her ear once she settled down, asked her, "What is it? What're you looking for?" Her hands still slid through the dirt, though less frantic.

Mama started crying again. "Blanche. Where did they put my sister?!"

I'd never seen my mother sob like that. Her outsides matched how my insides feel when she's angry. She was shaking like a scared dog.

Dad just kept holding Mama and rocking her. Eventually he stood her up and they came back in the house. He washed her hands and feet, and then put us all to bed. He curled around Mama like a warm shield, and I curled around Ethel.

◆ ◆ ◆

It's our last morning in North Dakota before we head back to Chicago. Mama doesn't look sad to be leaving. We bring a large breakfast to Grandma—scrambled eggs, fried potatoes and onions, link sausages, buttered toast—and she fusses over us like everything we do makes her happy. Mama tells her to sit, to let us wait on her for once. I'm not nervous when I set Grandma's table. She has so few dishes but they're the kind that can't break, even if you drop them on the floor, even if you throw them at the wall. They're blue enamel with speckles, as if they let a little kid drip white paint on the clean blue surface. When I squint at a dish the pattern swirls—it looks like the night sky has been trapped on a plate. Ethel whispers that I'd better get a move on and not be too dreamy.

When we're all chewing, even Grandma, who has a hard time working the false choppers she can pull out of her mouth, Mama says it's a shame she can't give us the grand tour.

"We went all over town," Dad says, "and up to Cannon Ball and other parts to see relatives. What did we miss?"

"Everything." Mama sighs and stabs a sausage link like it's to blame for her disappointment. "All the most significant places—the old cabin and Proposal Hill—are underwater. We can't get near them unless we're fish. That damned Oahe Dam!"

I expect Grandma to hush Mama for swearing, but she nods in agreement. "That's right! Oh, how we fought that project back in the forties. But in 1960, just a year before you were born"—Grandma points her lower lip at me—"they went ahead and evicted almost two hundred of us, put us in trailers. Then they flooded our homes and precious bottomlands. To them it was just another big land grab."

"You're not kidding, it was a terrible injustice! I even wrote a story about it at the time." Dad eyes his toast, like there's writing on it. "How tribes along the Missouri River paid the ultimate price for the project, while reaping few of the benefits."

"Oh, Jack would've had a *lot* to say about that travesty," Grandma says. "If he'd been here, he'd have written reams of protest letters."

"If he'd been here, he'd have gotten drunk and drowned."

Ethel jostles my arm and I spill my glass of water to cover Mama's words. No one scolds. I think they're relieved by the interruption. Mama grabs a dish towel to sop up the wet table. I thank Ethel in my head for rescuing the grown-ups from their bad moods and sad memories.

Saying goodbye to Grandma is hard. "Don't forget, we carry the same Dakhóta name," she whispers.

She holds my face in her hands. "Do you remember how to say it?"

I think carefully before speaking, not wanting to embarrass Grandma with a clunky mistake: "Wanáȟča Wašté Wiŋ." The words feel strange in my mouth, but make me proud, too.

"That's right." Grandma strokes my cheeks—her hands smell like sweet grass. "We give our name to only one person, and sometimes we keep it for ourselves. But the first time I saw you the name just came out of my mouth, so it was yours. Wanáȟča Wašté Wiŋ. 'Woman Whose Good Works Bring Flowers.' It's a beautiful name but can be heavy on one's back. I hope I didn't give you too great a burden."

I don't know what to say, so I just shake my head. Then I remember to ask her a question I've wondered for a long time. "What's Mama's Dakhóta name?" Mama tells me stories about her childhood, about practically *everything,* but she's never told me this, and for some reason I feel like I'm not supposed to ask.

Grandma looks surprised. She works her mouth like her teeth are slipping. "Your mother has a big name that came to her from *her* grandmother. Maybe it was to offer protection because she had a hole in the heart when she was little. We had to keep her still so she could mend; she couldn't run around and play with the other kids. Maybe that's why Iná called her Maȟpíya Boǧá Wiŋ, or 'Gathering of Stormclouds Woman,' as we'd say in English. Surely a person powerful enough to summon storms can heal an injured heart."

Ethel trusts my grandma enough to approve of most everything she says, but I can feel her shaking her head the tiniest bit. Silently, I agree with her, like Grandma is just trying to make a scary idea hide behind a nice one. I don't think Mama was given that name as protection, but maybe as a warning that she could bring thunder and lightning down on people's heads?

I feel Grandma's hand on my cheek again, her other hand smooths my forehead. "Whatever strength I have left is for you. Keep noticing everything. Keep that beautiful heart open. Someday it will save you." This kind of talk makes me embarrassed. As Mama often says, we're not a "mushy" family. But I lean into Grandma, holding the edge of her apron, which is worn soft from years of washing. Ethel whispers that I might not see her again, that I should say something just in case.

I motion Grandma to bend down so I can whisper in her ear. She smells cleaner than anyone, like the wind that's always blowing around her house. Now I'm stuck. I want to say something that will let her know all the feelings that are suddenly piling up in my heart and belly. I'm scared to think I might never see her again. I don't want to lose this chance to say something she'll remember. But the only thing I'm able to breathe into her ear is, "I miss your soft hands every night before I go to sleep."

I wave to Grandma from the back seat of our Ford after Dad gives it another pep talk. Ethel waves, too. I'm crying, and in my head, I tell Ethel that my goodbye words were stupid.

"Oh, no," she says. "They were just perfect."

◆ ◆ ◆

Mama is sad on my birthdays, so they make me sad, too. She usually spends the day in bed with a hot water bottle, and Dad takes
me to the drugstore to pick out a present. Dad says we're playing
a game where we try not to make a single sound until Mama is
up and about again. He reads, and Ethel and I talk to each other
without moving our lips. On this birthday, I show Ethel the gift
Dad bought me, something I've been wanting a long time: a set of
metal jacks with a ball. I can't play the game yet because it would
make too much noise, but the set is packed in a small cloth bag
that's tied to the belt of my pants. Every now and then I squeeze
the bundle, and it makes me happy. Mama told me that when
she's feeling better, she'll teach me how to play jacks, and that's
another birthday gift.

"We can wait for that," I whisper to Ethel, and Ethel scowls
because she's just a baby, so she isn't patient.

The next morning, after Dad leaves for work and Mama has
washed the breakfast dishes, she gets down on the floor with me.
The kitchen linoleum is so clean it makes the little rubber ball
bounce.

Mama scatters jacks on the floor and shows me how to toss
the ball and swipe the jacks into her hand before the ball bounces
two times. She makes it look easy, like magic. I make it look like a
disaster—one of my favorite words, which Mama uses when her
hair gets caught in a storm and she doesn't have a scarf. But I'll
practice, even if Ethel can't stop laughing.

The phone rings, and Mama gets up to answer. She likes to
talk to her friends, the ones Dad calls her "fellow rabble-rousers."
She drinks coffee and twists the phone cord around her fingers. I
practice and practice my game until I can swipe up one jack at a
time before the ball messes me up. After a while I don't even hear
Mama's voice anymore. I get the way I do when I'm learning a new

song. It's like I'm all alone in the world, and even Ethel is forgotten. Until I hear a crash! I've scattered my jacks too far, and Mama has tripped on some. She falls hard on her rump, and her shoe flies off. It knocks Ethel over, but Ethel doesn't make a sound. Neither do I. Either the clock has stopped, or the fridge that hums, or I've gone deaf and can't hear anything. Can't move. I'm stuck with fear.

Mama pulls herself up and stands over me. She's shouting, I guess, but there's still no sound. She is so tall, and her eyes are big. They get bigger and bigger and so red it looks like they're full of bleeding spiderwebs. Mama swipes a few jacks into her hand and places them in mine. She curls my hand into a fist and covers it with her own. Her face comes in close, and I can smell the coffee on her breath. She's telling me something, and I know they're angry words, but I can't hear them, and now I know why. My heart is roaring in my ears like a hundred drums. Her hand crushes mine, and the metal spikes of the jacks cut into me. She's squeezing my hand and staring into my eyes. I'm screaming on the inside, but Ethel is upside down somewhere under Mama's shoe, telling me to keep my head.

Just when I can't stand the pain anymore and think blood will start squishing out from between Mama's fingers, she lets go. I fall on my back and realize I'm wet all over, sweaty like it's a hot summer day. I start hearing sounds again, and Mama patches my bloody palm. She tells me the story we'll tell Dad about my hand and has me say it again until I get it right. Perfect. I teach the story to Ethel, but she won't say it back.

The week after my birthday is Columbus Day, so Dad doesn't have to go to work. My parents aren't fans of that particular holiday—they say there are too many things wrong with it. Mama says that he didn't discover anything beyond "his own stupidity and inability to navigate." Dad says he brought nothing but suffering to this continent, including diseases and slavery, and that you can't discover a place where folks are already living. I ask them why Columbus has his own day, then, so big that the mail won't come, Dad won't have to go to work, and Mayor Daley will celebrate it with a big parade. Mama says, "It's the celebration of a mediocre white man to make white people feel better about themselves." Dad bursts out laughing, but I just look at Ethel and shrug. She nods in a wise way like she agrees with my parents. "Prejudice," she says, which makes me feel lonesome.

"Why don't you take Sissy on an outing since you have a free day?" Mama asks Dad. "You don't spend much time together."

Dad looks hurt but he quickly changes his face into a smile.

"Would you like that?" he asks. I nod and a matching grin stretches my face. I try to encourage my father, try to fix the thing I can see him always adjusting, the same way he adjusts the tie clip he wears to work because he says a Lakȟóta journalist needs to look "sharp." I want my parents to be in love both ways, not Dad by himself. So I fall in love for them, over and over again.

Dad says our destination will be a surprise. Ethel tells me it's because he hasn't figured out where to take us yet, but she isn't fussing.

First, we go to the Field Museum of Natural History so I can visit the dinosaur bones and the stuffed buffalo I decide to name Nijinsky, after the famous ballet dancer. Grandma told me that buffalo are graceful even though they're large, so I like to imagine a herd of them dancing on the Plains. In my head they swoop in circles, making complicated patterns even better than those done by the June Taylor Dancers. The only exhibit I *don't* want to see is the whale skeleton strung up on the ceiling. I had a nightmare once that the massive jaws plunged down to grab me and wouldn't let go—I dangled from their bite. Dad says this kind of whale doesn't eat little girls, only tiny fish called krill. But Dad wasn't there in my dream, and no one saved me. So, we skip that room. Ethel enjoys the mummies best because she likes how Egyptians worshipped cats. I hold her up so she can see the cat mummies.

We eat lunch in the cafeteria and a woman at the next table stares at Ethel in a way that's not very friendly. I don't want Ethel's feelings to be hurt, so I switch her from the table to my lap, where the woman can't glare at her. She wears pretty cat eyeglasses with shiny diamonds at the outer edges—it's too bad she ruins them with her mean look. For some reason I think, *That's a Myrtle from the suburbs,* the kind of woman Mama says she isn't! Something tells me Mama wouldn't be allowed to join that particular group. Not that she'd want to.

Dad notices the glaring woman and lifts one of his eyebrows so high, it looks like it's going to run straight up his forehead and into his hair. I snicker, to let him know I notice he's trying to make me feel better.

"Some wašíčus can be very rude, can't they?" he asks, and I nod. "They *love* to watch us. But we don't care, do we?" I shake my head. "We've got nothing to hide." Then Dad smiles, and he's so handsome with his shining, happy eyes, I feel a swell of warmth inside.

Dad's use of that word in our language, "wašíču," reminds me of how few of them I know. If languages are alive and have a spirit, then English is my boss, while Dakhóta is more like a nice dream it's hard to remember. All you know is that something about it made you happy. Dad doesn't mind my questions, so I ask him, "How come you and Mama don't speak our language? Did you forget it, or is it against the law?"

My question makes Dad wince, and now I'm sorry I bothered him. I'm too curious for my own good. Though Ethel pats my hand to let me know she's on my side. She's pretty curious, too. Dad takes a sip of coffee like it will help him explain.

"That's a very intelligent, important question," he finally says, pressing his finger onto the table to pick up stray grains of sugar he brushes onto a napkin. Dad is so careful and neat. "The simple answer is that if you don't use a gift, like a language, eventually you'll lose parts of it, or most of it. But in our case, it wasn't due to laziness. We've had forces working to get rid of our culture and beliefs, our way of living, for many generations now. Wašíču want us to be like them because . . ."

I sense Dad is going down like a man I saw in a movie—sucked into a hole of quicksand until even his hat disappeared.

"Oh, it's complicated. Because they want our land and resources, so they say we're backward people who don't know how to live right. That makes it easier to commit theft and push us around. Like bullies, you know? Great big dangerous ones on a massive scale." Dad holds his arms apart and I imagine Godzilla stomping the thípi villages I've seen in pictures, until everything is flat. "I guess there's no simple answer, after all." Dad winks. I must look too serious. "The bottom line is that Mama and I went to schools where we got in trouble for speaking our original language, where English was all that was allowed. So gradually, it won. We remember fewer words with each generation, which is a shame."

Ethel sighs, and I know she's growing tired of this talk. She wants action! So, I let go of my question and make a silent promise that I'll work to remember each and every Dakhóta or Lakȟóta word my parents use, and maybe someday I'll spend more time with Grandma, who knows all the words.

Next Dad takes us to visit Lake Michigan, not to the beach since it's too cold to swim, but to a tumble of boulders beyond the sand that Dad calls a "breakwater." He helps me clamber onto a flat rock we use as a chair, though it's more like sitting on a table. Ethel says we should dig for shells, but Dad doesn't hear; he's staring at the lake, which is whipped up like a malt. I enjoy it when it's in this mood, playing tag with the shore but not smashing down like it's angry.

Dad must be thinking the same way. He says, "When the lake is playful like this it reminds me of my brother."

"Uncle Luther?"

"Yes."

Ethel is squirming in my lap, trying to reach for a shell she sees poking out of the sand between boulders, but now she stops. She's as curious to hear about Dad's brother as I am.

"Tell me a story about him." Oops, I forgot to be polite like Mama taught me. "Please," I add.

Dad pats my knee. "Let me see, I'm not as good as your mother when it comes to talking. That's why I became a writer. With a pencil in my hand, I can say what's in my head, but once my mouth gets going, I'm tongue-tied."

I shake my head. Dad talks just fine.

"Sissy, my big fan! Thank you for seeing some shine in your old man." Dad rubs his chin but keeps watching Lake Michigan lick the edges of sand with foamy bubbles. "You would've adored your uncle Luther."

I don't react in any way Dad can see, but on the inside, I'm thinking, *No*, out of loyalty.

"He was a year older than me and taught me everything I needed to know." Dad laughs. "But I didn't have his special magic. He had this extra spark in him like a flame turned high that never went out. He burned through his sleep, sweat breaking out on his forehead, and I'd wonder what dream adventures he was having that he never shared. He had so much energy he made me tired to watch. And he liked to laugh more than anything—a funny yip, like biting at joy. I couldn't even be jealous of him—how fast he could run, how good he was at sports, how much girls liked him—because he was my best friend."

Now I'm sorry I asked for a story about Luther. I want Dad to know *he's* the hero in my world, not his brother. I wonder if he's ever heard Mama's secret she whispered to me one night, that she was supposed to marry Luther and not him? That she's still missing him?

"One time our mother must've seen me watch Luther with a wistful look on my face, wishing I could be more high-energy fun, like him. She sat me down and told me a story of what happened when he was just a baby. Maybe to explain where the extra spark came from.

"You remember that movie *The Wizard of Oz?*" I nod, and immediately start humming "Ding Dong! The Witch Is Dead."

"So, you know what a tornado is. We have them in South Dakota sometimes, and a real bad one the evening I was born. I wasn't due for a while yet, but I guess the circumstances were such that even in my mother's womb I could feel that pressure, and it got me moving. So poor Mama gave birth to me in our root cellar. Can you imagine?"

I don't answer because I can tell Dad isn't talking to me so much as to his memory.

"But see, I'm telling this all wrong." Dad scrapes his hands together like they're sandy. "Okay. When the twister was first noticed, snuffling along the fields way in the distance, making a mess of everything in its path, my father sounded the alarm and got my mother and her sister and the unborn me into the root cellar for safety. But he couldn't find Luther. My brother had just been there, playing in the yard. He'd learned to walk at an early age, and by one year old he could run. Though our father said it was a funny, bowlegged run with a lot of falling down. The grasses were high around their place, and it was impossible to see him, to thrash through every inch of ground, though Até tried for a while.

"He called until he lost his voice. He had to give up, couldn't leave his wife without protection."

I'm getting nervous even though I know they all survived. Stories are funny that way. They can kick up your nerves even when you know the ending.

"Everyone was wild with panic about Luther. Fearing he'd be killed. My mother was apparently weeping, crying his name over and over. Then no one could hear her anymore since the tornado moved past our place, smashing everything that wasn't nailed down. They say it seemed to last forever, that fuming whirlwind. When it was gone, and they could hear again, could pat themselves down and know they were still alive, my mother went into labor. That took *more* time away from being able to search for Luther. Who knows how many hours he spent on his own? But eventually they found him, sitting in what was left of the yard, sucking on a chicken bone they couldn't account for since we didn't have any chickens. He grinned at them and waved the bone. He didn't have any injuries, not even a tiny scratch on his skin. The only physical change in him was that before he'd had one whorl of hair on his crown, and now he had two, both of them spinning counterclockwise."

I must look confused because Dad bends down so I can see his own single cowlick. But that's not what I'm scowling at. He's making his brother sound sacred, and I don't want Luther to have more than my father.

"What people said is that the wind claimed Luther for a relative, so he was more than just a baby boy after that day. They say he flew through the heart of a twister and the wind loved him and kept him safe. They said he would be able to marshal the winds at a critical time and maybe even save some lives." Dad pauses a long time, and I think it must be the end of the story, though he sits so still I freeze, too.

"Turns out they were right. He did marshal the wind at a critical time, make it his ally, and in doing so saved a lot of men in our unit. Just not Luther." Dad shakes himself the way dogs do after a bad dream. "But that's not a story for my Sissy to hear."

Dad reaches over and tickles me, then tickles Ethel. We're both giggling in a minute and my good feelings are restored. Luther is gone while my father is still here. Maybe he *was* magic like my father says, but in the end the wind took him, and let him blow out.

Mama argued with Dad last night. I couldn't hear what it was about, though I slept on the floor outside their bedroom to make sure everyone was safe. I'd already hidden the knives and heaviest pots, even the corn holders, which are small but could do damage if a person used one to jab somebody in the face. I've learned to pay attention to voice levels, how much anger signifies we should look out! I go into action when Mama's irritation builds, reminding me of warning sirens that blast through our neighborhood each month in a test. I stay close in case I need to go for help. Ethel says I worry too much, but it's my job to look out for the biggest people in my heart.

Dad must've carried me back to my bed in the night. I wake up hugging Ethel, the sheet and blanket tucked all around me the way Dad does when he kisses me good night. No one is speaking much at breakfast, but at least the spiky grumbles are gone. Everyone seems tired, like they're "nursing a hangover," which Dad says is a miserable thing to experience, and that you have to fight with a big greasy breakfast because alcohol's a poison. But my parents almost never drink. They barely eat anything this morning, just toast and Dad's favorite shredded wheat. He doesn't try to kiss

Mama when he leaves, her back to him while she's washing the dishes. He kisses me and pats Ethel on the head, then he's out the door—leaving behind a scent of soap and his aftershave that features the picture of a ship on the bottle. My face is wet from where his damp hair grazed me.

Ethel and I think this is going to be a gloomy day. We think I'll carry the hangover with me to school, and all my worries packed along with lunch. But Mama surprises us. When the dishes are washed and dried, she turns around and snatches her apron off in a flash. "Today is going to be our good day!" Mama crows, and I leap out of the chair and twirl in circles like my idea of a real ballerina, until Ethel warns me she's going to throw up. Mama phones the school to say I'm down with a cold, she winks at me and tries not to smile. Mama never winks! She tells them I won't be able to be in school today. Then she grabs the newspaper and looks at the movie listings.

"You like musicals, Sissy. Why don't we see this *Chitty Chitty Bang Bang* that's been hanging around forever?"

"Yes!"

"We'll have lunch at Stouffer's, which is right near the theater, then we'll see the movie, and if there's time afterward, we can go to the park."

Ethel and I stare at each other, our mouths hanging open. Mama laughs when she notices. "I'll take that as a confirmation." I nod and rush to her, grabbing her waist in a hug. Ethel is squished between us. Mama pats me on the back and tells me to change from my school clothes into slacks. If we move quickly, we can visit the main public library downtown—one of our favorite spots.

In my head I tick off all the wonders of the day: a visit to the library, where I found three books I can hardly wait to read, currently stowed in Mama's big purse, then lunch at Stouffer's, which has white tablecloths and special dishes like spinach soufflé—a fancy puff it was fun to eat. Next, we went to the movie that featured a nice grandpa, a beautiful flying car, a scary child catcher, and dancing dolls, which were Ethel's favorite. We were even given a program about the movie, with all kinds of pictures. Mama and I shared popcorn though I was still full from lunch.

Mama smiles down at me. "This was definitely our good day, Sissy." Tears pop into my eyes and I watch the ground so she won't see them. I twirl around her and it's a good thing I've got a tight grip on Ethel because she nearly goes flying. Mama laughs and catches Ethel's empty hand. We stroll through the park that way, Ethel swinging between us, scared at first, but then kicking out her legs with joy. I can't hear her over the noise of a group of crows strutting across the grass like kings as if this is Crow Park and not Lincoln Park, but I think she's giggling. Ethel *never* giggles around my mother.

Mama leads us over to President Lincoln. He's standing as tall as her, one hand behind his back and the other holding the edge of his jacket like someone wants to take it from him. He's looking down at his feet and I swear he's wondering if he should step off that pedestal and join us in a walk. One foot is close to the edge— he's so tempted. Mama narrows her eyes at Lincoln and halts our happy parade.

"You know who this is?" she asks.

"President Lincoln."

She remains silent so I add: "They shot him, and he died." I remember this from the exhibits about him at the Historical Society.

Mama nods. "He did some good things and some awful things."

I feel Ethel go limp. She's hanging between me and Mama, and suddenly it isn't so fun. I pet her hand with my thumb to let her know everything is okay.

Mama looks at me and gestures toward Lincoln with her lips. "He signed the death warrant for a lot of our people. Thirty-eight Dakhóta men were hanged the day after Christmas on *his* order, essentially for being Indian, for wanting to live as we'd always done before white people started swarming our territory, claiming it as theirs."

I peek at Lincoln's face, and he looks sad, like he would apologize to Mama if she'd just let him jump off that platform and explain. I know how he feels.

Mama shakes her head. "I can't feel right about him, and that's that." She lets go of Ethel's hand and I bring the doll close for a hug. Clouds slip over the face of the sun so now it's colder. Ethel shivers in my arms.

"Pretty lady!" a man shouts in our direction and he's so loud I almost drop Ethel.

"You, you!" He points at Mama and waggles his butt like a cat about to take a high leap.

The man wears a raincoat just like Dad's and his brown hair is combed nice. But there's something wrong with him. He's jumpy and wiggly, and his eyes are popped open too big.

Mama's forgotten all about Lincoln. She focuses on the stranger and pulls me behind her, though I peek around the strong wall of her.

The man opens his coat dramatically as if he's a magician on *The Ed Sullivan Show* who can make birds and rabbits appear, then disappear. "This is for you, pretty lady!" he screams. Something's hanging out of his pants, and it bounces from side to side as he jitters.

Mama makes a disgusted noise, the same as when she found a cockroach under the kitchen sink and squashed it. "You stay here," she commands. The harsh sound freezes me into a statue just like Lincoln. If a car was coming at me, I still wouldn't move. Ethel is so quiet I think she's holding her breath.

Mama digs in her purse for something and then charges at the stranger. His eyes get even bigger, which is hardly possible. He stops wriggling. Mama's good at getting people's attention. She's kicked off her shoes so she can run, and now she's just a few feet from the man, Dad's Swiss Army knife slashing from side to side like she's going to gut the stranger when she reaches him. He yelps and speeds off in the direction of Clark Street. Mama chases him to the edge of the park but stops once he makes it to the gas station across the street.

Mama finds her shoes and puts them back on. She complains she's ruined her nylons. She closes the knife and drops it back into her purse. She glares at me as if *I* invited the stranger to bother us in the park. "There are sick men in this world," she says. "You have to be careful, be prepared for anything. And whatever you do, don't stand down and let them win." She grabs my cold hand and shakes me, once, like that's meant to help me hear better.

We turn our backs on Lincoln and head home. Me, running to keep up with Mama, who is storming through the park. All that jostling gives Ethel the hiccups, but the funny sound doesn't make me laugh.

Our good day is officially over.

When Mama goes into fight mode she can get stuck there. Once we're home and it's time for her to start dinner, she paces instead, stalks from one end of the apartment to the other like a soldier ready for battle. She starts talking to herself, which makes me nervous. "He better not complain," she says. Mama opens the cupboard and pulls out a can of cream of mushroom soup, slams it on the kitchen counter. She does the same with a can of string beans.

Dinner's going to be simple tonight because she's in no mood to fuss over a meal. I know Dad won't mind, and neither do I. We both go along with Mama's moods because if you try to change them, things get worse. It's like asking a huge storm to simmer down when it wants to roar across the city and knock down trees. It'll howl even louder and maybe blast you with lightning.

Since dinner won't take long to fix, Mama has time to think. She pulls me into the living room and points for me to sit on the couch. I hold Ethel on my lap and gently stroke her hair. She's been nervous ever since Mama got mad at Lincoln.

Mama is still pacing back and forth in front of me. Then she gets still, like she's decided something. She settles in the chair across from me and Ethel, smooths the skirt of her dress with strong hands, then clutches her knees.

"There's something you need to understand," she says. I check her eyes, but the whites are still white, so I don't hold my breath the way Ethel does. "You are a soft little girl." I nod; I've heard this over and over for a hundred years. "You can get hurt being like that." Mama heads into a story that she likes to tell new friends, about how I'm too nice to live. *Sensitive.* I feel like I've known that word since the day I was born. She reminds me how when I was little, maybe three years old, I was playing in the park with a girl a lot bigger than me. I wanted to be friends with her. Problem was, she kept knocking me down. Not hard enough to hurt, so I'd get up, smile at her, and return for what Mama calls "another round of abuse." Mama told me to hit back. But I never did. After watching me get knocked down for the third time Mama lost her patience. She came over and walked me in front of the mean girl, grasped my baby wrists in her hands, and forced me to shove the girl to the ground. Mama being as strong as she is, the girl went flying into a tree and got a knot on her head. Her mother came running at the scream—caught up in a book or conversation with another parent, she hadn't noticed our doings until then. Mama explained that the girl tripped and took a tumble into the tree. Mama laughed at how the girl stared at her then, so surprised she stopped crying. But she didn't shake her head or tell her mother the truth.

"That little girl never messed with you again," Mama tells me. It's the moral of her story. I don't like hearing it though, since it doesn't feel fair. The other girl might not have been very nice, but she didn't hurt me. Mama forced me to be mean in a way that was worse.

"I want you to be strong, to be able to defend yourself. Our people have been pushed around for generations by dangerous bullies in greater numbers than us, who have more weapons. On top of that, you're a girl. Men of every kind take advantage of girls, try to get whatever they want from them. Like that sick jerk in the park." Mama chuckles. "I sure scared *him*, didn't I? He never expected a woman to fight back." I nod, but Ethel stays quiet. I can tell she doesn't want to be noticed.

"He'll consider long and hard before he ever pulls a stunt like that again."

I think the lesson might be over now, but Mama is just getting started. She pulls out a story I've never heard before, something that happened on her reservation when she was just a girl.

"There was a Rooshian farmer who married into our tribe—not many of them did, they were so down on Indians. He wasn't a great catch, and we felt sorry for his wife, who was sweet but always ailing. Turns out she had tuberculosis and died after giving him three girls. He taught them to speak German, just like him, and it was so odd to hear these Dakhóta girls, who looked like they could be my sisters, talking that way. The oldest daughter was so much like her mother, gentle and lovely. Her eyes such a beautiful golden brown and slanted like a cat's. Whenever we had any food to spare my mother would bring her a little something for the girls—they were so thin."

Mama clutches her hands together and stops talking. She looks at me and then notices Ethel, who is still perched on my lap. "I swear that doll stares at me sometimes," Mama says. Ethel is more still than she's ever been before, like she's dead and can't breathe. "There's something wrong with her." I want to defend Ethel, but I'm worried that will make things worse, whip Mama into a storm that blows out the windows, maybe carries Ethel into the sky. I sit tight and speak nicely to Ethel in my head.

Mama sends her a last glare and then picks up the story. "This is upsetting," she warns me, "but some kids have to live through events like this, which is worse. You're only hearing about it." I nod. I'm just like one of those puppets Julie Andrews made dance in that song "The Lonely Goatherd." My head agrees when Mama wants it to.

"Men have physical needs that can make them monsters," Mama continues. "They want to stick you with their privates whenever they feel like it, whether it's right or not." I'm not exactly sure what she's talking about, though I guess it has to do with the jiggling hot dogs I saw on Ben and the man in the park. Maybe what they do is something like Dr. Grant giving me shots with a needle? Which I hate. "That Rooshian farmer was missing his wife and started fooling with his own daughter, treating her like she was supposed to take her mother's place. We found out because she got pregnant with what people said was a 'catch colt.' When a girl is that thin you can see evidence of a child early on, like they've swallowed a whole cantaloupe that won't digest. The girl never left the farm, she was basically her father's prisoner, so we knew who put that baby inside her. We tried to get the priest to do something, but he was useless." Mama's hand moves to her arm, the place where she made a flesh sacrifice. It's like her body remembers another priest who wasn't much help when she argued with him in confession.

"Eventually the baby was born, and your grandmother was called out to their farm to help the girl. When she got there, Iná said the girl was so gray she thought she was dead. But her skin was warm. She was breathing. Iná looked for the baby and the farmer handed over a red bundle. He hadn't even washed the little thing. 'Tot,' he told her. She didn't need a translation; she could see the baby was dead. She has a soft heart like you, so she started to cry, though she knew it was probably for the best the child didn't live. She tended to the mother, made sure she was going to survive, before washing the infant. Once she turned to the baby, she noticed something strange in the soft spot." Mama places a finger on the top of her head. "A baby's head is open here, like a well, because the skull hasn't finished growing a hard shell. Iná said there was a small hole there, like a pin had been pushed inside to kill the child. Another girl. That farmer was full of girls."

I'm squeezing Ethel so hard at this point I make her breathe again. She nearly coughs. *I'm sorry,* I whisper in my head. Mama's story is making me feel like I have the stomach flu. I want to throw up but know I better not. I clamp down on the sick feeling to make it go away.

"Iná reported her suspicion to everyone she thought had power. But no one did anything. It was easier to look the other way. Besides, authorities didn't care about a dead Indian baby conceived in such a nasty way."

Mama stands up and begins pacing again. "I know it's an awful thing to tell you, but after what happened today, I need you to toughen up, to stop being so dreamy. Real life is ugly a lot of the time, and you have to protect yourself, so no one ever hurts you like that Rooshian farmer hurt his daughter, or like that man in the park wanted to hurt us."

Us. For some reason that small word makes me dizzy. It's like I'm back in the park and now the stranger is wiggling at me and not just Mama, maybe even wiggling at Ethel. This time I can't stop the sick from taking over. I set Ethel on the couch and race for the bathroom, making it just in time as breakfast and lunch and popcorn get thrown up into the toilet. At least Mama isn't mad after I tidy the bathroom and myself, brush my teeth, and sit a few minutes on the side of the tub until I feel calm.

By the time I return to the living room Mama is in the kitchen, opening the cans for dinner. I notice Ethel has moved from the couch to the top of Mama's hassock, which contains her sewing supplies in its hidden belly: spools of thread and her darning egg, needles, pins, extra buttons, snaps, and zippers, measuring tape. Ethel's hair is mussed so I get the brush.

"What were you doing over there?" I ask her, as we settle together on the couch, and I start to brush her hair the way she likes. Ethel cries out to stop me, but she won't talk. I turn her around so I can look into her eyes, and they are so dead it scares me. For the first time ever I shake my doll, hard, the way Mama does me when she's mad. Ethel starts breathing again, which makes tears run down my face.

Now I'm the one who can't breathe.

"My head!" Ethel cries. "My head!"

I don't know what's wrong. I pet her soft hair like a good mother should, kiss her right on the crown. That's when I find what's hurting her—my lip snags a bump that shouldn't be there. I check my doll like I'm looking for lice and find one of Mama's pins stuck all the way through Ethel's head so just the small flat top is showing. I pry the pin from her crown as gently as I can, the way Dad once worked a piece of glass from my foot. Little bit by little bit, I pull it out, find Mama's pincushion, and stick it there.

Ethel is quiet. She looks scared even though I rescued her. "You're fine now," I tell her, and she nods, just like me. "Why did Mama do that?" I ask myself, and don't have any idea.

But Ethel does: "Because she had to."

Mama surprises me for Halloween by making me the best costume I've ever worn! She knows I'm crazy about that musical we saw, *Chitty Chitty Bang Bang,* especially the song performed by Truly Scrumptious, pretending she's a doll on a music box so she can get inside the evil baron's castle. I've memorized the song and can do a pretty good imitation of the doll's funny, stiff dance. Right before the holiday Mama finds a frilly party dress at the Salvation Army. She said it cost almost nothing because it's no longer in style. It has a petticoat with layers of net that make the skirt of the dress stand out, nice and full. I can't help twirling when I put it on. Mama remakes the outfit on her sewing machine, adding a little black vest that laces up in front. When she's finished the job, she dresses me. She paints round circles on my face with her bright red lipstick and steps back, holding up the movie program to see how close I look to the dancing doll.

"Everything but the hairdo," she says. My hair has finally grown to the middle of my back, so Mama braids it. She says it's thin and fine, and tangles too easily, unlike her own thick hair. I agree. My braids aren't alive like Mama's would be if she still had long hair—mine look like tiny snakes. I smile up at Mama, who is so tall and magical; she knows exactly how to make dreams come true without my even telling her.

"What?" she asks. She sounds nervous.

"Nothing. Thank you, Mama." I rush over and hug her around the middle—that much touching is usually okay if I don't overdo it. She pats my head, plays with my braids like they're reins on a toy horse.

"Ribbons," she says, gently pushing me away. "We need ribbons to tie up your hair in loops."

"Yes! Like Truly Scrumptious." I hear Ethel snort from the chair where she's been watching me change into someone else. Ethel's tired of me pretending to be a doll.

"Just like," Mama says, as she heads for my bedroom. I have a stash of ribbons in my dresser drawer.

I pick up Ethel and swirl her around in a dance. Her cheeks puff out like she's going to vomit. "'What do you see, you people gazing at me?'" I sing.

"Stop! Stop!" Ethel's kicking her legs in protest.

I'm about to finish teasing her when a loud slam hushes us both. We hold our breath together.

"What's this?" Mama roars as she stomps from my bedroom. She's waving a fist at me, and it takes a second to see the glint of gold foil clutched in her hand. Mama's found my stash of toffee wrappers!

Mama hits me with questions: Have I been stealing? How did I get these? When I explain they were a gift from the druggist downstairs, she's even angrier, asking what he's done to me, how did I pay for them? She shouts over my explanations and throws the wrappers in my face. I stoop to gather them because even with Mama's anger, they're still my treasure. Ethel tugs on my arm, says I'd better hide until she calms down.

Hide where? My feet decide for me, running straight to the bathroom, which has a solid door with a big silver lock. I rush in and throw my body against the wood, click the latch. I've taken Mama by surprise so she's a few steps behind. She pounds on the door. "You open this right now!"

Bam bam bam! Mama beats on the wood. Ethel is shaking, so I hug her close to my chest and tell her we'll be okay. It's a lie. We both know this. But she looks at me with a sweet face of trust.

The bathroom keeps me and Ethel alive. No matter how much Mama pounds the door, or kicks it, or smashes it with the heavy living room phone she must've unplugged to use as a weapon, the lock holds, and the door doesn't break. At some point I open the window that looks out on nothing but the other side of the building. The ground is a ragged patch of grass covered in litter people have tossed there. I have a sudden idea! I offer my gold foil wrappings to God, as a payment for protection. I drop them out the window, one at a time, not too quickly so the prayer will last.

"Please keep me and Ethel safe," I whisper, not that Mama can hear me with all the noise she's making. "Please let Mama forgive me." The request must work, because soon after I drop the last piece of gold, watching it dip and float like a feather, Mama goes quiet.

Ethel tells me not to fall for any tricks. I won't. We wait until shadows begin to darken the room. I look at Ethel when I have the feeling it might be safe. Mama usually gets tired after being super angry and goes to bed with a hot water bottle. I click the lock open and pause. Silence. I turn the doorknob and hold my breath. No movement from outside. Bit by bit, moving slowly as a cat tracking a mouse, Ethel and I make our way out of the bathroom. And God answered my prayer.

The next day is Halloween, and my costume is neatly hanging in the closet where I put it before Dad and I had supper. When Mama said she wasn't feeling well, he cooked us all some grilled cheese sandwiches, served Mama hers in bed. I helped him scrape off the black bits that were burnt. I don't know if I'll be allowed to go trick-or-treating after school. Mama hasn't spoken to me at all since yesterday. She walks me to school in silence, which is noisier than the cars and the birds and a man singing "Cold Sweat" in the same exciting voice as James Brown. She squeezes my shoulder when we get to the front door and something in me relaxes. It's a sign that we'll be okay. I didn't even know how much my stomach was hurting until Mama does that, because now the pain begins to go away.

After school Mama meets me as usual, and we walk home. She isn't talking, but her quiet isn't noisy. She even brought Ethel with her, which she never does. She pulls Ethel out of a cloth shopping bag and hands her over. Ethel is wearing a new long-sleeved turquoise minidress made from fabric scraps, decorated at the neckline with white lace strips. Ethel's hair is smoothed back with a matching turquoise headband that really shows off her beautiful coffee skin. She's preening, I can tell. On the inside, I'm gushing, but I know that will annoy Mama, so I just say, "Thank you." She nods her head, and the three of us stroll down the street like we were never upset about anything.

Mama doesn't talk until we get home and I've finished my homework. She surprises me by breaking all the rules! Mama calls me into the living room, where she's settled on the couch. She holds out her hand for me to join her, and I notice a folder on her lap. Mama puts an arm around my shoulder, and we sit like that for a very long time, long enough for me to go from stiff to leaning against her side. Mama strokes my hair with one hand and pinches the folder with the other, like she's afraid it's going to run off.

"I want to share something with you before you get all dolled up in your costume."

I squeal inside to hear this news; I'll be celebrating Halloween after all!

"People can be dramatic sometimes," Mama continues. Now both her hands fidget with the manila folder. "We can overreact." At first I think she's smiling, then see she's chewing on a corner of her lip like she's nervous. She finally starts talking again. "You certainly know something about melodrama." I nod, though I'm not sure where this is heading.

"Even your grandma had times when she went around the bend. Though not very often."

Ethel gasps for me. I'm trying to keep quiet. I can't imagine Grandma pounding on doors.

"One time when her husband, Jack, was being awful to her—oh, he could be so mean—she did something I never would've expected. She had this bound book she kept in a special place, hidden away with other precious little things she'd take out every now and then to admire. I was so curious about that book—you know how much I love to read! The worst thing I ever did to my mother was invade her privacy and sneak into her parfleche box so I could see that volume. Turns out it was a diary, filled with hundreds of pages of her beautiful handwriting that looked like narrow birds flying across the lines. I didn't have time to read it, so the sin wasn't fulfilled. She never knew about my snooping. But I was punished all the same because after that, my curiosity was just about unbearable." Mama taps the folder in her lap. I understand. Secrets can be a nuisance, or even hurt like a twisted arm.

"That sad day seemed to go on forever. Jack was drunk and said one horrible thing after another. Eventually he passed out, but she didn't get going the way she usually did. She didn't start supper or tell the boys to wash up. None of us knew what to do, so we sat on our bed and waited. Mama finally rose and went to her special box. She brought out the diary and held it in her hands the way you might hold a baby, being careful of its head. In a flash she opened the door to our stove and tossed the book into the fire!"

I'm glad I'm holding Ethel's hand because she starts to topple over, and I catch her.

"I was the only one who got off the bed and ran over to wrestle with the flames. Mama just stood by, the knuckle of a finger caught between her lips. Completely frozen. I dug around with a poker and was able to stab the cover and a page beneath it and pull it out. The rest was lost."

Mama finally opens the folder and I see a scrap of ancient paper. Mama has to be careful because the edges are flaking. This must be the page Mama is talking about, the one she rescued. The writing slants like a man leaning over. It's more perfect than anything I've ever written. There's not enough left to read properly except for a grand title drawn at the top. It says: "Cora's Journal."

"I think your grandmother was so tired of being hurt, she threw her love in the fire to kill it, once and for all."

Tears slide down my face, but Ethel warns me to hide them. I might not understand everything Mama is saying, and I'm sure Grandma still loved everybody just the same after what she did. But it hurts to know she was sad enough to burn her flying birds, her leaning men. Sad enough to let go of whatever she thought was important to write down.

On my father's birthday, we celebrate by going to his favorite Italian restaurant in Piper's Alley. I like how the brick tunnel we walk through has torches on the walls, like we've left Chicago and stepped into a castle. We sit down, and Dad hands me a plastic menu, even though I always get the same thing: mostaccioli. It makes me feel grown-up to trace all the dishes' names with my finger. I ask Ethel what she would like to eat. She sits in my lap, on my napkin. I ask her to be polite; she only ever wants a meatball.

The nice waitress, Sylvia, isn't working tonight, so we have someone new. She says her name is Tricia, but she doesn't smile. And when she sees Ethel resting her small dark hand on my brown one, she makes a face. I squeeze Ethel's hand to make her feel better. Mama's lips pinch together, and I know it means she's chewing on the soft place inside her cheek. Dad tells Tricia what we all want, including Ethel's meatball, but he won't smile either, even though it's his birthday.

As soon as Tricia turns her back, Mama stops chewing her cheek. She says, "Ignorant!" like that's the waitress's real name. "I thought we left all this behind when we moved to Chicago." Her voice is angry air, like the hot steam inside her soup kettle.

Dad shrugs and piles up the plastic menus Tricia forgot to take. "Sometimes white people are just gonna be white people. Racism follows wherever you go."

Mama breaks all the breadsticks that are in a jar on the table. She snaps them to pieces, then mashes them to crumbs. Mama must be really upset to do this; she doesn't believe in wasting food. She and Dad are still talking, but I don't hear them. Ethel is whispering something, talking to herself the way Grandma used to when she forgot we were right there with her. I listen hard so I can hear what Ethel is saying. She copies what Dad said: "Racism follows wherever you go." But then she adds more: "Into your future. Into your soul." I don't know what she means, but the words make me cold. My arms get bumps like the skin of a chicken.

Seems like Mama heard Ethel, since all of a sudden, she glares at her. "Sissy, why do you have to bring that damn doll with you everywhere?" Now Mama is staring at me, hard, and I don't realize I'm squashing Ethel's arm like it's a breadstick I could snap until Ethel cries out, and I let her go.

The week after Dad's birthday, Mama says, "It's been too long since we've gone to a wačhípi," which I know means "dance." I jump so high into the air with excitement, I end up falling on the floor. Ethel smiles and shakes her head. Mama says I'm clumsy, though she helps me up and dusts me off. Mama organizes us so quickly! When we're a block away from the American Indian

Center we hear the sleigh bells worn by men dancers on their ankles. Though I'm still sitting in the car with Ethel on my lap, part of me is already running down the sidewalk and up the stairs to the massive building. Mama is slow to get out of the car because she has a big kettle of waštúŋkala she made for tonight's feast. Dad comes over to help but Mama's already placed it on the ground so she can pat down her sleek turquoise dress she made using a *Vogue* pattern. Dad likes to tease and say she's a "stylish Indian," but I can tell he's proud of her. He carries the kettle, and Mama sweeps ahead of us while we trot to keep up.

The first person we see when we climb to the second floor and enter Tribal Hall is Mama's friend Ethel. When we're in her company I think of her as Big Ethel, and my doll as Little Ethel.

"There you are, dear heart," she says, as she wraps me in a hug. Her husband, Lee, has saved chairs for us against the back wall. They're older than my parents but Mama says they "bounce around like teenagers." She likes this about them, that they're always up for games like bridge or Scrabble, though their favorite pastime is golf.

Lee is taller than Dad, so tall that folks tease and ask if he was stretched on a rack. He had to get a special set of golf clubs so he wouldn't have to stoop on the course. He and Dad root for the White Sox, not the Cubs, while Mama and Ethel don't follow baseball at all. Hockey is their favorite sport to watch. Lee says Ethel would've made a killer goalie if they'd let women play in the league, because "nothing gets past that woman." She reminds me of a squirrel—fast and light on her feet, nervous if she has to sit still for too long. When she plays bridge, she keeps getting up to stretch or replace empty bowls of snacks. Ethel was the first friend to hold me after I was born because Mama wanted her to be at the birth. Ethel told me once that she whispered something secret into my newborn ear that day, and when I'm older she'll share the message to remind me. She winked then, and I felt that whatever she said was something good, like she cast a spell of protection or promised that three of my wishes would come true. She's the closest thing I have to a fairy godmother—a Dakhóta one.

Lee is quieter than Ethel, he lets her do most of the talking. He watches her the way Dad watches Mama. He has a soft smile that looks like he has sad memories but they're from so long ago he can ignore them. Being around Ethel would cheer anyone, so maybe she's his happy ending? Tonight, though, he looks upset, like his stomach hurts. He leans over to Dad and says he wants to tell him something, so Dad and Big Ethel switch seats. I want to dance more than anything, get into the powwow arena, which is really a gymnasium with a polished wood floor. The bells always trigger my excitement, like I'm a pinball machine and someone has just popped the plunger, sending a steel ball rocketing through my system. But now I'm torn, both wanting to dance and wanting to hear what has Lee looking so worried. Little Ethel decides for me; she says we can dance as soon as we finish playing detective. So, I slide onto Dad's lap, pretend I'm sleepy and want to nap in his arms. I hug Ethel close, but make sure her ears aren't covered so she won't miss anything.

"What's going on?" Dad asks his friend. Lee scoots his wooden folding chair closer. My eyes are closed but I can hear the noise.

"I was raised to believe in spirits," he says. He pauses so long that Dad offers a little encouragement with, "Mmm hmm."

"I've heard ghost stories all my life and never made fun or thought they weren't true, but now I've had my own strange experience. Such a one last night." He goes on to tell Dad how he went golfing as he always does on weekends when the weather is decent. Big Ethel had to help out at a party and wasn't with him, so he stayed out later than usual.

"It was silly of me, trying to play when I could barely see the ball anymore. And it was chilly, too. Don't know what got into me, I just didn't want to leave."

I'm beginning to think I should go ahead and dance, this sounds like boring grown-up talk, but Ethel pats my hand in a sign to wait.

"Finally, I packed it in and started across the course. It was a bit of a hike back to the car. I was all alone, at least as far as the eye could tell."

I feel a shiver across my scalp and I'm glad now that I listened to Ethel.

"Cornelius, I heard a noise at my back that made me spin around—a wild, desperate panting like the ghost of a panther who's run a hundred miles to save its life. It was dark so I pulled out my lighter. Nothing to see. Then the flame scared me, because I didn't want to be seen by whatever was making that noise. So I snuffed it. I hustled along faster but the noise followed. Insistent. Then I heard a voice cry out—not in words, just fear, pain. No, bigger than that, sheer terror! It was horrible. Especially when I realized it wasn't the moaning cry of a wild cat but a frightened young woman. She chased me all the way back to my car. And I hated myself for not having the nerve to turn around and speak, to stop and give her comfort. I was that afraid."

"I'm so sorry." My father is mumbling. I can tell he's shocked; this isn't even close to what he thought Lee would share. "I don't know what I'd do in a situation like that. Sounds awful. But you're okay now?"

"No." Lee says that he and Big Ethel called a friend who's been using that golf course for a lot longer than they have, to see if there were any stories of strange happenings. Turns out there are. The friend said that a young woman was killed on that golf course back in the thirties. She broke things off with her boyfriend and he kidnapped her, determined to change her mind. He was driving them back to his place when she jumped out of the car and dashed to the course, trying to get away.

"He pulled off the road and chased her down, so angry that she was serious about leaving him. Once he caught up to her, he strangled her to death. Left her poor body there on the grass for others to find in the morning. The old man who found her had a heart attack in reaction and died the next day. So, there were two deaths that came of that evil."

"Oh, Lee." My father's voice is thick with sorrow.

"I couldn't sleep all night, swear I could feel her breath on my neck, still hear her gasping panic in my head. I kept thinking, I have to save her! Though of course she's long dead. Her story is done. But it isn't. I can't bear that some part of her is still playing out the worst moments of her life. It isn't fair! If anyone should be running up and down that course it should be her killer, chased back into hell each night!"

I don't want to hear more. Now I'm sorry I stayed to listen. I guess there are reasons why adults clam up around kids, don't want us to know all there is to know. If we had any idea of all the bad things that could be waiting for us, we might just give up and refuse to get older. I pretend to wake and move back to the safety of Big Ethel, though she has a serious face and is whispering, so I bet she's telling the same story. I close my ears and focus on the drum, change into my moccasins. Then I set Little Ethel on my chair so she can watch and see how it's done, watch me scrub with my favorite Ho-Chunk dancers, arms pumping up and down like I'm doing laundry the old-time way. I stick to Ho-Chunk style even though Mama is forever saying I should follow her friend Pauline and dance like her, since she's Dakhóta like us. I throw myself into music like it can save me—keep me out of the place where a girl died a long time ago, and is still dying, over and over again.

Dancing pauses for a dinner break, and Mama hands me a bowl of her waštúŋkala with a side of fry bread. I don't eat it right away. First, I enjoy inhaling the steam that smells so good, poke at the large white kernels of corn that will burst in my mouth like tender eggs. Strands of venison coax me to try a taste but I have to cool the soup first. I blow on the surface the way Mama showed me, not too hard or I'll make a mess and spatter myself. I ask Ethel if she wants a sip. She wrinkles her nose and says, "Bambi."

I promise her that Bambi is fine and not anywhere close to Mama's soup, but with each spoonful of my favorite dish, Ethel whispers, "Bambi," at me. I just ignore her. Most of the time she's my best friend in the world, but she has bad days like everybody else where she's all prickles and irritation and likes to tease.

Our emcee for the evening is a friend of my parents. Mama likes how funny he is, "that Dave is never at a loss for words," she says. He has a table set up onstage, high above us, so he can watch the action. If folks get restless, he calls out a specialty number, like he does now: "Ladies, find your man, we're asking our Chi-Town Drum to give us a Rabbit Dance!" He whoops playfully into the microphone and teases the men, tells them he's keeping an eye out and they better not run off. Rabbit Dance is always ladies' choice. I have a deal worked out with my buddy Mark, who's just a year older than I am. He does fancy dance style and is pretty good—he learned how to do the splits and likes showing off at the end of a song by landing that way, his arms thrown wide and head down. All dramatic. The deal is that I ask him to dance and in return he wipes down his hands so they're not sweaty when we take hold. Mark teases me too much though, making faces if I happen to look in his direction, calling me "Tiger Lily" like I'm some made-up Indian princess of the Disney tribe. Dad says it's because he likes me but that doesn't make any sense at all, so I keep warning Mark that I might not ask him to dance next time. He just makes kissy-kissy sounds at me and laughs.

Tonight, when the emcee calls for a Rabbit Dance, I note where Mark is and decide I'll take my time before moseying over to claim him. I'll let him sweat for a couple of minutes. Then I note Mama rising out of her chair, settling her black dance shawl across her shoulders. Mama never dances, and Dad only when there's an Honor Song for veterans. But Mama gathers herself, then turns to Dad with a mischievous look in her eye. "Will you do me the honor?" she asks. My heart does a ballet leap.

"The honor is all mine." Dad rises and takes her hand—she leads him onto the dance floor. They're the third couple in line. I'm glued to the floor and can watch only them as they two-step in perfect time with the drum, with each other, Mama smiling and Dad looking happy enough to cry. They know all the steps, how to separate and then find each other again, reach their arms high in the air to make an arch for other dancers to pass under, and then stoop to follow, moving gracefully beneath a tunnel of arms. They know when to dance backward, and when to step forward again, never losing a single beat. They're the most beautiful couple I've ever seen, including the ones in movies, and tonight in this dance they look crazy about each other. I'm sad when it ends, and only then remember to look for Mark. Turns out another girl asked him, one we both think is stuck-up because she's so unfriendly and never cracks a smile. Mark lifts his eyebrows at me in question, and I shrug, hoping my shoulders look apologetic. I'm not really sorry though. I could watch my parents dance together all night.

I think I've been able to push away the awful story I overheard. Ethel and I fall right to sleep after Dad tucks us in. But the scared lady catches me in a dream. I don't just hear her, I see her, trying to run in heels that keep tripping her up on the grass. She doesn't think to toss them off the way Mama would. I don't see a man chasing her, but I don't have to. I can feel his rage whipping all around us like the tornado Dad said tore up their homeplace when he was born. Then the dream changes so now *I'm* the girl he's chasing, and even though I kick off my shoes it isn't enough. I can feel his fingers touch my shoulder blades. Any second he'll grab me, and I'll be finished. I guess I cry out because Dad is suddenly there, hushing me and telling me I'm safe. He says nothing bad will ever hurt me while he's around. I know he means it, but my body doesn't believe him. Even with an extra blanket covering me and Ethel, it doesn't stop shaking until morning sun butters the walls and covers every shadow.

It's a week before Thanksgiving, that complicated holiday my parents both enjoy and hate. We all love the food: Mama's roast turkey with dressing, mashed potatoes and gravy, pumpkin pie with a big spoonful of whipped cream. We love the gathering of friends who join us, including Big Ethel and Lee. What my parents don't appreciate is the story behind the holiday, which they remind me each year is a cleanup job to hide the awful harm Pilgrims brought to tribes they first encountered. Thanksgiving is a tricky time of year for us—the weather's getting cold here in Chicago, and we're reminded how different our version of the truth is from that of other Americans who believe Pilgrims were satisfied with what our people gave them. So, I should have watched my step rather than be too sensitive, as Mama always warns. I should have been more careful. Now it's too late.

I don't tell Dad or the policeman what really happened because grown-ups don't believe us. They pretend to believe sometimes, but that's just play. You can tell because they're smiling or using a different voice that is too high. When the policeman keeps asking me questions, I just shrug and lean into Dad's side. His hand is resting on my head, and it's heavy but also nice. I wish I could tell him, but I don't think I will. I'm holding Ethel against my stomach, and every time I look down at her, she shakes her head just a little bit. She's warning me to keep quiet. Acting like she's my mother again. I put one hand on her head like Dad's rests on mine, and because I feel so safe like that, like a daisy in a beaded chain Mama taught me to make, the truth runs through me like it's happening all over again.

Mama and I are walking home from the A&P store. She's got her hands full with one big bag of groceries and a heavy glass jug of milk. She's wearing her pretty fall coat, which is as red as her lipstick, with large black buttons. I'm helping her by carrying a light bag packed with two cartons of eggs and a loaf of bread on top, the food she doesn't want to get squished. I grip the rolled-up top of the bag with all my might, trying to be careful, but I can't help kicking at leaves on the ground. They crunch when I stomp them flat, which makes me feel like a powerful giant! We're close to home when I see a small gray poodle in the park outside our building, just like Judy, the zombie dog from my nightmare. Judy grins at me and I'm sure she's that same dog. I'm not scared though, because I remember that she liked my singing. I want to pet her, but I don't have a free hand since I'm holding Ethel, who isn't a fan of dogs. Judy grins at me and I spin in her direction to at least say hello, when my feet don't work the way they would if I was a ballerina. They tangle and bring me down hard on my knees, right on top of the grocery bag I was supposed to be minding. I dropped the bag to save Ethel—she is my first worry. I don't want her to get a concussion like Dad did last year. Ethel whispers that she's just fine but I better peek at Mama because she *isn't*. Mama's standing above us, poking at the squashed bag with her foot. We don't have to look inside to know the eggs are busted and the bread is a flat pancake. Her mouth opens big, bigger, and for a second, I think she's going to keep opening her mouth until it's large enough to scoop me up and swallow me whole. Judy and the lady who was walking her have rushed away from us, and it's just me and Ethel and Mama, and the ruined bag that's proof I can't do *anything* right. Mama's mouth stays open but delivers no sound, which is scarier than her shouting things like I'm a clumsy mess and she can never trust me with the simplest thing, or that I'm selfish and don't appreciate her. Her mouth is shocked, but her eyes know what to do. They spin from midnight black to the color of Red Hots. Ethel whispers that Mama is so mad she can't even talk, and we better *do* something. I straighten my sore knees and untangle my enemy feet. I run for my life!

I'm not too fast. Ethel is heavier when I run. Her head is bouncing in a way I don't like; it might hurt her, but I don't have time to do anything else. Mama chases after me, slowed down by groceries and the big jug of milk. I hear her shoes slap the pave-ment, and each smack is as scary as a monster coming out of my dreams. Mama doesn't like running, doesn't appreciate my do-ing something without permission. Mama's calling at me in that voice that screams trouble, but I block her out. It's the only way to be brave enough to save my life and Ethel's. Then, because Ethel can read my thoughts, she says, "You might save your life only to lose it when Mama gets hold of you." Her voice shakes like my running has given her hiccups. She's right, but I can't stop. Fear's whipping me along, getting bigger, not smaller. Bigger when I gain the entrance to our building after going around the long way, thinking maybe I'll wear Mama out, and she'll cool off. Bigger when I hit the stairs. Bigger and bigger as I go up and up and up, past our second-floor apartment.

My hearing opens again—a drum is beating in my ears. Mama

hollers that Christian name we don't use anymore. Her voice is louder because she's in the entranceway below. There's a loud smash that finally makes me stop. I look through the bannister rails. There's a wide-open space where I can see all the way down to where Mama is standing, four stories below. She's dropped the jug, which has broken, splashing her legs with milk. I see shiny bits of glass. She sets down the groceries and sidesteps the mess. She starts chasing up the stairs, her red wool coat with black buttons flapping around her legs. I'm one floor from the top, and when I get there, I'll be stuck. There's just an open landing and doors to an apartment on either side. I don't know the folks who live there. I run up those last stairs anyway, then back up against the wall. Mama is so fast I don't have time to do anything else. She's near the top step. I'm scared to look at her face, but Ethel whispers that I better. So, I make myself. Her eyes are red like her coat.

Mama's anger is a second person on the stairs. Like it's so big it can't fit inside her anymore.

Mama's anger is fire red, smoking red, like coals for barbecues. Ethel keeps whispering scary things. For once she isn't helping. She says it looks like the Devil never left Mama when the nun let her out of the closet. She says Mama's going to hurt us, the Devil's going to hurt us. I don't think she's ever been this afraid before. I'm so crazy scared in my head that I'm screaming in there, though my lips are stuck together, so no one hears. The only thing to do is close my eyes and give up. Let whatever Mama does happen. Because she's big and I'm small, and Ethel is only a doll. I even raise my arms like bad guys do on TV shows when they've had enough.

Mama leaps up the top step. I feel the wind she makes as she rushes in front of me. I can smell her perfume—it's all over both of us. I'm gripping Ethel so hard in my raised hand, she squeaks. The last thing I remember is Ethel shouting, "Don't look!," as I choke on Mama's perfume that is too sweet, like medicine. I'm about to faint when I hear the noise, like another scuffle of tangled feet. A crack, a scream that's moving away from me. I make myself open my eyes. Mama's gone. It's just me and Ethel, standing there together. I'm squeezing Ethel so hard it hurts. She tells me to stop. Then she says, "I took care of it. Somebody had to." And I look at her little hands, smaller than mine, and I look through the bannister that runs along the landing like a fence. Mama is at the bottom, lying on top of milk and glass. The red from her eyes is all around her head, and she's staring up at me but doesn't see anything.

Dad is saying something now, and I'm glad because I don't like to remember how Mama looked.

He's giving the policeman information. Mama's age, our phone number. Mama's Christian name: Lillian.

"Just like this one here," he says with tears in his voice, and he strokes my hair. That's right, I'm Lillian, too, named after Mama because she said we have to have a Lillian in every generation. But later that night, once I stop crying for Mama, which has made my eyes swollen and burned by salt, I whisper to Ethel that I'm never gonna use that name. I want to be me, not Lillian. Ethel says that sounds right. She doesn't want to be anyone but Ethel. I crush her to my chest and start crying again. So she hushes me and tells me to sleep.

PART 2

Hole in the Heart

Lillian ~ 1930s

The Bureau of Indian Affairs doctor says I was born with a hole in the heart. It's the main thing I remember about myself and who I am. The first time I see a chicken heart, Iná making ready to cook it just for me when the other kids are running around outside and I'm stuck in a sawed-off beer keg with edges too high for me to climb, I beg her to let me hold it before it goes in the pan. Iná sighs but gives it to me. The meat fills my palm. I bring it to my ear because my own heart makes noise when I do anything too much, but this one is silent. Silent and perfect, there aren't any holes. I squeeze it and wish I could switch it for mine. I'm jealous of that heart in all its beauty. Glad now that Iná is going to fry it up for me to eat. I will swallow what I can't have.

Those first years I spend more time with Iná than my sisters and brothers. I grow up in that damn beer keg that smells like rotting fields. For years I can't get away from the smell because even when I'm lifted out of the keg I carry the stench on my clothes, skin, and hair. Alvina told me once that despite the stink, I'm the most special in our family because of my "affliction." Blanche made a face and when I asked my sisters why a defect would make me special, Blanche said, "It means you're spoiled! You get treats and no one shouts at you, because God bit you before you were born and didn't like the taste—he spit you out." Alvina hushed her. She's the oldest and acts like a fence between me and Blanche.

Eventually I learn why Blanche teases me so much—she's stuck in the middle between me and Alvina, and then there are twin boys right behind me, Oscar and Teddy, so she doesn't get noticed much. But if I'm so special I wonder why everyone calls me Waŋské, which isn't a name but a number, telling folks I'm the fourth child in this family, behind Alvina and Blanche and another girl who died before I was born. I complained about it once and Iná said I had a fancy name that sits on my birth certificate, and she brought it out of a drawer in our bureau to show me. I was only three then, so I couldn't read yet, but Iná promised that my Christian name was there on the paper: Lillian. To me it looked nothing more than a smudge.

I can read perfectly now. I taught myself from the one book we have in our cabin, left behind by an old "Wobbly" who passed through town a few years ago and stayed with us for a week because he found my parents interesting. They are politics people who follow the complicated disputes of leaders on our reservation, and even those in Bismarck, North Dakota, and Washington, D.C. I think he left that book behind as payment because we shared our food with him even though that meant no one had a full stomach. He had kind eyes in a cold color—silver ice. He showed me the book one night, brought it over to my beer keg and propped it on the edge so I could see the pictures.

"This is a book on child labor," he said, pointing to photographs of scrubby-looking white children with dirty faces and no smiles. "They are treated inhumanely by greedy bosses."

I wasn't interested in the bosses, but after the Wobbly left I liked to bring his book into the beer keg with me so I could visit with those children, who made me cry. That's how I thought of it, that we were friends now, with me peeking in the book's windows to wave at them. Some days I swear they waved back. When I'd memorized each face and had made up a name for every kid, they started talking to me in my head. They helped me pick out the words beneath their pictures, then words at the top of the page. By the time I was four I could read the whole thing, and people came to our cabin to test me, their mouths hanging open as I read and read about white children who were maybe as poor as us but looked more miserable.

Iná works a small shuttle in her hand to make magic. I like to watch her take something as plain as string and turn it into a lacy giant snowflake that drapes over her arm as it grows. She says this is "tatting," which she learned how to do at the Carlisle Indian Industrial School in faraway Pennsylvania. She sings Carlisle songs as she tats, tunes she said were performed by their marching band. She hums Dakhóta songs while she peels potatoes and cooks. She can be many people, just not at the same time. And she changes *again* whenever *he* is home. When he is in a good mood, she laughs and lets him pull her into a stiff-legged dance. When he is angry, smelling of hooch, she's so quiet you can barely see her. Iná melts into the walls.

I don't call our father "Até" or any English versions of the word. I call him "him" or "Jack." Even when he's nice to me I'm always keeping one eye on him because you need to watch what he's thinking.

Today when he comes home from no work, with no coins, and only a half-stink of hooch, he waves me over from my perch on the big bed I share with my sisters and little brothers. I've been reading the child labor book for the one millionth time. I tuck it under the blanket to keep those kids warm.

"I'm not going to steal your book," he says. He isn't frowning, so I take my time crossing the room.

"I know."

"What's in your noggin today?" He pats me on the head, and even though he means well, his hand is heavy, which makes my knees buckle.

Iná is here and not here.

"Me and Blanche made a graveyard," I tell him.

"Blanche and I." He pats me harder.

"Blanche and I." English is his second language, or maybe his fourth because he spoke all three dialects of our language before he ever went to school, but he hates English so much he's careful with it. He wants us to be careful, too.

"Go on."

"Blanche and I made a graveyard for the birds." With him it's best to say as little as possible because you never know what word will come at him like a punch and make him angry. So I don't tell him how we buried Julius, our pet magpie that died in the night, Iná giving us a piece of fabric to wrap him up with all the odds and ends of treasures he stole that aren't worth anything to anybody else. I also keep quiet about the second burial we performed once our bird was safely in the ground and properly mourned with testaments to his good character, thieving aside. Blanche said we should bury Jack, to keep Iná from falling pregnant every year and suffering miscarriages, to keep her from turning invisible each time he walked through the door. I looked around to make sure no one overheard my sister's mischief. Blanche brought a bucket of water from the well and poured it on the ground. I watched as she worked the mud in her hands, molding it into a man the size of a doll.

"I did this part, so you dig," she ordered. I was too surprised and nervous to argue with her. I grabbed Iná's garden spade and chipped at the dirt until I'd made a pit large enough to hold the mud father.

Blanche used the spade to scoop him up, and then paused in her work as if shocked by how little he weighed, how much she'd reduced him to child size with her mud magic. She let him slide into the hole, not seeming to care that he fell to pieces—the head smashed by the rest of him. She covered him up with the small hill of earth and patted down the grave.

Blanche crossed her arms, clutching her shoulders, and spoke as solemnly as the local priest: "Here lies our father, who art NOT in heaven, and piss be his name. We won't cry over you; you'll never be missed. You can drink with the Devil, and we don't care if he roasts your liver!"

My legs weren't shaking until she started saying "we." She included me in her angry medicine, and it made me feel unsafe, like we were the lone trees for miles, exposed on Proposal Hill as lightning slashed the sky, headed straight for us.

Jack has no idea we killed him today in our game. He mumbles, "A graveyard for the birds. That's the kind of thing my little sister would have created." His face turns sad, which makes him look handsome, like an Indian version of the actor John Gilbert. His eyes are soft instead of mean. And the silver stripe in his head of black hair adds a touch of mystery.

The doctor says the hole in my heart is closed now, but I don't believe him: first, because he drinks too much and can't walk straight without his fingers touching the hospital wall; second, because most of the time when I look at Jack, my heart spills out every good feeling like it's a broken tap. Usually there's nothing left to warm him, or me, and we stand together in the cold. But today he looks awfully sad, which stoppers my heart. He pulls me onto his knee and presses my hands between his. I feel guilty, like I'm betraying Iná by comforting the enemy, but Jack's tears fall onto the back of my shirt and my heart gets so big it scares me. Maybe his tears work medicine on me like old Mrs. Standing Cloud's bring-him-back love cure that is sure to lasso wayward husbands, so they don't run away from home anymore.

Jack stares at the pattern of our hands, laces our fingers together. He tells me a story that's hard to follow because tears make him pause and his breath flows past my ear, close enough for me to smell the good time he was having before things went sour. But the part I remember is how his sister died when she was little.

"They stole her from me," he says in a whisper that breaks into a sob. "I was the only one she believed in, and I let her down. I couldn't steal her back." I think the story is finished but Jack leans forward so the last words are just for me and my right ear: "She haunted me for ages. Every closet I opened, every drawer I dug through, I'd feel her little hand suddenly grab mine in the dark. One night I begged a tramp to chop them off, these damn hands. He said, 'Kid, you're drunk. Go home. You need your mitts.' What did *he* know? How'd *he* like it if the only person in the world who cared about him kept tugging on him to do the impossible— pull her back into this world, make her alive again?"

Jack lets me slide off his knee. He's nursing his misery now to the point where it's almost a pleasure and doesn't notice how I head over to Iná and sling an arm around her neck, so she'll know I'm on her side. I'm latched on to Iná but still following Jack in my head, wondering why he never thought of a different possibility for his sister's haunting. How maybe she didn't want to return to *this* world but was trying to haul him into hers.

It's late summer and we all feel the shadow of a new school year creep closer. Iná puts us to work in her garden on a hot morning with a furnace wind. The dry soil scrapes at our faces like sandpaper, and we sweat through our overalls. Blanche and I are at war with potato bugs. We're not squeamish, though we do get sick of the flies treating our cabin like it's theirs. But potato bugs are vile. Even Iná, who taught us to honor all beings, who made us return beans we stole from a field mouse's hidden cache, who insists we should *never* kill unktómi or ruin her webs, even *she* is no fan of the six-legged monster with a demon face. We have to inspect each plant near the root, and carefully remove the bug so its jaws don't chomp our fingers. To kill them, we snap off their heads and toss them in a jar of kerosene. We try to tempt Fairbanks with fresh corpses since he has a taste for beetles, but he hops away from us like we're trying to poison him, shrieking, "Bad! Bad!" in outrage. He's a fussier fellow than our last pet magpie. We shouldn't have named him after a movie star.

"Goodbye, Sister Frances. Goodbye, Sister Bernard. Ashes to ashes, dust to dust." Blanche is mumbling at the doomed bugs until I wonder if she has sunstroke.

"What're you talking about?"

She glares at me like I'm the one responsible for this chore. "I'm pretending that it's not just potato bugs I'm massacring."

"Oh." Next thing I know I'm copying Blanche. "Goodbye, Sister Nora. Goodbye, Sister Gertrude." It *is* very satisfying to eliminate the nuns from our garden as if we're actually removing them from their positions as teachers and overseers at our boarding school, so we'll never have to see them again.

There's only one we consider decent. We kill Sister Frances over and over, but Sister Anne escapes death. And maybe this game gets us in trouble with the mission school god? Maybe he's just as hot as we are, so his sense of humor has melted? Because pretty soon Jack is staggering toward us, shouting in a mix of languages all jumbled by hooch. He's carrying his ancient shotgun, which is as much a danger to him as any target.

Blanche grabs my wrist as if to steady me. We rise together, slowly, until our knees lock tight to help us feel brave.

Jack settles on raving in English, shouts that if we don't clear out, he'll shoot us into the next world. He screams that he's not going back to Carlisle, no one can take him back to Pennsylvania. "I'm not leaving my ma; I'm not leaving my sister. They need me!" He's ten feet away now, and swaying, the shotgun wavers between Blanche and me. "You can't take me away; I'll kill you first!"

He shouts and shouts, the words scraping his voice raw, how he's not a boy, he's a man. He starts blubbering and almost drops the gun as he swipes his eyes with one arm.

"Must've been a bad batch," my sister whispers. There have been a few times where Jack got his hands on hooch that is so dangerous it fries his brain, messes with his vision so he can't properly see. Hooch has blinded Jack, turned his girls into reservation agents or other officials who want to drag him across the country to kill the Indian part of him, turn him into a white man. As a kid he ran away from Indian boarding school so many times he was declared a delinquent and locked up in an adult jail for a whole year.

I hear movement behind me, see Alvina dart into a run just outside Jack's limited field of vision. She's no doubt headed for Little Soldier's place to get help—he's our grandpa, Indian way. He was a young fighter in the battle that wiped out Custer and his men, though he never brags about his war exploits or victories. If anyone can bring Jack out of his monster drunk, it's this sweet old man who refuses to sit in a chair or lie down on a bed. He carries a large square of canvas to spread on the ground when he wants to sit or nap, and his back is so straight Blanche told me a story about how his spine isn't human bone but the sapling trunk of a cottonwood tree. I knew she made that up but decided to believe it anyway because Grandpa Little Soldier deserves to be part tree.

I try not to stare at Jack, though I want to keep an eye on the gun. My sick heart feels kicked up like a herd of wild horses. I keep having to swallow—fear is greasy in my mouth. I'm sliding away from my body because it's too uncomfortable to stay inside it. Maybe Jack already killed me, and I'm a ghost looking back at myself and Blanche? The sun is behind me now, boring its heat through my skull. I can't be dead, or I wouldn't feel anything. Jack is gone because now I'm standing where he is, and the gun is heavy in my hands. I'm so confused. Why can't I just set the weapon down? Because Blanche is still holding my wrist like she's handcuffed to me. I slide back into my body just in time to hear Grandpa Little Soldier ride up on his horse. Before I learn how it's all going to turn out, find out if Jack murders us in the yard, my face rushes at the ground in a dead faint.

Jack is penitent for days after threatening to shoot me and Blanche. Grandpa Little Soldier confiscated his gun, but he hasn't made a peep to complain. He also hasn't had a drop of hooch, so by the third day he's sleeping most of the time, sweating and shivering under the blankets though it's still hot, his hands too shaky for him to hold a cup. Iná has to feed him like a baby.

This morning we all sleep late, just like Jack. Alvina finally rousts us from bed, takes over breakfast chores when Iná is nowhere to be found. She brings in water from the well and covers it with a flour sack to protect it while the dust settles to the bottom. The dirt is flying in from everywhere this summer to the point where our broom is useless though we still scrape at the floor out of habit.

Jack mews from the bedroom like a sick cat. Alvina tends to him. She's more patient and tenderhearted than me and Blanche. She hopes to be a nurse.

"If he wants anything bad enough, he can crawl out here and get it himself," Blanche mutters.

We're not going to wait on him.

Alvina must work some kind of healing magic because this morning Jack shows his face in the kitchen, leaning on her like she's a cane. She helps him to a chair. Blanche and I scatter to the other end of the cabin and watch him warily, listen to him sip the cold muddy coffee Iná left for him. He's like a wolf in a story, dressed up in a man's skin so he can fool people into trusting him. Only to show his true teeth right before he bites.

Jack can't seem to look any of us in the eye, just stares at his coffee like there's a world to be observed in its murky depths. I picture the Loch Ness Monster everyone was talking about last year, a miniature one, swimming in Jack's cup, thrashing its tiny tail to splash him. That would be exciting! While that doesn't happen, Jack does surprise us. When Alvina asks where our mother is, he begins talking.

"Your iná was called away for her good counsel." He thumbs the side of his cup like he's swiping it clean. Which is a funny thing for someone to do when you've seen them pass out with their face in the dirt, inhaling it.

"But why Iná and not you? You're the best speaker on the whole reservation." Alvina is like Jack's booster. Blanche shoots a glare at her.

He drops his head. I don't think it's a nod of agreement; maybe his skull is packed with thoughts and got heavy all of a sudden. But he doesn't ignore Alvina like he ordinarily would.

"I'm not . . . consistent," he finally says. "They know they can always count on Cora, but they can't count on me."

There's a sudden hush in our cabin. The boys who were playing in the corner with Fairbanks, chattering as they work to teach him more words than "bad" and "mine," have gone silent. Fairbanks is quiet, too, his clever eyes staring at our father. We're all used to Jack spouting nonsense, used to his rants, his jolly clowning, awful bullying, or crying jags. We're not used to Jack being honest.

Jack sighs. "I was given the gift of oration—not in English though. English doesn't have words for many of our concepts. When I was whipped for never letting go of my Dakhótiyapi, I'd think to myself: 'You could never learn my language. Your spirit isn't big enough to walk in our words. They hold mysteries you can only understand with the heart.' I thought all their talk talk talk was flat as a pancake, and you could understand anything they said even with a thin mind."

Blanche snickers, which startles me. Snaps me out of the trance Jack creates with words.

Jack takes a quick sideways glance at her. This small gesture of approval lifts him from his slumped pose.

"Words were my medicine when I was a boy, my power. Yet here were these people telling me to let that medicine go. You might as well just kill me then!" Jack slaps the table, and we all jump. Even Fairbanks hops closer to the boys. Jack notices the tension but doesn't apologize. He swirls the coffee in his cup in a mournful way.

"I was supposed to be a leader. Elders told my mother this when I was little. They saw good things in me. They encouraged me to listen when they were talking and reminiscing, when they analyzed challenges to see if there was another path that could preserve us. They would test me to see if I'd really heard them, and so I learned to speak in front of groups of people. And sometimes relatives visited from other regions, so I learned their dialects, too. The words made sense to me. I could see how they were related to each other, just as we were. How they could work together to tell a story or cut a new path through an old problem." Jack takes a sip of coffee and doesn't even make a face though it looks awful, which somehow feels like a kindness he's offering our mother.

"Sometimes when you lose every fight, you end up breaking. Your mother never breaks. She traveled the same roads I did, dealt with many of the same teachers and authorities. When she graduated from Carlisle, she hadn't seen her parents for nine years. Nine years away from home, each summer farmed out to live with a white family because she was a prize pupil, and they didn't want her going back to Indian ways. When she returned home, do you know what her parents did?" Jack doesn't wait for us to respond. He seems to be talking to himself now, lost in the past. "They built her a separate house since they feared she wouldn't be comfortable living the Indian way as they did. She lived all alone in that house, with people looking at her funny, full of suspicion, though at least she was slender then, so they didn't take her for a 'fort Indian.' Your iná was brokenhearted lonesome, maybe a bit lost at first. But she knew where she comes from, who she comes from. Her family, and yours, has a long line of hereditary chiefs, respected leaders. Ultimately, Cora's consistent honorable behavior showed everyone that she was still one of them, that she knew how to behave and understood what we owe one another in our thióšpaye, and beyond that, in our oyáte. She carries that deep trust on her shoulders, that responsibility. So when the people need help, they turn to her first. Sometimes they get my counsel as well when I can show up. But I'm not your iná."

Blanche surprises me by asking Jack a question. Usually, she does her best to deny his very existence. "How come you speak English with us all the time, though you hate it? And only speak Dakhóta with older folks?"

Jack blinks at her, twice, like he's trying to remember who she is. He gets so caught up in his memories and ideas, he floats away from us and talks more to himself than anyone.

"Challenging me, huh?" Jack pretend-growls, his hands shaking so much as he grips the cup; he can't scare anyone today.

Blanche shrugs. She's tough.

"Good question. I'll give you an answer, but it might not be true. Who knows?" Jack shrugs right back.

"Cora and I got into the practice once you started school, because you didn't understand us so well anymore. We know firsthand how that works, how you're punished for speaking our language. The constant policing of our ways and our words interrupts the ability to think fluently. Our thoughts get chopped up. We don't want that to happen to you. The hard fact is, we increasingly live in English, the language of those whose power directs our lives—or tries to."

I'm not as brave as my sister, but a question pops out of me before I have time to stop myself. "Why did you say that might not be the truth, your answer?"

"Getting it from all sides now?!" Jack looks tired, resigned. He keeps trying to muster some of his old vinegar, but the spark is dead. At least temporarily.

"What I meant is that we don't really understand half of what we do. We just go along and live. Maybe English is safer to me because it doesn't mean anything, because its words are empty to me. No heart. Sometimes when you lose a lot, you have to put your heart away to keep it ticking."

He raises his hands now—a great effort, which we know means, "Enough."

Even though Jack appears worn-out and humble as he shares truthful thoughts, in this moment he doesn't look broken at all. I feel a strange sensation in the region of my troubled heart, the beat unsteady, as if kicked out of rhythm. In a few breaths it arranges itself into the usual pulse, though I still feel strange, like I have to grow inside to make room for what might be new respect for my father.

Jack is finished talking when his hands begin to tremble so

violently he drops his cup. Being made of tin, it survives, and Alvina cleans up the spill. He motions for her to serve as his cane again, and she helps him back to bed. Blanche and I run outside, eager to discuss this morning's revelations! "Did you know Iná lived all by herself in a house?"

"Nope."

"I wonder what she did all day." Blanche is lying on the ground, feet in the air like she can walk on the clouds.

"Read," I say wistfully.

"Nah, I bet she went all over visiting people, seeing what they needed."

Blanche is right, that sounds more like Iná. I'm suddenly sad for her, wondering if she ever had fun, if she ever slipped off the halter of duty she wears so gracefully we forget it's there.

We talk about how Jack might've been an okay kid, someone who could've been our friend.

Blanche reads my mind, as usual. "Don't count on him to stay nice," she warns. "Feel a little bit better because now we know he wasn't always a son of a—"

"Blanche!" I interrupt where she's headed. Iná would be scandalized by such talk.

"Gun!" she says. "Son of a gun. Sheesh! Don't be such a goody-goody."

I stick my own feet in the air and kick my sister. We flail back and forth, bruise each other up and down our shins, but the pretend fight is a relief. We work out all the complicated feelings that can sit in the gut.

Blanche finishes what she was trying to say when I interrupted. "We can feel good that Jack has some . . . qualities. At least, he did once. But don't think today changes anything."

"I know." The words come out in a sad whisper that's almost

embarrassing, but Fairbanks swoops in for the rescue. The boys have taught him another word, and the magpie is eager to show off to anyone who will listen. He knows he's a smart, pretty boy. "Bird!" he shouts at us. "Bird bird bird!" He hops between us and spreads his wings. He's flashier than our last magpie friend, Julius. In addition to a black cap and white chest, he has blue tail feathers like he's wearing a piece of evening sky.

"We need to teach him some Dakhóta," Blanche growls, but she strokes the feathers at his throat. Her eyes widen. "What if we taught him to say 'čhesdí'?"

"Blanche!" Alvina overhears from the doorway. "Don't you dare! Don't be a headache for Iná."

For once my sister doesn't sass. She lies back and allows Fairbanks to strut up and down her torso, giggling when he tickles. He shows off his entire repertoire of English, punctuating each word with a dramatic ruffle of feathers.

"You're better than a movie star," Blanche tells him, and Fairbanks tips his head and accepts the compliment with grace. "Star!" he croaks and flies off as if to say the show is over, leaving us a little bit amazed.

For a week we have glimpses of who our father could be. But eventually old habits or demons capture him again and he's back to being Jack. One morning we wake to snores so violent they shake the walls—in a few places dried mud that plasters the chinks even falls out, as well as a shiny button Fairbanks stowed in one of his hiding places. He snatches it up before we can examine it, but none of us wears clothes with shiny buttons. Blanche says, "Good bird. Keep stealing from those BIA folks."

"Don't encourage him," Iná says, but it sounds like she's smiling.

Jack emits one last outrageously loud snort and falls silent.

"Go check on your father," Iná tells Blanche.

My sister grumbles under her breath, "To see if he's kicked the bucket." She walks to the bedroom in disgust.

Iná must've heard her but chooses to ignore the sass.

Alvina returns from the outhouse, wrapped in what looks like one of those fancy feather boas the film stars wear. When the thing flexes and creeps across her shoulder I see it's actually Bernice, her favorite bull snake. Bernice would be as tall as Alvina if she could stand on her tail, so she drapes around her in luxurious loops. Iná stops scrubbing the soup pot and wipes her hands on her apron. She strokes the snake with a finger until Bernice shivers, which Alvina explains is happiness. Bernice is a sleek beauty—creamy yellow with brown patches—but while we appreciate how she keeps down the rodent and rattlesnake populations surrounding our place, we're careful with her because in a bad mood she can get hissy. Though she has nothing but love for Alvina.

"Take her outside now, I don't want the boys to pester her."

When Alvina returns our mother motions for us to join her at the kitchen table. There are two chairs, both crafted by Jack, and two long benches so we can all fit. She hands each of us a small portion of kabúbu bread, made special by a dab of her homemade chokecherry jam. Alvina makes the treat last, taking tiny doll bites. In a few moments we're all staring at her, watching her eat.

"Don't stare," Iná scolds, but gently. She knows how hunger can interfere with manners.

Iná is so busy with work around the cabin, and answering the calls of community members, she disappears into her chores. Every now and then she drops her work to spend time with us. These are my favorite times—even the boys stop squirming and annoying each other, though I can feel the breeze as they swing their legs, which don't yet touch the ground.

"You know who made all our furniture?" Iná asks.

"Jack," says Blanche in a harsh, grudging voice.

"Your father." Iná can wilt us with the most inoffensive words.

"These are quality pieces. Plain, but look how everything lines up the way it should and is measured just right so there's no wobble from mismatched legs. He even worked grooves in the chairs to make it easier on our bottoms." Someone gasps. Iná takes such care with her language, raised as she was the old Dakhóta way, to be a lady. For our mother, "bottom" is racy.

Iná lifts a bundle from her lap and unwraps the package. It's her parfleche container of private treasures that no one is allowed to touch, not even Jack. She pulls out a small object we can't see because it's cupped in her hand. She holds it like a prayer stone.

"Your father and I were in school together," she says. "So far away from here, clear across the country in the East. We couldn't come home for visits, even in summer. One day I was homesick, severely blue. I didn't cry in front of anyone, but Jack knew me well and could see my tears even when they didn't fall. We had a secret hiding place where we would meet sometimes, though not often because nearly every minute was regimented like we were soldiers in the army."

We nod. It doesn't sound like school has changed that much, though we're glad we get to come home for visits and summer.

"I told Jack a story from when I was little. The buffalo had been hunted just about to extinction, slaughtered in the millions. Partly due to greed and partly because doing so undercut the strength of our tribes. But one autumn day we heard the blessed pounding of hooves in the distance, and a small herd rode over the hill behind my family's lodge. Oh, what a sight!"

I pretend I'm a small girl standing beside Iná, witnessing this wonder.

"They are magnificent beings, and so powerful. They tore off, skirting town like they knew exactly where to go. My parents started up an Honor Song though I was probably too excited to join them. I noticed a couple of stragglers, far behind the others. A mama buffalo and her little calf. The calf was having a hard time managing the hill and tumbled when it tried to run down to meet its mother. It cried in a way that would pain your heart, and when the mother came to the rescue, the calf couldn't stand up. He'd broken a leg."

Alvina is sniffling and I'm afraid I'll be doing the same any second. I can't bear the picture of the poor baby calf, scared and injured.

"You have to be careful around our buffalo relatives, respectful. They can kill a person with one toss of the head. But my mother went forward to counsel with the calf's mother. She walked very slowly, eyes forward, not staring at the being's face. She waited a small distance away and the mama buffalo remained calm, so she went up to her and stood beside her. She told her that we could look after the calf and maybe he would live. She promised we would take care of him until the herd returned. The buffalo took a long time making up her mind, figuring out if she could trust this human. Then she went over to her calf and licked his head. She turned so quickly we thought she was going to charge my mother after all, but instead she took off running in the direction of the herd. My father brought the calf home and we nursed him back to health. The sad thing was the herd never returned. Maybe they, too, were hunted out of existence."

Alvina is sobbing now, and Blanche screwing her lips to the side the way she does when she's fighting tears. I'm usually the crybaby, the one Jack calls a "hothouse flower," whatever that is. But I've gone strangely cold. Like I can clamp down on a feeling and kill it before it takes me over.

"That buffalo was like a brother to me, we grew up together, trusted each other. When he was full grown my father let our uncles take the buffalo away. People were too hungry for us to keep him, and a being like that was never meant to be a pet. He was so smart, he knew what was happening, and he looked me right in the eye to give me courage. We didn't talk through words, but I heard him all the same. He said this is the way of life. We live, we love, we give our bodies to the earth as food. We never really die. But he walked away slowly to let me know he was sad to be parted."

Iná's voice is thick with the memory. She opens her hand and lifts it forward so we can all see the beautiful carving of a buffalo that rests there. Teddy reaches for it, and quickly snatches his hand back. No one needs to tell him this is something more special than a toy. It's small enough to balance on a quarter. You can see details of hooves and horns, the shaggy mane of its head.

"Your father carved this for me when we were kids, after I told him the story. He said the buffalo came to him in a dream and told him to pass on the message that he's not really gone, and he'll always remember me." A single tear slides down Iná's beautiful face, slipping into her perfect mouth that looks as carved and lovely as the miniature my father made. "I don't mean to make us cry, just the opposite. The point is that even in difficult times, see how the light is always working to come in. Don't forget to notice."

She returns the buffalo to his nest in the parfleche packet. I stand shakily, understanding Iná just gave us a gift, but feeling lost in a swirl of emotions. There's so much to think about: Iná as a little girl still at home with her parents; an injured buffalo who becomes a member of the family; millions of our relatives massacred for the price of their hides; young Jack, talented and kind, offering Iná comfort. I wonder if her tear was for the lost buffalo, or for the memory of Jack. I'll have to think on what she said about the light, how it always comes in. Maybe. Problem is, so do the shadows.

♦ ♦ ♦

Floor space is limited in our cabin, so the walls are covered with practical items: tools, pails (including one for wathéča), braids of thíŋpsila, an ancient harness, a cradleboard. The one decorative piece Jack hammered into the wall is a photograph taken of Iná when she graduated from the Carlisle Indian Industrial School in 1909. It's printed on thick cardboard with inked curlicues on the border to make it look fancy. The picture has a hold on me though I see it every day. I never tire of kneeling on one of the chairs built by Jack, so I can better view the slim lady who holds a rolled-up document in a casual way. From her relaxed pose, you'd never know how hard it was to come by that particular piece of paper. She doesn't look like a Dakhóta woman at all except for the few flashes of skin—she's swaddled in white elegance from head to toe. I asked what her old-fashioned hairstyle was called, and she said a "bouffant bun," which was all the rage because of some girl named Gibson. She has the perfect features and clear-skin glow of the big stars in movie magazines. But beneath the floor-length white gown that covers her neck and even her arms, all the way past the wrist, is the strength and warm color of a Dakhóta woman. When Jack is coasting on a half-hooch buzz and catches the eye of that younger Iná, who lived so improbably before we kids were born, he says she is a "stunning model of contradictions." When Jack rockets through the place on a full bender he says Iná is a "wašíču pretender," and points as proof to the gold timepiece that's pinned to her graduation dress, since according to Jack only white people are arrogant enough to think they can capture Time. I'm drawn to the picture not for the reasons Jack mentions, but because this portrait is of someone who could never be invisible.

Jack is most dangerous when he's on the path between half-hooch and dead drunk. Dead drunk we can wash up if he pisses, and then put to bed. Dead drunk moans, and waves a weak hand from a prone position. Half-drunk is still in his body enough to remember love. But *full*-hooch is angry enough to hate everyone who crosses his path, and strong enough to do damage. Full-hooch will say things you can't take back, mean things that spray into a person like bird shot. Some of Jack's worst tantrums visit us when he's in that stage, and tension is all around him to the point you can almost see it, like a halo of lightning. My nerves act up when he's like that, my stomach clenched so tight it's not even hungry. The only way I can breathe sometimes is to pretend Jack is a writer, and this is a play he's writing for the stage. We're the folks he's hired to say our lines and move around as he commands, but in the end it's all make-believe and the curtain will come down when it's over, and everyone will still be alive for the next performance.

It's the final weekend before us kids head back to boarding school. Jack keeps going off with his friends to "chase his demons," as Iná calls his pursuit of liquor. Blanche mutters that you'd think he'd want to spend time with us before we're gone again, *not* that she cares. But Iná says that's exactly why he's running away—he can't bear these separations. When he finally does show up it's when we're all sleepy and Iná is pushing us to get ready for bed. We smell Jack as soon as he opens the door. He stands at the entrance like an unsteady sheriff about to make an arrest. He glances around the room like he's searching for the criminal who's caused such misery in his head. His hunt ends when he spies Iná's photograph. He staggers to it and leans so close I'm afraid he's going to take a bite.

"Who is this? No one I know!" He spins around to squint at us all, face after face. Iná sits on the edge of our big bed, an arm around each of my brothers. She's disappeared into being their mother. Jack walks before her and glares like she's the enemy.

"You think she's *you*?" he asks. Iná's posture is still as straight as the girl holding a diploma. She looks through Jack, like he's merely the ghost of her husband.

He snarls like a scared wolf backed into a corner. "Not anymore. Just look at you!"

When Jack is drunk, he loses his vocabulary and sounds like a bully in a schoolyard fight who knows maybe three words altogether. He goes on to mock Iná for losing her slender figure. She isn't fat. No one we know has much flesh on the bone. But I guess when you give birth to a bunch of kids, including ones who die, you don't look the way you did before.

Iná doesn't have many clothes, just two dresses and a skirt and top, but he snatches the skirt from where it sits on a peg. He barks for me and my sisters to come over. He holds the skirt open and tells us to step inside. Alvina cooperates, as always, and she pulls me in with her. Blanche glares at Jack, but she follows when I yank on her hand. His point is made—the three of us all fit inside. Is there room for another? He motions for the boys, and they approach warily, each measured step clearly painful, like they're condemned men being walked to the gallows. No one else fits. They shuffle backward to return to Iná on the bed.

Jack crows with triumph and jigs around the room. "Three children equal one of you, you lazy cow! Look how you've let yourself go. I thought you were supposed to be the pride of your family, the star of the tribe. And there you sit, your uŋzé wider than an ax handle. It's a wonder you fit through the door!" Jack goes on and on, snickering at his wit as we climb out of Iná's flower-print skirt. It's her favorite piece of clothing but I have the feeling she won't look at it the same anymore. I start to cry but clamp down on my heart until it freezes, and the tears return to the source. Blanche grabs my hand so hard it hurts. I look into her face—she's pale with fury. I'm scared she's going to make things worse, so I press her hand back in warning. Our grasp is so tight it feels like we're trying to break each other's bones.

The miserable play writes on, but at least the director refrains from adding violence. We don't give Jack anything to pounce on—maybe all of us are learning how to disappear. Eventually the curtain comes down and Jack weaves his way to the tiny bedroom he and Iná share. None of us washes up, which is practically a sin. We want to wink out like a candle that's spent its wax. Jack is snoring by the time Iná enters their room. She doesn't look back at us to wish us good dreams. She just lies down on the bed with a groan, the way she does when one of us is ready to be born, pushing at her insides with impatient feet. But there isn't any baby now unless you count Jack.

Because our parents have so little say in what schools we attend, this year Alvina and the boys are placed at the Flandreau Indian School in South Dakota, while Blanche and I return to Bismarck. This makes our leave-taking extra sad. Iná tells us to take heart as she helps us climb into Grandpa Little Soldier's wagon. Jack is nowhere to be found, which Blanche says suits her just fine, though she whispers it to me, wanting to spare our mother's feelings. Iná looks at us more closely than usual, tilts her head like she's puzzling out what we need.

"You've got storms at your back, but soon after arriving just wait, you're going to find a nice surprise. The sun will come out again." We nod respectfully. Sometimes Iná sees a little bit ahead, like she catches Time and races past him, then waits for the rest of us to catch up. Her words are a comfort in my head, but my sick heart still feels heavy as stone.

We begin our gray journey that even Grandpa Little Soldier can't fix with his sweet jokes. He takes us as far as the nearest railway branch, singing a song for warriors when we get close as if he wants to shore up our hearts with courage. A train will take us the near–fifty miles to our destination, the capitol of North Dakota, which has more wašíčus gathered in one place than anywhere else I've seen. Practically straight to the door of our school, situated on a high bluff a couple of miles out of town. We don't get to see the Bismarck sights very often, but we've walked past the famed Patterson Hotel, which is ten stories high! Iná's been there many times as an active member of the Nonpartisan League, attending meetings. I wish I could see her in action, apron left at home, wašíču men listening to her wise counsel. Even though Bismarck is an exciting place, with so many shops and the Paramount Theatre, my stomach begins to clench the closer we get to school. Sooner than I'd like, we're walking into the compound. Blanche marches ahead of me, determined to be stoic and accept our lot—we won't return home for months. I pause to prepare myself, like a knight in former times, strapping on his suit of armor. I look up—the color of the sky surprises me; it is such a beautiful blue and not the sickly yellow my eyes want it to be to match my heart. The clouds are pristine white, as if they've been plumped and bleached, and they float along as if they haven't any cares. Everything is the same as I remember: the stern-looking brick buildings, three stories tall, that house our classrooms, dormitory, and dining hall, and a scattering of small outbuildings like the barn and laundry. The most cheerful structure is the humble wooden chapel topped with a grand pointy steeple that seems like a mismatch, like someone putting on airs. Blanche said once that the steeple looks big enough to crush the building, and just might one of these days. She said it hopefully, though I always cross my fingers it won't when we're inside for Mass. What finally gives me the energy to push myself forward, into the new school year, is the steady voice of the Missouri River, which runs beneath this hill. Its powerful flow continues as it did before this place was built, before our teachers were born, before English words ever traveled across its waves. This water is my relative, and it's so much stronger than anyone inside these buildings.

As it turns out, Iná's prediction comes true. The Holy Thunder boys, like their name, bring an extra charge to our lives. Whenever they hang around me and Blanche, the stale air crackles with a brighter energy. They're new to the school, brought over from South Dakota after too many kids died of consumption at their last place. Luther is Blanche's age, and Cornelius is a month younger than me. They're brothers, but don't look related. Luther has a flat, moon face that's warm in color—his cheeks flushed like he just won a footrace. He's forever grinning, even when he's mad, and skittish as a coyote. The kind to run up to you, and then away, like he was never there. He teases. Cornelius is probably more handsome—a lot of girls sneak glances at him throughout the day. He has what I think of as regal features, strong and fine, and soft eyes that can't keep a secret. I can practically read his thoughts and feelings just by looking at them. He laughs at his brother's jokes but is quieter. He likes to draw pictures, even in the dirt when he can't scrounge extra paper.

Luther sits in front of me in class, and I notice the two whorls at the back of his head, spinning like twisters through his thick black hair. His earlobes are long and plump, and one morning I'm so eager to press those soft pads of flesh between my fingers I reach for one before catching myself just in time.

Blanche notices and shoots her eyebrows higher than I've ever seen, like she's shouting at me, *What are you doing?!* Blanche has no interest in touching boys or being touched by them, unless it's a brawl or a wrestling match, where she gets to pin them down and make them plead for mercy. People say the two of us look like twins, though Blanche is the tougher version, more muscle and bone and frustration, more skinned knees and chewed fingernails. Boys like her the way they like their other friends, and that's fine with her. But I'm not Blanche.

We become friends with the Holy Thunders when Blanche calls them over during exercise period, where we're allowed to leave the school buildings and play tag or our version of football, which is missing the ball. They're slow to respond, wary, not yet sure who they can trust.

Blanche can be diplomatic when she wants to be. She kills two birds with one stone in her opening salutation, a nod to both hospitality and mutiny by her use of the boys' Lakȟóta dialect in addressing them, though our Indian languages are strictly forbidden in this place. The brothers immediately light up at familiar words and whisper back. Luther talks the most, as they both watch the ground or our knees, in the polite way we're taught at home. No staring like white people do. They are more fluent in Lakȟóta than we are. We all switch to English once we've covered the niceties, and Blanche tells them this place is haunted by a demon in the basement.

"Try not to get locked in the punishment box, 'cause that's where the demon lives," she says. "But if you do, just tell him stories. That'll keep him distracted from chewing you up." She points to a dent in her shin that I know she's had since birth. "I fell asleep in the box one time, and the damn thing took a bite out of me. Look!" The boys examine what they can see of her leg through heavy wool stockings.

Their eyes widen and they nod at her with respect. I roll my eyes, but no one notices.

Cornelius makes a gesture for us to come closer, like what he has to say is important and secret. We huddle together and he tells us that in their last school they found something awful in one of the closets. I hear Blanche's breath hitch; she loves this kind of excitement, anything dark and spooky.

"That's right," says Luther. "I almost forgot."

"I'll never forget." Cornelius tells us that a teacher asked them to move boxes of supplies to the closet, to store them until they were needed. They didn't think anything of it until they were stacking the boxes inside and the overhead light went out.

"No big deal. It was day, so we could see enough to finish the job."

"But then . . ." Luther interjects, making his voice thick with suspense like actors' on the radio.

"But then," Cornelius says, following his brother's lead, "a cold rush of air brushed our faces and the light clicked on again. Then off. We heard crying from the darkest corner way in the back."

"It was so sad, the way women cry at funerals."

"It was brokenhearted." Cornelius pauses too long so Blanche steps on his foot. "Then whatever was there, was gone."

"Yeah. We could feel the difference. It wasn't cold or sad anymore."

Blanche twists her lips to the side. I can tell she's disappointed.

"Wait, there's more!" Cornelius must've caught that, too. "The light came back on, and I noticed scribbles on the wall, back in the corner where the crying was. I moved boxes to get a better look. There was writing in pencil, but messy, like from a little kid."

"What did it say?" Blanche is interested again. So am I.

"The same couple of words written over and over in a small patch." Cornelius kneels on the ground and uses his finger to trace words in the dirt. He draws the letters, so they look childish and wobbly, which makes them even sadder. We read: **HELP HOME HELP HOME HELP HOME**. He straightens up and dusts off his hand.

"Some kid," Luther finally says, and we shuffle in nervous agreement. No one wants to say what we're all thinking. That the kid was probably one of us and for all we know is now dead and buried, forever trapped in the school closet.

Sister Frances has a nose for everything good; she can smell out friendships and the rare moments when our hearts smile. She aims to squash our fleeting joys, and make sure the students under her watch never become allies. So, she quickly notices the attachment that develops between the pair of us sisters and the new boys from South Dakota. She breaks us up whenever she can, sending us on separate errands, which of course makes us only more determined to stick together. After a month of futile interference, Sister Frances calls me and Blanche into her tiny office. The three of us barely fit together in the space. There isn't room for more than her desk and chair and one bookcase, which is mostly empty. We stand in front of her desk and wait for the lecture.

Sister Frances is old, but the kind of old that could've happened when she was a kid. She's old in the way of the rare chokecherry that goes sour as soon as you pluck it. Unhappy old, not singing, smiling old like some of the elders back home. She's a thin stalk of dry grass locked inside the drapes of her habit. The black robe and wimple that seems screwed onto her head don't look like a uniform on her, rather a new skin she grew to stop being human.

Sister Frances taps the empty plane of her desk with her crucifix. Jesus's toes knock against the wood, and I can't imagine he's happy being shaken like that as he hangs there in agony. She doesn't seem to notice what she's doing. She's glaring at us with blue eyes that go pale when she's angry. Right now, they're near bleached, and her whole face looks to me like a colorless snow monster.

"I am *very* concerned about you," she tells us. The crucifix tap

tap taps and I think if Jesus could look up at me, he'd roll his eyes. "You're on your way to becoming lost girls."

I can't see Blanche's face, but I can *hear* her biting her cheek to keep from smiling. Blanche is going to wear that description, "lost girls," as a badge of honor.

Sister Frances launches into a lecture about how boys are bad, the whole lot of them except for the Pope and others who have taken vows to serve God. All of them want nothing more than to stick their Things in us, their filthy Things, which we should *not* allow until we're married and ready to be mothers. Even then we should limit contact with their Things. And above all we should never look at them because we might go blind from the shock and evil.

Sister Frances doesn't know it, but she isn't getting anywhere with us except to give Blanche a juicy speech she'll be performing behind the nun's back for weeks to come, complete with rude hand gestures and bottom-wriggling.

Sister Frances promises that if she ever catches us touching the boys or letting them touch us with their filthy hands (I guess she thinks boys never wash), we'll be making friends with her strap. She points to the wall where a heavy strap hangs on a nail—an angry being, greedy for bare flesh, that nearly all us students have intimate relations with from the first week of school. The strap is part of Sister Frances's body that she can take on and off like Old Man Archambault and his wooden leg. She uses it on us until the strap tastes blood, it won't settle for stripes and welts, so Blanche and I have learned never to cry when it comes after us. The noise and tears will only give Sister Frances what *she* craves, and we don't want to feed her anything, not even our misery.

Hours after Sister Frances harangues us on the wrongness of our friendship with the Holy Thunders, Blanche hands down an assignment: the four of us are going to be master spies like the ones she heard on a radio program—we're going to hatch a plan to subvert the regular business of this mission school. We're going to come up with something so shocking, so unexpected and devious, everyone will be talking about the action for generations to come.

"We'll be legend," Blanche declares, and I swear there's a fire burning behind her eyes, I see flames shoot past the irises. The boys are nodding. "I like it," says Luther. "We'll do it," Cornelius promises, his face serious like he's taken an oath.

To be honest, I'm betting that Blanche and I will be the ones to dream up a scheme nefarious and interesting enough to meet Blanche's high standards. But in the end, it's the Holy Thunders who bring the perfect idea.

The next time we're able to meet behind the boys' dormitory, an area with only a narrow strip of grass that after a few steps drops into a sharp slope to the river—our safe spot because Sister Frances never patrols here, perhaps afraid of tumbling into the water—Luther breaks into a triumphant grin full of coyote satisfaction.

"We've got it," he says, slapping Cornelius on the back. "You tell them." Luther can be as bossy as Blanche.

Cornelius smiles, too, more cautiously than his brother. He strokes his chin in an old man way, thoughtful, considering where to start. I instantly know that if Luther told the tale, the two of them would shine as heroes, but that Cornelius will be humble and give credit where it's due.

"We remembered a story a relative told us, our ma's uncle Melvin—"

"He's a Two Bulls," Luther interrupts. Like us, they've been taught it's important we map our family connections since these branches say more about where we come from than the names of towns.

"Yeah. Uncle Mel wasn't crazy about the mission priest who sort of took over our community. The priest favored converts who left our Lakȟóta ways and took up the rosary and would talk down to them about relatives who stayed true. Where people once got along and helped each other out, there was now bad blood, and Mel blamed the priest for what he thought of as dark medicine."

"*Very* dark," Luther says, looking serious for once.

"Right. Mel wasn't a true believer in the Jesus way. He bore scars from the Sun Dance we make in secret. He wanted to test the power of this priest's god. He said it took him a while to figure something out, and in the meantime, he went to Mass—listened, watched, pretended his heart was open to conversion."

Luther barks a harsh laugh, which tells us something about Uncle Melvin and his devotion to our traditional ways.

"He noticed the priest seemed to prize one thing above everything else, a small gold box he kept on the altar, where he locked up the Holy Eucharist."

"Mel didn't call it that, he called it the Holy Cracker," Luther says. Blanche snickers.

"He didn't want to ask the priest about it directly, being smart and careful, so he had one of his women friends do the asking. She found out it was pretty old and came from a church in Ireland that burned down though the tabernacle survived, unscorched. It made the crossing to America and kept moving west till it reached South Dakota. Mel said he guessed it was pretty—gold leaf picturing a big cross with rays of light shining off it, and a small dove floating on top. The priest kept it chained to a hook on the altar so no one would take it, and he talked to the Host in its belly every time he passed."

"The Holy Cracker," Luther reminds us. *Yes, we know.* We ignore him.

"Mel decided that all the religious power of the priest seemed to be locked in that little box. He thought of all it survived, like a fire and an ocean crossing, travels through the Plains. *This* was the thing to test, to see if it could beat him. If the tabernacle beat him, then maybe he'd listen to the priest. So he broke into the chapel one night and pried the box from the altar. He said it was easy. That night he slept with the box near his head in case Jesus had something to tell him in his dreams. But the only thing that came to him when he woke was that he had to pee."

We all laugh for show, but even Blanche is a bit shocked that he slept with the holy of holies and lived to tell the tale.

"After a bite to eat he wrapped the box in a blanket and walked it over to the creek—small compared to this river, but pretty fast." Cornelius gestures at the Missouri below us. "He tossed the tabernacle into the water to see if it would sink or float, test if it could grow wings and fly back to the priest, maybe even take revenge on him, bring him bad luck."

To my surprise, my skin has gone cold. I'm more nervous than I would've thought, just imagining the gold-leaf tabernacle arcing into the water. I hear the splash, like I'm standing there beside the boys' uncle. I wait with him to see what will happen.

Blanche finally says what I'm thinking. "So, what happened?"

"Nothing," Cornelius answers. "Nothing," Luther echoes and shrugs his shoulders.

"He saw the thing tumble around—the water was too busy and strong for it to just sink, though it disappeared when it got way ahead of him. The priest and his followers were shocked by its loss, but never solved it. The tabernacle didn't return. And Mel ended up marrying the woman who'd passed along the information to him in the first place. They were happy together until she died by the time they had grandkids. That was so many years later he didn't think the tabernacle had anything to do with it—

just her heart, which never ticked right. So he kept following our ways, though he had to keep quiet about it."

"And that gets to *us*," Luther says, eyebrows raised dramatically. "We don't have to hurt the tabernacle, just set it free." In my head I see our own wooden tabernacle suddenly sprout wings like a hawk, watch it soar over Sister Frances's head and down the chapel aisle, coasting through the open door into sunshine that never reaches it on the altar. When I describe that vision to Blanche later, she likes it, though she adds something to make it her own: "I see it pooping slimy bird shit on Sister Frances's head *before* it flies out the door." We crumple into hysterics, and I have to agree that Blanche's version is better.

As so often happens in this place, even though we succeed in our plans, we fail. We choose a random night to break in and steal the tabernacle, though the chapel isn't locked so it's easy to stroll right through the door, bold and grinning, elbowing each other with excitement. When Blanche and I sneak out of our dorm we only wake one Ree girl who might not like us very much but won't bother to snitch. The Holy Thunders don't wake anyone since apparently the boys in their dorm sleep like they've all been clubbed in the head. The grown-ups are resting in their rooms, or what the nuns call "cells," and the one assigned to keep watch on our peace is snoring in the kitchen. Blanche wishes we could spy on Sister Frances and see if she snoozes upside down like a bat hanging from its toes, but I steer her along. The best part of the adventure is the four of us standing together in the night air, watching the moon that hangs full in the sky like a woman carrying twins. We lace arms around each other's necks and just breathe like we never can during the day. We listen as the Missouri River sings a rushing song of encouragement, like it approves of this mission. Then Blanche whaps me in the uŋzé with a Charleston-like sideways kick, and it's time to move on.

The tabernacle is modest—a plain square box made of cherrywood, inlaid with a black walnut cross. It shines in the dark, which spooks me a little until I notice a small oil lamp alight on the altar, as if the Holy Eucharist is afraid of the dark. The crowbar Cornelius borrowed from the workshop turns out to be unnecessary. Father Mahoney doesn't chain up his tabernacle like a prisoner. We're almost disappointed. This doesn't seem like the grand caper we imagined. The box is locked, but we never intended to bust into the tabernacle itself—even Blanche is wary of messing directly with the Holy Cracker. We're just here to liberate its house.

"Who's gonna take it?" Cornelius fidgets with the crowbar.

"*I* will," Blanche says, but Luther is already hoisting the box into his arms.

"Is it heavy?" his brother asks.

"Nah."

Blanche and I make sure that nothing is disturbed on the altar or in the chapel, not a single votive candle missing. We don't want to leave tracks—it's supposed to look like forces of God, or the Devil, have visited the chapel tonight.

Luther lifts the box onto his shoulder, and we follow behind in a formal procession we never planned. Luther sets the box onto the grass and moonlight picks out red tones in the polished wood.

The tabernacle is beautiful and somehow alive—I half expect it to take flight as it did in my head. Maybe Cornelius picks up on my thoughts. He gestures to the limbs of an ash tree, says, "We should set it up there, like it flew away and picked that tree for a nest."

Blanche insists on climbing the tree with the boys while I hold on to the box, ready to hand it up to them. This is the most precarious part of the whole night, watching the three move the box from limb to limb while managing to keep their balance. When they succeed, I can't help but think that Sister Frances's god is more tolerant and good-natured than his servant. We stand together one last time to admire our work, observe how the tabernacle glows in the moonlight and watches over the school from its roost in the tree.

The grown-ups don't raise a fuss after all our trouble, our hoping to shake them up and make a statement. Maybe they don't want to give the other students ideas. The incident is almost completely hushed up and the tabernacle back in its place by the next time we attend chapel, though Father Mahoney slips a little when he hammers us about "profanation" in his sermon. I might be the only student who knows what the heck he's talking about when he uses that word.

Blanche is sour but I tell her to buck up because Sister Frances is on the prowl even more than usual. When we're headed to lunch, she actually comes over and sniffs the air around us as if hunting for a whiff of guilt. We stare at the ground until she snaps her fingers, which means we can go. The only change brought about by our night adventure is that the Holy Thunder boys are now solidly family, and the little cherry tabernacle feels like a friend.

Sister Frances sends us home for the Christmas holidays with a letter she writes to our parents, telling them we are "incorrigible" and well on our way to becoming "floozies." We know what she says because she reads the page aloud before folding it into an envelope and handing it to Blanche. We're commanded to bring back their response when school resumes in February. You'd think we'd be nervous on the journey home, through hours on a train, then jostled in Grandpa Little Soldier's wagon, which groans so much we expect it to balk someday and fall apart. But we're not the least bit worried.

The next morning Iná is called away to help a young mother

with some mysterious trouble Iná refuses to share with us. "Don't be so nosy," she scolds. Secretly, we're thrilled by this development. We wait for Jack to begin his day, and flutter around him with more attention than he usually gets from us. He's no dummy.

"So, what're you plotting now?" he growls.

Blanche hands him the letter. We watch his face as he reads Sister Frances's missive. When he finishes and turns to us, eyebrows raised, we do what Blanche said we should: we take deep, formal bows, like men wearing tuxedo suits and top hats.

Sure enough, Jack claps for us.

"Well done!" he says. He jumps from the chair and leads us in a jig. "I knew there had to be some of me percolating inside you," he crows. When the celebration tires him, he drops into the chair and writes a response in gorgeous penmanship that makes Sister Frances's ink scratches look meager. He writes that he is "delighted" we are of "independent minds, unassailed, unconverted, and not unduly influenced by the likes of such a limited mind as yours, totally lacking in imagination." He says we are members of a sovereign nation far older than hers, and who is she to decide our worth? Jack enjoys the joust, reading his words several times over and chuckling each time. We don't have an envelope, but he folds the paper neatly and seals it with candle wax.

"Problem solved," he says with a wink.

I've wanted a doll ever since I can remember. I've seen pictures of them in a tattered old Sears catalog Iná keeps in the parfleche container that folds painted wings over her few precious items. I think that catalog is as old as Iná. She calls it "tókša, Black Hills" because the only way we'd be able to buy anything in it would be if the United States came down with amnesia and gave us back everything it took. Though we kids all know Iná is teasing—we would never accept mázaska for the Black Hills. That would be like selling your ancestors' bones.

To Blanche's everlasting disgust, I get my wish for a doll on the Christmas Eve before my tenth birthday. We're all back from school now, helping Iná make festive garlands of popcorn and cranberries. I'm featured in the town production of *A Christmas Carol*, playing the poor little lame child, Tiny Tim. We all have the bowl haircuts we're given at boarding school, so I can pass for a boy. Whenever I practice my most important line, "God bless us, every one!" Blanche falls on the floor and shakes her whole body like you can actually die of embarrassment and my acting has killed her.

Both Iná and Jack laugh at my sister's antics. My brothers skip circles around her body and toss a few kernels of popcorn at her face. Everyone is in a fine mood—we have wood for the stove, and a kettle of simmering corn soup that Iná's been cooking for what seems like days. We all smell good enough to eat.

Blanche makes a miraculous recovery, and we bundle up for the walk to Tribal Hall for our community Christmas party, though it won't be Christmas for two more days. The boys throw snowballs at each other on the way there, joined by friends along the way. They're all wet by the time we get to the hall, and Iná scrubs their faces with a flour-sack towel, which leaves scratches. My legs wobble with nerves when I see how the whole town has shown up tonight, but Alvina grabs my arm and holds me steady. She's playing my older sister in the production and I'm glad now to have her here with me.

Somehow, I manage to get through the play without causing Blanche, or anyone else, to fall down in a fit of shame. I even re-member my lines. After we all take a bow and I think I'm safe for the night, the white director, who is really a teacher from the high school, puts his hand on my shoulder and asks me to wait. I wonder if I did something wrong, though his touch is light and gentle.

The crowd quiets and watches the two of us—we have the stage to ourselves and are trapped in the bright eye of a spotlight. I'm glad I can't see anyone past the glare; Blanche is probably making sour faces.

The director clears his throat and speaks to the audience. His hands press on my shoulders.

"I'm sure everyone knows this little girl," he says. "We're told that she taught herself to read, and her comprehension is years beyond her age."

Oh, no! I will never live this down. Blanche will use that word against me for the rest of my life. She will tease about my "comprehension," say I'm so backward I can't even comprehend a million things she'll never tire of inventing. Why do adults ruin our lives in these careless ways?

Turns out my job as entertainment for the night isn't over. The director hands me a copy of the Charles Dickens novel *A Tale of Two Cities*. I've never read it, but when he points to the opening page, I begin to read. He has me perform all of Chapter One, and I don't know how I make it through the unfamiliar words, like "epoch," "incredulity," "requisition," and "atrocious," but maybe the unhappy children in the book on cruel labor have pooled their magic into one big dose. I somehow know this language, these rhythms and pronunciations, and when I finish there is silence. I'm not able to see who starts the polite applause but Alvina tells me later it was Blanche. I can't believe her. "It *was*," she insists, and I know Alvina isn't a liar so I guess it must be true, though Blanche starts in on me with "comprehension" jokes as soon as I get off the stage.

Later that night, when we're sandwiched together with Alvina in our bed, Blanche puts her arm around me and tells me to make it warm. I place it under the wing of my own cold arm and gradually we stop shaking. As I'm about to fall asleep Blanche whispers in my ear, her lips so close they tickle.

"You're smarter than they think." I catch my breath in utter shock. Is this compliment a joke or a trap?

"They like you to perform because to them, it's a trick. They think when we learn from them and their books it's like we're a puppy you can make bow or dance on its back legs. They look at us like fractions. We're fractions, not whole as them."

I'm still barely breathing since Blanche is never this serious. She must be really mad.

"That's why our people didn't clap at first, even though you did a good job. They could feel something was wrong. But that's not your fault." Blanche squeezes me and drops her forehead against the back of my neck. I'm not sure how she can breathe that way, but she falls asleep inhaling my skin. I think about what she said. I think about how she simmers all day like Iná's kettle of soup. I may be the trick pony but I'm beginning to think my sister Blanche is smarter. The idea doesn't make me feel bad at all. I wouldn't like to see three layers deep into everything. The deeper you go, the darker things get.

The next day is Christmas Eve. Mama surprises us—she and Jack must've given up sugar for a year to collect enough for her to make gingerbread cookies. They're shaped like men in warbonnets so at first we're afraid to eat them even though we've never seen anything so tempting.

"They won't mind," Iná reassures us. She laughs. "They're happy to see Dakhóta children enjoy a treat."

"What if they're Chippewa?" asks Blanche.

"Wisenheimer," Jack says, but there's a smile in his eyes.

"Chippewas don't wear warbonnets like that. Theirs stand up different," Alvina says, always the earnest one in the family.

For some reason that sends Blanche into howls of laughter. She's gripping a not-Chippewa gingerbread man and keeps steering him toward her mouth but can't take a bite until she's back in control.

Then we all quiet down for a few minutes to enjoy the cookies. Even Jack looks like he's bitten a piece of heaven. The noise of our chewing, the tang of sweet ginger, the satisfying snap of each tasty piece, is a wonder.

After our first round of cookies, Iná pulls out a basket hidden under her bed. The basket looks to me like something church ladies from the Catholic mission have donated to the poor. I know we don't have much, and sometimes at school we're hungry enough to smear peanut butter in our pockets so we can lick it off our fingers long after lunch is finished. But I don't ever see my family as "poor," and don't like us being trapped under that term. "Poor" makes me think of kids whose mother doesn't order them to get in the washtub all the time, doesn't check behind their ears to make sure there's no dirt there for potatoes to grow, a mother who doesn't keep a careful garden, a mother who doesn't know so much about elections she's been asked to help count votes to keep everyone honest. I have a feeling there's something special in the basket, but whatever it is won't make up for the slight in how it arrived. Alvina would say I'm too proud. She's the good girl who gives everyone a chance. But I'm not her.

The boys speed over to Iná in a flash of red and black, looking like plaid birds in the shirts she sewed from an old blanket. A basket means treats—they grab her hands in excitement, try to drag them lower so they can see what's coming. The rare taste of sugar has turned them giddy and wild.

"Pshhh!" Iná sounds like a mama snake. The boys back away, but with a bounce; they're rubber balls with big eyes.

Iná brings the basket to our kitchen table, which is used for eating, for Iná and Jack's important political papers that we know we should *never* touch, for sewing projects, for supporting Jack's head when memories make it too heavy to hold up on his own. She sets down the basket—a pretty, embroidered dish towel covers the contents. Ina knows how to draw out happy suspense. She slips a hand beneath the towel and removes one perfect orange.

"An orange!" Alvina cries. The boys are jumping up and down even though they've never seen one before. The last one to enter this cabin arrived when I was still living in the beer keg, and the boys were folded up together in Iná's womb. Ina plucks them out, one by one, four oranges in all! Her hand scrabbles in the basket again and pulls out a tin of hard candy, the kind you can suck on three times and then stow away to enjoy later. We know how to make it last. There's an old *St. Nicholas Magazine* that my fingers ache to touch, and a tin of sliced ham. Jack looks more cheerful than I've ever seen him.

Blanche and I sneak a glance at each other and it's like we've signed a treaty in our minds; today we will be friends, not enemies. But that's before Iná produces the last item in the basket, something that took up the most space. "Looks like we have a new member of the family." Iná removes the towel now and uses both hands to lift up the final offering—the most beautiful doll I've ever seen. The doll wears a tag around her neck: "For the little girl who reads so well."

Even though Blanche doesn't like dolls, never yearned for one as I do, our truce is dead. There are things you know about your sister, especially one so close in age that people mistake you for twins. There are unspoken agreements that keep the peace, like we're supposed to be equals, perfectly even, we're supposed to rise and fall together. And when one of us tilts away from that accepted order, it's a declaration of war!

The doll has no inkling she brings a storm. Her painted lips are parted in a laugh that shows a top row of baby teeth, and a sweet dimple is pressed into each cheek. Her light skin glows, flushed with happiness. Reddish-blond hair springs from her head in glossy ringlets, and she wears a festive white dress with red polka dots. How can such a joyful being darken any mood? But she does.

Iná hands me the doll. I shake my head, not ready to accept what I doubt is real.

"Go ahead, she's yours." Iná presses the doll on me, and I take her into my arms. I let out a shaky breath and learn an awful lesson I still don't understand. How when a dream comes true you have to feel deserving or else it brings only guilt and shame. I hear the doll's voice in my head, but it's quiet beneath my roar of nerves. She says my name, the one no one else utters though it lives on my birth certificate. She shortens it to say: *Hello, Lily. I love you.* Her words make me cringe, though I smile at her, so I won't hurt her feelings. I try to say I love her back, try talking in my mind to this beautiful creation, entrusted to my care. But the only words that come to me are a question: *Who am I to be loved?* I can't say.

Later that day Blanche and I argue about the doll's name. "She's Shirley Temple," Blanche says, shaking her head like I'm too stupid to live. We've never seen a Shirley Temple movie ourselves, but we've heard her sing on our neighbor's radio, and seen pictures of her dancing her heart out in film magazines that folks who work for the Bureau of Indian Affairs toss out when they've read them just one time. We collect their cast-off reading material for Jack, and for ourselves. Jack will read anything his eyes land on, he's desperate for news and information even when it comes in the language of his enemy. One time when Blanche glared at Jack with contempt, his head laid out on the table and pants dark with piss, Iná moved between them as if Blanche was some kind of killer about to strike. Blanche backed up, confused. After all, we're Iná's allies and protectors—well, as much as we can be. We're on the same side.

"Don't judge your father," Iná scolded. "Learn from his mistakes. But don't judge."

Tears squirted from Blanche's eyes, which was a shock. She fights anything "mushy" or soft—I think she'd rather peel off a layer of skin than give up one tear.

"Your father is the most intelligent man in the entire state. That's why politicians come to seek his counsel. He remembers everything he's ever read, turns it in his mind so he can see it from a hundred different directions. His mind is strong, but his heart is weak. Or maybe it's the opposite—he has a strong heart, but his mind lets him down. You don't know all that broke him. Don't judge."

When Iná finally noticed Blanche wiping her face, realized there were tears, she opened her arms.

"Come here, my girl." She combed Blanche's shorn hair with her fingers, rubbed her scalp like she could smooth any hurt thoughts.

Blanche is more wary of Iná now, like maybe she can switch sides midway through the battle. Blanche is a little more ferocious ever since that day she cried. She has to be respectful of grown-ups, though, so I catch most of her scorn. Which is why she insists that my doll is Shirley, and it doesn't matter what I want to call her.

My voice sounds like it's pleading when I argue, "I know she looks like Shirley Temple, but there's only one actual version of her, the movie star, so this one's different. She's her own person, and I have to figure out her real name."

"Her own person?! Sheesh, how'd I ever get such a sister? What do you want with a white doll anyway? If she were really alive, do you think she'd be friends with you? She'd turn up her nose and flounce off. Though the laugh's on her because she's not even new, she's an old used doll!"

I don't answer Blanche's questions, and she doesn't wait around for me to try. She turns on her heel and does her tough-girl impression of flouncing off. I'm glad to have this space of quiet. Everything inside me has been so noisy since the doll arrived. I can't stop touching her ringlets, which make me think of the story of Rumpelstiltskin I read in a tattered book of fairy tales at school, how he gave a girl magic so she could spin straw into gold—this gold that is now between my fingers, but soft and alive, not something you want to spend. She has clean white anklets, the fanciest I've ever seen, and white leather shoes that button up on the side. They're a little scuffed, and her hair is a bit messy at the scalp, though the ringlets bounce just the way they should. Even though Blanche hasn't touched the doll, nothing escapes her notice, so she quickly saw this gift isn't brand-new, straight from the box. She's been cared for by somebody else already. And that's what's different about me and Blanche, I don't take this as a flaw—it just tells me that the doll has love in the bank and a heart big with practice.

I ask the doll what no one ever asks kids: "What do you want your name to be?"

The doll doesn't even have to think about it. She says, "Mae," in a voice that is solid and warm, not the squeak of a peppy little girl.

The week after Christmas warm air from the west chases winter away. The snow melts and we can play outside without coats, which is lucky since we've outgrown the ones Iná made us from blankets, and Mae doesn't have any coat at all. I'm not sure how much a little white girl from somewhere else knows about Dakhóta people and our reservation, our history. I'm guessing, nothing at all. So I act as Mae's tour guide. The first place I bring her is the nearest and most important: Lalá's grave, which is just across the road from our cabin. We kids are the guardian of his resting place, though when Blanche hears me call it that she corrects me like she's a teacher: "How can he rest? They massacred him, treated his body with disrespect, spread quicklime to make him disappear like he never existed. I bet he's planning his revenge."

"Lalá isn't vengeful," I say, like I know him personally even though he was gone thirty-five years before I was born.

Blanche flicks her fingers at me in a gesture that would get her in trouble if Iná could see.

Sitting Bull probably wouldn't approve either. But Mae just smiles at Blanche like they're friends, smiles at Sitting Bull's grave like she agrees with us that he is wonderful and deserving of our protection. We don't let other kids get noisy around him or horse around. We keep our eyes on tourists because they're liable to steal one of the prayer rocks placed on the concrete slab that holds him under the ground.

Lalá knows our secrets. Even though all us girls in the family have made our Holy Communion, and march into confession, where we're expected to unload our sins and mistakes, we bring our pains and fears to Lalá. Iná says he was a good listener. She should know; her father was one of his interpreters, who took his daughter with him everywhere, so she sat in on many conversations with the old chief. I share these stories with Mae, and it turns out she's a good listener, too. She remembers what I say and never laughs at my thoughts. I walk her through town, hold her up so she can look through the window of the Luger's store to see all the merchandise. There are so many things a person can own it confounds the mind! Mae is most curious about the dolls featured in the window; one of them looks just like her. Mae waves at them, but none of them waves back. She looks at me, her forehead wrinkled in confusion.

"Don't they like me?" she asks. She's still smiling and showing her dimples, but her eyes look sad.

"They're not alive, like you."

"Oh." That's another thing I appreciate about Mae—she doesn't make me explain what I'm not sure I could. I walk her past Tribal Hall, and the statue of a woman they say turned to stone because she was pouting. Mae says she doesn't approve of pouting either; it's childish. I walk her all over our small creation, which seems bigger now through the doll's eyes. I realize my world must be immense to this being who hibernated for so long, until I came along and woke her up.

We know better than to grumble as we watch Iná whittle away the small portion of beef that Grandpa Little Soldier brought us on his visit. The meat is a rich, glistening purple that makes my stomach cave in even more from anticipation. She's carving it into smaller sections to be shared with neighbors. I can hear my sister's thoughts—it's like they jump from her head to mine since she's standing right beside me, her own stomach roaring like a bear: *I know we're responsible for the welfare of our relatives, but do we have to have so many?*

I think right back at her: *Sometimes they come through for us though, like Grandpa Little Soldier. We haven't starved yet!*

Blanche pinches me then, like she heard me mimic Iná's favorite line when we're all so hungry we could eat dirt. One time the boys even tried when Blanche told them mud pies were "delicious!" The boys ate her pies and paid the price by living in the outhouse for a while.

I have a large imagination, everyone says so, but one thing I find hard to conjure in my mind is having so much to eat I'd need to push back the plate and stop chewing.

Iná finishes cutting the beef into shares she wraps in newspaper. Jack will be sorry for the loss of the pages, even though they're pretty well memorized. She tells us to wash up before we go visiting, and to check our brothers to make sure they clean the backs of their necks. Ordinarily I'd bring Mae with me; she likes these outings and has interesting things to say about the people she meets. But today I tuck her into the big bed and explain that she can't come along because one of the people we're visiting is a little girl who will feel heartbroken with wishing.

"You mean she'd wish for me?" Mae whispers, her eyes wide with surprise.

"Oh, yes, she'd think you're a miracle!" Mae smiles and her dimples pucker.

"Okay. Tell me everything later."

Iná walks us all over town, dropping off small packets of beef that will strengthen our neighbors' stew. Old lady Gray Bull, who is like a khúŋši to us, is so overwhelmed by the gift she covers her mouth and cries. When she can speak, she says that she'll soak that meat as long as it takes. She has maybe three teeth left in her mouth, but I bet she'll tear through that beef with her bare gums if she has to.

Our final stop is both my favorite and the one I dread. A girl I think of as my own child, at least my pretend child, lives here with her parents and older brother. She's six but looks years younger and isn't much taller than Mae. She's always been sickly, which Iná says stunted her growth. Ada is beautiful enough to be a doll herself, and once I was finally liberated from the beer keg, I used to love to hold her and tell her stories about the sad little white children in my book. She has wavy brown hair that curls above her forehead, a sweet nose, and eyes that make folks stare because they're so unusual—a color that changes from gold to brown to black, fringed with the longest lashes. Iná says that Ada has consumption now, which is catching, so we're not allowed to hold her, or share a dipper of water.

But we can sit a few feet away and horse around to make her laugh.

The reason I dread seeing Ada these days is because *I'm* the one who had her wish come true. Ada loves the idea of dolls as much as I do, though she's seen few examples. Today I feel particularly heavy inside and keep clearing my throat like I'm chewing a cud of guilt. Ada brandishes something in her small hand, moving it up and down so vigorously it's hard for me to make out what it is.

"I have a doll!" she crows, but the words make her cough. She settles enough for me to view the thing—what turns out to be a thick carrot with a face drawn in ink, large eyes spiked with lashes just like Ada's. I smile at her excitement even as I swallow my cud again, thinking of Mae and her golden ringlets, her shoes made of real leather and her dress with red polka dots. Ada would lose her mind with joy in the presence of such an impossible being.

Ada chatters more than usual, excited to tell me everything she knows about Glory. A thick cough slows her down, but she doesn't give up. She says that Glory was born in the yard on a full moon and rescued by her brother. He drops his head in embarrassment. His cheeks are permanently red when we're around, which Iná says is because he's shy. We don't have room for anyone to be shy at our place. Ada says that Glory is funny and likes to tell jokes, though she doesn't feel like it just now. Also, she likes to be cuddled and fed milk. I think the milk part is made up since we have so little of it.

Seeing how delighted Ada's mother is to receive the packet of meat, I can't help but worry about Glory. I'm not sure she's going to last long before ending up in the soup.

All during Ada's talk I can feel Blanche taking bossy sister glances at me. They're almost noisy, like her neck is squawking as it turns. Again, I can read her thoughts: *How can you let this úŋšika girl have a doll like this when you're sitting on top of manna from heaven?* Blanche has taken to throwing in that expression from our religious studies whenever there's a wrong way to use it, as in, "Seeing that crosspatch Fischer get knocked off his horse was sheer manna from heaven!" So in my head I have her throw it at me in the right way.

As all this is going on I make a decision: I'd rather carry the load of guilt than say goodbye to Mae. I don't want to even picture what that would look like. Mae is evidence of my magic—proof that what I think, and even hope, can become real. I don't want to give that medicine back, even for a dear lonesome girl. I wish I could hug Ada when we leave, but we can only wave from the door. She smiles and waggles Glory at us. When we're outside Blanche knocks her hip into mine, and I go flying. Alvina helps me up and dusts me off. Iná ignores what she calls "the sister scuffle." As long as no blood is shed, she lets us figure things out for ourselves.

I don't ask Blanche what the shove was for, and she doesn't tell me. We already know.

Two weeks later when we hear that Ada is dying, my first crazy thought is of Glory. I wonder if the carrot has been eaten yet. Iná asks if we'd like to visit the girl one last time. We understand that she wants us to say yes, but that if we don't, she'll never raise the subject again or try to make us feel bad.

Iná doesn't carry grudges. We all nod, no one comfortable enough to speak.

Iná has trained us well, so even the boys rummage through their nonexistent store of belongings to find something to bring Ada as she starts her journey. We girls all have a piece of hard candy left from Christmas, but the boys have nothing but round stones they use as marbles. Iná takes pity on them and gives them a treasured ball of sweet wasná they can offer jointly. As we're making ready to leave, Iná pulls me aside and takes hold of my hands. Her grasp is gentle, no squeezes or pressure, no clamorous thoughts jumping from her head to mine the way it happens with Blanche. She's searching my face, truly reading it, like there's a question only my expression can answer. I look sideways at the floor. I know what she's hoping I'll do. She won't ask, not for something this big. Iná can sense that if my heart isn't really healed like the doctor said it is, Mae's presence does something to repair the trouble. The cud of guilt is back in my throat, tears burn my eyes but don't fall. I feel damned because though I'm awfully sad about Ada, I know the tears aren't for her. It's clear to me that I'll never be able to hold up my head again in this family if I don't bring Mae and place her in Ada's arms.

I don't hear Mae's voice anymore. She stopped talking to me as soon as she heard I was giving her away. Blanche, on the other hand, was actually nice to me for two days in a row. I don't like to think about that final visit with Ada, even though the shock of her happiness was so great we were all a little afraid she might die right then. Glory was no more. We didn't dare ask. A few days later we attended Ada's funeral, watched as a small plain box was lowered into the ground. Her mother thanked me, again, for the miracle of a gift. I think she meant to make me feel better by saying they'd placed Mae in Ada's arms before fastening the casket so the two could hold each other forever. But I began weeping and Iná had to guide me away, walk me slowly home. Mae was here for such a short time, but the hole she leaves feels bigger than the one in my heart. Nights are hard. As soon as I close my eyes, I see Mae resting in the arms of a dead girl. She's trapped there, alive. One night I have a nightmare that the small coffin collapses under the weight of earth and Mae's head is mashed in. She screams, "Lily!!!" and then goes quiet, her mouth filled with dirt. I must scream, too, because when I wake Blanche is stroking my arm in the gentlest way, usually reserved for pet magpies and owlets.

◆ ◆ ◆

Blanche and I steel ourselves for the return to school in Bismarck. I feel the loss of Ada and Mae like a wire wrapped around my heart—pinching me, hurting. The Holy Thunder boys are waiting for us when we arrive, both of them flashing big smiles when they see us enter the compound. The next moment they turn bashful and begin thumping each other in a pretend fight to hide their feelings. The following day Cornelius presents me with a small fan he's made of assorted feathers. The quills are lodged inside a small carved handle that might've originally been a cooking spoon, and a scrap of hide covers the wood—I can smell its smoky fragrance as soon as I touch it. He created a pretty design that moves from ivory feathers on the outer edges to tawny brown in the middle. It's a fan fit for a doll like Mae, as if he knows all about her, though not that she's gone. I sense the warning pressure of tears, but freeze them, imagine they've turned to chips of ice. I don't want to give Cornelius the wrong idea. I'll be polite and thank him for the gift the way Iná taught us, but don't want him to think I match his special feelings. Maybe from the years I spent stuck in a beer keg, where all I could do was observe the ways of other people living their lives, I perceive things about them. Things they might not want me to see.

What I know from the very beginning of our dealings with the Holy Thunder boys is that both of them love me. And *not* like a sister. Not even like a friend, in the way of Blanche. What I also know is that their love isn't the same strength or concentration. A voice in my head says that I mean the world to Cornelius— I'm the first one he looks to when he walks in a room, he faces my direction like I'm the sun and he's a helpless plant that will shrivel without my light. Somehow, I'm convinced that Cornelius will love me for the rest of his life, and the idea makes sweat break out on my forehead. The thought turns me spitting mad. It's different with Luther. I shine to him like a coin he wishes he had in his pocket. A coin he can finger and flip in the air to show off what he's got. A coin he might spend or someday lose, and only miss for a moment. I don't know if he'll love me much longer and that feels safe somehow. I can relax with Luther and let him play coyote with me—run off in a playful lope and then circle back when I don't expect him. Luther won't work as hard to please me and that's just fine. I choose him.

Blanche warns me that my nemesis is out for blood. Well, what she actually says is: "You better be careful. Sister Frances is looking for any excuse to take you down."

I already know. When I won the statewide spelling bee this week, up against adults from all over North Dakota, you'd think from the nun's face that I'd just taken the Lord's name in vain while shooting up the room. She acts like I'm a gangster, the hidden Dakhóta stepdaughter of Baby Face Nelson. Sister Frances should be happy that my winning word was "canonical" and not something embarrassing like "scatological" or "gynecology." She'd probably faint if she even heard a term like that. According to her, we're not supposed to have bodies all riddled with sin but turn ourselves into holy spirits that rise above life and blood and childbirth. The problem is, *her* holy spirit might be starved clean of every physical comfort or desire, but it's just plain mean as a rattlesnake, no, worse. As Blanche says, she is "pure hell."

The other teachers at school are proud of me, like I won because they do such a good job with backward Indian kids, turning us from hoodlum savages into respectable citizens. As a result of my win, I'm given special privileges to borrow a book from our small library, to take it with me instead of having to skim it right there in the few minutes of free time between chores and classes. Sister Frances catches me mooning over a new box of books donated to the school. I'm clutching a thick hardcover novel to my chest, *A Girl of the Limberlost,* which looks like heaven compared to the dreary titles on most of the shelves.

Sister Frances points her long finger at me, something Iná taught us is severely rude. "That is theft!", she cries. "Those books haven't been cataloged yet. How dare you touch them." She snatches the wonderful book from me and glances at the title page. It's gloriously illustrated with flowers and butterflies that look as if they could fly off the paper and swarm her face. The very existence of such a book is no doubt an abomination in her eyes.

"You are no better than a criminal," she says. The charge makes me gasp, though I could kick myself for not exerting more self-control. I understand Sister Frances. I know her language. This isn't personal, which makes it worse. The only reason she singles me out is because of my magic when it comes to words, the way they're never mysterious to me, and always friends. How my ability to learn them, to weave them together, puts the lie to her beliefs and prejudices. If she could stamp me out, she would. I stain her world.

Sister Frances has strong fingers that can grip the back of the neck like metal pliers. She nabs me like this and escorts me to the basement, where she tosses me into her favorite room—the dark punishment box that makes you feel like you're dead and buried, and the rest of the world is gone. I know I've seen the last of the *Limberlost,* the last of the beautiful ink butterflies and any stories they carry on their bright wings. The nun will no doubt tear the book to pieces and feed it to the kitchen stove.

She doesn't leave right away. I don't hear the clack of her boots on the stone floor. She must be listening at the door, waiting for me to cry and wail. Or at least sniffle. She forgot to slap me this time before shoving me into the shadows. I'm sure her hand is burning over that lapse. The thought makes me smile. I never give her the satisfaction of tears. In the face of Sister Frances's anger,

I turn myself into Blanche. Eventually I hear the sharp noise of her steps walking away. Each click like someone dropped a silver dollar. My head begins to spin a story of magical coins left in the wake of a villain's footsteps, so they end up making everyone rich, despite their miserable actions. "God gets the last word," I say aloud, and laugh. Because of course I don't mean Sister Frances's god, a being who creates a body only to ask it to stop being one, a deity who would choose the likes of her to be his "bride." That's a god I don't want to believe in because he makes no sense.

Hours pass and I'm out of stories. Turns out my stomach is more powerful than my brain, and in a shouting match hunger is the loudest. I even take off my dress so I can lick inside the pocket where I smeared a dab of peanut butter from yesterday's sandwich. I lick along the seams and suck every last bit of fat and sugar from the fabric. I'm cold and hungry and lonesome. Iná says that school is good for me, but I don't think so. School makes me think mean thoughts, makes my sick heart open new holes. I'm afraid the last bit of love in the soft meat will bleed away, and I'll be just like Sister Frances. To endure the chill I imagine my body being its match—the cold rock of me lying on the cold rock of the floor. "We are twins," I say aloud and it's too dark in here for me to see the words. There are layers of shadow, but I squeeze my eyes shut because I've learned they can conjure ghosts and demons.

Is it day? Is it night? Is Blanche worried about me? I suck on a knuckle and pretend it's a piece of hard candy. What is the Limberlost, and how can I find it? I realize I'm crying because my face warms in patches. I think of Mae and wonder if she's scared, too, in the dark of the dead girl's grave.

Just like that, the words in my head produce magic! Thoughts go walking outside me and bring help.

"Lily?" The voice of a girl is suddenly with me in this punishment box. Only one being has ever called me that.

"Mae?" I hear the scuffle of running feet and a small figure launches itself against me, like it's going to tunnel straight through me. I can't see much in the shadows, but when I lean close to the bundle, ringlets tickle my nose and make me sneeze. I don't know how she did it, but Mae has returned, just like Bossy, our old cow, who stubbornly walked home every time we had to sell her off.

I trace Mae's features with my finger to make sure she's not a demon fooling me with cruel tricks. I pat down her dress, cup her foot in my palm. It's my doll come back again, raised from the dead! Even Blanche would approve of this excitement.

Mae settles in the crook of my arm. "Tell me what happened," I say.

She sighs. "It was rough. I didn't like the dark or the bugs. There are bugs, you know, too many of them!" Mae tells me that there are ways she's like her Hollywood counterpart—she, too, has courage and pluck, as well as very strong legs from tap dancing, even up and down the stairs. She says the coffin box was cheap wood that rotted soon enough, so she could pick it apart like wet paper. Then she kicked her way upward, through layers of earth. "I just thought of it as swimming," she says, though there's a hint of tears in her voice. "I'm very dirty now. You'll be surprised."

I hug Mae tighter. "I don't care. I'm just happy you found me. How'd you know where to look?"

"I walked home first and peeked in the door. Iná looked sad and the place was too quiet. So I knew you must be back at school."

A horrifying thought makes me double over and squeeze Mae too hard. She squawks. I don't have the breath to apologize yet. My head is showing me Sister Frances tossing a mud-splattered Mae into the kitchen stove. It's like the doll witnesses that same vision. She whispers, "No one can see me now, only you."

I want to ask her how that's possible, how she even knows for sure. But something stops me. In all the stories I've read and heard about magic, people do best when they just believe. It's when they start poking at it, asking too many questions, that everything unravels. So all I say is: "Good." And I kiss the doll's forehead.

Mae's company warms this cold season that drags on without sunshine. I mean to tell Blanche about the surprise magic, but she's crabbier than usual, and I never find the right moment. I don't want her to wreck the one thing in my life that shimmers. Mae follows me everywhere, either perched on my shoulders with her small hands holding my neck like a chin strap, or riding one of my feet, her arms wrapped around my leg. She mocks Sister Frances by repeating everything she says in a prissy voice.

Sometimes it's so hard for me to keep from laughing I bite a hole in my cheek.

One morning when Sister Anne is called away from our mathematics lesson and we're left alone in the classroom, Mae runs to the sister's desk and climbs one of the legs as easily as if it's a rope. She hauls herself to the desktop and pats the skirt of her dress, which is splotchy with stains. She taps one foot like it's considering. She taps the other, like it's answering back. Then she's off in a blur of dancing, twirling across Sister Anne's papers without mussing them, kicking at a pile of books that somehow doesn't topple. She isn't dancing for me, but for herself. I can see that fever of concentration and happiness on her shiny face. Probably the way I look when I'm lost in reading. Mae taps and spins, leaps over pieces of chalk. Her ringlets bounce with joy, her expression fierce, like maybe this is some kind of rebellion. She makes enough racket to draw everyone's attention, but no one else looks, no one else seems to notice. Even Blanche just sits, elbows on her desk, head in hands. Scowling like there's nothing good in the world. For a moment she reminds me of Jack. She misses Mae's finale, which is a tremendous leap, so high above the desk it's like invisible birds have plucked her into the air. She lands on the floor and immediately drops into the prettiest curtsy, smiling at the room to show off her dimples. I half rise out of my chair, ready to clap, then remember myself. Blanche glares me a questioning look. I shrug back. Mae doesn't seem upset by the lack of applause. She saunters down the aisle and rejoins me, clambering up my leg so she can settle in my lap. She looks at me, still smiling.

Her teeth have somehow remained perfectly white.

"I'm your secret," she says, and I nod. She falls asleep as I work on multiplying large numbers the way Sister Anne showed us. I want to tell Mae that it's interesting how some numbers feel like friends, while others aren't trustworthy at all, how I like zero best because it stands for everything we don't yet see. But I keep quiet. I don't want anyone to think I'm crazy when instead I'm just kind of magic.

Sister Frances wakes us earlier than usual. She says it's Ash Wednesday and we need to prepare our hearts and minds as we head into Lent.

"She wants us to pray *before* we pray," Blanche grumbles. "Like we're not good enough to get dirty ashes drawn on our foreheads."

Blanche has seemed angrier every day of this school year, but today her grumps are more habit. She looks like she might bust into a smile as we sit over a cup of thin gray lumps that are supposedly oatmeal.

"What?" I ask, hoping for good news.

"Lalá came to me in a dream," she whispers. It must've been a *great* dream because she doesn't even smirk to lord it over me.

"Really? What did he say?" I'm feeling envy, like someone spooned it right on top of my breakfast mush. But I swipe it away as unworthy. Lalá wouldn't like me to be jealous of my sister.

"It's not what he *said*." Blanche pauses. Maybe she's drawing out the suspense, or maybe she's actually thinking. I tell myself to be patient and not get cranky. "It's how he looked. Young and strong, and no wounds that I could see. He waved his arm for me to join him. We were walking along the Grand River and the quiet suddenly got loud." Blanche squints like she's trying to remember perfectly.

"Lalá wasn't speaking, but I heard his breath, calm and steady. I heard the water join in like it was breathing, then the wind. Then I heard *myself* breathing with Lalá, with everything. I know this sounds dumb, but it wasn't!" Blanche scowls at me as if daring me to say something mean. Which I won't. "Lalá made me part of his whole world, and I was every bit as good as the rest. We all breathed the same." Tears rise in the corners of my sister's eyes. I think of how creeks swell after a rain. Blanche wills her own creek of emotions to stay down, but I surprise myself with how I react to her final words on the matter. When Blanche says, "I'm fine now," I'm the one who starts crying.

Sister Frances leads us into the chapel for morning Mass and the ritual of receiving ashes. She walks faster than usual, almost bouncing, and I know it's because she'll be in the presence of Father Mahoney. The way she flutters around that man you'd think she's in love. If he weren't a priest, Father Mahoney would be handsome. He has thick silver hair though he's not old, and a strong, balanced face like the few actors I've seen. What makes me wary of him is his eyes, which are so black they blend into the pupil, so it's like staring into an eternity of night.

Blanche doesn't think there's anything attractive about the priest. She calls him "Father Baloney," or when she's really mad, "Father Phony." But we march to our seats in the pews and try not to squirm through the service that's so familiar it's become automatic. The only thing different today is Father Mahoney's sermon, and the ashes he'll draw on us later that Blanche says will burn, like she always does. The first time she told me when I was little, I was actually scared.

Father Mahoney seems more excited than usual as he starts up his sermon. His expression is stern, as if he's heard bad news, and his voice sharp. He sounds like we've all failed him. Oh, no, can he read minds? Instead of the usual lesson from the Bible, he's harping on the life of Sitting Bull. I half believe he was able to see into Blanche's dream and trailed behind like a spy as Lalá brought her back to herself.

We're used to white folks telling us how lucky we are that they are in our lives, telling us that we didn't know how to live until they came along. We're used to being made to feel dirty, backward, feeble-minded, lax in our conduct, nasty in our manners— just one tiny hair from being a beast in the zoo. Jack calls this "propaganda," and one of his favorite sayings when sober is: "Don't believe the propaganda." Though I think part of him does. So Father Mahoney isn't shocking anyone in the chapel today with the swipes he takes at Indian people as a whole, and the Sioux Nation in particular (which makes our Ree classmates quietly snicker). But me and my sister aren't the only ones bristling when he launches into an attack on Sitting Bull. He says he suspects that some of us were taught to revere the "old chief," perhaps even see him as a holy man. "But there's *nothing* holy about that scoundrel," Father Mahoney blasts, slapping the lectern with his pink hand. "He defied a just power. He ignored the inevitable and organized brutal fighters to rebel against our powerful nation. But who brought him down in the end? His own people. Patriots who knew the right thing to do, who wanted to end his stranglehold on a few remaining followers. The Indian police are the heroes of this story, the ones who propelled you on the path of salvation.

Always hold to the path of Our Lord who suffered and died for your very souls, whether society deems you deserving or not. The Lord deems you worthy of his sacrifice, and you must prove it to him every day, in every thought and action. Think of yourself as turning your back on the past. Envision yourself turning your back on dangerous miscreants like Sitting Bull, and the lost souls who trusted him. Turn your back even on family members should they continue a wayward road. Do not romanticize what is rightfully gone, rightfully dead. Face forward and head into the light that is Jesus Christ, Our Holy Redeemer. You will never be sorry!"

Oh, but we're already sorry, I'm thinking, as Father Mahoney rambles on. Blanche has heated so quick I'm amazed she hasn't gone up in flames. I swear I can *hear* her sizzling beside me. Mae sneaks a glance at her, worried, like me. I'm afraid when it comes time to receive our cross of ashes, Blanche will attack Father Mahoney and bloody his nose. But she's docile in the end, almost suspiciously calm as she walks demurely before the priest and kneels for his benediction: "Remember that you are dust, and to dust you shall return." She lets him thumb a mark on her forehead that we're not allowed to rub off. She keeps her hands pressed together in prayer and is so solemn she brings on a ripple of raised eyebrows. Mae whispers what I'm thinking: "I don't like this one little bit."

Blanche doesn't launch her rebellion right away. I don't even think it's planned. Maybe her meek act was intended to buy time until she could design the perfect revenge. But instead of her brain cooking up grand schemes, something in her snaps while we're doing our kitchen chores. Blanche scrubs the floor while I peel potatoes. Mae is napping, curled around my ankle like a cat. She hums a peppy tune in her sleep that doesn't match the mood of the room. Maybe Blanche catches some wisp of music in the heavy air?

Now she's humming, too, as she scrubs, though not the same song as Mae. She's on her hands and knees, wielding the brush with so much force I think she might plunge it through the planks. She scrubs in rhythm to her song, her upward push the downbeat of a drum. Oh, no! My heart may or may not still bear an open hole, but right now it's feeling solid as rock—a petrified thing frozen with fear. I recognize my sister's quiet tune—a song that honors Sitting Bull, our lalá. Blanche's hum streams quietly from her nose through several rounds of the song. I know better than to say anything. When she's mad she can be perverse and do the opposite of what she's told. I remind myself to breathe, to keep breathing for all of us. My knife slips on the potato and I'm lucky I don't cut myself. "Be careful," I say to myself, to my sister, under my breath. I don't know how much time passes. Whenever I'm most afraid, time slides right off the clock and becomes something else—a slow, oozing paste that makes each moment work to unstick itself. How many minutes pass before Blanche adds words to her song? Lakȟóta words we learned from Grandpa Little Soldier, that tell the story of Lalá and his courageous heart. How many minutes before her song gets louder, the scrub brush pounding the floor in accompaniment? I finally unlock myself and force my legs to stand. "Blanche, stop!" I cry. Mae wakes and grabs my leg tight as if she, too, is scared.

Blanche doesn't hear me. Her anger has torched all sense of fear. Or maybe it's devotion that fills her now so there's no room for anything else? She's like a girl martyr who can't feel the first lick of an executioner's flames because she's wild with spirit. Maybe Blanche isn't here in this kitchen but walking with Lalá beside the Grand River, flowing with it, and matching its sweet song with their steps.

Soon Blanche is loud enough to bring nuns on the run—skirts flying, some clutching the long crucifix they wear so it won't bounce obscenely against their bodies. I find myself standing over my sister. I grab her scrub brush, but her grip is too tight. I let go. I hear myself beg her to stop, to be quiet, as if it's someone else who pleads. I kick over Blanche's bucket to get her attention, but she doesn't seem to notice. Sister Anne is the first to reach Blanche—she's the gentlest of this order of nuns. She's crying like me, like she can't bear to see this girl throw her life away. When Blanche sings louder Sister Anne tries to stuff a dish towel in her mouth, but Blanche is too quick. She's on her feet, dashing past. She can sing and race around the room at the same time. She leaps onto a chair and from the chair onto the massive table. She kicks the potatoes I was peeling onto the floor. She breaks so many rules at once, beginning with the use of our language, I'm ready to faint. This feels a bit like the end of the world. Some part of me says that's crazy. Why should a girl singing in a kitchen be the end of the world? Or did Mae say that? She looks at me like I'm expected to answer.

Nuns pile on top of my sister and I can't see her anymore. Sometimes her song is muffled, but she must be biting the sisters' hands because the song always breaks through again, defiant as any warrior's battle cry.

I'm shaking so hard I can barely stand, and it's Mae who comes to my rescue. She can't seem to do anything to help Blanche but is determined to keep me safe. She raises her hand in the air and waves it at me. I reach down and as soon as we clasp hands the magic takes over. Mae and I become weightless beings who can float on air. We rise up, up, passing the table and the massive stove, higher than the windows, so high our heads gently bump the ceiling where we rest against it like carnival balloons.

We have a bird's-eye view of the skirmish. My sister is covered with nuns, the way ants swarm a beetle trapped on its back, or crows peck apart a downed squirrel. I can't tell if she's still singing because there's a roar in my ears, as if the Missouri River has flooded its banks and is about to smash through the kitchen. My emotions are flat in this weightless space and can't upset me. All I can do is watch. Sister Frances is trying to thrust soap in Blanche's mouth, her homemade industrial soap that can burn for days. But Blanche is a thrashing buffalo spirit no one can subdue. The nun points, commands; Sister Bernard is heating water in a cauldron. Not too hot, Sister Frances must order, since it doesn't take long. She bends over the cauldron, working the soap with her hands in the heated water. What is she doing? I wonder. Mae works out the puzzle ahead of me: "Soap soup!" she chirps, like what's happening is a game.

It turns out Sister Frances's imagination is every bit as large and diabolical as my own. She gets soap in Blanche's mouth by pouring it in, one full ladle of the melted stuff after the other. And even though I'm held by magic that soothes the edges of panic, I can't help hollering down to the cluster of nuns that they'd better stop, or they'll drown my Blanche.

Hours later, when Mae has brought us down from the ceiling and allowed the sisters to lead me to bed, she tells me what happened. How Sister Frances poisoned Blanche with lye from strong soap. How Sister Anne held the girl and wept but couldn't save her after hours of Blanche vomiting blood. How the doctor arrived too late and wrote down whatever Sister Frances told him to write on the death certificate because it was the middle of the night and he wanted to return to sleep. How Sister Frances told the other nuns what happened was tragic, but no doubt a censure from the Lord brought down on Blanche for her wickedness.

I'm too numb to believe the doll. The horror of her words divides at the top of my skull and drips down each side, falling away from me. I listen like I'm dreaming, and the dream is a nightmare, but nothing that can truly hurt me once I wake.

PART 3

Ghost Dance

Cora ~ 1900s

CORA'S JOURNAL

People say the season of our birth predicts our nature. I was born in bitter cold, and Iná says my first breath was smoke. She went into labor as a blizzard bore down on the Plains, the storm arriving alongside me as if we were twins. Many children died that day, the familiar road they walked between home and school suddenly obscured by my cold brother's heart of snow. He buried them in lonesome mounds, his grievances piling up against homesteads and schoolhouses, covering fences and caving in roofs. I used to dream of my storm brother—the one place he could visit me long after his rage was spent, and the dead buried. He was a wild spirit, a sparkling white twister, frustrated in his attempts to embrace me or hold my hand. He slipped through my fingers, coated my lashes with frost, swept my hair into knots—his furious love could never set. I melted him.

I wonder who I would be if I was born in calm. My brother brought fair warning of what was to come, he readied me for danger and ice. When I was little, I thought we were opposites because my flesh was warm and I was able to sit quiet, but always there's a frozen distance between me and the ones I love. They flow through my fingers just the same.

At the time of my birth my parents were living near the Cannonball River in a small clapboard house with a thípi lodge pitched in the back. Their nearest neighbor was a massive burr oak called the Council Tree because it had witnessed hundreds of years of human affairs: our arguments and treaties. What fate brought me to earth at such a confluence of contradictions—war and compromise? The place stamped itself on my infant heart so always I'm of two minds and strategies: learning when to fight and when to surrender. Before I was old enough to walk we moved farther south, closer to Fort Yates, the reservation agency town.

My earliest memory is of the doll, Winona, bound up with me in the cradleboard as if Iná had given birth to a second daughter and wanted us to look after each other. I came to realize that she was older—I could tell from the weathered skin of her body sewn of deer hide, and the overworked area of her eyes, which had once been formed of porcupine quills but were now sparked to life with indigo beads. Her braids were thick and long even as my own hair was still fluff, and she wore dentalium shell earrings sewn just behind the deerskin ears, which were too delicate to hold them. She was so pretty and elegant, certainly the boss of me and not the other way around.

On nights when I was too restless to sleep, I remember Iná's gentle voice whispering, "Ábu, ábu." Sometimes she drowsed off to her own spell, and then it was the doll that took over, chanting the same lullaby though it chimed differently coming from a beaded mouth. The two of them pillowed me, surrounded me with what softness they could spare, for we lived in sharp times.

My first experience with sorrow came when I was three years old. We were at home, wintering in a cabin built by my father, Saswe. He was enjoying eggs fried up with potatoes and I was gnawing on the jerked beef I favored, which took patience to conquer with baby teeth but soothed their ache. We were sitting in chairs because we'd quit our thípi lodge for the winter, and it still felt strange to me, balancing on that thick plank of wood, my nose barely level with the table unless Iná boosted me with folded blankets. Winona sat in a chair beside me. She was a dainty eater who politely nibbled whatever I offered but feasted on little more than air. She tensed before I did when we heard the clamor of horse and rider streaking toward our place. The reckless speed frightened me; our friends and relatives didn't drive their ponies so cruelly. We thought the rider would stop when he reached us, but he only slowed a little, called for Saswe, alerted him that there was terrible news: our lalá, Sitting Bull, had been arrested by our own Indian police and witnesses claimed he was dead. Then he took off, continuing his alarm. Iná didn't move—she seemed frozen to her chair—but Saswe leapt into action. He grabbed a thick buffalo robe and his best rifle and told Iná he was going to see if the news was true. "Dead or alive, they'll bring him to the agency. If he's dead . . ." My father shook himself and made ready to ride into town. He stepped to the door, then came back for me. I reached for Winona and Iná noticed. She tucked the slim doll inside the finger-woven belt cinching my dress, pulled it tight to keep her safe. Saswe said that if Lalá was truly dead this would change everything.

"But why bring our daughter into such awful business?"

"This one is wise. She'll remember." He had no more to say than that, and I thought at the time he meant Winona, my doll, for she had survived the love of other children before me, and even the worst event suffered by our ancestors: the massacre at Whitestone Hill. Nearly thirty years earlier, as federal troops shot down entire families in an unprovoked attack, a desperate mother lashed her wounded baby to a travois pulled by their dog.

He followed the scent of survivors and came across Winona lying on the ground near a great fire that scorched her original hair. The dog bit down on her and carried her away, perhaps thinking she was another child in need of rescue, or being a dog, understood the importance of a beloved toy. When Winona whispered her memories to me in later years, she said that Whitestone Hill was the day the world ended. I never asked what she meant, how the world could be gone when the sun was still in the sky and my parents alive. I felt such a question would diminish her pain, which was clear to see from the stain of ancient tears trailing her indigo eyes.

My father set me on his tall pony and climbed behind me, wrapping us in the buffalo robe. The morning air was cold enough to scrape our skin and stab each breath. Iná looked worried as she watched us go, but I didn't know enough to be frightened, and felt safe nestled between my father and Winona. As we got closer to town we heard layers of conflicting noise—wails of grief, several songs that rang out in defiance, the creak of wagons and pounding of horses being run at a gallop. People were everywhere, surrounding a wagon protected by soldiers and Indian police. My father rode straight to the wagon, his pony delicately weaving its way through the crowd. When our neighbors saw it was Saswe coming through, one of Tȟatȟáŋka Íyotake's trusted interpreters, they parted to let him pass. We could smell the devastation before seeing it, the familiar odor that comes with butchering, and another smell I couldn't place that was sour enough to turn my stomach. When I was older, I realized it was the smell of whiskey, which the Indian police had been drinking the night before and into the early morning to give them nerve to arrest Lalá.

Finally, we stood before the wagon, looking down into its contents. A gruesome snarl of bodies was heaped together. We learned that more than a dozen men were killed that dawn, several of them members of the police. In his shock my father neglected to cover my face; I had a clear view of the carnage. I wouldn't have known the mashed blob of flesh was our lalá—his face crudely destroyed and at least seven gunshot wounds splintering the body. But I recognized his hands, which were raised in defense and frozen there. Those terrible claws were once warm palms that stroked my cheek and wild tuft of hair. The ruined face had smiled at me and teased.

"Don't look!" Winona said, too late. She told me to cover my eyes, but I was a shocked creek of anguish overrunning my banks—I couldn't move.

I heard the keening of voices all around me—Lalá's people, our oyáte, weeping and singing Honor Songs to comfort the great chief's spirit and let his ancestors know he would soon join them, also to comfort themselves and keep their minds strong. Those who sang were brave to do this publicly since our ceremonies and songs were now illegal. Some of them would no doubt end up being locked in the stockade as punishment. Misery hung in the air. Young as I was, I could feel the tension of thick emotions that even a slicing cold couldn't shatter. The air warmed with horror and anger, thoughts of revenge. Our pony began nervously shifting his back legs and my father had to reach down and pat his strong neck, whisper calm words in his ear to stop the shuffle. I think the horse wanted to back away from the smell of danger in the air, the iron tang of frozen blood. Observing the ruined flesh touched us; we felt coated in Tȟatȟáŋka Íyotake's gore.

The story of that terrible morning came to me in pieces, what I overheard then and in days to come. Little of it understood by me, as young as I was, yet I listened because my father had brought me to bear witness. The friend who shared the most reliable version of events was Little Soldier, who had been working for the agency, wearing the silver badge of the Indian police until the day he was ordered to join a party that would arrest Sitting Bull. Lalá had adopted Little Soldier as another son, and he would not take up arms against his father. So Little Soldier removed his badge and his heavy blue uniform and said he would never work for the agency again. He said there were a couple of other Indian police who did the same, but the rest were persuaded by personal grudges, or warnings of the violence Sitting Bull would bring upon us if he joined with Oglálas who were making the Ghost Dance at Pine Ridge Agency. They were also coaxed with a large shipment of whiskey the army supplied them, which they started drinking that night. Agent James McLaughlin, who wore a thick brush of hair beneath his nose that I thought of as an angry caterpillar, was determined to break Lalá's influence among our people. So he sent out more than forty men to arrest Sitting Bull, consisting of police and four volunteers, with a company of army soldiers waiting nearby in case support was needed. They arrived at Lalá's cabin so early in the morning the old chief was still in bed. The policemen were nervous and rude, pounding on his door in a commanding way, and when they saw he was naked beneath the blanket they didn't let him dress himself but started roughly pulling a shirt over his head. Those who followed Lalá were beginning to gather outside, worried for his safety. When he appeared in the doorway of his cabin and paused there, getting his bearings, two of the policemen became rough, trying to kick him through the door. Catch-the-Bear, who was loyal to Sitting Bull, aimed his rifle at a police captain named Bull Head and they faced off. Catch-the-Bear shot Bull Head, who then opened fire on Lalá. A battle broke out. Sitting Bull's young son, Crow Foot, was killed though he begged for his life. The police might have been overwhelmed by Lalá's supporters if it weren't for the army soldiers who showed up when they heard sounds of violence. They shelled the yard with their Hotchkiss gun, which scared off supporters.

Bodies of the dead were piled into a wagon and brought to town, attracting Dakȟóta and Lakȟóta people throughout the territory as word spread. One of the saddest moments of that awful morning involved Lalá's horse, who'd learned to perform during the months Sitting Bull spent working for Buffalo Bill Cody in his Wild West Show. The horse was trained to dance on his hind legs, then fall to the ground at the sound of gunfire as if he'd been shot. While Lalá was being murdered, the horse carried out his routine, thinking his dramatic caper was nothing more than a clever act.

Little Soldier wept as he told my parents the events of that terrible day, which survivors on both sides of the conflict had shared with him. He'd experienced the carnage of battles before, including the one that finished General Custer, but only where our people were fighting a common threat. To see a family broken apart and killing each other, all because a white agent pressured them into it or because they left our ways, broke our friend's heart. My father later said that Lalá's death was the end of more than a sacred life, significant as it was; he said that wašíčus had pushed us so out of balance we were now capable of turning against each other, capable of betrayal within the oyáte.

My father is an Indian rancher with a small herd of cattle, but I observe how much he works with his voice—interpreting for Lalá while he was still alive, as well as for other Lakȟóta and Dakȟóta leaders, advising those who seek his counsel. His mind is a clear sky; there is nothing he's afraid to consider, he's open to reason from all sides. I've heard him warn our leaders that the wašíčus we deal with have minds that move stubbornly in one direction— marching always toward what they want, impatient when you point out tributary paths or hills with a better view. "We must walk them up the hill with careful speech," he says. "Lead them step by step to a higher plain so we can point out all that will be affected by one decision. It's difficult because they want to focus on their nose." My father taps his nose whenever he says this, and his audience laughs, though nervously.

Iná works mainly with her hands, skinning the animals we eat for food, scraping their hides to prepare them for a variety of uses, planting corn and beans, sewing, beading, cooking, collecting plants for healing. Her hands are as clever as my father's tongue. She doesn't talk much, preferring to share stories through what she beads on our moccasins and leggings, what she paints on our parfleche containers. But when she does speak, she makes sense. Her words are deeply felt and long remembered.

Years after Lalá was killed, which was soon followed by the horrors of the Wounded Knee massacre, I ask my father why Agent McLaughlin and other wašíčus are so frightened of the Ghost Dance, which to me looks just like a Round Dance. He takes a long time considering the question. He is seldom in a rush. "Their ways and ours are far apart." He moves his hands, so they are opposite one another, like enemies faced off in battle. "They want our territory and wish we would disappear—they wouldn't have to think about us again. But here we are, remembering a world without their presence, our ancestors' abundant world which the Ghost Dance promises to restore. We are a threat to wašíču designs. For them, there is no such thing as enough."

Iná sets down her work on new moccasins for my growing feet. She holds out her hands and I slip onto her lap, where she wraps me in warm arms that smell of smoke. She rocks me so gently we're barely moving. I imagine us as cattails nudged by a warm breeze. When she speaks, I feel the breath of her words on the part in my hair. "What is wakháŋ can never be fully understood.

"We're just pitiful humans whose mind has limits. So, when we're given a vision, it's a small piece of something much larger.

The Ghost Dance is said to bring back everything that was lost, our former world made whole again—the dead reborn and singing alongside us. The wašíčus gone, as if they never arrived. Prophets said this would happen immediately, if we dream hard enough and dance in the proper way. It's a beautiful dream for us, but a terrible one for wašíčus, who want to keep what they have and take what's left. But maybe the Ghost Dance works apart from Time, and the dance will take generations to complete? By then maybe some wašíčus will have joined our family, and then they, too, will take up the dance? What is wakháŋ is powerful beyond comprehension. Maybe we should dance and dream and pray for the good of everything in the world because we're meant to restore it together."

My father says that we should welcome all stories to see if they are worth remembering. "You can put ideas on and off just like moccasins. You can wear them and set them aside, hold on to those you find meaningful. Don't be afraid of learning something beyond what we're able to teach you. Even the wisest person doesn't know everything. But it's also important to preserve the ideas that make sense to you, even in the face of resistance—someone telling you that you're wrong and only *they* know the truth. Such boasting is evidence of a fool, perhaps a dangerous one."

My parents were educated in two conflicting traditions, raised on Dakhóta stories and ways of thinking, as well as learning to read wašíču books and newspapers. Iná is related to a beloved hereditary chief of our band, Mathó Núŋpa, who died before I was born though I've heard so many stories about him he is as familiar to me as the sun in the sky. Because of this connection she was sent to a Catholic ladies' school in St. Joseph, Missouri, living there from the age of seven until she was eighteen. At this school she became fluent in English and French and applied her prodigious talents for beadwork to the needlework she was taught there. She returned home when Mathó Núŋpa was dying and requested to see his favorite niece again. She confesses that after being gone so long, she was a little afraid to return home, wondering if she would know how to behave, if she would be accepted. She says that within a few days it was like she had never left. She was with her uncle when he died, singing a funny little song to him in French, which made him smile. Iná says she didn't realize that for eleven years she had been holding her breath, careful not to make mistakes, wanting to make a good impression so others would respect Dakhóta ladies and see how capable we are. When she was home, standing atop a prairie hill where the wind seemed to flow toward her from every direction, she was able to breathe all the way through her body. "I came back to life again," she says, and I can't help but cry a little to think of Iná strapped so tight she was a living ghost. When I'm old enough to read for myself, Iná shows me an article clipped from a newspaper. I cringe at the insulting title: "The Relapse of an Indian Princess into Barbarity." I skim through the opening paragraph and realize the author is referring to Iná though his words are awful and don't describe the warm, dignified woman I know so well.

"You don't have to read it," she says, and I gladly hand the page over to her as if it burns. "I just want you to know that what strangers make of you means nothing. Your heart knows the truth."

As I'm falling asleep that night, I ask Winona what she thinks of the article and the little bit I was able to read before disgust turned my stomach. "Everything I see is colored by my eyes. When they were sewn of dyed black porcupine quills, the world was dark, and now that they are indigo glass beads the vision is clear but always twilight. We don't *see* the truth. But our heart feels it if we listen."

Winona sounds like Iná and not a doll. She's experienced more than I have. She survived the end of one world and is learning what it's like to live in another. I don't think she trusts this new time. She never sleeps. I take her hand between my fingers and hold on, grateful she is here as a guardian of my dreams. I know she will wake me before I'm ever lost.

Winona is even more suspicious of wašíčus than my parents. When I'm twelve years old and they are being counseled to send me to the Carlisle Indian Industrial School in Pennsylvania because I'm intelligent and can learn what I need there to make my way in our changing world, my parents don't dismiss the idea, but instead give it serious consideration. My father says we must be realistic—it's no longer possible for us to live as we did for thousands of years beyond memory. And it's important to know English because it's the only way for our views to bear any weight with those who think they're superior. How can they twist our words or misunderstand them if we express ourselves as fluently in their language as they do? He argues—seemingly with himself since no one around him openly objects—that I won't experience the same shock many of our children do, including my own mother, who was sent to Missouri, since I'm already well versed in English and even write lengthy dramatic poems I enjoy performing for our family's amusement.

Winona is horrified by this talk. She whispers to me at night that wašíčus are more interested in remaking us to fit their image than in offering us successful lives; she insists they're also attempting to control our leaders by persuading them to hand over their children. How can there be an effective rebellion if one's children are held by the enemy? Why is this school so far from home, doesn't the distance destroy families? Why must we be kept away for years at a time, rather than allowed to return for visits? She seeks to make me fearful enough to beg my parents to stay, something I know I cannot do, even though it's my secret wish. I was raised to honor courage, to never fear adventure or a new path. Winona is so frustrated, so concerned for me given this line of thinking, she says she would like to tear out her hair, which

I know came from Iná's own head when she repaired the doll. She cries out that she is of no use! She sees me walking straight into the fire and cannot pull me back. I cradle her then, as if I am her mother. I stroke her braids and the darker patch of skin beneath her eyes, stained by tears from before I was born. I assure her I'm strong enough to survive the challenge, and that she'll be right there with me, guiding my every move.

I'm working to finally arrive at the present in this narration, though there are still significant events between the last episode and this one, including how I attained the means to begin this journal. I write when I can. I've been kept so busy at school I didn't have the luxury of reflection until now. I've come to see the dangers of routine, how easily we're trapped in its oppressive monotony, mesmerized by sameness so we march through the days like we're half-asleep. Captain Pratt, the silver-haired founder of this school, drills us as if we're soldiers in his army, organizes us by military rank. Yes, we are here to be educated in basic subjects he maintains are important, but also to labor so we'll graduate with a trade that fits into the wašíču notion of proper industry fit for Indians. I've been selected to focus on sewing and tatting, taught to craft school uniforms, the long dresses wašíču women wear, as well as produce lace collars, shawls, and doilies.

Now that I've caught my breath, adjusted to this stifling air, I can think back on all that has transpired since I first stepped on a train. The morning I left for Carlisle, just one of a crowd of Dakhóta children—each of us surrounded by family as if we were pods of a flower about to shed our petals—I took a long time studying the faces of my loved ones. I drew them in memory, aware this might be the last time I saw them with my eyes. For all I knew we were headed to our deaths—there were other children who never returned to their families, who were instead buried in a graveyard of the distant school, disappeared forever. We hoped not to land in that ground but were promised nothing.

Though it was Wasúthuŋ Wi, usually offering the warmest days, the morning we left, skies brought a cold slanted rain that stung our faces. The season mocked us, bringing an early chill on a morning already shivery with leave-taking. Still, my mother remained calm and organized food for me—a packet of bread and jerked beef for the journey. We said our farewells at home to avoid crying in public, but I noted the glimmer of tears my parents fought back as they watched me as carefully as I watched them. The moment was so painful I told myself it was a bad dream that wouldn't last forever.

I expected my friend Marie to sit beside me on the train, but we weren't allowed to choose companions, perhaps to prepare us for a life of grim regulations and commands. A stout man with a white beard so wild it looked like he'd been struck with a cluster of porcupine quills shoved us into seats, two by two, as we appeared before him. And when a boy named Alphonse tried to switch seats to look after his sister, the man shoved him down and wagged a thick finger at the boy's nose. My seatmate was a boy I'd seen now and then at town functions, but he was different from us, a cut-hair whose father was a white soldier in the same army that killed us at Whitestone Hill. I was uncomfortable to be paired with him and hoped we'd be able to make changes as the journey progressed. He was such a wriggler! He rubbed his hands together in busy circles like a raccoon's and cracked his knuckles. His legs bounced nervously as if they wanted to run away from him. He turned to look out the window, then turned to face the aisle. I was next to the window, so one of the times he leaned forward to see past me he sneaked a look right at my face. I caught him, which embarrassed us both, but then his face opened into the broadest smile I'd ever seen, the kind that makes you think of the juice of ripe berries on a sunny day—everything sweet and alive and comfortable.

He stuck out his hand for me to shake, and we shook solemnly like leaders forging an agreement.

"My name is Jack," he said. "You're Cora."

"Yes."

"I know you, but I don't know her. Who is she?" He indicated my doll with his chin.

"This is Winona," I said, sounding as formal as my parents during introductions. "She's very old. She survived a massacre."

Then Jack surprised me; he shifted for a moment, the squirming boy replaced by the old man he would grow into. "Didn't we all?" he said firmly, like it wasn't really a question.

During the long days of travel, including a stint in Chicago's Union Station, where we were roped together so no one would wander off and also attracted gawkers who thought we were some kind of performance group since one man kept shouting at us to do a "rain dance," I became friends with Jack to the point where the next time we boarded a train we made sure to stand next to each other so we could sit together. I fell asleep on his shoulder. He fell asleep on mine. He shocked me by saying he hated his father, that the man was mean to his mother and little sister, and was so against Indians Jack wondered why he ever bothered to marry one. Better for them all if he were to run off and leave! I wasn't used to children speaking out against their elders, criticizing them. Nor used to young ones sharing strong opinions about private family matters. I felt my parents wouldn't approve of Jack being my friend, so in those early days I was always defending him in my head, explaining why they should overlook this or that failure of decorum. In my imagined talks with them I explained that there was something quite noble about Jack, his vehement love for the women in his family, his protectiveness of them. And there was an intelligence in his words that showed his mind was as busy as his twitchy body—nothing escaped his notice. But what most drew me was how alive he was, his fingers drumming the wooden seat, his eyes smiling and staring right into mine though I should have looked away to be modest. His eyes captured me from the first day, what he called "Irish black, not Indian black." When I asked him the difference, he said that Irish black had a cold shine like the barrel of a gun, but Indian black was soft and warm like the muzzle of a deer. I think he was talking of his father's eyes and not his own, for I saw them switch from cold to warm depending on what he was thinking, and who he was remembering.

Jack's hands were seldom still but when he fell asleep, I studied them. They were nicked with scars and scabbed scratches, like a boy who'd gone through battles. They were rough, wrinkled hands, unlike his face, which was fawn smooth. He looked like our people in his features, which were elegant Dakhóta lines—straight nose and high forehead, mouth graceful as a long bow—though when our hands were close, I could see that his were a lighter shade. His hair was thick as a black broom, and a spray stood up in cheerful protest—a cowlick none could tame.

I asked Winona what she thought of him, and she said she didn't know yet. This surprised me for we are nearly always in agreement when it comes to our assessment of people, as if we think the same thoughts and share a single heart.

"*I* trust him," I told her, as if that were the issue.

"I know," she said. She stared at Jack with indigo eyes that painted everything twilight. She could sense I wanted more from her, and as we were family, she extended herself for my sake, though I think it made her uncomfortable. "He's a puzzle," she finally said, and then went quiet.

I fell asleep with her words swirling round and round in my head. My father carved me a wooden puzzle when I was just a baby. It was simple to complete though probably not simple to make—circles within circles. The lesson, according to my father, was not how to place the disks, but to remember what they stood for. The smallest inner button he said was me, his beloved daughter. She was held in a band of wood that represented him and my mother. The circle that held all three of us was the thióśpaye, our close relations. The circle beyond that signified our Iháŋkthuŋwaŋna Dakhóta and Húŋkpapȟa Lakȟóta heritage—two bands of the Očhéthi Šakówiŋ. The next circle was the oyáte, our nation complete, while the final circle and thickest piece of wood represented the world and all of its beings, who lived with us in accordance with agreements made before we were born. The puzzle was no larger than my infant hand and my father made sure to carefully smooth the wood, so no splinter would pierce my skin. We both enjoyed settling the pieces together to form a single orb like the slice of a carved full moon, but we used a different approach. My father started with the outer world and gradually filled it in. He said, "Here is the world, beginning with the sky and everything it watches, but where are its favorite people, the Dakhóta Nation? Here they are. And where are the two bands within our larger confederacy? Right here. Tell me where to find that close family of many relatives living in Dakota Territory. Here it is. And where are those parents who try to teach their daughter everything she needs for a good life? There they are. But the circle can never be complete without their Cora. The world is missing its dearest girl." He would set the small button of me into the center, and the satisfaction that click of wholeness gave me would last for hours. Still, it never felt right for me to put the toy together in that order. Instead, I started with my small, lonesome self and built protection around me, one encompassing circle at a time, like providing wider arms to hold me the farther away the world became. I fell asleep with memories of this puzzle, which collided with Winona's words about Jack. I spent a night of dreams trying to find the space where Jack belonged, but the piece of him I held in my hand was jagged and didn't fit no matter how hard I tried to jam him into our world.

I thought the journey to Carlisle would be the hardest part of leaving home, being jostled on endless tracks a constant reminder of the growing miles between my parents and me, a warning that I was getting closer and closer to the strange new life still hidden behind a mysterious blanket of miles. But the performance of arrival was so much harder. How we were herded together and made to stand perfectly still for a group photograph, nearly everyone clutching something precious from home, some item pressed into our hand at the last minute as a talisman against disease or other harm. Most of us dressed in traditional garb or a mix of wašíču clothes in our own style. Except for Jack, who showed up dressed as a cut-hair, hands empty but for the nicks and scratches. Then the shock of a new baptism, more violent than the one my family agreed to in order to pacify our local mission. Girls and boys pulled apart into separate buildings where we were made to drop our clothes and step into cold baths where matrons with scrub brushes tried to wash the Indian brown off our skin. Scratchy new clothes awaited us as we dried, and everything we'd carried across the country, everything we'd worn and hidden in pockets or moccasins, each belt and dress and shirt, each medal and feather and bead, was taken away, loaded into baskets. We had the appearance of strangers, even our hair clipped short while the boys' was shorn to the skin. We looked like a village in mourning. So now we are all cut-hairs, against our will. One girl tried to rescue her long braids from the ground, wound them around her fist. But a stern woman rapped her hand with a wooden brush. I could hear the crack against her knuckles, and her braids fell to the floor like dead snakes.

Before we were allowed to eat and rest, we were marched onto the parade ground, made nervous by a constant bark of orders for us to get in line and not be such a ragged lot! I understood the sharp commands, but most of my fellow students staggered in a daze, the words a meaningless drone. I attempted to translate for the younger ones around me but was shouted down. I quickly learned that the utterance of a single Dakhóta word, even offered to be helpful, is a serious offense. They treat our language like a sickness so contagious it must be cut from our tongues and minds. So, I marched for a while in silence while children faltered around me, begging me with their eyes to please explain. Eventually I used my hands to indicate what they should do, careful to keep the movements subtle to avoid detection from the ones doing all the shouting, fellow students who appear to be of high rank and responsibility and seem to be constantly angry with us. Many children are familiar with the hand language we developed to communicate with other tribes in our territory and rely on it when speech is impossible.

An older man, dressed in the suit of a teacher, his expression and movements stiff as a heavy stick, perused the baskets of precious belongings—picking out an item here and there to observe with curiosity, only to drop it as if it soiled his fingers. In the end our clothes and treasured items were thrown into metal drums lined up before us. My fellow students and I glanced at each other, wondering what this meant. Even after flames leapt from the full barrels, my mind refused to believe what was happening. It wasn't possible that my doll Winona was part of this ceremony, the burning away of our past. She had survived the conflagration of Whitestone Hill when the soldiers destroyed our lodges and food, cooking utensils and clothes, our bridles and buffalo robes, everything that helps a people live. She would survive these Carlisle people and the grim lessons they doled out like punishment. I told myself she was safe. But then I heard her shout from the depths of the fire closest to me, one cry that rose above the noise of consuming flames: "Šíča!" she shouted in warning. So I knew these wicked people were trying to kill my doll.

I understood her well enough to grasp the entirety of her message—that this place was not what it pretended, and what was sterile could also be filthy. But none of it yet made sense. All I knew was a relative was dying, being burned alive, and I needed to save her. I rushed at the barrel and pawed through flames, my sleeves catching fire. Teachers pulled me away and a matron later tended my injured hands. I'm sure I was scolded for the wild rescue attempt, and for me there was no language barrier, but my heart couldn't comprehend a single word. Already a dear relative had been sacrificed to this place, and that made it an enemy.

I will say this for Carlisle: its grounds are impressive, almost like a bustling town. The train runs right past the school, and when I first entered the campus, I thought the hospital building was the entire academy. Not at all! There are so many buildings I was afraid I would wander into the wrong one, though it turns out that's impossible what with all the marching we do from place to place. We are seldom alone. At the heart of the campus is the bandstand, which I must admit is cheerful in its aspect, surrounded by shrubs. An older student who gave us a tour waved his hand at the structure and told us the school band is very famous. Student members have marched in presidential inaugural parades and traveled to other cities to perform. I'm not sure how many of us followed his speech, but no one dared fidget. North of the bandstand is the girls' dormitory, behind which is a large gymnasium. This athletic building separates our quarters from the older boys' dormitory on the other side, almost like a monitor keeping watch, though the younger boys' dormitory is just east of where the girls live. The disciplinarian's quarters are adjacent to the dormitory for older boys, since they're deemed more troublesome. There are stables and trade shops, a laundry and printing office, the superintendent's quarters, where Captain Pratt resides, and an administration building, as well as a dining hall where some of our classes are held. There is staff housing, a chapel, a guardhouse from when the place was a military barracks, a large athletic field, and at the northernmost edge of the campus, quiet and alone, there's a cemetery for students who didn't survive this place.

The first week after our arrival, Jack and I only glimpsed one another across the parade ground when we marched and worked our muscles with Indian clubs. Already I was cynical, thinking the exercise wasn't for our health so much as to build us to endure hard labor. As advanced speakers of English, Jack and I were placed in the same classes, but were shy of each other, become strangers again in this new version of life. To be honest, I wear humiliation now along with the complicated layers of undergarments. Shame invades one's thoughts like a parasite, twists them like wet laundry until all sense is wrung out. I feel shame at being pushed around and worked like clay as if I had no earlier form. I'm not mortified by the Dakhóta girl I was at home, rather by this new creature who obeys rules that don't make sense, and whose natural inclinations for sympathy are roundly discouraged. How they dislike our defense of one another, our natural affection! How much they want us to bow our backs as far as they will bend without breaking. This place upends my childhood teachings, and what my parents value is denounced: personal dignity becomes defiance, generosity is foolishness, sympathy seen as weakness, too much curiosity considered impudent, and courage is the highest offense, being viewed as rebellion. I wonder how these people have flourished on the earth; they can be so unkind and perverse.

My hands were still blistered a few days after the burning of Winona so I was limited in what chores I could do—I was allowed to study in an empty classroom while other students were attending their studies to learn a trade, what I'm quickly apprehending is actually work to sustain this school and pay its bills. One afternoon I heard a funny "tsss" sound, which pulled me from an infuriating essay on how Christian values transformed the world. I looked to the window and there was Jack, waving at me. He looked younger without his thick cap of wavy hair, scalp tender with nicks from the shears. I walked slowly to the window, battling an inner chime of warning that said this connection might not be the best idea. But his expression was so serious it worried me.

The window was open only a few inches to air the stale room. I carefully opened it more, using the bandaged backs of my hands, which were less injured. Now that he had my attention, Jack kicked at the building in a sullen way, hands in his pockets and face turned from me. "Are you all right?"

He shrugged.

"Where are you supposed to be?"

"Digging trenches to bury our property they destroyed. I'll go back in a minute."

I couldn't help but smile at him. That word "property"—he sounded like a wašíču.

"I found something. It was tucked inside what was left of your doll." He stood on tiptoe to hand me a small black stone, no larger than my fingernail. It was shiny black, slippery to the touch. A fanciful idea crossed my mind, that this is what stars look like when they've burned and fallen to earth. There is still light that shines from their scorched depths.

"It's what's left of her heart."

Jack's words startled me, and I almost dropped the stone. But in another moment, I believed him. I always knew that Winona wasn't just any doll—she was alive until these people killed her. I was grateful for the artifact and thanked Jack in a hushed voice that was all I could manage without crying.

Jack looked so glum I wanted to say something consoling. "At least *you* didn't lose anything. I'm glad of that."

He lifted one shoulder, looked like he was fighting tears.

"Did you?" A nod.

"What did they burn?"

Jack gave the building a ferocious kick that must've hurt. "They took my letter, the one Ma wrote about how they'd miss me, and what I should think of if I get upset. And my sister is too little to write so she drew an outline of her hand on the paper. Ma said it was Alice's way of promising that she's always holding my hand, even this far away. And now she's not!"

Jack bolted across the lawn, no doubt to cry in private. I wept for him, for all of us, cut off from everything that made sense in our world. I held on to the stone heart, pressed it until it was warm, and maybe it was my own pulse I felt in my fingertips, but I'm convinced it began to flutter, rapid as the heart of a tiny bird. I felt guilty for the mistake with Jack, not realizing how much he was one of us despite being a cut-hair. This place was already testing him, just as it was the rest of us. And here I'd thought he had nothing to lose.

One month after arriving at Carlisle I have written a thousand letters to my parents in my head, while only three with an actual pen. We are encouraged to immerse ourselves in the business of this place, to leave home in the past. So, I keep my loyalties secret. Every morning upon waking, I face the rising sun and silently ask that powerful being to shine health on those I love, to nourish them with strength. I like to think they're also facing the sun and praying for my safety, that we are united even across vast miles of territory.

Perhaps because I'm now living in close proximity to children from various parts of the country, so many of them coughing through the long nights, their health compromised by grief and a poor diet that leaves us hungry, I come down with a sickness more serious than any before. I must be powerfully ill for I end up in the infirmary, even though many of the girls in my dormitory have eyes glazed with fever and an unnatural, crackling breath. They say I have pneumonia, but the word means nothing. All I know is that breathing has become my sole focus; I work at it, sucking tiny sips of air and begging my lungs to accept them. I alternately boil from fevers, imagining I've fallen into Iná's soup kettle, then freeze, shivering beneath the blankets, dreaming that I rest at the bottom of a frozen creek. I have no taste for food or water, only air. How many days do I fight like this? Breath by breath by breath. There is no one to pray over me here, as they would do at home. No one to sing encouraging songs that give me strength. I have the desperate thought that my struggle is ceremony—I'm crying for a vision in this empty place that has flattened me to nothing. Does the idea summon a vision, or did one wait for me all along? As I'm lying awake tonight, watching the ceiling pulse as if it will lower itself and squash what's left of my body, a young woman floats into view directly above me. She is beautiful in the way of my mother—they could be sisters, though this woman's hair isn't combed but hangs down in snarled strings. She's wrapped in a blanket she holds tight to her body. I wonder how she can hover there, stretched out like a fish floating in calm water. She smiles at me but I'm too confused to respond. I can only stare like a curious wašíču. My breathing suddenly eases, the pressure on my lungs relents. I can focus more clearly on the woman because I'm no longer struggling for air. Then the woman opens her blanket, and her presence becomes a nightmare—she's wholly naked, her breasts hanging down like udders on a cow. Her body might have been beautiful once, but now it's sliced and gun-shot—I don't understand how she's still alive given all her wounds. I want to close my eyes, but she makes a curious noise like a strangled hiss and I'm too afraid to disobey. She wants me to look. She lowers herself until she's so close I could reach up and touch her. She drops the blanket, or it disappears. Her hands are free and she's using them to open the mouths of the most awful cuts that look like stabs from a bayonet. She probes them and I cry out when a finger goes deep inside, past the knuckle. How can she bear the pain?

She tilts her head and it's like she heard my question. She speaks without using her tongue—she's opened her mouth to show me she has none. It's been taken for a trophy. I hear her in my head, telling me to have no fear, she is a relative from a long time before when our people were massacred. She wants me to see how they desecrated her body. Her silent voice soothes me. In my fever I imagine her tortured body as protection—she has flown here to stand between me and a foreign grave. She becomes a welcome presence, a comfort. I'm no longer frightened of the gore, though I'm sorry for her suffering. She wants me to know that she fingers her injuries not because she is depraved or wanting to be seen as pitiful. She picks her wounds to keep them open because the survivor's way is to allow flesh to sew its mouth closed, to forget, though scars mound atop what will never be the same, what will never be as whole as it was before.

There is no true healing without remembering, she tells me in her silent way, and she guides my finger inside a bullet hole that has ripped through her heart. I know I should be horrified, but I'm honored by this connection, this intimacy across death and Time. There is something she wants me to do, and when I'm well I'll figure it out. I promise her this in my head. She rises back to the ceiling and then through it. I wonder if the children on that upper floor will see her, too? Or is she here just for me, blood of my blood? The finger that touched her wound is warm, as she was. She moves like a ghost, but pain has kept her alive. There is a puzzle in this but I'm too tired to understand. I fall asleep thinking that her pain is mine even though my body is whole and unblemished. Her pain is mine. I carry it now.

I'm grateful for this bound journal, where I've recounted memories of earlier years and my arrival at Carlisle, where I've written what my heart is truly thinking. It's a gift from Miss Feld, who runs the Susan Longstreth Literary Society, of which I am a selected member for my "gift of English." I'm the youngest girl in the group, most of them in their final years at the school, and they treat me like their little sister and pet. Miss Feld handed me the treasure on my thirteenth birthday, showed me what she inscribed on the inside cover: "For dear Cora, Sioux Priestess of the Highest Order, whose language lifts her above peers, whose sensibility is a wonder. A magnificent flower grown from corrupt soil. You are my miracle. From your proudly devoted teacher, Miss Caroline Feld."

I was of two instincts when Miss Feld handed me the gift: grateful for her clear generosity, frustrated by the heedless insult. I thanked her most courteously, which pinked her cheeks and brought shine to her expression, but I wasn't effusive though the gift is considerable and offered more than she ever dreamed. She is a long-waisted wisp of a woman whose sympathies run deep and show on her face, which is narrow but pleasing in its features, in particular her green eyes that darken to brown when filled with emotion. She is the youngest member of the faculty, seemingly unaware of the disapproving air some colleagues bring to their interactions. I sense she is barely tolerated, and that more than a few of them would never miss her. She is too fanciful for their tastes.

Though I am homesick each moment I have energy for reflection, on the whole I'm adjusting to my new situation. Or at least, I accept it without too much fight in my heart. Jack doesn't fare as well. He was excited when he learned there was a printing press at the school and publications written by students—though with careful editing performed by staff to keep the authors within strict margins of acceptable content. He was certain he'd be allowed to work in the pressroom given his talent for communication. But perhaps his nicked hands betrayed him, or the bright mischief in his eyes? Instead it was declared he would learn the carpentry trade, a decision that brought him grave disappointment. He says it's like they want to knock him down from his true talents. We rarely find moments alone to talk, and when we do, he watches the ground rather than look me straight in the eyes as he did on the train. He has learned to carve in his new trade, but it's as if he whittles himself rather than wood, and there is less of him with each passing month.

I have a new friend here at school. On cold-wind days when we march, march, march, like prisoners I've seen in chains, and the world seems drained of every color but gray, she is like the surprise of a crimson wood lily in snow. Her friendship is better than any medicine poured into spoons. Grace is Cheyenne, which automatically brings favor since her nation is allied with mine—there is a natural trust between us. Though we're the same age, she is taller; perhaps because of this she's inclined to stoop as if looking for something on the ground. She has the loveliest uptilted eyes, and a small square forehead framed by wisps of brown curls that stubbornly grow back as soon as Matron trims them. We chatter during every spare moment—she attended a mission school before this one, so she is nearly fluent in speaking English, though not writing it. Our favorite time together is during the weekly gymnasium privileges allowed us girls. We take over the runner's walk, which magically floats above us on the second floor of the building—a circular track that goes nowhere at all. We trot along with linked arms, giggling as our hips bang into each other until we find our rhythm that turns us into a team of horses hitched together, pulling along our freight of stories. She cheers me with her fancy for an older boy, Micah, who is shy and studious, though handsome in the perfect balance of his Navajo features. Each week there is a drama of some kind, as she does or doesn't gain his attention. I think he admires her but is too embarrassed to make a show of it.

She says her real name isn't Grace, which was given to her by a local priest, but that she doesn't mind the change since her own name is a burden on her heart. She whispers it so quietly in her language, it's like the real name is hidden and her breath merely scatters the dust off its top. But I hear the translation: "Many Kills Woman." Our pace slows as she tells me how a relative gave her this honored name, after a woman who fought bravely defending her family. "Now it feels like a curse," she confides, "because I once had four older brothers." I hear, rather than see, tears gathering in her eyes. "All of them gone. I am the last child standing." Though I'm certain she had nothing to do with their deaths, which she cannot discuss, I understand the weight of guilt when we survive what others don't. Winona has taught me that misery, with her stories of outliving the end of the world.

I show Grace what remains of my beloved doll, her stone heart, which I keep safe in a drawer. The girl's eyes widen as she strokes the small, burnt marble. "She bit me!" Grace cries and explains that's the best way she can describe the shock of life she felt pass from the object to her skin.

"Her spirit is unquenchable," I say. And when Grace furrows her brow at the strange word, I add: "It cannot die."

I begin carrying Winona with me in my pocket, rather than leave her confined. She warms up to being in the world again, listening to the action, making plain her approval or objection. She likes Grace, though she wants to know what killed her brothers. I've noticed my doll is a collector of tragedy, as if she hopes to learn every variation of doomed failure so she can ward it off in the future. Maybe it's her way of arming herself, so she can better protect those she loves.

As the school year closes, Captain Pratt announces that those of us in good standing who are interested in a field trip may sign up to visit Gettysburg, which is about thirty miles from here. He gives a speech on the significance of the place, how there were something like fifty thousand casualties by the end of that single Civil War battle—a number that slips through my head as too great to comprehend. He says the Union side ultimately won the terrible struggle, and the victory was critical in shifting the war. He reads us the entirety of the Gettysburg Address, originally delivered by the man who was then president: Abraham Lincoln. I find my hands have curled into tight fists at the words, which though elegant, spare no thought or shame for the travesty this leader brought on our heads six months before Gettysburg—when he signed the death warrants for many of my people, hanged so wretchedly and unjustly together in the town of Mankato, while onlookers jeered. The real culprit in the affair being the very government that condemned these thirty-eight Dakhóta men, the very government that didn't abide by its solemn promises, which allowed our children to starve. When Captain Pratt rattles off dates in recounting the great battle, my brain immediately works out the timing, calculates that only two months later the victorious element of this army would try to annihilate my people at Whitestone Hill. I have no interest in the graveyard of soldiers who were once my enemy, and for all I can tell, still are.

Jack notices my tension and nods. He brushes the back of my fist with his knuckles.

"I'll never go," he whispers angrily. "They can rot with their glory. It has nothing to do with us." In the confusion of sorting out excited volunteers for the trip, Jack and I slip away to a quiet space behind the printer's office.

"A trip would be fun," I admit. "If we were going somewhere else." We sit on the grass, which is overgrown in this neglected patch.

"Sure. But we have to make a stand wherever we can."

"Do you feel *any* connection to the American soldiers, given that your father is in the same army?" My question is offered in a rush because Jack seldom mentions his father.

"No!" His answer is immediate. He punches the ground so hard I worry he might break his hand. "I could face even *him* in battle and end his days."

I stifle a gasp, not wanting to judge him.

"That sounds terrible, I know. But he hates us. The longer he's been in our territory, the more he wishes he never came. He thinks our people are dirt. One time when he was real drunk, he told my mother he'd put good seed in her, the best to be found in good old County Mayo. But she birthed a litter of dogs." Jack's voice is shaking, and a single tear is caught in his dark lashes. "My sister was too young to understand, so she smiled at him and placed her cheek on his knee. Mean as he is, he couldn't push her away, she is so—" He doesn't finish the thought, overcome by emotion, but I understand. His sister makes everyone feel loved, even him. I place a hand on Jack's leather boot, which is separate enough from him to be safe, chaste.

"He is to be pitied, more than hated. Such cruelty is a sickness." I remove my hand. I'm surprised to hear Iná's voice come from my own mouth, what she would advise this crushed boy. Though to be honest, I would hate such a man myself.

Jack's mood changes so fast, it's like lightning has struck us on this ground. He does a backward somersault and leaps to his feet. He pulls a string of beads from his pocket, then cups it in his hands. "I made you something," he says, and his smile is so full of the day's bright sun that my heart catches and flutters. He places the string in my hand and then shoots away from me as if chased by the wind of a storm. When my heart calms, I examine the gift: it's a necklace of small wooden stars he must have carved for me, each one held apart by a knot between them, seven in all. With this small gesture he has given me the world—a promise that our Očhéthi Šakówiŋ, our mighty council fires, still burn brightly in this cosmos.

Later that night, as I'm about to fall asleep, I hear Winona's voice in my ear. I've taken to placing the stone of her beneath my pillow, so she can visit my dreams. She's been quiet all day, even after my private conversation with Jack. She must have been musing on everything that happened.

"I know for certain now," she says, though she pauses before delivering her verdict: "Jack is trouble."

I whisper that it's impossible for anyone to be untroubled in this strange place, which purposely unravels the fabric of its students to remake them into something they might not recognize.

"But he is different," Winona insists. "Not whole like you, where the enemy is on the outside. Remember, he is half his father. Half his anger, and his sickness. He has so much to prove to himself. He will always unravel faster than you."

I am too tired to argue with Winona, and never want to upset her. With one hand I stroke her heart's face beneath the pillow, and with the other I clutch a necklace of stars, hidden beneath my nightdress. I dream all night of string, of large spools thrust in my lap for me to loop and hook until it becomes the most beautiful shroud of lace.

It's the summer of our first experience with the Outing Program, where students live with white families in local counties, and work at jobs like farming and housekeeping. Some of the older boys quietly complain that they're used as cheap labor for farms, and that their wages are often held back with one excuse or another. Jack and I are heartened to learn that we'll be stationed in the same county, though I'll be living in town, and he'll be on a potato farm. My host family, the Greeveses, are Quakers who run a small school. In return for a bed and meals, I'll clean their rooms and help with cooking, laundry, mending, gardening. I have no illusions about the purpose behind the program, designed by our founder, Captain Pratt. We're told it's to help us practice the skills we've been taught at school, but the main reason is to keep us from returning home, where we might lose what gains we've made in becoming "civilized." Still, my parents have agreed that I will be here for at least the next five years, so I'll pretend to be fooled with as much grace as I can muster.

Mr. Greeves has offered to transport both me and Jack to his town about an hour's ride from Carlisle. Jack's host will pick him up there and bring him to the farm. The two of us stand together in the warm morning sun, our few belongings packed in small traveling cases that were donated to the school. Jack kicks at the earth, as if to punish this Pennsylvania soil. But when I nudge him, he looks up and smiles.

"Are you nervous?"

"Naw. Whatever the situation, it can't be worse than this place."

"Well, I am. I'm nervous," I confess.

"Don't be. The family will surely like you. Everyone does!" He says this with such vehemence, he turns shy.

Before we've had the chance to talk more a wagon pulls up, driven by a man who is all sharp lines and angles as if he were drawn with a ruler. But once he sees us, he smiles, and the warmth of his expression softens his face. He doesn't look very old, maybe my father's age, but there's a formality about him that adds years. We quickly load onto the wagon and are off, heading into the next adventure! I enjoy the breeze of our swift movement, and the chance to see more of this territory that is so different from home. The trees here bunch together, their heads bowed close like gossips. And the grasses are greener, so lavishly bright they almost look painted. Both Jack and I keep craning our necks, not wanting to miss any of the sights. Mr. Greeves doesn't interrupt our pleasure with questions or attempts at conversation, for which I'm grateful. We arrive too soon at our destination, and lean into each other subtly so no one will notice, our arms pressing sentiments we'd be too bashful to speak.

I worry about Jack when I see the man who is waiting to transport him to a farm outside of town. Mr. Taylor appears about twice the size of Mr. Greeves and has nothing of his friendly air. He is all muscle and angry beard. He doesn't offer any thanks for Jack being brought to him, just nods his head, and tells Jack to get up in the wagon. When Jack takes a last look at me, Mr. Taylor barks, "Hurry up, boy, lots of work waiting for us!" I feel a pain in my heart but there's nothing I can do, so I wave to Jack and send up a prayer that he will be protected.

Mr. Greeves tells me that we'll be home in a short while. There's a generosity in him offering that word, "home," like he wants it to be mine, too. When we arrive, I am greeted by his wife, who is strikingly like him in her narrow shape, but just as warm, and their daughter, who is hopping up and down. In her excitement she accidentally steps on the tail of her cat, an orange marmalade-striped being I'll learn is named Chloe. Chloe cries and runs straight up the tree in their front yard, looking unimpressed when the daughter offers an apology.

The girl who will share her room with me is Susanna Greeves and we are exactly the same age, though she was born in spring. While I'm wary of new people, there is something so friendly about the scatter of freckles across her nose I offer an open smile upon our introduction, which she returns. She wears her dark blond hair in neat braids and has eyes the same pleasant color— a mix of honey and brown. I'm still studying her features and how much she looks like her long-nosed parents, though on her the feature is appealing, a neat refinement, when she hooks my arm in hers and tells me, "Run!"

I'm so jolted with surprise I stumble, but then we're sprinting through the field beside her house, and I realize this is just what I needed after bouncing around in the wagon for an hour; after saying goodbye to Jack and watching him leave with a sour-faced man; after a year of being captured in binding clothes and nonsensical rules. We fall into the grass and lie on our backs, careless as old friends. We hear the determined drill of a woodpecker though we can't see him, and both of us burst out laughing at the same time.

"I'm glad you're here!" Susanna gushes, reaching for my hand. "I wish I had a sister."

I'm not used to such frankness, especially after a year of being guarded, so I say only, "Thank you," though with a smile I hope will show my sincerity. Within the hour we are the best of friends and I realize this girl is the first white person I like.

All my nerves about the summer are quickly gone. I am most

fortunate in this appointment as the Greeves family are kind. They expect me to do my work, certainly, but it's nothing more than I would do at school, or even at home to help Iná with household chores. Susanna is my companion in each task; she doesn't shirk her share of the labor, and somehow it all gets done in a merry way that makes us feel sturdy and accomplished. Though I must admit, the laundry is our least favorite enterprise since it works up a lather of sweat. Then we find relief in a small pond behind my hosts' house. Susanna and I like to sit on the banks, our feet cooling in still water. Sometimes she'll kick up a spray aimed at me, and we splash-fight until we're drenched. Then what's to be done but lie on our backs and let the sun dry us off while we study the clouds and tell their stories.

"That one is Elias." Susanna points to a cloud resembling a man with a puffed-up chest. "And he's in love with Sarah." She points to a wispy series of clouds that curl in waves. The romantic chase is on! We so easily lose time in each other's company, feeling free to imagine and just be. Though I yearn for my family and for familiar hills beneath home skies that first taught me about Eternity, this is the next place in the world to make me content. Since I'm a respected member of the Susan Longstreth Literary Society, where we exercise our minds beneath a banner reading "Labor Conquers All Things," and because I like to find the right word for every thought, I try to define what is happening in my body and emotions, try to understand the precise feeling. And maybe because I'm fingering Winona's scorched heart, which is always in a small pocket of my dress, I hear her voice inside my head, joining the run of thoughts: "This place nourishes you," she says. "We all need love."

One night when we're lying in Susanna's bed, she grasps my hand and asks me about Jack. I must have talked about him more than I intended. Her hand squeezes mine, then she raises our

arms in the air, pulses them back and forth in a way that is sooth-
ing. Susanna is the most physical girl I've ever known. She speaks
with the body as much as her voice. I'm sad when she lets go and
we tuck our arms back into place like dignified ladies.

"He's special to you," she says, not asking a question.

"Mmmm . . ." I buy time with empty noise. I don't want to be
reserved with Susanna, but there are so many taboos surrounding
my connection with Jack I don't know how to voice them without
betraying him and myself.

"You're special to *him*," she says. The simple words open a
door beneath my back as if the bed has a mouth that wants to de-
vour me. My stomach clenches with the fall, tears leak from my
eyes. I can't stop falling, so I grab her hand to steady myself.

"You don't have to say anything," she finally whispers. She re-
leases my hand so she can stroke my hair. I almost hear my mother's voice singing, "Ábu, ábu."

"Go to sleep and dream of Jack." Susanna pets my hair until
I sleep. But I don't dream of Jack.

Instead, I dream of the injured woman who works hard to
keep her wounds alive, no matter the misery. She's curled up
in the corner of Susanna's room. I can see her shadow. She isn't
wearing any blanket, just her tortured flesh. Her hair is matted
and covers much of her face, but I can see one bloodshot eye peek
through the strands. I'm not scared this time; I remember that
she's my relative, who would never hurt me, the one who helped
me catch my breath when I was sick with pneumonia. Three of
her fingers are dug inside a cluster of holes someone made in her
body. I can feel a mild discomfort in the same part of my torso and
then remember: *her pain is mine,* though certainly diminished by
comparison. I wonder if I'm actually dreaming or if she traveled
here to find me, if my unexpected friendship with Susanna has
made her all the more lonesome. I extend my hand in the dark,

offering it in her direction. She drifts toward me like a shredded cloud, her own hand reaching for mine. When we clasp palms, a jolt runs through my system. I'm falling again, as I did when Jack was mentioned, but this time there's pain and grief and terror, until rage blasts through me, smothering everything else. My heart is a fist that wants to pound and pound and pound, never stop fighting. The injured woman covers me now, our faces no more than an inch apart, her breath flowing into my mouth, my breath flowing into hers. She is my relative, who loves me, I remind myself, as her breath becomes cold, as my heart kicks over from rage to fear.

"Yes, but her love is terrible," a voice says—I think it's Winona's heart. "You don't have to accept what she brings."

"Too late," I tell the dark, and the woman inhales my words. "It's already happened. Her pain is mine."

A frightened gasp breaks the spell of connection. Susanna grabs my arm and shakes me. The injured ancestor is gone, wafting away like smoke.

"Something attacked you!" Susanna sounds like she's about to cry.

"I'm fine." I do my best to reassure her, to suggest she dreamed the hovering figure. Eventually the girl calms enough to sleep again, and she is all smiles and friendliness in the morning. But there's a caution behind her eyes that wasn't there before; a tiny splinter has pricked our friendship and remains lodged there, though we go through the motions of work and play. The injured woman has come between us with her suffering, and the more I think on it, the more I suspect that is why she came.

I've been living with the Greeveses for four weeks when I hear distressing news. Mr. Taylor of the dour expression and ferocious beard pounds on the front door while we're eating breakfast.

Mr. Greeves offers a polite invitation for him to join us though there's nothing civil in Taylor's manner. He shakes his head and says he just wants to state his business, he's wasting precious time.

"I'm here to see if that Indian girl knows anything about the boy," he says. He juts his chin at me in a way I find insulting.

Mr. Greeves intervenes. "This lady is Miss Cora, and you may direct a question to her if she has no objection?"

I nod my head and then push myself to match my host's courtesy: "I have no objection."

Mr. Taylor must be grinding his teeth; his jaw muscle twitches.

"The boy run off!" he barks. "I want to know if he's sheltered here, or if *she* knows anything about it." He jerks his chin at me again. I know he'd like to shake me.

Mr. Greeves is masterful at remaining calm; his voice soothes like the sweet rumble of their cat's purr. "I assure you we're not harboring anyone other than the people you see. Miss Cora, is there anything you can contribute to this inquiry?"

"No, sir." I look at Mr. Greeves while answering, so he'll know that "sir" is meant for him.

"He's not been here, telling stories?" Mr. Taylor bites the edge of his mustache as if to keep from saying more.

"What stories would he have to tell?" Mr. Greeves asks, his voice calm but clearly challenging this edgy man.

"None that's true!" Mr. Taylor barks.

"I'm sorry, we can't help you."

Mr. Taylor pumps his hands into fists and his jaw muscle jumps again, but there's nothing to be done but stomp away.

Once he's gone, I have space and breath to be terrified for Jack.

"I honestly don't know anything about this," I tell the room. I want to say that after witnessing Mr. Taylor in action I can easily understand why Jack would bolt; what on earth must have happened to him? Something more than a whipping, which he's used to from school and his soldier father. But I catch myself. The Greeveses are kind but I'm not sure of their limits, the point marking the edge of their sympathies. I'm left alone in my fears and worries. *Oh, Jack!* I keep thinking, wondering where he is and how he's faring. I want to search for him but know that will never be allowed. Yet I can't imagine going on as usual, as if nothing's happened. As soon as I can gracefully be alone, I head to the pond. I wash my hands and face in the clear water. I cool the back of my neck. Then I sit at the base of a beautiful dogwood tree I think of as a gracious lady, my back against her trunk to give me strength, maturity. I speak to the lady in the tree, ask her to help my friend, my wild Jack. I don't even hear myself chanting until a cloud passes over the sun and alerts me to pay attention to time. I can't be gone for long. "Let him be safe, let him be safe," I murmur to the tree, though I don't use raw English. I offer my request in Dakhóta because that is the language of my heart and Jack's.

The summer is over now and I'm back at Carlisle, living this year with a girl from the Territory of Alaska who can't yet say who she is though her eyes tell some of her story, and my dear friend Grace, who is now like family. We are never allowed to live with a member of our own tribe since Captain Pratt decreed that "Carlisle has always planted treason to the tribe and loyalty to the nation at large."

Though why we should be loyal to a nation that has yet to make us citizens is questionable. We are meant to be splintered here, driven from each other and our languages, which hold powerful medicine.

Susanna and I have promised to correspond, though we were shy after saying it, suspecting that our friendship was still interrupted since the visit of my injured ancestor, and not likely to continue now that I'm gone.

I put off mentioning Jack here. Not because I think Miss Feld will break her vow to never examine this volume, rather because it takes such control to live with the bad things that happen to those we love. I've crossed out that last bit several times, the fragment about love, and keep writing it back in, each time smaller and smaller. But this journal is the space of my truth, so I must speak plain and stop scratching out my feelings. Iná taught me that a Dakhóta woman is modest and dignified, and we don't throw our hearts at men until they have well earned them. I don't know what Jack deserves, he is a complicated case, but at risk of sounding like some lovestruck girl who giggles over boys and connects our names together in doodled hearts like the ones in wašíču valentines, I will admit: Cora loves Jack.

And though Jack is a mystery to most, never what you expect him to be from one moment to the next, I'll stake my life on this hunch: Jack loves Cora.

There are times in the dining hall when I feel a pinch at the back of my neck, a quick wave of heat like a lit match has been whisked past my skin. If I turn to look behind me, always I catch Jack's eyes latched on me, prying, watching. There are invisible lines strung between us; we are reined together. But here I am, still avoiding the story. Some of which I know. Some of which I can only guess.

Jack's outing was nothing like mine. His host family treated him like a farm animal to be driven to exhaustion. He ate in the kitchen after the family finished their meal, and slept in the loft of the barn, though that arrangement was a blessing because he shared those quarters with a pup. He did her the favor of changing her name. The Taylors called her Bone since she was terribly thin and nervous, but Jack called her Peg after the warm character Peggotty in his favorite novel, *David Copperfield*. And just as we grow into our names, so Peg plumped under Jack's care and even showed flashes of joy. She flourished while Jack declined, though she was a great comfort.

Jack is returned now. The police caught him just outside Pittsburgh, where he was following the railroad tracks in the direction of home. Authorities along the trail had been alerted to keep watch for an Indian runaway, more specifically, a "Sioux," which might have made them extra cautious since we are considered notorious after the demolition of Custer's 7th Cavalry. Some days he walked, some days he hopped a train. Peg had taken off with him and when she was tired, he buttoned her up in his shirt and made it a sling so he could carry her. He left the farm in the night after something happened that he refuses to explain to anyone. He was interrogated several times, but only shook his head and wouldn't speak. As a consequence, there was no mercy. But later, when Jack recovered from the brutal whipping dished out by the discipline master, supposedly on order from a tribunal of fellow students, he said the pain washed him clean. He spent many days and nights locked in the guardhouse, which sits beside the older boys' quarters. The man in charge of his discipline taunted him, said he was practicing his future since a worthless boy like him would surely end up in prison someday. I cried every night throughout the ordeal, though never told him. I prayed and prayed that he would be granted comfort. What's strange is he wrote me a letter, too shy to speak the piece aloud, where he said there were nights he didn't think he was asleep yet, but swore I walked through the wall and covered him with a blanket. No words were spoken between us, and the visits were brief, but they were just what he needed to hold himself together. I don't know what to think about that. The idea makes me glad, but also a little afraid.

One final note on the sad episode offers a sweet gesture: the little dog Peg was gathered up with Jack and returned to the school as if she, too, were an insubordinate pupil. She was rescued by

Man-on-the-Bandstand, who is of course not a man at all, rather the woman editor of our publication, *The Indian Helper,* who uses that alias, a play on her initials. Miss Burgess allows Peg to wander where she likes, so Jack is permitted brief reunions with his friend. He is her dearest favorite. The moment she spies him the entire back end of her wags joyfully along with her tail, and Jack suffers face baths from her rough little tongue. She is tan like a fawn with triangular ears that flop over when she's happy. I doubt she'll grow very big. She's the most popular figure on campus and not a few of the students look more fondly upon Jack for having brought her.

Before moving on, I'd like to share a further note on Miss Burgess, our rigorous editor. Though students are encouraged to shares stories of their progress and adventures in publications, they're not given much latitude in expressing opinions or voicing criticisms. Each time I look upon a newly published article, I can't help but see it as a patch of garden that's been vigorously pruned and weeded until only the barest stem remains. Miss Burgess diligently oversees this process of muzzling the truth, which is one reason this journal is so precious to me. These words are as much my own as I can make them, given that I write in a language poured in from the outside, rather than rising from my own heart.

Perhaps to combat this stifling of voices, I'm inspired to insinuate myself into the post of assisting Miss Feld in her perusal of student letters, ostensibly to mark their progress in learning English. Other faculty members are involved in the process, and I can't approach them all, but maybe I can help at least a few students send truth through the mail. I feel protective of these missives, some of them speaking with a forced kind of jollity if the author doesn't want parents to worry, which is my own habit when writing home, some of them despairing and pleading. I've yet to hold one back for further inspection and feel a thrill of excitement each time a new batch is prepared for mailing. There might be repercussions eventually, if too many parents write their concerns to the captain. But until such time, I will happily continue this minor rebellion.

I'm increasingly worried about my Alaskan roommate, whose Carlisle name is Beth. I suspect her actual name has something to do with crows or the color black; she's tried to act it out for me and Grace. Though when we get too fixated on the crow part of the demonstration, she becomes frustrated. The reason for my concern is how much weight she's lost since arriving. The unvaried food served at our tables makes her ill; she can't seem to keep much of it in her stomach. Many of the students suffer from the severe change in their diet, used to fresh protein and berries, an abundance of wild greens. At Carlisle we're served mainly dense bread and thin soup, certainly never enough. She is so thin now the blades of her cheeks look sharp, as if they'll slice through her skin. Grace and I confer about the problem and try to learn what food she'd like to eat. She draws a picture of what appear to be tiny eggs all piled together. We don't know what it means. Poor Beth is beside herself with vexation, though not aimed at us, rather at herself. I fear she begins to feel stupid, which is one of the problems of this place when we're stripped of language. We cautiously show the picture to Linus, a member of the football team who is also from Alaska, ask if he knows what the drawing depicts. His eyes widen and he stuffs a knuckle in his mouth. Grace and I are worried we've somehow insulted him, but he grabs the picture and brings it to his nose quite tenderly as if he can smell what's depicted there. He whispers words we don't understand but would be reported if we were the kind to police fellow students as we've been ordered to do—military rules. He shakes himself to return from wherever he went and smiles. "These are fish eggs," he explains. "Over here, these are from salmon"—he points to a tumble of the larger variety—"and these are from herring. They are . . ." He can't seem to find the right word but the look on his face tells us these tiny eggs are delicacies. After we explain the reason for our errand he smiles. "She misses fish." Then Linus jogs away, though we note he keeps the drawing.

A small group of us, which includes Jack, put our heads together to devise a scheme to secure fish for Beth. There's no use talking to anyone in the kitchen—their brutal budget has already caused several students to waste away, sent home before the end of the year so if they should die, the school won't be blamed. The dietary needs of one girl from Alaska won't change the system, even if the child's life is at stake. Jack consults with older boys who are friendlier to him now because of Peg. If anyone knows what's possible to do outside the strict rules and rhythms of this place it's the boys who still find ways to smoke tobacco.

Jack says the boys scoffed at the idea that fish were hard to come by. "They told me there are trout in Letort Creek," he said, his eyes bright with excitement that reminds me of the boy I first met on the train. "That's the stream behind the athletic field and cemetery. They go fishing there all the time with Prune, and he gets the older girls in domestic courses to fry them up."

Prune is a handsome Seneca footballer whose athletic efforts on the field are more like dancing than sport. I've seen him leap over a fallen player and catch the ball midair, tuck it close to his middle and barely land before pivoting in another direction to confound the defense. I don't know why he's called "Prune," no one will say, though the older boys smirk when we ask. We introduce Prune to Beth at a debate, one of the few events where the sexes are allowed to mingle. She's too shy to look up at him or shake his hand, though she gently taps his proffered hand with her fist in a way that is clearly a gesture of respect. He seems touched. His face, which is usually taken up with whatever mood suits him as a much-admired school leader—boredom, insolence, ridicule—softens.

"She is so thin," he says. Her wrist is a flesh-covered twig, and her eyes are enormous black ponds in a starved face. In that moment Prune becomes our ally and organizes his team to produce a steady supply of fish for Beth from Alaska—to tide her over until she adapts to this new, limited diet. It's quite a commitment made by the boys, requiring negotiations with the older girls that I suspect involve secret kisses. I'm so proud of them and how, in this instance, we will fight for one another.

I pester Jack for details on this grand conspiracy: How does it work? He explains that the boys involved are high-ranking, some of them serving as campus patrol guards meant to prevent us from running. They can move through the campus more freely and steal away for a check of clever traps they learned to make at home. Though they also drop a line and hook for the pleasure of it, whenever possible. I already understand the cooking part, how the older girls who help teach Domestic Arts have a stream of ready excuses as to why they're teaching others to prepare fish. And somehow Beth is their favorite pupil to serve as taster. She might not yet have English words to express her appreciation, but each bite is such an event by the look on her face, everyone is convinced of their success!

Within a month Beth has more flesh on the bone and is once again alert, better able to focus on learning English. Turns out she's a chatterbox and was dying inside to be unable to communicate. Pretty soon Grace and I make jokes about tossing her in Letort Creek with the fish to bring us peace, but really she's a pesty little sister we would do anything to protect.

A grim day though the weather mocks us with autumn heat and pure skies as blue as Iná's favorite periwinkle beads. A young

Cheyenne boy who no one knew well hanged himself in the night. He'd stripped down to his undergarments, perhaps to finally rid himself of the scratchy clothes and hated uniform that duplicates the ones worn by soldiers who massacred his people at Sand Creek just a year after our own relatives were struck down at White-stone Hill. The boy who discovered him hanging from the stair railing said there was something else on his person, a paper with a drawing. Our guess is that the picture illustrates his real name, as it depicts a horse leaping for the sun, its forelegs on the rise and never falling. Beth appears shocked and spent breakfast holding herself while rocking. Grace and I did our best to block the view any teacher or matron might have of her. She has settled now.

My pen is too heavy to write more. I feel old today.

The school is decorated for Christmas, and we have more visitors who troop through campus to see what Captain Pratt has been up to in turning so-called "wild Indians" into darker versions of white people. There are times I feel on exhibit when groups of wealthy Easterners watch us move about our day in the var-ious workshops—they examine my tatting and the extravagant ladies' hats I create to be sold. On weekends I'm called upon to declaim, reciting "The Wreck of the Hesperus," and other poems and speeches from memory. I enjoy this chance to display my full range of emotions under the guise of performance. I can rage and weep and thunder. I can threaten and glower. For those minutes I feel powerful and truthful, and it doesn't matter if the audience thinks me a trained monkey, for I know it was my parents who taught me to read, and to write with a careful hand. Anything I am comes from them.

Jack lives for what reading he can manage in the library, mak-ing his way through a treasure trove of novels bequeathed to the school by a patron, and for the visits we arrange during school functions that allow the mingling of boys and girls. Our days are filled with work and study, drills, and roll call—the routine deadens him but is also a mercy. The less time he has to think, the better. He surprises me with a holiday gift he made in woodshop, bookends for my few volumes, including this journal. Carved into the aspen wood are delicate prairie grasses, gracefully bent by the wind. I'm touched by the gesture and hug them to my chest, which makes Jack blush. "The grasses are so real! Like they're about to move. These are really fine, Jack. You're an artist." He smiles, but no longer looks me in the eye as he once did on the train.

Jack brings Home to this place, however he can. In my own way, maybe I do as well. Both of us tireless agitators, though our arena of protest is limited to the mind. We go along with the program and serve our time but neither of us is convinced. Still, the season is a cheerful one: the caroling is quite beautiful and I sing along with everyone else in praise of a baby born in dangerous times. I make sweet popcorn balls with syrup, and small coconut cakes that look like snowmen. I write Jack a poem for Christmas and then rip it to pieces. In the end I give him a book I purchase in town with money I've saved from my summer work—*Wuthering Heights,* because there's a touch of Heathcliff in this troubled boy. I want him to leave the moors for these few years and survive the unnatural smothering of his spirit.

Winter has passed, and the early blooming of plants and flowers makes routine-filled days more bearable. Though I'm forever homesick for the plains and the kind faces of my parents.

Jack passes me a note after supper. The message is simple, but cryptic: "I have to do something. Don't worry. It's important." Fear squeezes my heart and though he wouldn't like it, my first thought is, *Oh, no! What is he up to now?* I find out soon enough.

The next morning the school hums with whispered gossip—

we're insects sawing our wings together to share the same song: "Where's Jack? Where's Jack?"

I'm told by Grace, who heard it from her secret boyfriend, Cyrus (she finally gave up on Micah), that Jack ran off in the night, climbing out the second-story window and dropping all the way from the porch to the ground. He can't have been hurt, at least not badly, since he's nowhere to be found.

I'm fearful and angry, and also, if I'm honest, a bit proud of him. I want to shake, hug, and rescue him all at once. I run my finger across the tall prairie grasses he carved into my bookends, press inside the grooves and run my nail through the stems. I pray to Wakháŋ Tháŋka that Jack be protected, that he lands in a good place, that I learn where he is. I pray that Jack be guided so he does the right thing, whatever Wakháŋ Tháŋka determines that to be. Pictures rise in my head of secret wishes that have no business attaching themselves to prayer—to push them away I rub my temples. There is so much I want with Jack when we're older. I go about my studies and work as usual, my every move as unremarkable as I can manage, but inside the blizzard of my birth returns—cold winds squeeze my heart, so I work all the harder in order to keep warm. I live this way for a week, a girl of ice and tears. I can barely focus on my lessons from the worry.

Eight days have passed since Jack's disappearance, and it is nearly May. The Literary Society is busy planning entertainments that will attend various May celebrations. More opportunities to show off for wealthy friends of Captain Pratt, though we enjoy the galas for our own sake. During supper as I poke at my meal and try to force myself to eat, again I hear the insect buzz of gossip sweep through the place. The chatter of news begins at the teachers' table and travels down the rows until I hear it for myself: Jack is found! Captain Pratt received a telegram from Ohio. He will be returning on the train. My hands begin to shake, so I quickly hide them in my lap. My fingers pinch the napkin—they are creatures apart from me that *will* show how flustered they are. I give up all pretense of eating; I would only choke on the stew. I don't know what to feel.

Jack returns in manacles that had to be specially altered to fit his slight wrists. A police captain in Youngstown personally accompanied him to the train, and he was chained to his seat for the ride's duration. The conductor passed the key to an agent from our end, and only then was Jack unchained and allowed to stand, though the manacles remained in place all the way to our parade ground, where he is brought as a kind of exhibit at morning roll call.

I was afraid he would look defeated, but Jack struts behind Mr. Fuller, Master General of Disciplinary Headquarters, as if he's a prisoner of war who will remain defiant to the end. We've been studying the American Revolution in our readers, and Jack's dramatic entrance calls to mind the words of Patrick Henry from 1775: "Give me liberty, or give me death!" Which I consider a mere echo of any Dakhóta warrior's battle cry. Jack is only a gaunt boy with a wild brush of hair and emperor's straight nose, but I know I'm not the only one in the crowd who admires his courageous bearing.

Mr. Fuller will make an example of him, restrict his diet to bread and water while he's kept in the guardhouse. And of course there will be a heavy dose of corporal punishment. He will be shunned for a time, with everyone discouraged from acknowledging his existence—something I will never do, even if they lock me up in the next cell. But he stands straight through all the public denunciation and shaming, and when the manacles are finally removed, he pumps his arms in the air and unleashes a war cry so powerfully chilling that my tongue trills in support before I know what I'm doing. Then, there is dead silence on the field until Beth collapses in a faint. I'm convinced she did this on purpose, to shift everyone's horrified attention from the delinquent behavior of her friends.

It is rare for a girl to be placed in a guardhouse cell, but my offense was so flagrant and outrageous, according to staff and a tribunal of fellow students, there is nothing to be done but treat me like a ruffian boy. Not only did I make noise in support of Jack, I used the Dakhóta-style ululation our women trill to denote approval. Hence, I've dragged my backward ways into the pristine future we are forced to march toward. I can't help but be a little nervous, though it's a comfort to know Jack is across the narrow aisle from me, locked up in his own cell. When we're left alone, he's able to tell me of his adventures.

Jack insists his escape was orchestrated by the spirits. One night he dreamed he was back home, standing in line with his mother and little sister as they waited for necessary supplies to be distributed. Each woman holding her precious ration ticket or wearing it round her neck in a beaded case. These goods were usually a spare amount of foodstuffs, soap, sometimes cloth, owed to us by treaty for all the theft of land that once sustained us. His mother was nervous that everything would be gone by the time they got to the head of the line, yet there was nothing to do but wait. Then little Alice noticed a strange formation in the sky. She tugged on Jack's hand to show him. It was an isolated cloud in a clear sky, traveling straight for the reservation agency. Soon everyone was watching the odd sight, gaping at its speed. Then, crack! Lightning shot from the cloud, plunging its energy deep into the earth.

"It was like Crazy Horse's spirit came to take revenge," Jack loud-whispers at me, careful to protect our conversation, but wanting to be heard. I'm leaning into the solid door, my ear pressed so hard against the wood it hurts. "Everyone scattered, including my ma, except for me and Alice. We were curious. She's brave and drew me forward to see what the lightning had done. I approached the spot carefully; we could still feel a charge in the air that lifted the hair off our scalp and arms, and the whole area smelled like gunpowder. Alice got there first and peeked in a hole blasted by the bolt. The lip of it was glazed, like the earth had been seared. Alice liked the shine. Before I could stop her, she bent over to rub it with a finger. That's when she noticed something inside the pit."

Jack's voice falters. I'm not sure if he's stopped talking or gone too quiet for me to hear.

"What was there?" I ask, to urge him on or let him know I've missed what he said.

"Me."

In a voice thick with awe, the most reverent I've ever heard him, Jack describes how he saw himself curled up in the pit, which was much larger than it first appeared. He was sleeping, naked but for a blanket, hand clutching a pipe. Alice's eyes grew big as she stared from her brother in the hole to her brother standing beside her.

"You know what that means?"

"Yes." Now I understand his urgency, the meaning of his scribbled note that told me so little. These are things he couldn't share in a hurried, disrespectful way.

"I was called to perform haŋbdéčheya. That was certain. But there's something else in the dream that was significant. As we stood there, it began to rain. But not the normal kind. What stormed out of the sky and mounded like dry snow were shreds of paper. I snatched a few from the air, lines of Wordsworth and Dickens, stanzas from the Bible. Pieces of documents with legal language, and numbers all stacked together like from an account ledger. All that paper was filling up the hole, piled up on the sleeping version of me, until it woke him. He stood up in a hurry, so quick he made Alice squeak. But as soon as he was on his feet, his hands offering the pipe to whatever spirits had summoned the pages, the paper snow was sucked up into the air and popped back inside the cloud that still lurked above us, like it was watching. *I* made it all go away."

This is a sacred dream; I can recognize that plainly. All my worry and anger and spent emotions that have gripped me since Jack ran off spill from my heart to the ground where I sit. He is as remarkable as I've thought him to be, despite the nay-saying that goes on in my head in my parents' voices. This is a powerful call to action, though I'm not sure what that would be—it's the kind of dream Jack would share with elders back home who are adept at interpretation.

What happens next is something I don't want to write or remember. My punishment is solely dietary in the form of bread and water, and to be locked up for three days. But older boys who have been selected by committee are dispatched to Jack's cell to carry out his other discipline. They are there to hold him down while Mr. Fuller whips him, using a heavy strap, and though I cover my ears and curl up on a bench as far from the door as possible, I hear things I can't forget. Deep friendships are formed here; love grows in both abundant soil and dry chalk. But the school was also organized to foster enmity. We are urged to be spies and bullies, to resist allegiance to any but those who bring us the wašíču dream. Former tribal enemies are set against each other, settling old grudges when approved by the school. So, Jack is made to pay in blood.

There's more to his story I hear while he's recovering from the beating. To my relief he is the same, undaunted Jack, though his voice quivers at the start. Whatever happened when he sought his vision has given him strength and purpose.

I tell Jack to rest, but he insists on finishing his story, though his breathing is rough: "When I set out to honor the message of the dream, I got my hands on some food from the kitchen, stole Mr. Temple's fancy German pipe, though it's not as good as one of ours. I figured the spirits would overlook something like that. Grabbed some other things and the blanket off my bed. A couple of friends helped lower me out the window, though don't tell anyone that."

"Of course not," I promise. That should be obvious.

"I hopped a train till I was far enough away to feel safe. Sat up top so I could watch for the right place. I needed a hill, but not so open that I'd be noticed. I guess the hill I chose was in Ohio, though I wasn't paying attention to state lines or sign markers. When I saw the wooded hill, I could feel the rightness of it calling me, though it was scary to jump off even though the train was slowing into a curve." I shudder to hear this, can't help but imagine all that could've gone wrong with Jack's leap off the train.

"I camped out in that place until I felt ready to perform what was asked of me." Jack's voice softens and he suddenly sounds older. "I was nervous, you see, that I wouldn't be able to go through with it. But I did. Finished before anybody found me. Rigged up a small sweat lodge that barely fit to purify myself. Four days and four nights without food or water, standing in a pit I scratched out of the earth, praying, and offering the pipe, asking for guidance or whatever Wakháŋ Tháŋka and the spirits wanted to show me. The first day was so hard, not because of the body, but the mind. It was . . . dull." Jack draws out the last word, as if it's a shameful secret.

"I prayed and sang, tried to focus on what I was there to do, but all that happened was a family of deer came over to watch me.

They seemed to know I wasn't any threat. It was cold once the sun went down, so cold. I stood as long as I could and then rolled up in the blanket. If there were dreams, I don't remember them. I was so ashamed of the silence. Even the birds were quiet around me. I wondered if it was because I had the wrong pipe; maybe the spirits were insulted and thought I didn't know better than to use a foreign instrument and not our sacred pipestone. The one thing I can say for myself is that I didn't give up. I decided that if I completed the ceremony without receiving any vision, any message, I would accept that the spirits called me out there to prove I was devoted, and nothing more. But on the final night, I was no longer alone."

Jack coughs, sounding battered. I remind myself that he will heal. He always does.

"There was so much I was shown, it was like my eyes were never open before that night. I can't tell you all of it, I think I'm not supposed to, but I can share this one part because it involves you." I feel squeezed from within, no air, no heartbeat. I'll be suspended like this until Jack continues.

"Nothing bad," he says, perhaps sensing my nerves. "Someone I'm pretty sure was an ancestor from way back suddenly stood before me. He opened his hands like he was holding a great book in them. And as I watched, I saw he held all of it, wings of pages from the earliest illuminated manuscripts painted by monks in Europe, to history texts and cookbooks and farm manuals, all these pages flying between his hands. He smiled at me, like he was proud of his medicine, and then tossed the pages in the air, where they turned into white birds, flying from us into the tops of trees. The man touched my forehead and all of a sudden I could see pictures in my head, of myself grown up, standing in front of important-looking men, men with power, and I was Dakhóta but they were listening to me. Then he chuckled and gestured for the pipe. I handed it over. He examined it like it was the strangest creature he'd ever seen but smoked a few puffs to try it out. Before he left, he gently touched my eyelids to close them. He sang to me, but it wasn't a prayer. It was an old love song. The last thing I was shown was your face, but older, and I knew that we were . . . connected." Jack's voice trails off in embarrassment. I can feel my face flush from neck to hairline.

Jack's narrative has tired him. He needs to sleep. But he says something so quietly I'm only half certain it was spoken, not dreamed: "We're meant to be together to help restore our world."

Stunning news: Jack is lauded as one of the most improved students Carlisle has ever seen! He receives top marks in all his classes, as well as in carpentry. He's a valued member of the debate team, who demolishes everyone else when it comes to his preparation and quick-minded rebuttals that confound the opposition. Captain Pratt parades him before visitors, impresses them with the spectacle of a Sioux Indian who can discuss the writings of Dickens, Irving, and Hawthorne. Jack is beginning to look happy and confident, more like the boy I first met on the train. For an entire school year, we shine together like white stars. I'm even allowed to invite him over for tea. Our future blinds us with light, though we carry ourselves with humility to cover the mutiny that still lives in our hearts. We have only to look in one another's eyes to see the resolution there. As Jack whispered to me one afternoon before finishing off a slice of toast, "We're here to complete the Ghost Dance."

Perhaps we are too proud, too certain of success. Certainty is a smug creature that begs to have his legs kicked out from under him. Perhaps we tempt the spirits to bring us back to earth. Or maybe it's simply life having its way with us, rolling on as it does, unmindful of how its course impacts anyone. We're in the final weeks of our second year at Carlisle when Jack collapses at the supper table. He holds his neck like he's choking. Fellows on either side of him pound his back in case a piece of food has lodged in his throat, but he continues to thrash like a panicked fish jerked out of water. The fit lasts for several long minutes. When he calms, he's rushed off to the infirmary for an examination. As a star pupil at Carlisle, extra precautions will be taken to ensure his health. I can only observe the disturbance from my table on the girls' side of the hall. My hands tremble to match the nervous pounding of my heart. *Why Jack?* I think. *Why always Jack?*

He comes to me later, as I work through a lesson in the library without being able to concentrate. He gives me a pleading look and I slip outside into the evening air. We hide ourselves in the back of the building for privacy. "I've written you something." Jack hands me a sheaf of folded pages. "I have to leave now, there's no choice." It takes every shred of self-control not to scream at him. He must see the despair in my eyes.

"You don't understand. Something's happened to Alice."

"What? How do you know?"

"I could feel it, like it was happening to me, too. She was choking. I could feel the hands around my neck, her neck. She cried out for me. I *must* go! There's no choice," he says again.

"But the captain could telegraph the reservation agent, ask him to check on your family. He would do that for you. Maybe we'd know by tomorrow, faster than you hopping trains and walking." What I don't say is I suspect the captain would go to the trouble of a telegram for Jack, given that his father is a wašíču soldier. We are all ranked in his eyes, some higher than others. This would only turn Jack against the plan.

Jack is listening. *Oh, please, do listen!*

"Maybe . . ."

I convince him to stay and do as I suggest. His face is difficult to watch, so filled with pain. I'm struck with the sensation of falling, then realize it's his own floundering that I've absorbed through sympathy. Concern makes me bold. I grab his hands and the pages he gave me fall to the ground at our feet. We clutch each other for stability and hope. A full moon rises above our heads and we're gray in that light, shadowed. My heart opens like the injured woman's wounds and speaks to Jack in ways I've never talked before. We are both crying by the time I close, telling him he is never alone because I am ever loyal. We raise our clasped hands so they're bathed in the moon's light. We take comfort in knowing that this mothering light can be seen just as well back home. She loves us wherever we are.

Captain Pratt calls Jack into his office the next day to relay the difficult news. He admits he was willing to go to the trouble of seeking information to prove the boy's superstitious hunch was nonsense. Alas, Jack was right to have fears for his sister. The captain says she's dead. She choked on a piece of beef in their mother's stew. He says he's sorry, son, he's sorry. He leaves it go and doesn't censure Jack when the boy tears out of his office like he's chased by demons. Maybe no one can see them, but he's being chased, all right. He comes straight to me, where I'm working in the laundry. He tells me what he's learned, and then swears to me it's wrong. My hands are soaked from wringing out undergarments, but he won't even let me dry them. He clutches at them, and I pull him over to a private niche in the large room so no one will see this breach of decorum. The other girls look away and go on with their work; they understand sorrow.

"It didn't happen the way they said." Jack squeezes my wrists so tight I'm worried he'll break me.

"I *felt* it when it happened. She didn't choke on the inside; the force came from the *outside*. Like this." He lifts his hands to my neck, and I push them away.

"You don't have to show me. I believe you." Something in Jack has spilled, and he feels dangerous. I step back so we're an arm's length apart. He doesn't seem to notice.

"He killed her; I can feel it! He finally killed one of us, and I wasn't there to stop it." Jack spins and punches the wall with such fury the entire building seems to hold its breath, not only the girls but also the walls and floor and ceiling, the sparkling windows.

Ordinarily I would go to him, assess the physical damage, but instead I back away another step, and then another. I reach in my pocket to finger Winona's heart. A voice in my head says: *If he breaks, he will destroy you.*

Rather than push me farther from Jack, the voice propels me forward to examine his hand, his injured fist. I walk him to a sink and wash off the blood, wrap his knuckles in a handkerchief. If Winona is seeking to protect me, she chose the wrong words. I am here to keep Jack from breaking. I will not allow the puzzle of Jack to fracture. I'll bind the pieces together, so he remains forever and always my brilliant wild boy, my heart's future.

I'm too tired to write, and too lonesome not to. Every time I close my eyes or look at the blank page I see Jack spinning, caught in a kind of whirlpool like the one I witnessed at the base of a waterfall. He's trapped, going round and round. And I can't seem to drag him out—he doesn't even let me try. He took off again, as I knew he would. Students aren't given leave to go home for funerals. The policy is, better they mourn here where they're protected from Indian ways of dispatching the dead. Though these days our traditional ceremonies of grief are illegal, so who knows what little Alice's burial will be like? I think Jack even realizes he won't make it home in time, if at all. But he must try. He needs to be in motion with his grief, rather than still. All I can do is move through the days and make sure I don't become a puzzle like Jack. One of us must remain whole.

I'm teaching Beth to tat; her fingers are so quick and clever. She's able to speak English well enough now to tell stories of her life back home. She misses the song of ocean waters early in the morning when the sun is moving through its brilliant colors. She is a squirrel dancer, difficult to keep plugged in a chair. She acts out her descriptions, unfolding from the floor to become a risen sun, imitating a mischievous raven she knew who pretended to be injured so other ravens would feed him, only to run off laughing once his belly was full. She can move like an old bear woman, or a newborn otter pup; she can leap like a salmon. Home is ever alive in her, and we roommates help protect that spark. Carlisle is many things I don't appreciate, but I can say about it that I found sisters here.

Miss Feld pulls me aside after one of my performances for visitors. She had prevailed upon me to learn "The Song of Hiawatha," but I selected a lengthy passage from *Jane Eyre* instead because her honest voice was the only one I could stand to inhabit in my present state of mind. Miss Feld is agitated though the entertainment and reception went well. She is so pale, in contrast to the coppery fire of her hair, how much it blazes across her head.

"There are developments," she whispers dramatically, and she leads me outside for privacy. I've no doubt this pertains to Jack, so I stand as straight as I can, as if good posture can somehow ward off bad news.

"I overheard a conversation. Oh, my, this is just like Shakespeare!" I hold myself still, impassive. Miss Feld has good intentions but for her this is merely intrigue. She catches herself and smiles an upside-down apology.

"He returned home. Well, he got as far as Bismarck and then the agent was called to fetch him and bring him to the reservation. Apparently, he was in a rough state. Shoes stolen, near-starved. But he was able to see his mother and visit his sister's grave."

Tears are falling and I'm at such a distance from myself I could be the waterfall we came across when I was little. Something that spills water without reason.

"He and his father had *words*." I can tell from the way she emphasizes "words" that Miss Feld means they came to blows. "He's been arrested and signed over to the authorities for being disorderly. That's all I know right now, but I'll pass along any further knowledge as I learn more."

I remember to thank my teacher for her kindness and concern. I float back to my room and sit on the edge of the bed. After Grace and Beth return, they leave me alone when I don't show any interest in talking. I wish I could return to an earlier hour when I was the orphan, Jane Eyre, struggling to survive uncaring relations and a cruel boarding school. I felt for her then, but now I'm envious of the heroine, whose ending was so much more promising than mine looks to be. Her beloved Rochester may have been blinded and maimed by the burning of his home, but he is hers at long last, and they will be together. I sit like a stone for hours, until Grace takes my hand to help me rise and prepare for bed. I'm glad to leave off walking through my mind, each thought bringing me nowhere good. I pray I do not dream.

I don't see the injured woman until the room is dark and the other girls are sleeping. She sits beneath the window, chin on her knees, watching me. Her legs are gashed and bleeding—she traces the seams with a fingernail. It's strange how commanding she is in her silence. It feels disrespectful to remain in bed with a relative huddled on the floor, so I go to her, and kneel beside her. She takes my hand and runs it across a cut on her leg, digs in with my fingernail where a scab was beginning to form.

"I don't want to hurt you," I whisper.

The answer rings in my head: *It was already done.*

I ask her a question that drags me under on the most difficult days: "Does the pain never end?"

She tilts her head like she's listening to something. Finally she responds, *Not here.*

We sit together all night, though at some point I lay my head against her knees. She combs my hair with her fingers and though she can't sing, she breathes softly on my forehead in a way that soothes. I fall into a doze with my hand covering her slashed ankle, open to the bone. I want to thank her, but I'm held down by sleep and can't move. I want her to know that I see she brings more than the burden of pain; she also brings comfort.

Grace finds me curled on the floor but doesn't ask questions. I check my hand and nightdress for blood, but my ancestor has left no trace of her suffering. We go through the motions of our rigid schedule, and I try not to think of Jack until Miss Feld finds me later and offers a more full report.

"Prepare yourself," she whispers. She places an arm around my waist and guides me into the room where we have our Literary Society meetings. Perhaps it's unkind of me, but I can't help feeling that this episode is the most excitement Miss Feld has had in her life; she projects such an air of breathless titillation. I stare at the banner draped across the front wall that reads, "Labor Conquers All Things." An irreverent thought streaks through my head: *I'm not sure Jane would agree.* I bid her be my ally today, bid her leave the pages of Brontë's book and sit beside me while I hear what new misery has landed upon Jack. She would understand my passion and yet be sensible, helping me remain tethered to earth rather than stolen by fearful thoughts. I vow to be impassive, no matter what I hear.

Miss Feld sits me in a chair while she paces before me. She spins dramatically, like an actress in a play about to divulge the whole of a plot. "He's been formally charged! Yes, his father signed a complaint against him, claiming assault and attempted murder! Both parents have made written statements that he's incorrigible, and they attest not even Captain Pratt at this fine institution can save him, so he'll be brought over to some prison in Minnesota, to remove him from connections both here and at home. It is so shocking!"

"How long?" The only words that form. I'm running a fingernail across the back of my hand, creating a cut that will bleed.

"Stop that," Miss Feld admonishes. She pulls my hand away and holds it, but I can't bear the cold sweat of her palm, her thrill. I wriggle my hand free.

"How long?"

"One year. Which is unthinkable and horribly unfair, but on the other hand, at your age these months will fly. He'll be back before you know it! The captain is still interested in the boy and maintains he won't give up on him."

I thank Miss Feld for her friendship, for relaying the news, blush at her with a warmth that is born of ice. I'm purposely obsequious for the first time in my life. Rather than a show of respect, it's the opposite. I'm insincere because I don't believe this teacher deserves my true heart. I can't think of anyone in authority here who does. Only fellow students who have become friends, my roommates, who have become sisters, sweet jolly Peg with her triangular ears, and Jack. He'll be locked up in jail for a year, possibly the youngest prisoner in the place. He's just fourteen. What friends will he find? How will he protect himself from men who might be thieves and killers? Why would his mother go along with such a thing? From what he's said, she loves him dearly. Then I recall Jack's fit in the dining hall, how he spasmed on the floor, holding his neck as if a person none of us could see was throttling the life out of him. I'm sure I've seen his mother in town before, but never paid attention to her. Maybe it was easy to miss her, to overlook her figure as she scurried past on an errand. Maybe she is similar to Jack's little dog when she was still a haunted thing named Bone. Maybe without Jack his mother has lost even more ground and is little more than a shadow against the wall.

In coming days, I take advantage of Miss Feld's romantic fascination with my predicament and Jack's. She learns where he'll be sent, and even receives permission from Captain Pratt to write him there, on the pretense of keeping him engaged with his literary studies. So, I'll be able to write to Jack through the intercession of this teacher. I should be grateful, and on some level I am. I only wish she weren't enjoying herself so much. I think of Jack's burnt letter, the one that was taken when we first arrived, where his mother offered comfort and Alice traced the outline of her hand, so he'd know it was always held out to him. How does he manage his heart? Is the puzzle of him holding together? Does he feel betrayed by everyone he loves? I will do what I can from this distance, write letters that I think of as sewing projects, where I use the careful needlework of my pen to stitch the boy into a suit that will keep him in one solid piece.

I've neglected this journal for many months and have just now returned from the summer Outing Program, where I once again stayed at the Greeveses' home and renewed a friendship with Susanna. Things are no longer strained between us though we are older now, so we behave with less abandon. It was impossible to write Jack until school was back in session, for my letters are folded into a note written by Miss Feld. His yearlong sentence is nearly finished, and I've dedicated myself to work and study and friendships, but I'm like Jack's little sister—my hand always reaching out for his, even when he can't feel it. I haven't received a single letter in return, nor has Miss Feld, but she says that could be the rules of the place, or perhaps prisoners are expected to pay for their own paper and postage. About six months into his sentence, I had to let go of worry and learn to squash these thoughts. I return to *Jane Eyre* for solace, and also Anne Elliot from the novel *Persuasion,* for she knows how to be patient. In the past my little-girl motto would probably have been something like: *Live!* These days it is the less ambitious: *Endure.* Though the way I envision that word nestled in a patch of ominous purple-black clouds, perhaps it is more so.

I no longer carry Winona's stone heart in my pocket. She is wrapped in a handkerchief in my drawer. What I hear in her voice is too full of warnings I'm unable to heed. My heart is my compass; where it points I cannot help but follow.

I attend chapel regularly here since part of our schooling is to become good members of the Christian faith. I absorb the teachings, stories, and tenets, can pass a test on many aspects of this religion, but for me it's just another subject, like mathematics and literature. I'm like my parents when it comes to the wašíču gods—my father, who holds Christianity in his mind but not his heart and spirit; Iná, who holds Christianity in her ability to perform the rituals, and nowhere else. We were born with strong spirits that are related to all other beings in our territory, related to the hills and rivers, the sun and moon. The inner light my teachers wish to give me is already here, though some of them do their best to snuff it out.

From my studies I gather wašíčus wish to know everything there is to know. That isn't our way. We understand that aspects of the world are so wonderfully mysterious we aren't capable of comprehending the whole of it. Even our wisest counselors and most gifted medicine people can only graze the deepest mysteries with fingertip thoughts. And they do not press, because to do so is a god's privilege. What is sacred, what is wakháŋ, speaks to us, shares what we need to know, and no more. Are we to be trusted with the power of perfect knowledge? Can our minds expand enough to contain star language? Can the voice of water fill us with the fierce pull of its secrets and yet we do not drown? Can we bear to hear the full store of earth's memory? Can we hold our tongues still enough, when necessary, to avoid singing the world down?

I write papers for Religious Studies that are dead words on a page, a repetition of what my teachers want me to say. I give them these words and not my Truth because I'm not recklessly bold like Jack. I'm an ant moving my grains of sand each day, moving my pencil across paper to record what is drilled into me. I reserve honest thoughts for this private journal, which I've taken to hiding beneath my mattress. There is a danger here in being fully seen and known. The captain thinks that to "save" Indian people he must run a factory that produces shades—children who no longer recognize themselves or believe in their existence.

The year is up, though the months have crawled, not flown. Miss Feld's excitement has dampened, though she still plays my sponsor in this connection. If anything, my own feelings have grown during the absence, and I've gently rebuffed the gifts and gestures held out by other boys, including a Harvard pennant our football team won when they bested the Crimson in a match. My roommates were quite annoyed with me when I refused that offering.

Tomorrow Jack is scheduled to arrive and resume his studies. On the outside I try to behave like a proper Dakhóta lady, or at the very least an Austen heroine, while on the inside I'm a colliding flock of butterflies. I imagine I won't be able to sleep but I'm so worn by nerves I shut down as soon as my eyes close.

Hours later I wake quite suddenly as if someone has shaken my bed. No. The room is silent and still. My roommates are breathing softly in their own beds against the opposite wall. I close my eyes again and begin to doze until certainty jolts through me that I'm being watched. My lids open and I nearly scream. The injured woman is laid out above me, our noses nearly touching, her eyes peering directly into mine. She takes my head in her hands, tilts it as she moves hers, so we are a mirror, though I don't share the bullet wound that mars her forehead. Her breath is cold enough that I can see it make its way past my lips. We exchange breath until mine is as chilled as hers. She pulls back then and grips her own face, slips fingers in her mouth and, with one wrench, breaks her jaw. Her mouth is torn open so I can see past broken teeth and the useless root of her tongue, I can see past her voice. The emptiness draws me; there might be comfort in the absence of everything. But in the back of the injured woman's throat there is a prick of light, maybe a star, and then another star, and she isn't empty at all but is the sky beyond this sky. I don't understand what she's showing me. She must hear the confusion for she uses her hands to snap her jaws back in place, and I am shut out of the world of her mouth.

The injured woman is not Anne Elliot, the sensible British heroine surrounded by silly relatives. She is tired and frustrated; she is tortured with pain. She grips her head and shakes it in a frenzy that truly frightens me. Thoughts or visions splash like a mess of droplets: I see her whole and beautiful, laughing. I see her held by a mother, charging on a horse, smudging herself with sage. I see her harvesting corn and reading the stars. Words come to me though they're mine and not hers. *She's looking for the way past pain.*

Maybe I'm too young to understand, or maybe these are sacred matters that will always be deeper than my capacity to unravel. All I have is a feeling. When the injured woman stops spattering me with her cherished memories, I realize she's just a girl, not much older than I am now. She could be another Carlisle student yearning for home, ready to make the journey but unable to remember how to get there. Agony is a dreadful companion but at least it keeps her sharp, keeps her from surrendering to oblivion, where there's no memory of the time before pain.

My musings give me courage, and I reach out to this troubled ancestor as if she is my future daughter. I pull her to me, her body light as a bundle of sticks. Her battered skull nestles against my neck, and I stroke her matted hair, singing, "Ábu, ábu," until we both sleep.

I've anticipated this moment for a year now, imagining what it will feel like. I have a scrap of paper that never leaves my pocket, where I draw a tiny slash for each day that passes, bundling them in groups of five like we've been taught. The paper is at last filled with stacks upon stacks of black-inked wheat. I'm both thrilled and frightened. Happy to finally see the face of a boy who is more family to me than anyone, but worried that his heart no longer carries me.

I linger on the porch of the administration building, knowing Jack will be brought here first to commence with all the paperwork that's needed to track us. I couldn't eat today, my throat constricted with nerves, and as I pace back and forth, I feel light, empty, scoured clean inside. I fancy I've exchanged my heart and lungs for windstorms, become my blizzard brother on the inside, a tempest of swirling flakes. I'm both frozen and overheated; the cold of a snowstorm, the heat generated by motion.

I hear the noise of a wagon pulling up the drive. Each clop of the horse's hooves rings out: *Jack Jack Jack*. Mr. Fuller reins in the horse and it stops. I watch him as he alights from the wagon, rather than glance at the other figure, because I want to take in all of Jack once he's in front of me. The two walk toward the building and Mr. Fuller charges up the steps. The other person stalls at the bottom. I make myself look at him and my heart returns to its place in my chest, though the storm is there, too, whipping all around. Jack is taller than he was but stooped like an older man. And so thin. His profile is a chiseling of his ancestors', regal and strong, but he won't look at me.

Mr. Fuller calls, "Get a move on, boy. Say hello to your friend and then we have a lot of business ahead of us."

Jack mounts the steps, slowly, so I count them in my head: *one, two, three, four*. His shoes are too small for his feet and are broken at the seams. *Five, six, seven*. He stands next to me, still facing away.

"Jack." I can barely hear myself, the whisper light as a flake of snow.

He sighs like an old man, his lungs thick with noise. At last, he turns to me.

I catch myself from gasping when I see the white streak that paints his hair. Most of it the same thick black, except for that jagged scar. He watches my feet, won't look me in the eye. So I step closer, which I know is too bold, not the way Iná taught me to behave. I reach for Jack, extend open hands as we did before, when we latched them together beneath a full moon to become a single Dakhóta being far from home. Jack finally looks at me. It's all I can do to keep from crying. His warm black eyes the color of clean earth are closed doors. They say they do not know me. He walks into the administration building and I'm left standing alone with hands raised in the air, fingers apart to leave room for Jack's to join them.

PART 4

A Council of Dolls

Jesse ~ 2010s

I'm thinking it's just another ordinary day in the strangely unten-
able twenty-first century, a time when my species seems determined to end our brief run on this planet, when the past comes
knocking. I've been searching eBay for pristine first editions of
novels authored by my favorite Native writers, one of my rare
indulgences on a careful budget. Though I haven't touched the
keyboard for several seconds as I examine a decent-looking volume of *Celia's Song* by Lee Maracle, a different book suddenly
appears and fills the computer screen: *Baby-Boomer Dolls*. It's
so off topic it seems difficult to attribute to the site's crafty algo-
rithm. Irritated by the disruption, I'm about to move on but the
cover photograph stops me: a close-up shot of Tiny Thumbelina,
a fourteen-inch baby doll produced by Ideal in the 1960s. She
looks familiar, her unsmiling face and chubby cheeks, her chin-
length hair straight as straw. And then I remember: Ethel. The
doll on the cover of this book is white, all the featured dolls are,
but my Ethel was Black. *Is* Black. She's stored in an old trunk my
father bought to pack up my belongings when I left Chicago for
college. I didn't bring Ethel with me to Harvard, of course, but
now that trunk has become a kind of mausoleum for my childhood. The novel I'd been examining is forgotten. I head to the

bedroom where the trunk sits against the wall, covered by a Pendleton Water Blanket given to me for work I did as board member for a Native American arts organization. I set the blanket on my bed and then kneel before the trunk, ignoring the sudden band of tension that squeezes my chest. I unlatch the brass draw bolts only to realize the main lock requires a key. During the hunt for the key my heart hitches in a way that makes me pause to check my rabbity pulse. It's been months since my last anxiety attack. I will myself to calm down. *Breathe, Jesse, breathe.*

By the time I find the key and open the damn lock, at least a half hour has passed since eBay first brought me face-to-face with Tiny Thumbelina. I lift the trunk lid and am overwhelmed by a fragrance that nearly makes me cry—Chanel No. 5. It's like Mama is with me, her spirit wafting from this trunk Dad purchased with such hopeful excitement for my future. I'm holding the edges of it as if kneeling at the lip of a treacherously deep cave or White Rabbit's hole, and I don't want to fall out of my life into some other world. I close my eyes, trying to remember if I kept Mama's last bottle of Chanel—the one stowed in the top drawer of her dresser. I wouldn't have used it, ever. It was her scent, not mine. She swore she'd never worn perfume until Dad bought her a small bottle of Chanel soon after they married. She complained about the expense, always registered a few words of annoyed protest when he bought it for her, but she wore it carefully to make it last. I can see her dabbing the bottle's mouth at her pulse points and the tip of a finger so she could apply it behind each ear. Back then I used to wish my mother could just accept a gift with good grace rather than pitch a minor fit. Now that I have a better understanding of why she did this, I find the routine more poignant. Mama never felt deserving of precious gifts, or even deserving of love. On top of which was her ingrained "scarcity mindset"; she was convinced our family was always on the brink of economic disaster. Even if we'd had thousands of dollars in savings (which we never did), Mama would still have fretted that it wasn't enough to make her feel safe. Though to be fair, growing up on an Indian reservation during the Depression would probably instill that perspective in anyone.

Memories are already swirling through me, and I haven't even peeked at the contents of this box. I take a deep, cleansing breath and am about to begin the inspection when Prince swoops ahead of me, grasps something with his feet, and carries it over to the bed.

"My hair! My hair!" The voice is familiar, but I don't allow myself to process who it belongs to. I focus on the intruder, Prince, a mischievous Moluccan cockatoo with unclipped wings. He's hunched over his prey and tries to keep his back to me when I get up to investigate.

"Give up the goods, buddy, I'm not playing."

Prince turns to look at me—he's smart enough to know when I'm serious. He holds up a foot that appears to be tangled in thread, bows his head as if he's the injured party. When I get a good view of what he snatched from the trunk I realize it's Ethel, my Tiny Thumbelina doll from childhood, the very object that launched my search. Her dark brown hair is still shiny after all these decades, but a hank of it is caught up in Prince's toes. He allows me to free Ethel, then flutters off to avoid a scolding. I hear him muttering to himself in the living room, no doubt peeved that I confiscated his prize. Prince has a habit of walking off disappointments in a lengthy pout. In a half hour or so he'll forgive me.

With no more distractions, I face Ethel. She's still wearing the same drab green dress she wore when Dad bought her for me, annoyed because the saleslady kept trying to direct him to the white version of the doll. My ever-polite and patient father says he had to get grumpily insistent for her to ring up the toy, and the rest of the transaction was carried out in stony silence between the two. *Poor Ethel*, I think. *How must that have made her feel?* Then the bottom floor of me opens and I'm in free fall, spinning dizzily through years and memories until I launch myself onto the bed, trying to stop the momentum. My hands are clutching the comforter and Ethel is squashed somewhere beneath me—an uncomfortable lump against my hip. The discomfort is more than physical.

Was that really her voice? I fret. She used to speak to me when I was little, but of course that was only my imagination. I try to recall when Ethel went quiet. Around the time I turned eleven and had to work so hard because I won a scholarship to attend a private school. *Ethel didn't want to get in the way of my studies*, is what I'm thinking, which unnerves me. How quickly I've fallen back into my little-girl belief that Ethel is a live being, not just a cloth-bodied preemie with molded vinyl head, arms, and legs, and a mechanism that makes her wriggle when you pull the cord, though it's broken now.

Cautiously I sit up on the bed and rescue Ethel from her smothered position. My hands are shaking as I straighten her hair and dress. She's at once so familiar and deeply unsettling. I want to know if it was an actual voice I heard cry out, but I'm terrified of that being the case. It's a comfort to hear Prince still grousing in the next room. I've been careful not to cuss around him, so his most irate expletive is, "Jeez!" He's tossing it around like birdseed.

"Ethel?" My voice sounds pitifully young, not at all like that of a writer capable of giving talks and readings before a large audience. I study her warm brown face, run a finger across her cheek. She is expressionless, her painted eyes staring past me, through me, unengaged. Her hands are so small, molded into an active pose—open, reaching, like there's something in front of her she wants yet never touches. I hold one of them in my fingers, to offer something. "Ethel, are you there?"

To my relief, and also disappointment, she remains silent. Dead. I sit her up on the bed, against one of the pillows, and turn back to the trunk to continue searching through my past.

I lose a couple of hours. I find Liddle Kiddle dolls: Peter Pan, Alice in Wonderland, and Cinderella, strange creatures who fit in the palm of my hand and whose heads are as large as their bodies. I'd forgotten they even existed. There's a set of Nancy Drew mysteries Dad bought secondhand (an edition published in the 1930s), and my high school yearbooks as well as programs from the plays I performed in back then. I uncover the original Barbie doll as well as her boyfriend, Ken, though they were handed down to me from an older friend with Ken's hair already rubbed off, so I used a black marker to color his scalp. I did my best to convince him and Barbie that he was Lakȟóta like my father, though he seemed too stiff and formal to be one of us. I stored them holding each other, which I find rather sweet, though I don't remember doing it. My boxed set of the *Chronicles of Narnia* are in here, as well as the *Chronicles of Prydain* series, which I pull out to reread. There are a dozen diaries, the kind with delicate locks, and a ballerina music box that holds all the tiny keys. My hands caress the white cover of the music box, where a painted ballerina still leans gracefully into her high arabesque. Inside there's another dancer that turns in circles in time to the music, watching herself in a small triangular mirror. I have a sense memory of the taste of glue on S&H Green Stamps Mama collected from grocery stores and gas stations. It was my job to paste them into booklets. Licking worked better than a sponge, which crinkled the stamps too much. Mama and I dreamed about what we'd select from the redemption center if we could only fill enough booklets for big purchases like a color television or a dollhouse. Imagining was lovely escapism, but we always ended up with something boring, practical: a steak knife set or a new baking dish. The one whimsical purchase Mama made with a stack of booklets was this music box, which plays a sweet version of "Swan Lake," my favorite ballet. It wasn't even my birthday or Christmas. Just a regular day where after school I saw it sitting on the kitchen table and didn't dare touch it until Mama said I could, because I thought surely it was a gift for someone else. What I do next surprises me: I kiss the keepsake and whisper, "Thank you, Mama." The box is fragrant with Chanel No. 5. I hurriedly set it aside, so I won't cry. I can practically hear Mama's voice scolding, "Don't make a fuss." To distract myself I pull out a thick pile of record albums—the expected soundtracks of musicals but also numerous Buffy Ste. Marie discs and *Custer Died for Your Sins* by Lakȟóta singer Floyd Westerman.

At the bottom of the trunk, wrapped carefully in bubble wrap, is an object that brings a jolt when I make it through layers of protection: Mama's Hopi pottery bird, the one I accidentally busted as a little girl. I can see the hairline crack that cuts straight through her, down her fine back. I wonder why she's stowed away rather than displayed on one of my shelves? I'm about to rectify that, she's really very striking, when something stops me. Her coloring is burnt sienna, which resembles dried blood. An inner voice whispers, "You killed her." I hurriedly rewrap the artwork and squash the tape back in place, thrust her down the side of the trunk so she's hidden by a nest of Liddle Kiddles. *It's* hidden, I correct myself. *It* is just an old piece of pottery, not *she*. "You killed her just the same," a voice insists. I slam the trunk closed and latch all the locks. Cover it with the Pendleton blanket, making sure the dragonfly image is centered. I tell myself I'm a fiction writer with a strong imagination that has always owned me. But I could cry with relief when Prince stalks into the bedroom to remind me it's time for supper. His voice cracks out four notes over and over, the introductory beats of "When Doves Cry." He's clearly in the mood for the greatest hits of the musical genius he was named after. He takes note of Ethel but doesn't make a grab for her, so I turn off the bedroom light and leave her alone in the dark. Prince and I will have supper and then tear up the joint with rejuvenating rhythms by Prince and the Revolution, which will banish all the weirdness of the last few hours. I don't allow myself to consider the mystery of how my mother's fragrance was all over the contents of the trunk though there wasn't an ancient bottle of perfume anywhere to be found. The scent lingered during my inspection as if Mama were kneeling beside me, leaning into the past.

The cockatoo has worn himself out with a half-dozen performances of his favorite song, Prince's "Kiss," complete with noisy smooches aimed in my direction. He stomp-danced, showed off his crest with its vibrant salmon-colored feathers, beat his wings like he was about to take off for another planet. He's nearly as dramatic as I was as a kid. Now he's curled up in my lap, his beak clicking softly with pleasure as I gently scratch his neck and chest. Feather dust is everywhere. I never thought I'd live with a bird, but when my close friend begged me to take him after his negative reaction to her newborn baby, I gladly offered refuge. We were already buddies—he had me wrapped around his strange reptilian toes. The transition was smooth, and he never seemed upset to move on, though he cuddles with Heather when she visits, sans baby. Prince is a sweetheart when he's the center of attention but jealous as an evil queen when confronted with competition. The way I live these days, he doesn't have a thing to worry about.

I'm reading my tattered childhood journals from the days when I didn't know for sure who I was, given the many names I was called, and all that was projected onto my moony self. My mother's strong personality dominated our household, and I was like an appendage to her powerful energy—another arm that seldom went rogue. My legal name was Lillian, after my mother: Lillian Holy Thunder. So there were two of us until she died. But the name never felt like mine and when I was in high school, I asked my father if I could change it. He consented, though I could see the very mention of my mother caused him pain. He was used to calling me "Sissy," one of my nicknames, which helped us skirt the subject of Mama and any mention of the name Lillian.

"So, who does my girl want to be?" Dad asked quite innocently, though the question opened doors beyond doors in my head. That's the exhaustion of how my brain works—I read between every line.

I didn't blink an eye though: "Jesse."

Dad scratched his head like a stock character in a film, which made me laugh. "Dad, you're scratching your head. Who does that?"

"Uh, someone who doesn't wash his hair." He winked at me. "But seriously, that's not what I was expecting. It's nice, though . . . Jesse. Where does it come from? Why that name?"

I shrugged. "I want something that could work for a man or a woman because when I'm a writer I want to be taken seriously."

"Well, then." Dad looked at me more closely than usual, as if he realized there was a lot more going on inside my head than he knew. But he helped me put the paperwork together and jump through the legal hoops. Since the age of fourteen I've been Jesse Holy Thunder, and while I haven't even begun to live up to that name, I know that version of me is in here somewhere, waiting to come out.

The diary I'm skimming through dates back to the year I was ten. I'd just read *Harriet the Spy* by Louise Fitzhugh and was trying to write my own scathingly honest remarks in imitation of Harriet, even though that practice hadn't worked out so well for her. I quickly realized that tactless honesty is basically unsympathetic observation. Not that I used those words. All I knew was that documenting what the most ruthless part of my brain noticed about the world and other people made me feel sad and mean. So I stopped. If I didn't like someone at school, I tried to imagine what things were like for them at home, what might be going on behind closed doors that no one else could see. If Dad was worn out and distant, I reminded myself that he loved me and always showed up, even if what was left of him at the end of the day was often a bit thin. One time my teacher, Mrs. Cooper, scolded me for writing an activist poem about poverty in Chicago's Indian ghetto, rather than one about flowers budding in spring (her favorite topic), her red pen bleeding angrily all over the page: "Such a waste of your talent! There is wonderful beauty all around us, why focus on ugliness?" Instead of calling her poisonous names in my private pages, I told Dad that maybe we could have a talk with her about artistic freedom, which turned into a somewhat productive conversation. At least, she stuck to grading me on craft rather than subject.

I'm touched by what I chose to write about in the journal: the friendships, minor dramas, secret crushes. I'm amused by the blood oath I made back then, complete with a dried smear pressed onto the page, which was gathered by scratching one of my mosquito bites until it bled. I vowed that one day I'd be a published author—must have doubted myself enough to perform the dramatic ritual. When you've gone that far out on a limb, you don't want to embarrass yourself with achieving less than what's promised in your own blood.

Near the end of the journal, I'm suddenly stopped by an entry that pertains to Ethel: "Ethel's been quiet lately. Sometimes I catch her watching me in that old way, where she's alive in her eyes. But as soon as I notice, she shuts down again. It's like she can power up her batteries or flick them off. I wish she'd talk to me now that I'm older. I need to know what *really* happened."

"Really" is underlined seven times. I remember that for the first few days after Mama died Ethel acted like she'd done something to protect me. But then she clammed up and didn't want to talk about Mama anymore. She never shared details. I'm both glad and sorry that my eyes were squeezed shut when whatever happened, happened. Alive or dead, Ethel is a vault that won't reveal the truth, which means either a living Ethel is still operating as my protector, or a dead doll is the device I use to hide from something I already know.

Prince is wheezing softly in his snuggle hideaway sleeping cave, a plush triangular cocoon in bright purple, of course, that hangs from inside his massive rolling cage. I never lock him up except at bedtime. If I didn't, he'd run up and down the halls, pull out his toys and play, and then get sick from lack of sleep. He always complains at first, blasts me with "Jeez!" and "Holy Goat, no!" I'm not sure where he picked that up. Not from me or Heather. But despite the protest, as soon as he's ensconced in his fuzzy hideaway hut, he immediately falls asleep. Meanwhile, it takes me an hour or so to shut down my brain, which does its own version of running up and down the halls.

I'm convinced I'm still in this noisily musing awake stage when I have what I would classify as a fully conscious dream. I guess it's what you'd call a "vision," though that feels a bit pretentious or exalted, like I'm some kind of medicine person—which I'm not. I hear a rustling sound over by the window, so I open my eyes, peer into the darkness of the bedroom. A small figure emerges from the wall, a shadow stepping beyond shadows. Part of me wants to scream but the survivor in me takes over. I quietly sit up, making ready to defend myself. What stops me is an energy blast, a powerful burst of emotion that is so palpable I'm surprised it doesn't knock me down: naked sorrow—the dangerous kind, with hidden suckers like an undertow that can drown you. The feeling is pure torture; I begin gasping for breath. Calmly, apparently heedless of my distress, the figure steps close enough that pale light from the window falls across it, illuminating a girl's face and intense, staring eyes. She looks Native, like a younger version of me or my many cousins. She's wearing a blanket but in reaching her hands toward me, it drops, and I see her mutilated flesh, glistening as if the injuries were inflicted moments ago, on the other side of the wall she stepped through. All fear drops away and the unbearable sorrow transforms into concern and protectiveness. I push the covers aside and touch my feet to the floor, sit on the edge of the bed. Waiting. Some part of me acknowledges this is spirit turf, but I've spent so many years being trained in the academy and later teaching, I take a moment to confirm I'm truly awake. Yes.

"Are we relatives?" I ask the figure. Not sure if the words are spoken or transferred through thought.

She tips her head, which feels like an affirmation, opens her mouth to show me her tongue is gone. She cannot speak as she once did. Someone did more than kill her, he destroyed her.

Yet here I am, she conveys to me with her mind. *We only think we're destroyed.*

She observes my reaction to that message. Goose bumps break out all over my body and I shiver, fold arms across my chest to mimic strength. My teeth chatter. Why is this declaration of survival so frightening to me?

She answers firmly, her eyes latched on to mine in a connection that can't be broken: *Because when you realize how much power you have, you must use it.*

She continues to watch me, even as she moves backward gracefully, carefully, her bare feet bleeding from where a toe was slashed away, returning her to the wall, where she melts into its shadows. As soon as she's gone, I begin sobbing—the ugly, heaving, nose-running kind of cries that leave you wrung out in a grief hangover. I'm not even clear on what I'm mourning, though part of me suggests I might be blocking myself from facing whatever it is. One thing is clear, I'm being called to live. I'm being nudged to come out of my own snuggle hideaway lair where I've been hibernating my entire life.

I can't bear to put Ethel back in the trunk, so she remains on my bed, facing a bank of windows that overlook the glorious garden behind our house. I live in an upstairs condominium, and a wealthy retired couple live downstairs. They maintain the backyard, which looks like the tame edge of a great forest, though the wooded acres are deceptive and don't go very far before dropping off steeply to join Interstate-35E at the base of the cliff. We live on Crocus Hill—a private cul-de-sac in Saint Paul, Minnesota. I feel like I've infiltrated the wealthy, having lucked into the purchase before condo prices skyrocketed in the area. What money I made off my first novel I spent on this place and paying off my student loans. I can't afford the expensive cruises and European tours my neighbors tell me about, though sometimes I'm flown to interesting places for literary festivals and conferences, all expenses paid. I've seen more of the world than my budget would suggest, when I occasionally push myself out of hibernation.

I wonder what Ethel thinks of the view. Does she worry about the baby foxes that slink along with their mother at dusk, learning to hunt? Does she follow the antics of an albino squirrel's family as they feud with a pileated woodpecker defending his territory within a massive eastern cottonwood tree? I hope she isn't bored or lonesome. Prince has lost interest in her for some unknown reason. Goodness knows he has enough of his own toys to keep him occupied—items like an octopus piñata and a Beakasaurus contraption he loves to nibble. Though his favorite possession is a plush SpongeBob SquarePants pillow he alternately harasses and cuddles.

Inspired by the unexpected reunion with Ethel and other cherished items from my past, I decide to investigate another Pandora's box of history. This one is a large vinyl tub, hidden so effectively it takes an hour to find it at the back of my deep walk-in closet. Several other tubs are stacked on top, so I've worked up a light sweat by the time I drag it into my bedroom. I've pasted a label on its side which reads simply: "Mom stuff." A flashing thought teases that I, myself, am "Mom stuff," if you think about it; thankfully not folded and smothered in a modular tub from Target. I reach for the lid but pull back. I haven't opened this thing in decades. Then, like a guardian angel sent to compose my nerves, I hear Prince warbling "I Left My Heart in San Francisco," which I had no idea was even part of his repertoire. He's channeling Tony Bennett, the singer's smooth delivery and vibrato, though with a tinny cockatoo timbre and boozy pronunciation. I burst out laughing, have to stuff the edge of a pillow in my mouth to keep quiet so he won't hear my hysteria from his perch in the living room. I wouldn't like to insult him. Courage restored by my crooner of a bird!

I hurriedly tug the lid off the container. There it is again, the overpowering fragrance of Chanel No. 5, though at least its presence makes sense this time since these are Mama's things. There aren't as many items as I'd expected—two of them take up a lot of space. The first one I remove and unpack from a garment bag is the bright red coat with large black buttons she was wearing when she died. Thankfully Dad didn't preserve it as it was; it's been properly cleaned and pressed. How strange of him to hold on to such a ghoulish keepsake. On impulse I try it on. A trifle long, since Mama was taller than I am, but when I close the buttons there's a satisfying security I feel in its encompassing warmth. Mama wasn't a hugger, but her coat is holding me together. I continue wearing it as I retrieve a shoebox filled with smaller items: Mama's red lipstick, which is now flaking like an old cake; her hairbrush with a few dusty strands of black hair; a wooden darning egg; a tarnished round medal picturing a flying bee; and a small photo album, pages frustratingly empty except for a slip of ancient-looking paper that reads, simply, "Cora's Journal," in graceful handwriting. Oh, my! I remember this charred fragment, and Mama's story of how Khúŋši burned her diary. Still, I have so few photographs of my childhood, I'm disappointed there's nothing more. The final two items are stored in long boxes that remind me of coffins, each one tied with butcher's twine. How long ago were these packed? Perhaps they've not been opened since my mother died. I have no idea what they contain.

Since I feel a bit like an archaeologist uncovering sacred artifacts, I try to untie the string rather than cut it. Failure brings scissors. I lift the lid off the largest box, shift through wrapping paper, and am stunned to see the cheerful face of Shirley Temple smiling up at me. My breath hitches. The doll stares sweetly, innocently—I'm horrified by an impulse to shake her because her presence triggers so many conflicting emotions and memories that begin to play in my head like a documentary film I never wished to make. But none of this is her fault, so I lift her from the box and carry her to a plush armchair in my bedroom where we can sit together and allow me time to gather my wits.

I examine the doll carefully, note that despite her age, she appears to be in very good shape. A small, yellowed tag is tied to her wrist, which reads in a handwritten script: "Vintage 1930s Shirley Temple doll, modeled after role in *Bright Eyes*—$5."

My godmother, Big Ethel, is suddenly so present it's as if she strolls into the room. I hear her term for me, "dear heart." We bought this doll together for Mama. Well, Ethel forked over the money, which was a great sum to us in the 1960s. Mama was having a bad day where she couldn't get out of bed, and Big Ethel just happened to visit. Mama was embarrassed—back then you were expected to be prepared for company, apartment clean, baked goods ready to serve, hair properly coiffed. Not watching television from bed in the middle of the day, hugging a hot water bottle. But Ethel didn't judge, said she had energy to burn, and could she take me for a walk to let my mother rest? We rushed off together and in my excitement, it was a rare time I didn't bring Ethel, my doll. Big Ethel and I walked all over creation, window-shopping on Wells Street, which had such funky, interesting stores, and on our return trip we popped into a favorite thrift shop on Division Street because of the doll we saw in the window, her arm raised as if she were waving at us. Big Ethel said we must have been guided there that day. We bought the doll for Mama, to replace one she'd been pressured to give to a dying girl who was eventually buried with the treasure. On the return trip home, we were giddy with pleasure, imagining Mama's reaction!

I'm sure she was polite to Big Ethel, and graciously thanked her. But once my godmother left, Mama wasn't at all happy. She was back in bed, Shirley seated on her lap; Mama's hands gripped the doll's arms like unfriendly restraints. She said something about how the doll wasn't able to save her sister and let her die. But I thought she must mean her friend who died of tuberculosis. "Mama is confused," I concluded. Now I'm not so sure.

Mama was still holding on to Shirley in a stiff way when she said she never got over the loss of that doll, and it crushed her when she learned it was buried. I remember her scolding herself as soon as she made that confession: "Can you imagine? My being so selfish, I almost cared more for that doll than the poor little girl. But you see, I never owned a toy before, certainly nothing so fine.

When mission ladies gave her to me one Christmas, it was like being touched by magic. Then the magic went away."

I think a part of my mother was always scolding herself, never offering a moment's peace. She ultimately thrust the gift onto me, told me to put the doll away somewhere she wouldn't see it. "She isn't Mae," she whispered. The only place I could think of was the back corner of my closet, so I set a folded towel there, to serve as her couch. When I left for school in the morning, I'd place Ethel inside with her so they could talk, though I left the door open a crack to give them fresh air. They were so alive to me. Ethel said Shirley had all kinds of stories to tell about what she'd seen through the store window. "She's better than a soap opera," Ethel claimed, which was a great compliment. But there I go, acting as if I had real conversations with my fourteen-inch Tiny Thumbelina from Sears.

I suddenly recall Mama elaborating on the story of her lost doll. She and my father seldom drank alcohol but one time, a few days before Christmas, Mama and Big Ethel were trying out a recipe for rum balls. Problem was, they kept tasting the batch as they baked, then skipped the cookies altogether and polished off the bottle of rum. I sat in a corner where I wouldn't be noticed, eavesdropping on their talk that became more open and intimate as the booze disappeared. Mama told Big Ethel the story of the doll, how she handed her over to a dying friend, but this time added that the doll returned to her when she was at school, or her ghost returned since no one else seemed able to see her.

"Oh, dear heart, that's remarkable." The way Big Ethel said "remarkable" wasn't remotely skeptical or unduly surprised, instead supportive. But at the first whiff of sentiment, of her friend's compassion filling the space between them, cutting through the haze of rum, Mama snapped shut and changed the subject. I wonder why this conversation slipped past me, momentous as it now feels. Perhaps as a kid I thought everyone had dolls that were fully alive to them and didn't find it strange that Mama had a similar experience.

I've been musing over the Shirley Temple doll for a good while, fingers unconsciously stroking her strawberry-blond ringlets, before realizing there's still another box left to open. I set her on the chair and check on Prince, who's been suspiciously quiet since his Tony Bennett serenade. He's watching some drama in my neighbor's yard, beak clicking against the window in his mysterious code. Good, I can sneak off to continue my investigation.

I cut the string on the second coffin-like box, dig through similar wrappings. This time I'm so unprepared for what I find, I actually back away as if to flee. Which is ridiculous, I know! I'm becoming as operatic as Prince. I make myself stare at the object. How could I have forgotten this second doll? Information floods through me, like someone's handed me her biography. Her name is Winona, and she was given to Mama, well, to both of us, after our last visit together with Grandma. I didn't know it at the time because Mama wasn't ready to show her to me yet. But after Mama died, my father brought her out and told me as much of the story as he knew. How she was the replica of a very old Dakhóta-style doll, originally created in the mid-1800s. The doll had been destroyed by fire at the Carlisle Indian School, and my khúŋši was heartbroken, preserving all that remained of her—a small, charred stone placed inside her for a heart. When Khúŋši returned from boarding school, her mother surprised her with a graduation gift—this copy of the doll she had lovingly made by hand to replace the one that was "killed." I recall my father using that word because it sounded so dramatic and strange. Khúŋši treasured the doll for itself, and for what the gift said about the quality of her mother's love. I finally remove Winona from her box so I can carefully study the figure. While she might not be the original artifact, she has now reached a great age in her own right and must be at least one hundred years old. Her body is sewn of the finest deer hide, using sinew as thread. The features of her face are beaded, and dentalium shell earrings hang from behind her deerskin ears, sewn there. She wears a buckskin dress, fringed along the sleeve cuffs and bottom hem. The yoke of the dress is completely beaded—an expanse of dazzling azure with white crosses representing the morning star visible in the sky. A woven belt cinches her narrow waist and tiny beaded moccasins don her feet. Her long braids are made of human hair, no doubt from the head of my great-grandmother. The doll's expression is wary. There's an air of strength about her, she's clearly a survivor, yet I read fear in her dark beaded eyes. It's as if she can feel my observing gaze and wonders what I think of her. I give her a gentle squeeze of reassurance and gasp at the zap of energy that emanates from her body. My khúŋši said that everything has spirit, everything is alive, and here is the best proof held in my own hands. I'm convinced this doll is more than a family heirloom—she's a relative. So I introduce myself to her and welcome her back to the land of the living.

I figure that since Shirley and Winona have already spent decades sharing the tomb of an airless tub, there must be a comfortable familiarity between them. I place them together in my guest bedroom, seated cozily on the bed. As if he can smell the newcomers, Prince rushes into the room and flutters onto the tall dresser, gazing down on the pair from on high like a presiding judge. He tilts his sleek head and stares at me with his inquisitive black eye circled by a distinctive eye ring. Something is up, he can tell, and he hates being left out.

"Aren't they beautiful?" I ask, indicating the powerful duo.

"Holy Goat, no!" Prince cries, and stomp-dances his feet. Before I can respond, he dive-bombs the two, his feet brushing the tops of their heads, then flies off and hides in a niche behind the open door, peeking out at me. His ritual when he knows he's been naughty.

"Oh, you're just jealous. But I love you anyway." Realizing he's forgiven, Prince runs off to play with his toys. Hours later I find him napping on my bed, his creamy pink head nestled in Ethel's small lap. Her open hand rests on his neck as if she's been scratching him the way he likes. The seemingly innocent tableau makes me cold. I grab a sweater to put on over my shirt though I'm Minnesota-tough when it comes to chilly weather and it's a gorgeous spring day in the forties, which we consider to be summer temperatures.

Strange things have been happening ever since the day I checked eBay for first-edition volumes by Native authors. If spirits are at work here, I have to smile at their reliance on technology. I keep teetering between my spirit self and my skeptical self. If I'm honest, I know my heart believes my khúŋši and her acceptance of sacred mystery, of the realm that exists not only within our hearts, but because of them. My chattering mind has always been the trouble. It's a being that wretchedly interrogates anything wondrous that could make me happy but requires surrender. My chattering mind can't help herself, so I treat her with compassion. She's witnessed what happens when I raise my hands and accept whatever is coming.

Within days of exploring my old trunk, I've become obsessed with dolls. Through eBay I've ordered another Black Tiny Thumbelina. She's not in as good shape as Ethel; her hair's a bit ragged and her body collapsed, needing added stuffing, but her face bears the same sensible expression and adorable chubby cheeks. If someone asked me why I bid on her, my instinctive answer would be: to keep Ethel company. Which I know is ridiculous. But something about Ethel, an air of wistful nobility, reminds me of Ishi—the last member of the Yahi tribe in California. I don't want her to feel alone in a world of white dolls. On a whim, I also order a Mary Poppins doll circa the 1960s like the one I so admired when I was little—only the doll, not her trunk with an entire wardrobe. I don't intend to actually play with her.

When each of the parcels arrives and the dolls are unpacked and brought together with Ethel, Shirley, and Winona, I laugh to myself that they look like a minor coven of witches, ready to share their secret spells and shake up the world.

Being thrust into my personal history, and that of my family, shakes me out of the static routine I've been trapped in for so long. Decades have run through my fingers as I withdrew from my own life like a convalescent. I've been an arts person since earliest memory, first imagining myself to be a ballerina in the grand tradition of my idol, Maria Tallchief, then a star of the Broadway musical theater like Rita Moreno. But always there was my love of literature as well as a paralyzing shyness that Mama called "being backward." She would swat at me when I followed too close behind her in new situations with people I didn't know. "Come show yourself and be polite!" she'd scold. "Stop being so backward." Early on it struck me that being a fiction writer was a safer route for an introvert than being a performer on the stage. My secret plan, sometimes secret even to myself, was always to be a published author. But I didn't get there in a straight, determined line. I decided to major in psychology early on during my freshman year in college, not because I intended to pursue it as a career, but rather to try to understand my family's dynamics and figure out what was wrong with me. I guess I was looking for a private cure for the hypersensitivity and depression that had plagued me since my mother's death. I was asked to write several papers that focused on childhood experiences, then explain the patterns I noted using what I'd learned from assigned texts and studies. I received

A's on these papers but the grades never cheered me, rather struck me with guilt for revealing what went on behind closed doors, for sharing scenes of my parents, well, my mother, when she wasn't on her best behavior. I had the impulse to defend her when a professor's comment intimated that some action she took was "abusive." I stopped writing these papers and instead focused on other areas of psychology that were less personally intrusive. That's when I became serious about writing fiction, thinking I could escape the past through imagining other stories, a happier outcome. After college I moved to Iowa to earn a master's of fine arts. Fiction was my obsession, and I wrote story after story until enough pages accumulated to complete a novel.

The act of writing was my safe place for several years, the one realm where I could open myself completely to inspiration in an unconscious, trusting way that felt a bit like magic. I hurled myself at the work like a fearless dancer throwing her body across a stage. I wrote and wrote—novels, stories, essays. My first book won a major award and I met several of my literary heroes. But when you harbor an inner script that treats you like the enemy, it doesn't allow you to soar for very long. Doubts nibble at the edges of your thoughts until they're the only voice left. Imposter syndrome secures its triumph and ushers in an era of self-sabotage. Then the carnival shuts down, packs up, moves to another town. And you're alone, hiding in the dark. For a few years my fictional characters had been so noisy in my imagination they drowned out the sly voice that had whispered to me since my mother's death. But now the sly voice was in charge. This is where I was the day that Ethel found me again via the book on baby-boomer dolls—alive without living.

I'm writing again, but not sure this new project is healthy. I didn't even consciously *choose* the material, which is closer to the bone than anything I've written before. I'm immersed in the past;

in fact, it's hijacked me. After a lifetime of running from uncomfortable memories which can trigger anxiety attacks or months of prolonged depression that shut down my life, it's like I've been dropped in the ocean of everything I avoided. No land in sight, no friend to pull me to shore. I must swim through each moment and episode to keep afloat and get anywhere. Of course, maybe I did choose this, on some deeper level. Maybe a grounded, secure part of me decided, it's time, confident that nothing I remember will actually kill me. Perhaps that solid version of myself (for some reason I envision her wearing old-school, original Earth Shoes) woke Ethel, my formidable ally. Who knows? All I'm aware of is emerging from hours-long sessions of furious typing, to find document files filled with stories. Some of them events that happened in my childhood, and some of them family experiences I apparently remember in minute detail though they happened before I was born; it's like they live in my body, swirl through the coiled rope of my DNA.

One evening the wind picks up and begins snapping through my apartment. A door slams, startling Prince, who squawks with indignation and comes running to find me. But he isn't alone. He's got something clutched in his beak, tripping over it, which slows him down. I'm horrified to see that it's Winona. He's kidnapped her from the guest bedroom and is dragging her by a braid. I'm about to scold him when he looks up at me, his expression serious, earnest. This isn't mischief. He drops her at my feet, nudges her body closer so I'll understand he brought her to me with a purpose. I have the sudden feeling that the rogue breeze wasn't random, and that the doll herself might have orchestrated this moment where I pick her up, smooth her hair, ask her what she wants. I carry her into the office, the room with the slammed door. No breezes now. There's an empty vase on my desk and I set her inside there so she can stand without falling over. The vase comes up to her shoulders, containing her in a way that reminds me of the beer keg Mama was kept in when she was little because her folks didn't have anything fancy like a playpen and they needed to keep her from running around with her siblings so she could heal the hole in her heart. Prince floats onto the desk and stands beside the doll, as if they're allies now. He bobs to inner music, watching me all the time like there's something I'm expected to do that I'm not doing.

I give up, glad there's no one around to watch what happens next. I ask the doll and the rocking cockatoo if they have a message for me. His job done, Prince immediately flutters out of the room. The doll, on the other hand, seems to straighten in the vase and catch my eye with her beaded stare. She begins to speak in my head, show me images from the distant past that flicker from one to the other like the projection of an old-time film. Inspired, I dutifully type her story.

BITTER DOLL

The doll is born as summer dies. The village of her birth is on the move, fleeing reports of a deadly sickness ravaging their enemies. Earlier in the day a hunting party returned with stories of lodges filled with the dead, their faces so disfigured the young men's hearts churned with sorrow for these úŋšika ones they might have killed on another day. The village is already in mourning for the death of a baby who lived for a mere handful of heartbeats, her young mother gone cold and silent as if she can will herself to follow the child. She is watched by older sisters determined to keep her alive, though she refuses even the smallest morsel of food. She can't bear to tell them that all she sees anymore is the sweet perfection of her baby's mouth, the tiny lips that will never open to feed or cry. Wičháŋȟpi Wiŋ becomes a ghost, and her name no longer suits her, named as she was after a brilliant star in the sky on the night of her birth. There is no longer light or color in this girl, she has lost every smile. Sometimes a sister places a hand on her heart to make sure it isn't frozen—she barely breathes. After weeks of this behavior the eldest sister scolds her gently, reminding Wičháŋȟpi Wiŋ that she is surrounded by children in the thióšpaye who need care and attention, that she will surely give birth to other babies. The words slip past her ears without comprehension. Grandparents who are revered for their sensible counsel tell the sisters to be patient with Wičháŋȟpi Wiŋ, that the path of grief is as mysterious as the ways of love. We cannot *force* our heart to heal when grievously wounded. So the sisters wait, as the hair they slashed short in sorrow grows long again.

The sister who is only a year older than Wičháŋȟpi Wiŋ, who taught her how to stand, how to run, how to listen, dreams one night of her sister carrying a doll in a cradleboard. The doll helps her speak again and eat—the doll sleeps next to her heart and makes it warm again. When she wakes, the sister digs out the finely tanned deer hide she intended to transform into a shirt for her son. These are survival times, so the doll must wait. She is birthed slowly, like a real child, each piece of her growing under the young woman's hands as she has time to do the work. The doll's slender body is fashioned from deer hide, filled with the down of cottonwood trees. Her eyes and mouth are stitched into place using dyed porcupine quills her creator carefully flattened. Her waist-length hair is plucked from the sister's own head, organized into braids. She is dressed like Wičháŋȟpi Wiŋ in her best finery—beaded buckskin dress and leggings, tiny moccasins that fit the tips of a woman's fingers. When she is finished the sisters pass her from hand to hand, inspecting the fine details of her creator's work. They approve, though are wary with guilt—this toy is such an indulgence. The sisters are ready to present the doll to the one still silent with grief. She sits on a mat in her thípi lodge, hands empty of the work that needs her attention, her shorn head bowed low— she will not allow her hair to grow long again. The sister who designed the doll places the small being in Wičháŋȟpi Wiŋ's open, idle hands. The doll begins to slip away but at the last moment before it plunges headfirst to the woven mat, Wičháŋȟpi Wiŋ grabs it by the ankle. She clutches the doll on her lap, inspecting it not with the eyes, but with gentle fingertip strokes. Wičháŋȟpi Wiŋ weeps then, softly. The flow of tears is a release, a cleansing—warm drops fall from her swollen eyes, landing on the doll's fresh face. The rain of tears stains her deerskin flesh, so it looks like she was born crying—a sorrowful doll.

Wičháŋȟpi Wiŋ is rescued by the gift, stunned back to life by this gesture of love. She knows the stitched being isn't alive in the same way as other children, who change and grow, but she certainly isn't lifeless. Wičháŋȟpi Wiŋ adds her own element to the doll, a spark of inspiration that makes her smile to think of it. Her secret. For weeks she's kept a small stone tucked in a pouch that dangles from her belt. The stone is one that came into her hand as she scrabbled for support from the earth while straining to bring her baby into the world. The baby that didn't live. The stone is unusual—slick as if wet, black at first glance though with a sheen of dark crimson like it bleeds from within. The stone is warm to the touch; she imagines it has stolen some of her own spark of life, pressed into it through obsessive fondling and smoothing for long catatonic hours. Wičháŋȟpi Wiŋ opens the doll under the left arm, cutting through her sister's careful stitches, then reaches inside to add the stone she nestles in a bed of fluff. She sews the doll closed again, satisfied. She's given the doll a heart.

The sisters name the small being Winona, because she is the first daughter to live among them, she will always be the first daughter even after Wičháŋȟpi Wiŋ gives birth to a girl who lives to adulthood.

Winona is a serious companion, loving but never playful. The girls who inherit her from one generation to the next sense her somber mood and air of responsibility. They are careful around her as they are with other elders, aware she is watching, that her cautious heart worries over them. They don't laugh much in her presence or tumble her about in lively games. But they trust her with their secrets and turn to her for comfort. She is a trustworthy doll.

Winona is two generations old when Čhumní is killed, the one named after glistening dew for the shine of her smile, a girl whose parents dressed her in moccasins with beaded soles to show how much they loved her, that her feet would never touch earth. The doll remembers being birthed by the hands of a Dakhóta woman to ease a mother's grief, so she considers them her people though she's made of tanned hide that is never warm to the touch in the way of the living. Her own moccasins have beaded soles—she is carried everywhere.

The doll has crescent deerskin ears and dentalium shell earrings. She is an attentive listener, especially in these lightning times, when the air is forever charged with tension. She's never heard such noise as she does this September

morning when General Sully and his Northern troops surround Čhumní's camp. There have been negotiations—the
band's chief and his eldest son have offered themselves as
hostages so the angry wašíčus will understand they offer no
threat. But the Blue Coats are bristling with shiny weapons;
they dismiss appeasing words and answer with the sharp
music of attack.

Čhumní's parents and brother face the onslaught of rushing soldiers with empty hands. Her older sister pushes the girl
behind her, but a stranger whose face is no more than a smear
against the sky, he moves so quickly, snatches the young
woman by the hair and drags her into the family's lodge.

Čhumní stands helpless, squeezing the doll so tightly she
feels the lump of stone buried where a heart should be, but
the doll is packed with nothing more than the fluff of cottonwood seeds. She has no life to give this girl who is frozen,
staring at the mangled hill of her parents and brother, dying together. The doll thinks the sky itself weeps blood as
Čhumní closes her eyes against this mist of death. A rifle shot
brings her to her knees. The doll slides from Čhumní's hand
and falls onto the grass. Winona watches a bloody rain paint
the prairie mounds of Whitestone Hill. She's glad she can't
turn her head to see the girl—she doesn't want to witness this
death.

General Sully's men destroy what the dead and their
survivors leave behind, gathering buffalo meat, thípi lodges,
utensils, and blankets, roasting it all in a great fire so any
survivors of today's murder will have nothing left to sustain
them. Someone tramples the doll as he tosses Čhumní onto a
cart, but she escapes notice. All she can do is watch.

The doll is pained by her survival. She strains to leap
into the flames, wishes she'd been sewn teeth so she could

chew herself into leather strips. She cannot close her eyes made of the dark indigo Italian beads Čhumní's mother sewed in place of the frayed porcupine quills from another generation, telling the doll she deserved "fresh eyes." She prays they will melt if she stares at the blaze. She feels her hair scorch, the air is so hungry. Braids fly from her head like burning twists of grass. She doesn't mind this loss, thinking it's right to be shorn in grief.

A terrified dog appears, dragging a gun-shot baby on a travois strapped to its shoulders. He must think the doll is another child to save—he bites down on her gently and runs from the carnage. Winona doesn't want to be rescued, but the loyal dog who carries her from the massacre ground, following a blood trail of survivors, refuses to release her until an old woman pets him on the head and insists.

"Šúŋka wašté," the woman gently praises, rubbing between his cocked ears, though the baby he sought to save is dead. The elder holds Winona on her lap, smooths the scorched stub of what hair remains. Today she has lost three generations that came from her womb, so she is broken open like a prairie night that reeks of smoke. She is swept so clean of every thought and memory, grief has nowhere to settle. She clings to the doll as if Winona can hold her in place, keep her from spinning away with the scorched wind. She crawls through the night with others who are shocked and injured, the doll tucked into her belt. Later, she adopts Winona and feeds her spirit, offers her the compassion she can't give herself for outliving an entire branch of loved ones.

Winona is too much for any child—her indigo eyes have witnessed the end of one world, how it burned for days, how mourners had to change direction and walk a broken path filled with dead earth and stones.

♦ ♦ ♦

Another generation passes and Winona is passed down to Cora, who is such a serious baby, scowling with fierce curiosity, her mother feels she belongs with the lonesome doll. Winona's heart is never light, but she watches the girl as if the stone is whole and without cracks, capable of swelling with love that fills her entire deerskin body.

Winona bears witness to each moment of Cora's young life, never far from the girl's company. Today Cora clutches the doll as they ride their first train. An older man with a stern white beard marches up and down the lurching aisle. He stares at the children with hard eyes, cold as rocks. He speaks English to scores of children who pack the compartment. Few of them understand him. Winona follows what he is saying, fluent as she is in his aggressive language that bangs the children's ears. He tells them to praise the Almighty for their great fortune—they will find him fifteen hundred miles hence when they step from the train and their backward ways into the world of Pennsylvania. They are headed to the Carlisle Indian Industrial School so they can shed the way of the blanket and take up the way of the plow.

Most of the children are dressed in traditional Dakhóta finery and carry precious objects like talismans to protect them. A few girls wear belts with pouches that contain tools for sewing. Everything familiar brings comfort in this foreign space. The doll has never felt as useful as she does now. Cora sing-whispers songs to Winona as if the doll is frightened. Or maybe she sings them to the boy who sits beside her, cracking his knuckles. Jack. The boy speaks respectfully to Cora, the two are quickly becoming friends, but the doll is nervous about their connection. She wants to holler a warning into her dear girl's ears, tell her to be careful! She doesn't want Cora to smile and warm to this boy who wears trouble like a white man's jacket. Winona wonders if the beads of her eyes are cracked because that's how she sees Jack—a child in pieces stuck haphazardly together like an ill-made thing that is easily shattered. She doesn't mean to be cruel, but she hopes the long train ride will shake him apart with its relentless rocking and sudden jolts, that he will fall from his seat beside Cora so the shards of him break, land in a heap at the girl's small feet. This will protect her from the danger of Jack's mischievous smile. But the doll's hopes are dashed—he remains in his seat, neither whole nor busted, and when the train jostles the children, they grab hands and hold on to each other in a way that makes the doll heavy with foreboding.

Winona is wary throughout the trip that carries her girl clear across the country, but she is firm in herself, nothing scares her now. She has already witnessed several lifetimes of atrocities. Still, she isn't prepared for what meets her at train's end, and neither is Cora. How the children are photographed in their original garb as soon as they arrive, allowed to hold cherished items from home, only to have everything taken from them and ceremonially burned directly after. It is in this way that the doll, who survived the massacre at Whitestone Hill, is thrown into the fire.

The doll doesn't understand how she remains, knowing little of spirit and how abiding loyalty will never reduce to ash. She's stronger now that fire has scoured her body. She is a new creature who sees through all the doors and windows of this dangerous place. She steps from cooling embers and for the first time feels what it's like to walk on beaded soles. She is so light she doesn't crack the glass. Her braids are restored, trailing down her back and tied off at the bottom with sinew. They're heavier than she remembers. She thinks she has a real heart now—there is a tiny drum inside, fluttering its music.

She holds out her hands and looks at them, inky blue as seen through the prism of her eyes. They offer two roads. She can go left and follow her new heart on a path of warm peace. She can choose right and step into war, avenge her abused children.

Her hands are jointed now, fingers nimble. She selects a charred splinter from the burnt bones of sacred objects, paints her face for battle. She is small and stealthy and can lift more than her weight. She spies an awl revealed by the burnt wreckage of its quilled sheath. The doll grasps its slim handle and thrusts it like a spear. Yes, she can do damage. She knows how vulnerable these large people are when they're sleeping. Their imaginations sleep with them, believing she is certainly destroyed. They will be defenseless as she visits them tonight, as she moves from room to room, gouging life from the matrons and teachers, the minister who slams small hands with his Bible.

The devouring flames have brought her deep knowledge; she understands all the languages of the betrayed children whose belongings were taken from them and destroyed, the ones she hears crying in their beds. Winona has become a doll for the collective—she can comfort them and say they don't have to cry anymore. She will protect them.

Except.

Winona's visions of physical life dissolve as she realizes even her thoughts are aflame. She tries to pull a grim smile but there is no mouth to move, there are no arms or legs or beaded moccasins on tiny feet, there are no braids or earrings or glass eyes. She is burned to nothing, finally killed, a doll without a trace of existence except for a blackened stone settled in warm ash.

The doll allows her thoughts to drift, to go wherever they do at the close of one's story. She yearns for silence, for the end to worries she can't address. She wonders if nothingness is the same as peace. But a finger stirs what is left of her— some essence of love. A child's hand plucks her free of the burn pile and drops her into his trouser pocket. Wonder of wonders, it's the dangerous boy who rescues her, or at least, the scorched lump of her heart. It is Jack who risks harm to find her and restore her to dear Cora, who is so shocked by this new territory, this confounding enemy of a school, she barely feels the pain of injured hands, burned when she tried to save Winona. And though the doll should be grateful to Jack for this kind gesture, her grudge against him only deepens. She knows this act of favor is the final element that blasts open the doors to Cora's heart, and once inside this broken boy will never let her go.

As I type the last sentence, a warning that the child version of my grandfather has captured my beloved grandmother in a way that will bring her enormous pain, I realize I'm crying. I close the file abruptly, as if it's haunted. I wonder if I'm writing fiction or being pulled into conversation with ancestors who never had their say; they were too busy surviving. Ridiculous as it sounds, I'm afraid to look at Winona, who I can tell from the periphery of my vision is still planted upright in the vase like a drooping flower. I make myself turn and face her. She isn't my grandmother's doll, lost to young Cora at the Carlisle Indian Industrial School, burned along with everything else she'd brought from home, every garment her mother lovingly sewed and beaded. But she carries Winona's story in the way of a respectful relative. This is such fanciful thinking, I nearly grimace at myself! Winona's face stops me—her dignified expression and the ancient wear of her skin, soft with compassion. This doll no doubt passed through the hands of many children who visited my khúŋši's home; Dakhóta girls who lived in the same broken times.

The next day I resolve to remain firmly in the twenty-first century. I'm wrapping up another semester teaching Native American Literature at nearby Macalester College. My students' final papers rise like a tower on the desk, requiring my attention. Winona is in another room, settled on a bed with the other dolls who have taken over my life in recent days. Out of sight, out of mind. At least that's how the strategy is supposed to work. I manage to critique and grade five lengthy papers before Prince interrupts by streaking onto the desk. He lands on the very next paper to be read, atop a pile that still looks formidably tall. He nibbles at the binder clip that holds the manuscript together, tries to wrench it off. This is a signal that it's time for lunch.

I've attended to Prince—fed him and played appreciative audience to his showstopper extravaganza. Today he was in a *Riverdance* mood and pounded his skeletal feet in his best imitation of Irish dancing. I have to admit he has a remarkable sense of rhythm, and if I were a more outgoing person, I could probably turn him into the next YouTube sensation. I return to my desk and begin reading the next paper but can't shake the remembered noise of Prince's stomping rhythm, the click click click of his nails on my wood floor. Quick fiddle music keeps looping through my head and I have to read the opening sentence of a student's manuscript over and over. The words won't penetrate.

A soft voice comments over the earworm that refuses to hush: "I miss dancing." I'm so startled, I jump to my feet and the office chair spins away from me as if it has its own choreographic aspirations. The voice has breath to it, feels very real, but there's no one else in the room.

"We're all here." There it is again, a girl's voice, bright with confidence. "Though we haven't been formally introduced." I swear she sounds like she's pouting. "But I'm happy to tell you my story, if you'll listen."

I have several options but in reality, feel there are only two: I can run away from the voice and her story, do whatever it takes to shut her down, or I can open a new document file and write what she wants to share.

The voice seems to read my thoughts—once I agree to listen, she tells me to bring her in from the bedroom because she can think better without the distraction of the other dolls, who might want to add their two cents. I wander into the back bedroom, skimming the floor as if I'm the ghost. I don't have to ask which doll summons me—my hand automatically reaches for Mama's doll, the one fashioned after Shirley Temple. While the original toy is surely still buried in a young girl's North Dakota grave, the spirits of these dolls have become strong in my imagination. I have no doubt the stories they have to tell are inspired by their original twin. I bring her into my workroom, and as soon as I settle her on the desk, she is alert and vibrant, eyes shining with life. I invite her to speak, and she immediately launches into her tale. She is chattering so quickly I beg her to pause so I can set up the file. Once I indicate I'm ready, Shirley is off and running, far more verbose than Winona. The pages quickly form until my hands are cramped from tapping keys for hours. Later I will read them with fascination even beyond the content of the story, for this approach is new to me. Always, my writing process is bumpy, a constant stop and start. I read paragraphs aloud to listen to their rhythm, look up synonyms in the online thesaurus when I rely on the same word too much, like it's the day's unconscious addiction. But this script falls directly into my imagination, my "memory," as if I'm taking dictation in an interview. That said, I trust the words that flow through my fingers, and the narrative they form. I title the new document "Wicked Taps."

WICKED TAPS

The doll is born in Long Island City, in a Queens factory within view of the East River. She's a composition doll, her flesh organized from humble materials like glue, sawdust, resin, and wood flour. Glazed with varnish to protect her smile. The god of her design is stamped on her small back, "Ideal N & T Co.," and they've provided her with a name pressed into her shiny skin: "Shirley Temple."

She has no way of knowing if her thoughts mirror those of an army of Shirley Temple dolls being birthed around her, all of them crafted with open-mouthed grins that show an upper row of baby teeth. They have strawberry-blond ringlets and hazel eyes, fully jointed arms and legs, which is good, because the doll has an impulse for movement thrumming in her solid limbs, a memory of dance in her bones that are not truly bones. Do the others want to join her in a musical number, create a spectacularly enormous chorus line, a chorus platoon?! Perhaps they're a bit short compared to the workers in this plant who coax them into being. But twenty-two inches of sparkling enthusiasm and musicality, well, that has to be worth something!

Her spirits plunge as she looks around her; the other Shirleys appear so complacent as to be dead. Are they thinking the same about her? Does her perpetual dimpled smile fool them to believe she has no heart? Questions blur through her mind, stacks of them riffle-shuffled together, including how she knows what a "riffle-shuffle" looks like? But she does—a thin scratch of memory of men on a break playing gin rummy, slapping cards down on a barrel top. She will go crazy if she doesn't slow the inner noise, pause the avalanche. She decides to focus on a single question that feels the most urgent: Are the fellow Shirleys who surround her in this gloomy cavern that smells like sawdust and faintly of fish once a window is opened, are they her sisters, or are they inanimate look-alikes without a hankering for anything, including love?

You might never know the answer, she tells herself. She wants to pump her arms in frustration or stamp her foot, but something tells her to be cautious. She's only just been born and doesn't know the rules yet. Maybe she should lie still and be patient. Listen and learn. Dream.

Once the doll is fully clothed in underwear, a white dress sprinkled with red polka dots, anklet socks, leather shoes, even a perky bow in her hair, she's wrapped in paper and placed in a box that fits her perfectly like a cardboard coffin. You'd think it would be easier for the doll to quiet her mind in this situation where there's nothing to see but the backs of her eyelids, which can open and close with the aid of metal rockers, and the paper that is shadow-colored like everything in this box, where even the noise of the world is muffled. But the opposite happens. The doll's thoughts collect and collide, interrupt. They're numerous as motes of dust she watched fall from a beam of light when she was still outside the box. Adding to the confusion are competing voices she seeks to recognize and separate so she'll know who is talking. There is her own chatterbox voice that loops incessantly like her dim recall of a roller coaster; there is a steadier, chirpy voice that's possibly the memories' owner, like maybe the doll is seeing glimpses of the *real* Shirley's life. Finally, a few days after her birth, another voice joins the racket—this one bringing emotions more than words. The doll feels a pull on her heart, though she's not sure she has one, a tug on her limbs and torso, even a tug on her clever feet that are convinced they can dance. A girl bids her to please *Come home,* but the doll can do nothing to answer. *Where is home?* she wonders.

Soon she's in motion, her box being trundled from conveyer belts to motor vehicles to the juddering motion of a train that makes the doll happy she doesn't eat food since it probably wouldn't set well in her tummy. She's clearly on the move, perhaps to find the voice that keeps summoning her to a mysterious homeplace? Now is the perfect time for her to test her abilities—she doesn't have to worry about someone seeing her, hidden as she is in the confining box, which feels like it's been packed into an even larger container. She can try to wriggle her fingers and toes, turn her head a little, though the paper wrapping is packed tight around her. She keeps deciding she's going to move, then doesn't. She suspects she is special but doesn't know for sure. She might be the only doll who is this close to being alive like the human-flesh girl whose face and memories she carries. If it turns out she's locked up in this body and will never be able to clap her hands or perform a tap routine like the ones she envisions in her head, that will be very sad. Right now, she'd rather live in suspense, with all kinds of adventures still possible and feeling a bit like magic, than know for sure she's just like one of those other dolls in the factory, who looked empty-headed and dull. Spiritless. So she holds still and lives in her mind, following the different voices that sometimes talk over each other and make her head hurt with confusion.

The doll eventually arrives. She is loaded off the freight train, placed inside a truck and driven miles down a bumpy road. She's taken out of the vehicle and walked up a short set of stairs.

"Here's your special order," a man's voice says. Oh, that makes the doll smile inside, a real smile and not the one her face was made to hold. "Don't see much of this sort," the man continues. "Label says we've got a Shirley Temple doll here, what a thing! While most of us are trying to keep body and soul together. You have royalty around here I don't know about?"

Another man laughs. "You could say that. The kid's so spoiled I stuff cotton in my ears soon as I see her coming. The kind that screams for everything and gets it most of the time."

"Uff da! Well, that's a shame."

The deliveryman must leave because the conversation ends. The doll is kept wrapped and her box slipped onto what feels like a low shelf, close to the floor.

"Someone will be glad to see you," a voice says, probably the storekeeper. The doll feels more like crying than celebrating. The person who summoned her doesn't sound very nice. She muses on this for a while, wondering if a friendly doll can make someone unspoiled? Maybe she has a job to do here?

The doll begins her new life after another journey—she's brought by car to what she guesses is a house, though she can't see it yet. It's Florence's birthday, though everyone calls her "Florrie." She's just turned seven years old, and has a big party planned for the day with all her friends, who aren't really friends, though they'll pretend for the chance to eat chicken, corn, mashed potatoes with gravy and biscuits, and even a fat slice of three-tiered chocolate cake. Florrie is a pincher, a hard pincher, and nearly every child who attends the party will leave with an angry bruise that bleeds a little where Florrie twisted their skin. But these are children who survived catastrophic dust storms where even their parents thought maybe the world was on its last legs or going through the great plagues of Egypt that Moses set on Pharaoh. They've survived pneumonia, consumption, hunger, and demoralized parents. So a little pain dished out by an unpleasant girl only merits a shrug. They not only get the best meal any of them has had in a good stretch, and the wonder of seeing a rich kid open present after present until she seems bored by the process, they also get party-favor bags that make it feel like Christmas though it's only October: a handful of Tootsie Rolls and Mary Jane taffy, Magic Slates with stylus pens, paper doll sets for the girls and marbles for the boys. The only unhappy child on Florrie's seventh birthday is Florrie.

Despite the abundance of gifts, which awe the partygoers, the appearance of the doll generates extra squeals and gasps that she can't help but find gratifying. Even the boys are impressed by how much the doll looks like the actual movie star she's modeled after. Many of the children are thinking, *Oh, can I hold her?* But silently because Florrie doesn't share. They don't want to give her the gift of their yearning only to be cruelly snubbed. Florrie makes a show of crushing the doll to her chest and kissing her on the forehead.

"Be a good baby," she says and plops the doll on a chair with a needlepoint seat cover. The other girls circle the doll, though no one touches. They point out her details and lean close to view her perfect teeth. The doll wishes they would reach for her, there's a warmth she feels from their eyes. But no one dares.

In coming weeks, the doll learns a great deal about the Thomson family, who have brought her all the way from the East Coast to what they call "the wilds of North Dakota." They're originally from Pittsburgh, a minister and his wife. Reverend Thomson is the so-called black sheep of his family, the rest of whom are capitalist businessmen determined to amass an even greater fortune than the one they inherited. Reverend Thomson was able to weather the disastrous stock market crash of 1929 because of his ignorance when it came to finances. He'd stowed cash and gold in safety deposit boxes, and was a strong believer in government bonds, which made sense to him. As a result, his losses were minimal while some of his relatives who had speculated more daringly were wiped out and had to start from scratch. Reverend Thomson maintains the Lord protected him, which has made him even less popular with his relations. He and his wife are true believers and choose to practice their ministry in a place they consider godforsaken—a condition they're working to remedy. They are kind to their neighbors and the members of their church, though no one understands their excessive indulgence of Florence, their only child. They live modestly, sensitive to the privations all around them, except when it comes to this small tyrant. The doll learns what the neighbors don't know: Mrs. Thomson suffered a devastating series of miscarriages in the early years of their marriage, and Florence is the only child who survived long enough to be born. She is their field of flowers.

Two months after she arrives in North Dakota the doll

finds herself upside down on the floor, dress over her head and white underpants exposed to the world. She is left there for hours, nerves ablaze with humiliation. Florrie spanked her for some make-believe reason the doll has already forgotten, a punishment that didn't hurt much beyond her pride, though Florrie made herself cry because she hit the doll so hard her hand burned. When Mrs. Thomson finds the doll in this compromised position, the lady rescues her, and decides the time has come to teach Florrie a lesson about gratitude. She collects all the girl's toys and packs them into boxes, then stores them in the attic until they can be picked up by friends and distributed to children on the nearby Indian reservation for Christmas. Before closing the attic door, the woman whispers an apology to the toys, saying they've done their job and it's not their fault her little girl doesn't appreciate them. Maybe now she'll learn to value what is offered with love. This whimsical gesture brings embarrassment, so she locks the door in a rush and hurries away. But the toys are grateful, especially the doll, who feels she was brought here on some sacred mission, only to become the abused sidekick of a disagreeable child. She is needed, she can feel it in her core.

The first time the doll meets Waŋské, the one she calls Lily, she knows she's come home. "You were calling me from the time I was born," the doll confides. Lily understands her perfectly—they speak the same heart language. Lily even asks her what she wants to be called. The doll knows immediately without thinking, the consequence of another memory that isn't her own, someone Shirley Temple has met in the industry. Rather than being charmed by the cute kid stars, or fascinated by the bombshell sirens like Jean Harlow, the doll admires an independent woman in the movie pictures who speaks with a saucy drawl: Mae West. A woman who takes charge and calls the shots. Lily adopts that name for the doll, and it feels right.

Life with Lily is about as different from the Thomsons' world as you can get. Lily's family doesn't have money, not even as much as the kids who attended Florrie's birthday party. But the mother is kind, and the children are sharp, interesting. Mae has to keep on her toes around Lily's sister Blanche, who views the doll with suspicion. But she doesn't take it as a personal snub, rather Blanche just seeing more than most, and picking up on Mae's awareness. One time when Mae is seated on the big bed where the children sleep, she finds herself alone with Blanche. The girl looks so much like Lily in her features, yet they're a bit harder on her, like the carver cut a little deeper in chiseling this one's face. Blanche watches the doll as if she's trying to catch her in a fidget. Mae sits quietly, pretending she's as dead as the skinned rabbit Cora is working on for supper.

Blanche finally tires of the spy game. She leans in close to Mae and whispers, "You don't fool me for a second. I know you're in there. Watching. I'll leave you alone, long as you don't mess with me."

The doll wants to shake her head no, she won't mess around, but she sits firm like an actor playing a death scene. She respects the girl and would never dream of tangling with her. If she didn't have to pretend to be a doll, Mae would stick out her hand and say, "Let's be friends."

Mae studies Lily so she'll understand her. The girl is pensive, serious, also imaginative. Her thoughts are as noisy as the doll's, and very often angry or disappointed. Lily wonders why she's expected to walk through life with her arms tied behind her back; at least that's how it feels. Sometimes she tells herself to be patient, that most children are dragged down from the floating balloon of their dreams, where they really want to be, and made to sit straight, parrot what they're told to say, or clam up like they're not even present. The problem is when she looks at her parents and how hemmed in they are from anything that looks like freedom, well, she loses hope in the future, can't even see past the figure of a stern nun at her school—the awful Sister Frances looming above her.

Mae is content with Lily and her family, happier than she was when she lived in a home of greater material abundance. She cheers her girl as best she can, thinks to herself that she has an important job, just like the film star who inspired her creation. But her satisfaction doesn't last for long. Lily is urged to hand over her precious friend, or protector, as Mae thinks of herself, to a little girl named Ada who is dying of consumption. Mae chastises herself for resisting the change, similar to how Lily scolds her own heart for breaking. Mae is gentle with Ada, and sorry when she passes away only days after they first meet. But Ada isn't her girl; she can feel it. There is someone who still needs Mae, someone who is very much alive.

The burial is traumatic. Mae is nestled in Ada's arms, which shift from weakness to a rigid strength—the grip of death. There are hours where the doll wonders if she, too, is dead since there's little to hear or see. But during the weeks Mae spends in the coffin, tucked in the arms of a sweet little girl who never stirs, she grows in wisdom and sensitivity. She feels her magic expand once she opens her heart to the experience, well, her metaphorical heart, and stops cringing each time she imagines a creepy-crawly moving across her skin. She recalls fewer of Shirley Temple's memories and more of her own. She has fleeting wisps of foreboding, a nagging fear of violence that will forever change Lily's life. Each hour the worry grows until Mae realizes she's going to have to escape this box in an effort to save her girl. The next moment Mae is standing on the ground atop the grave, not sure how she pulled this off other than through mere desire and helpless love. The area looks undisturbed. She makes up a story that sounds plausible, something to tell Lily when she finds her, confident now she will see her again given the magic of her return to the world.

The reunion of Mae and Lily is a patching of hearts. Mae finds her girl locked up in the school basement, in the punishment box that is cold and lonesome. Too many hours in there can make a child feel utterly alone and forgotten, as if the world has tipped them out of its story. They begin to think they'll remain there forever, until flesh melts from bone. It's a terrible place, a bit like the grave Mae just recently escaped. Somehow Mae is able to defy petty obstacles like locks and doors; she has powers that never worked before. So she's able to join Lily in the box and soothe the girl, keep her company in the long hours.

Mae's relief at being reunited with Lily lasts only for the duration of time they spend in the punishment box. When Sister Frances returns to send the girl to bed without supper, though Lily is hungry enough to eat the pocket of her dress, the doll's sense of a looming threat grows stronger. She now identifies the source: the enemy is Sister Frances and Mae plans to stop her. The woman is a menace—she sees her young charges as uncivilized, untrustworthy heathens, barely in possession of souls. To her mind, if they have souls, surely they're as stained and withered as a coal miner's lungs. It appears her role is not only to keep the children in line, crushed and obedient, but to demoralize them so they'll forever accept their lowly position in her prediction of grim futures. Mae thinks the nun takes pleasure in hurting the students—their feelings, their bodies, their spirits. The doll is determined to use her new powers to transfigure Sister Frances, turn the hardhanded woman with cold eyes into a more cottony version of herself—someone patient and tenderhearted.

Mae tries softening the nun by haunting her at night when she's asleep. The doll gently whispers in the woman's ear, praising Lily and Blanche for hours. She promises Sister Frances the girls are brave and intelligent, industrious, generous. Insists they're deserving of the nun's respect and kindness. She shares stories of the sisters that show them at their best. Mae works to influence the woman's opinion in this way for more than a week, and roundly fails. The nun seems impervious to tender cajoling.

Mae isn't the least bit discouraged; she decides to go gangster on Sister Frances. This is, after all, the era of John Dillinger, Bonnie and Clyde, Al Capone, and a mob of others—Mae's heard radio programs where their violent exploits are recounted in breathless detail. These are bad people, according to all reports, and Mae doesn't want to be bad, but she's becoming desperate just like those outlaws. She has children to save.

Mae breaks out in a performance one sleepy afternoon, while the children are studying math with Sister Anne. The nun is called out of the room and Mae can no longer hold still. She has memories of dazzling tap dance routines where her legs shuffle and piston, clapping the floor with metal chimes that sound like the rapid fire of a machine gun. Some part of her still feels like a star! So she leaves Lily and shinnies up the leg of Sister Anne's plain desk, which is hardly a glamorous stage but will have to serve. Mae tests her impatient feet that want to tap, hesitantly begins a soft-shoe slide, then gains momentum, whipping out time steps and double flaps, even a set of tricky wings. She's twirling and kicking; she leaps with effortless grace. If only everyone could see her and not just Lily! What a show she's performing in the patch of sun that shines on her face like a spotlight. She taps out love for Lily, and sadness for the sweet girl buried in a child's coffin; she taps out anger at Sister Frances, thinking her dance moves are magic that can expand her power. "Look at my wicked taps!" she shouts in her mind. "Surely I can conquer the enemy now." Her legs move with joy, neither wicked nor holy, just the limbs of a doll determined to win.

This time when Mae haunts the nun, she doesn't talk about the girls whose lives she seeks to protect, but instead focuses on Sister Frances. Mae whispers to the nun that she has a vicious temper, that misery and cruelty flow from her every word and gesture throughout the day, crushing the spirit of anyone unfortunate enough to interact with her. Mae recounts specific incidents to support her claims, asks the nun how a supposed child of God can pardon herself for all the harm she's caused? The doll has a soft, breathy tone; she doesn't scold, rather seduces—Mae's words slide into the nun's wrinkled ears that hang from her head like dried apples.

"You are wicked, and your heart is a tiny raisin. You'll spend eternity as the handmaiden of Satan, his accountant who records the lost souls who file into hell. He'll crush your foot beneath his hoof, he'll scald you with his glare, he'll skewer your hand with his long pinky fingernail. If there aren't enough souls in the flaming ledger, he'll nab one of your eyes and eat it right there before you. Sister Frances, you are as evil as they come; forever cruel, you aren't fit to live anymore on this green earth. You kill hope and joy, and no one will miss you when you're gone. You are death itself, and the rotten smell follows you wherever you go."

Mae can't view herself tormenting the nun, but she might be surprised at the peaceful expression she wears on her adorable, dimpled face. Though part of her is stunned by the hateful words that leave her mouth, her bright hazel eyes gleam with good humor. She's surprised at how easy it is to bedevil this persecutor. Sometimes after a lengthy monologue that is particularly graphic in detailing the future that awaits Sister Frances in hell, the doll places her hands on the area where a heart should be, as if astonished and remorseful for this harassment.

"My goodness," she breathes to herself at these times, and pats her small chest as if to comfort the heart that is missing there.

Mae's new strategy works. The nun's tortured nights begin to take a toll on her health—she looks haggard and wary; she no longer strides through the hallways with clack-heeled confidence but instead wobbles out of balance. Her voice wavers now when she utters a command, and sometimes she calls it back, hesitant, unsure of herself. She loses her appetite and becomes stick thin as the crude figures that are sometimes drawn of her behind her back. One day while she stands at the top of the main stairwell, pointing at Luther Holy Thunder to tie his shoe as she spots him on the landing below, the outside door is swept open and a strong breeze travels down the hall. It's a scorching afternoon outside, and that single blast of heat so reminds the nun of the yawning mouth of hell that preoccupies her thoughts, she staggers and falls headfirst down the long flight of stairs. Luther jumps to the side at the last moment before she collides with him, and so she smashes into the wall and breaks her neck. Sister Frances dies instantly, her hands curled like claws around the crucifix as if it could save her. This event seemingly closes the chapter on the nun's reign, and the danger she posed.

Except.

Mae discovers the limitations of her magic, how it's tethered by love. She is Lily's secret companion and protector, chief comforter, and friend. But she can't venture far from the girl's side or impact anyone else. Even clever, sensitive Blanche is no longer able to see the doll now that she's returned from Ada's grave. Each night when Lily sleeps, hugging Mae to her chest, the doll dreams of heroic deeds, imagining that she defeats the wretched Sister Frances and anyone else who poses a threat to the girl who is her true home. But when morning comes, the sky still dark as angry bells ring the children awake, Mae is brought back to humble earth. There is little she can do to stop the worst from happening. On the terrible day when Blanche defies the school and its cruel program, doing nothing more than sing an Honor Song in the first language she heard spoken, the doll can't trip the nuns or shout them down. She can't stop Sister Frances from poisoning Blanche with a stomachful of melted lye soap. All she can do is distract Lily's mind so it floats to safety, and remain with her when she slams back into her body.

Mae's silence is abrupt and unsettling—her story ends without warning. I glance where she sits beside a pile of books on my desk, her legs poked out from the skirt of a frilly dress. She is still in good shape, her ringlets neat and bouncy, but the dimpled cheer has gone out of her sculpted smile. I look at the Shirley Temple doll differently now after hearing what she shared. There are depths to her I wouldn't have believed if not for her pages of testimony. If what's happening is real beyond my imagination, these dolls are like a council coming together to address old problems that still strike them as urgent. They yet hope to save their girls.

Through all this writing I'm able to fully communicate with Ethel again. At least, that's what it feels like. Creativity that comes from our most courageous, authentic heart opens us to the Flow, an unseen river of images, insights, and visions where we connect across time with all that has ever lived. I close my eyes before wading into the waters of story, imagine myself standing in a creek that initially is nothing more than a trickle of clear water over a bed of polished stones. Behind me I hear the noise of water on the move, and the next thing I know the creek becomes a river that covers my ankles, my knees, my hips, finally carrying me off in a thrilling whoosh of tumbling energy. I can breathe in this water. I can see everything. I can hear my heart drumming its song in time with other hearts going back to our earliest mother. I can hear Ethel's voice.

"I waved at your father with my mind," Ethel says as I type. She sits on my desk, leaned against a photograph of the original Ethel and her husband, Lee, my godparents, who passed away before I finished college. She slumps a bit and for a moment her posture reminds me of an elder with a slight dowager's hump. Her small painted mouth remains still, her lips faded over time to a chalky pink. Yet I hear her voice easily now, the way I did more than forty years ago.

"I'd been sitting on that Sears shelf for so long, and he looked like a nice man. I could see you hovering at the edges of his spirit—he carried you everywhere though you probably didn't know it—and I liked you from the first. He noticed the wave and came straight to me, touched the glassine window of my box. I tried to look bright and interesting so he would bring me home to you for Christmas. He picked up my box and the joy swooped through me! So big, I think my gleeful shivers jiggled the package. I didn't want to scare him off, so I told myself to simmer down. Then there was that scary episode where the saleslady didn't want him to buy me. I could hear what she was thinking. She thought he was a man who didn't know the first thing about what a girl would like in a doll friend, and figured his child had a hankering for the Thumbelinas she saw on television commercials, who were all white. But I knew you'd love me even better than the white dolls! They looked fine, but none of them had a single thing to say that would've interested you. Every time I tried to get them to talk, to ease the boredom, they chattered about the clothes people wore and how because it was winter, we saw only coats. And what a shame that was. Green coat. Red coat. Persian lamb coat, ooh, they squealed over that one. I didn't care two cents about fashion. Hmph." I'd forgotten the sound Ethel made when she was exasperated—something between a sigh and a snort that was pretty adorable coming from a baby. I smile to myself and hope she doesn't notice. Ethel is all about respect.

"I liked your father even more when he saved me from that Butterick crowd, and when he pushed back against the saleslady's racist pressure. He told her I was the most beautiful doll he'd ever seen and that his little girl would love me." Ethel's voice is suddenly thick with emotion and my own eyes fill with tears. I blink them back so I can keep typing. She pauses to regain her composure and I pretend not to notice.

"He brought me home! Though I had to spend a few days hidden behind gift wrap. I was so excited. From the closet I could hear the sounds of a family moving through its day, hear Christmas music played on the stereo and your own beautiful voice." Ethel's compliment makes me blush, but I don't thank her, not wanting to interrupt her flow of memories. "Your heart was in your voice, so I already knew you before I ever set eyes on your face. From the very beginning there was love. The only thing that made me nervous about the situation was your mother. I could tell from her conversation that she was a roller coaster we'd all have to ride if we didn't want to crash. If she was up, then she'd take us along for a wild loop in the sky, and if she slumped, we'd have to tiptoe, and keep close to the ground. Forgive me for saying this, but that woman made me glad I was too young to drink coffee! Though Lord knows there were times I wished for something stronger in that little bottle of water you gave me. Oof! She could frazzle my nerves."

I don't disagree with Ethel's assessment of my mother, but it's still painful to hear. When Mama was up, there was no place better to be than in her company, though if I'm radically honest I'd have to say that even in those good times there was a crimp of worry at the edges from knowing that cheer would eventually plunge to become despairing rage.

"I can hear you hollering at me in your thoughts." Ethel appears to watch me from her slouched position, head bowed, like she's trying to read how much of the past I can handle.

Everything! I say silently. *I'm so much stronger now.*

"That was a terrible day. The very worst. I'd been dreading that sort of outcome. Your mother was burning hotter and hotter. She loved you and your father as much as she could, but her heart held no love for her own self, so what spilled onto others was destructive and erratic. She scraped herself together for as long as she could. She didn't want to bust all over everyone. Those days she spent in bed on your birthday? You might've thought she was regretting your birth, but that was never the case. Your birthdays reminded her that she was a mother with a precious being in her care, and she would dig inside, dig inside, trying to convince herself she could do the job. She wanted to be good for you. She lived with so much mean noise in her head. Well, I guess you know something about that yourself." I nod, but just keep typing. It's a relief to focus on a task and not linger on memories of my own inner script, which pretty much took me apart year in and year out, until recently.

"That awful day you came back from the grocery store and dropped one of the bags, your mother knew it was no big deal. But that's not how she *felt,* and she would ride whatever emotion rose up and took her over. She knew you were sensitive, regretful when you made a mistake, which we all do. She knew better than to explode in rage. But sometimes those chiding thoughts that tried to break through the anger only made things worse. 'Cause they flipped the guilty switch in her, and *that* made her really mad."

Ethel whispers the last word, "mad." It's such a small, ridiculous word when you think about it, when it covers a range of feelings that lead all the way up to violence.

"When she dropped that jug of milk and it broke—the liquid slopped up against her legs, splashing her nylons—whooo, she was *mad.* With each step she took up those stairs, chasing after us, some part of her knew she was going to hurt you. Her hands could feel it. *I* could feel it. I'm talking a kind of hurt she might never be able to take back. I had to do something quick. I had to protect you."

Ethel's voice is hushed but shaking with emotion. Urgent. She pauses so we can collect ourselves. Her baby chin slumps lower on her chest.

"Just so you know, neither one of us set a finger on your mother. All I did when she caught up to us and you closed your eyes, hands up like you were surrendering, which brought me high enough to look her straight in the face—all I did was mirror back to her what was in her heart at that moment. She'd sensed a power in me which made her uncomfortable, so I unleashed it. She saw the poison that kept pumping inside like a bitter snake gliding through her bloodstream. And it scared her.

"Your mama backed away from her own sickness and for a moment she had enough balance to catch herself from tipping over the edge. She chose not to. She let herself fall. She didn't ever want to take you with her."

She almost did, a voice says in my head.

Ethel hears. "That's right. She almost did. But 'almost' doesn't make it so."

Now I'm the one to slouch in my chair. I allow myself to cry. Prince has been unusually quiet this afternoon, leaving me and Ethel to our private business. But now he struts into the office, his head bopping to some tune no one else can hear. Always inner music with this one, the way I was as a little girl. He could easily fly onto my lap, but he climbs up instead, perhaps to show me he's willing to put in the work and not take the easy route. He perches on my knee and looks into my face, clicks his beak. Then, in a loud voice that startles both me and Ethel, who falls onto her side, he begins shouting the chorus of Prince's song "Let's Go Crazy" in mangled cockatoo pronunciation. My tears become hiccupping laughter. I probably sound a little bit cracked. That makes Prince cackle—he's so proud of himself for changing my mood. We laugh and sing, and I set Ethel upright again to restore her dignity.

We're an odd trio, but the air feels cleaner now. A vinyl doll and a wild cockatoo have helped me move through something that's been hanging over my heart for more than forty years. Which just goes to show, all beings are capable of providing love medicine.

The phone rings not five minutes after Prince's antics soothe my nerves. It's my best friend, Izzy. Between us are heart-lines like strings on a musical instrument that sound a deep note when the other needs support. I almost laugh when I see her number show up on caller ID. Her radar is sharp.

"What are you doing?" Izzy's tone is stern, but only because something in the air worries her. I find such comfort in her strong voice and faint drawl of vowels, courtesy of Oklahoma.

"Well, to be honest, my Tiny Thumbelina doll from child-hood is talking to me. Is that strange?" I say this with a laugh because speaking the words aloud is unnerving.

"I'm coming over there. Just hang on. I'll leave first thing tomorrow and should pull in by dinnertime. Is that okay?"

"That sounds perfect. Thank you!"

"What are sisters for? And I miss you."

Izzy and I have been rescuing each other since we met at a Native American Literature conference years ago. She sat down beside me as we waited for a panel discussion to begin, pulled out a package of Reese's Peanut Butter Cups, and offered me one. I'm usually painfully shy, but her warmth spread wings of cover over both of us, and I eagerly accepted, saying, "These just happen to be my favorite!"

Sharing that sweetness from the beginning made us quick confidantes.

Izzy's actual name is Dr. Isabelle Parker, born and raised in Bartlesville—a small city in the northeastern part of Oklahoma. She is Osage on her mother's side, tall like her from the family photographs I've seen. Isabelle's long silver hair is the first thing people notice about her, long enough that she has to take care when she sits down or she'll yank the braid. Her pale green eyes, which she says come down to her from her father, though she never knew him, are an unusual color—a soft jade. She's two years older than I am, her face as smooth as when I first met her decades ago; only the early silvering of hair signifies she might have been around for half a century. She's currently teaching at the University of Illinois in Champaign-Urbana, which is about a day's drive from Saint Paul, so we get to see each other fairly often.

I do a quick clean of my place, which excites Prince and makes him feel like dancing. I beg him to take a break for a while or go it alone, which turns him pouty. At least I can't hear his complaints over the noise of the vacuum. I despise cleaning more than just about any other job because of its utter futility. I dust the surfaces of a room and by the time I move on to the next location, dust is already snowing down. The sense of accomplishment is horribly short-lived. But having put my place in order, at least on the surface, I distract myself for the long hours until Izzy's arrival—pretending I'm still living my old life, where forgotten dolls are packed in trunks and ancestors remain quiet.

In accordance with tradition, as soon as Izzy parks in the Crocus Hill driveway and has deposited her suitcase in the guest bedroom, I formally greet her with a glass of champagne and dark chocolate truffles with sea salt. As an added treat, I set out the box of homemade petit fours given to me by one of my students after our final class of the semester. Izzy is a dessert-first kind of person; we'll eat supper later.

We curl up on my large chenille sofa, which is conveniently dark mauve to hide any spills. Prince watches quietly from his perch near my ancient CD sound system—he's subdued and careful around Izzy as if she's a magician who could turn him into one of the thousand-leggers that petrify him when they scuttle across the wall at freakish speeds. He has a special centipede squawk he makes to sound the alarm, then comes running to me for safety.

Izzy isn't one for small talk, she gets right down to business. She puts a hand on my arm. "Are you okay?"

It's like she flicks a switch in me and the polite hostessing goes right out the window. Tears spill in such a steady stream they feel artificial, like I'm a lawn with automated sprinklers. She sets our champagne flutes on the coffee table and wraps me in her arms. It's taken years for me to accept hugs. We used to tease that I'm uncomfortable with physical affection because I'm from a Northern Plains tribe, as opposed to her Southern Plains sunshiny warmth. But we both know it has something to do with Mama, and how she didn't like to be touched. I was trained to keep myself to myself.

I tell Izzy about how I "bumped" into Ethel through scrolling on eBay, and how I've started hearing her again after all these years of silence. I relate what Ethel told me about my mother's death, how I had nothing to do with it. Izzy knows I've spent a lifetime wondering what caused Mama's fall. Did I push her? Or the madly absurd alternative that it might've been my baby doll. I tell her about the fragrance of Chanel No. 5 that invaded my trunk for a few hours though there wasn't any visible source. Izzy does what few do well—she listens, without judgment or interruption, without rejecting anything as impossible. When I finish my weepy monologue, we scoot apart and take a few sips of champagne. I'm trying to steel myself, afraid of her reaction.

"As Granny would say, whoo, that's a big fat pipe full of misery. I'm so sorry, dear sister, that's a lot to unpack and process." She looks into the bottom of her champagne flute; I can tell she's considering whether or not to tell me a specific something.

"It's okay, go ahead. I've gotten to the point where I need to know. I promise I'm more solid than I look."

Izzy nods and sets down her glass. Fortifies herself with another truffle. Her beautiful sharp face, shaped like a diamond, relaxes into open pleasure. Izzy can be bribed into doing most anything legal with high-quality chocolate.

"I've been wondering when you would sense your mother's presence. I started seeing her hovering around you about a year ago. I think she's always been there, but with more urgency now, which made her visible, at least to some of us. She wants you to fully receive the messages that are coming your way, and to set down all that guilt. How can she set hers down when you're still hauling that burden?"

"She probably doesn't want me to waste more of my life than I already have." I finish off the champagne and bring in the bottle to pour us another glass.

"Survival is never a waste." Izzy's statement brings me to tears again, though this time I refuse them. "You couldn't help having depression, anxiety, PTSD. You didn't even know what was wrong most of your life, given that aversion to therapy. Remember what you told me one time, how you felt your main job some years was to stay alive? Well, you did your job, you made it through. Not everyone does. It takes fortitude."

"And a little help from your friends."

"Yes. You are loved. That didn't come out of nowhere. And look at your résumé, which is impressive as hell—not that I agree with the American habit of using a CV as some kind of measuring stick of worth. You've created a meaningful footprint, heartprint, soulprint, in this world, all the while fighting an inner script that wanted to take you down. Isn't it awful what we say to ourselves? I know that song-and-dance routine. Like a slow death, plucking out our feathers one painful yank at a time." Izzy remembers Prince, who is still watching us closely as if he's on a stakeout. "Sorry," she tells the bird. He doesn't even blink.

"I've always been curious . . ."

"Yes? Go ahead, please feel safe to ask or say anything. You're my trusted sister."

Izzy's cheeks develop a sweet flush of pink and her jade-green eyes soften, but she isn't someone who gets teary. "Thank you, and of course that's how I feel, too." She reaches across to squeeze my arm. Prince straightens in jealous alert. He doesn't like others getting too friendly with me in his presence. Izzy notices. "Ah, don't get your feathers twisted, Your Purple Highness. My, isn't he a character?"

"Understatement of the year."

"Okay. What I've often wondered is where your father fits into all of this. Your mother takes up most of the oxygen in the room, in your head; she's the constant focus. But what about him? Did he recognize that she needed help? Did he ever talk to you about her death?"

The most apt term for what's going on inside my body is: "swoon." It feels like bees have penetrated my skull and set up a hive there, and I'm riding one of those super-speed trains as we head into a tunnel, my vision narrowing to a point of light. Roaring sound is all I can hear—a part of me thinks it's my heart shouting. I'm frozen in gray shadows. I don't lose consciousness, just slide into another state where my body's panic becomes the only reality. I'm a freaked-out planet of one.

Then I hear Izzy's voice at the edges of my inner wall of sound. Gentle commands to "breathe." I'm not sure how long I crater in that agitated place, but eventually my vision begins to open, my ears hear more than the wrecked noise of the heart.

"Well, that was frightening. I think I need another chocolate." Izzy smiles tightly.

"I'm so sorry. I thought I was handling all this okay. Guess I wasn't expecting the conversation to move in that direction."

"And *I'm* sorry for triggering an episode but thank goodness you've come back. There must be something in there to look at when you're ready. Or you wouldn't have had such a big reaction."

"Oh, there is, I'm sure. Please don't worry, I'm grateful you asked what you did. That's a piece of the story I never interrogate. Why don't we have some proper food, and if I feel up to it, we can poke around the Dad stuff later?"

Together we whip up a meal of creamy mushroom pasta, asparagus salad, and fresh focaccia bread I picked up at Cossetta's on West 7th Street. Ordinarily we'd enjoy our supper in the dining room, but this evening we want to be cozy, so we head back to the couch and eat there. I put on some music, a favorite CD of Annie Humphrey's album *The Heron Smiled*. She's a Leech Lake Ojibwe musical artist who collaborated with John Trudell on a few of the tracks. Her voice is open, vulnerable; nothing slick. The perfect model for where I need to be in my healing practice.

Perhaps I'm procrastinating, not ready to jump into a discussion of my father, but after the dishes are scraped off and placed in the dishwasher, I lead Izzy into the master bedroom so she can meet the group I think of as "the Council of Dolls." I don't explain to her who each of them is, or the circumstances surrounding their acquisition. I let her sort through them on her own.

Izzy pats the top of Mary Poppins's head, which is covered by a black hat—she's wearing her outdoors clothes, including the floor-length blue coat. Her palm brushes the face of the extra Tiny Thumbelina I bought so Ethel wouldn't be completely outnumbered. She picks up the Shirley Temple doll, tips her over until her eyes close. Only two dolls receive more serious attention: Ethel and Winona.

"There's something special about these two," she says. "No offense"—offered to the other dolls, who lean against the pillows on my bed, arranged in a straight line like members of a jury.

"They've got extra mojo. I can feel it in my hands like an electric buzz, or sonic emotion."

"Your intuition is severely on point." I nudge her foot with mine. I can rarely be physically affectionate in a way that isn't childlike teasing. "Izzy, meet Ethel, my original baby doll that Dad got me for Christmas." Izzy strokes Ethel's hair. "And this one is very old, created by my great-grandmother as a graduation gift to her daughter. I call her Winona since that name designates the eldest daughter in a Dakhóta family. She's definitely the elder here." Izzy shakes Winona's hand, gives it a little squeeze.

"This is going to sound freaky, but I detect a rhythm when I touch her. If dolls had a pulse, I'd swear that's what it is—a slow, steady heartbeat."

I gesture to the window seats that look out on the back garden. Izzy sits down holding Winona on her lap.

"I have a confession to make."

"Do tell." Izzy smiles at me encouragingly and holds Winona's deerskin hands to help her wave at me. It's like they're both cheering me on.

"Even though Winona is a valuable heirloom, and I'm not just talking about material value, I couldn't help but carry out a minor surgery: open her up via a seam beneath her dress. To check something. Sure enough, I found a pouch sewn in her chest that contained a small stone. Holding it in my hand felt strange, like I clutched a live jewel. It's the most stunning, deep black, with a soft polish to it. But if you hold it up to the light the black looks more like burnt red. Strangest of all is what you feel when you pinch it between your fingers—a faint heartbeat as if from a tiny creature far away at the bottom of the sea." I shake my head at how bizarre I know this sounds.

Izzy doesn't seem the least bit surprised, bless her. She rolls with the story. "Did you return the stone, is it still there?" I nod.

Izzy looks down at the doll and gently, respectfully squeezes her chest like she's a paramedic trying to resuscitate a patient. "I feel it! There *is* a pulse, I wasn't imagining it. My gosh . . ." Izzy is rarely flummoxed, but she is now. Her eyes widen into a field of surprise.

"There's more—a scratch at the back of my memory the longer I held the doll. Something Dad told me when we drove to Harvard before sophomore year. He wanted to make sure to tell me about the gift my grandmother gave me and Mama, which I'd left in his care. I couldn't recall everything he said so I recently dug out an old journal from back then, crossing my fingers I'd documented the conversation. And sure enough, I found it! As we drove, Dad asked if I knew the story about the stone inside the Dakhóta doll, why it was so special to Grandma. He always got on with her really well and enjoyed visiting with her. Mama wasn't interested in the past, well, at least not when it came to mention of her father, so she'd gone for a walk as Grandma reminisced. He said she showed him all the contents of the parfleche envelope—that's what it looked like, with wings you could fold over and tuck in to protect the objects. They pored over the items, and she explained what everything was until she got to the doll and her hidden heart. She let him hold Winona and he experienced that odd pulsation. She told Dad that she'd brought her beloved doll with her to Carlisle, but as soon as the kids were all photographed to set up a sickening before-and-after series, their belongings were collected and burned. Including the doll. She was devastated, feeling like her last physical connection to home was torn away."

"Bastards!"

For the first time in an hour Prince chimes in: "Bats! Turds!" We hadn't realized he was listening.

"Sorry."

"It's okay. He's been exposed to a lot worse via my HBO programs. But, yes, such horrific treatment of our children. Soon after that her new friend, the boy she would marry, who became my grandpa, brought her a little stone he said he found in the ashes of the fire that destroyed their things. He said it was all that was left of the doll—her scorched heart."

Izzy gasps, which I find gratifying. Sometimes I wonder if I make too much of these family stories, these mysteries I desperately want to solve. I castigate myself for living too much in the past, worrying at it with my mind.

"The heart was given a new home," Izzy says. She caresses Winona's face, strokes her hair.

"Yes. The other doll was burned, but this one is enough like her that the heart feels comfortable in this skin."

"Does she speak to you, the way Ethel does?"

"She didn't at first, not until I asked. Then she showed me some of her story, like a film I was watching in my head. I think she's the one bringing me dreams. Or nightmares, I should say. Of the three dolls that belonged to us—me, Mama, and Grandma—I think she's the most traumatized."

Izzy and I are so often on the same wavelength, we automatically move to what feels like the next thing to do—no conversation needed. We shelve further conversation about my family matters and return to the living room to give Prince some attention before he explodes. We dance with him, and he settles on the couch with us when we need a break, dragging his SpongeBob SquarePants pillow along with him. Izzy catches me up on her news, all the gossip from Native Academia World, which she's privy to as her self-proclaimed title, "Venus-in-Gemini Social Butterfly," would predict. She attends nearly every conference. She starts yanking on a silver bracelet I gave her years ago—etched with gorgeous Tlingit imagery. A nervous tic.

This gesture signifies more intimate news, so I press her for details. "I met someone." Izzy has no difficulty launching new relationships with fascinating men who always impress me as contenders for something lasting—I've liked all of them. But as soon as a romantic connection grows serious, Izzy becomes restless. I used to think there was an issue here, something that needed healing, but now it seems it's just her seasonal migration pattern and when she moves on, no hearts are broken, and a deep fondness remains. I celebrate her latest adventure and glory in the details. I particularly appreciate the guy's name: Lucifer. Apparently, his father was a classics professor who adored Latin, and Lucifer is a reference to Venus, the morning star, in that language. According to Izzy he's a sweetheart, and he kept the name because he couldn't bear to disappoint his proud father. Privately I'm rooting for Lucifer to be "the one" for Izzy, then scold myself for projecting my own wishes for her onto the situation. She doesn't want a One and Only.

"What about you?" she asks.

I try to duck the question. "I've got my hands full with Prince. I think if I brought a guy home, he'd beak him to death."

"People have asked me about you, expressing interest. Guys. A couple of women, too. You might not realize it, but you're eminently snaggable."

"Ha!" I'm desperately uncomfortable with compliments.

"You agree that your mother was beautiful?"

"Very much! Everyone said so. I always thought she looked like a Dakhóta version of Hedy Lamarr."

"As you get older, you look more and more like her. Don't you see the resemblance?"

"Nope." I'm lying. But that word, "resemblance," makes me nervous. I've spent a lifetime working to come out from under my mother's long shadow. Izzy senses my discomfort and shifts the conversation. Still, her words follow me. The next time I excuse myself and head to the bathroom, I stand for a time peering at my face in the mirror. I see now what I refused to notice before: I've become an older version of my mother. I grew into her once my face thinned and my bone structure became more prominent. Though on me, I don't think the arrangement is beautiful. I'm presentable, possibly attractive, but not the striking vision my mother was as she stunned a room with her bold entrance. And maybe that's the difference, her emphatic presence and energy, her ability to seemingly electrify particles of air. Perhaps I'm too hard on myself, and my mother would have looked just as I do now, if she'd reached my age. I wonder if she would've mourned the loss of her power, or if nothing could dim it?

When I return to Izzy, the two of us lounging so comfortably on the couch, I decide to make up for ducking the conversation about relationships. I take a sip of water and open up to my best friend in the world. "I'm sorry for shutting you down when you brought up the possibility of romance in my life."

Izzy squeezes my shoulder. "No worries. I can be pushy, I know."

I find myself spilling a story I haven't told anyone except my journal. How I used to have relationships, like everyone else, boyfriends who were nice enough, a couple of whom I think I loved. But at the risk of sounding like a trite meme from social media, when you're not yet capable of loving yourself, what you offer someone else is messy: complicated and exhausting, and ultimately not good for anyone involved. Not that the failure of these connections was wholly my fault. Injured people attract others like them, and we hobbled along together the best we could until things would inevitably blow up. That much Izzy already knows; she was a shoulder to cry on in the worst of times. I assumed I'd marry, have a child, who always turned up in my imagination as a girl I'd encourage to be as sensitive as she wished. (Given life's perversity, she'd probably look askance at my vulnerability every bit as much as Mama did.) I wanted that chance to break the chain of passing on harmful inner scripts, the self-loathing that comes from brutally effective colonization. The passage of too much time, where I lived in a cocoon as smothering as a doll's cardboard coffin, removed one of those opportunities; I'm fifty now, long past childbearing. I don't mourn the situation, as some would. No doubt part of me suspects that despite my good intentions (what parents *don't* have good intentions?), I wasn't healed enough to break any chains. To be honest, *I* am my own child, the one I'm still seeking to raise.

I tell Izzy not to give up on me, because I have the feeling my life is just now getting started.

She playfully pumps fists in the air and grins; for a second there the mischievous gleam in her eye reminds me of Prince. "What's the scoop? Who've you got hidden in some love nest?"

I burst out laughing, and Prince flies over, perhaps jealous that someone else has brought me laughter. He settles in my lap, nips my hand with his beak.

"You mean other than *this* monster?" I gently scratch Prince's neck and he surprises me by purring just like a cat.

"Where'd he pick that up?"

"Lord knows. Television? This guy . . . But as for a 'love nest,' not even close. I do have a pretty good track record, though, when it comes to dreams being predictive of coming events."

"I remember. You were concerned about that trip I headed off to in Madrid a few years back. You told me to avoid public transportation at all costs. The day after our arrival: mayhem, horrible blasts that killed so many on the commuter trains. Thank goodness I listened."

"Yes! I'm so glad you did! But this 'talent' scared me as a kid, how all the dark stuff came true: earthquakes, tsunamis, attacks. Felt more like a liability. I wondered what the use was of dreaming terrible things you can't prevent happening. I also wondered why I couldn't summon happier events, and dream of *them*. Remember that line from *The Wizard of Oz*: 'Are you a good witch or a bad witch?' I definitely thought I was some kind of bad witch, and that's why Mama died." This last confession takes me by surprise. There's so much we don't admit to ourselves, in order to keep our little boats afloat.

"Oh, my sister." Izzy would wrap me in another hug if Prince hadn't taken me over. She pats my arm.

"Me and my gloom and doom. But wait, this time I've dreamed something positive! As a matter of fact, I've had a series of dreams where a man stands with his back to me, not being rude, just unaware because we haven't met. I can't see his face, but the sky around him is shimmering and I hear Big Ethel's voice, telling me to keep an eye out for this one. He's the keeper. In the first dream he was far in the distance, but he gets closer each time. Last time he whirled around, like he felt my presence, but I woke up before I could see his face." The little-girl version of me, the one named Sissy who wished to inhabit a dreamy musical of her own making, is suddenly very present. On cue, I begin singing "Something's Coming," from *West Side Story*. Then Prince picks up the tune, and in a few moments, we're blasting poor Izzy with a bizarre, garbled duet, because Prince doesn't know the words, but he refuses to be left out, so he makes up whatever sounds good to him. Izzy doesn't care; she jumps from the couch and dances to our eccentric music, which fills the air with the brightest hope.

Breakfast with Izzy is so relaxing and indulgent—sweet melons and white chocolate macadamia scones—I feel ready to talk about my father, Cornelius Holy Thunder. I set Ethel in a clear space on the table because she's so much a part of the story it would feel strange to leave her out. She slumps against a vase of flowers arranged in a vibrant mix of colors—peonies, tulips, and ranunculus. It almost looks like she's wearing a joyful crown.

"I've been thinking about the issues you raised last night, focusing on my father."

Izzy sips her coffee, offers a nod of encouragement.

"He was the easier parent to love, though I was crazy about them both. Our temperaments were more compatible—both of us really triggered by angry noise and any hint of violence. We wanted peace and quiet, an easy flow. He had a good excuse for being conflict-avoidant, after what he experienced in the Korean War. Not that I know the specifics. I don't think he shared the details with *anyone* once he returned home. As for what he thought of Mama's behavior? If he knew she had problems? Yes, he must have. Why else would he ask if Mama was good to me when he wasn't around?"

"He asked you that? When? What did you say?"

"This was after we left the church, so I was around seven years old. It was one of our rare times alone together—Mama was at some Indian Center meeting or protest rally. She loved being in the thick of the action! I wasn't at all prepared for a question like that. I think it scared me. I lied to him, said, yes, things were just fine, even though Mama was unraveling before my eyes. I couldn't betray her.

"And it wasn't an all-out lie since there were times she could be loving and patient, and so much fun! Plus, I felt guilty."

"What? Why?"

"Mama had it so hard growing up—I heard the awful stories. She was obviously traumatized and even if we could've afforded a therapist, she didn't trust them. Dad brought up the subject a few times, suggesting they get help as a couple. She said they'd be prejudiced at worst and ignorant at best—unable to comprehend where she was coming from as a Native person. There's some truth to that, certainly, especially given the era."

"You're not kidding! Our people have been pathologized from the very beginning. Still are."

"Absolutely. But as for Mama, her bad memories and pain were always evident to me. I think my privileges made her angry sometimes. She used to say she was a jealous-hearted person, but I never thought that could mean she was jealous of me. Now I'm not so sure. I had a father with a steady job, who rarely took a drink, who was loving and dependable. He always showed up for me. I went to good schools where teachers encouraged my talents for the most part. I had regular meals and clean water. I was her baby who hit the jackpot, yet instead of being obviously grateful I was sensitive as hell, which is why she called me a 'hothouse flower.'"

I laugh, but Izzy doesn't. "You could say she was dumping a lot of her anger on you, from earliest babyhood. Think of all you were having to navigate before you could even walk. At least she had a stable mother who was loving and reliable, who did her best to feed the kids. I hope I'm not offending you, but I hate it when people make suffering into a competition: Who had it worse?"

"Not offended. Yep, Mama was all about that kind of competition—even with Dad. But back to him. I think he expended an awful lot of energy trying to keep her happy, because he truly adored her from the first time they met as kids, and because he thought she deserved happiness. We both did. I guess he hoped that if he didn't make any missteps, we'd be okay. But that wasn't enough for Mama. She could get triggered by things that weren't even real. Dad and I weren't perfect, but her rages were never really about us; she was acting out all her pain and disappointments and trauma on us because she knew we loved her, so we were safe targets. It's taken me decades to figure that much out—I'm clearly not the fastest learner when it comes to this stuff."

"None of that, now. I had so many issues staring me straight in the face, yet couldn't identify a single one until I'd had years of counseling. Our blind spots are legion," Izzy adds.

"I guess as long as we eventually figure ourselves out, that's the important thing. Which reminds me, there's another aspect of guilt that kept me from seeking help. Mama used to say that the people she knew who were in therapy were self-absorbed complainers with a poor-me complex. And she never saw any improvement in them after all that analysis and expense. She said navel-gazing was for rich white folks with nothing better to do. The best thing to combat the blues was to get out of yourself and help someone else."

"And how'd that work out for her?" A beat later Izzy gasps, horrified at her snap. She comes up behind me and gives me a hug. "I'm so sorry. I should never have said that. So insensitive! But I was pissed."

I hug her arms, awkwardly, from my seated position, wanting her to feel how much there's no harm done. I trust Izzy's heart is always in the right place. "No worries! Now that I'm older I can see how this was an easy out for Mama, so she didn't have to face herself. While she did many laudable things for the community by throwing herself into activism and meetings and causes, and I've no doubt she sincerely cared about combating injustice, it was also a convenient strategy for someone who wants to run away from themselves. You can't run forever, though. Eventually you're going to pay the price for not attending to your innermost business."

Prince climbs onto my lap and makes himself comfortable. I hand-feed him pieces of melon, distracted by a memory that flies in like cross-breezes bringing the scent of lilacs into the room.

"Wow, just remembered a minor episode I don't think I've thought about since it happened. This showcases how ridiculously nutty I could be as a kid. So, we were all in the car, heading down Lake Shore Drive. I was probably about six. Something triggered Mama, and she started hollering at Dad, shouted that he better pull over by the lake or she was going to jump out of the moving car. Of course he got off at the next exit and pulled into a parking lot near the water. Mama popped out of the car and said she was going to throw herself into the lake because we didn't appreciate her. Here's the embarrassing bit: back then I was petrified of sticker-burr weeds I'd first encountered in North Dakota. I have no idea why. It's like I thought of them as a nefarious alien species, out to get me, possibly even kill me or take me over like the pods in *Invasion of the Body Snatchers*. The way they would stick to my socks and pants, and my fingers when I tried to get them off. Like they were determined to cover me all over, never let me go. So, I saw my parents arguing over by the water's edge, though at least the lake wasn't riled that day—no major wave action. I wanted to join them because sometimes my presence could calm things down and keep a heated moment from blowing up. The problem was the path I would have to take to reach them was a thick carpet of sticker-burr plants! I was beside myself with frustrated panic. I figured out a solution in the end. Always had a book or two with me, and I'd just started reading *The Green Fairy Book* I'd gotten from the library along with *The Red Fairy Book*. Can you believe I remember those titles? I can't recall the plots to my favorite books, but I remember that."

"Trauma hard-wires certain memories," Izzy says softly. She feeds Prince a small piece of macadamia nut that fell off her scone. He's really cleaning up this morning with the treats.

"You're right, that's what I've been told. Trauma can also damage a child's brain development, causing the kinds of memory lapses I've experienced. Anyhow, what I did to reach my folks was use the library books as stepping-stones across the field of stickers. Step on one, retrieve the other and place it ahead of me. Lordy, it took me a good while to reach them and once I did, Mama burst out laughing. She'd flung her purse into the lake, was threatening to follow it and drown herself, Dad trying to hold her back. Then she saw me doing my bizarre little routine with the books. That's what broke the tension. Dad waded out to fetch her purse, then picked me and my books up so I didn't have to navigate the hell-scape again, and Mama laughed the whole time, making fun of what a big baby I was, afraid of everything!"

Izzy is quiet and doesn't seem to find humor in my anecdote. "I know this isn't helpful, or even fair, but sometimes I really don't like your mother."

I start to defend Mama, who isn't here to explain herself. But Izzy continues: "You do realize she was projecting all her own insecurities and disrespect onto you? How do you make fun of a kid who's trying to help, even push through her fears to show up, when you're the drama queen threatening to kill yourself in front of your family? And for no good reason."

A purple tulip petal falls from the floral bouquet onto Ethel's head, like a random thought landed there that she wants me to notice. "I just remembered. This was supposed to be about my father, and I've slipped away from him again. I feel protective of him because it was his love that grounded me the most. Not sure I'd have survived if not for him. It's hard for me to hold him ac-countable in any of what happened because he was the safe parent. I'm always letting him off the hook because he shored me up. But I realize that's not fair to Mama. She had dreams and ambitions she set aside for us, while Dad got to go out in the world and fight for his place in it.

"Still, it's hard not to adore him; he had such sweet ways. It's interesting how he always treated Ethel with great care and respect. He never locked her up in a trunk, that was me! After I left for college, he kept her out on my bed, sitting primly in the middle like she was waiting for me to return."

"Did he try to talk with you about what happened when your mother died?"

"Believe it or not, no. The police questioned me, but no one pushed. I was so young and distraught. Everyone chalked it up to a horrible accident. Dad was wrecked but kept going for my sake. Mama had always been the center of his universe. He said once that if my uncle Luther had survived the war and married her as they planned, he would've remained single the rest of his life. And I suspect that's true."

"Did he ever go out with anyone after she died?"

"He had a 'woman friend' who was chasing him, though he didn't seem to understand that's what was going on. They were part of a bowling league and would go to movies, eat at a restaurant now and again. It never went anywhere because he was oblivious, and she didn't want to hurt their friendship. At least, that's my guess from observing them together. It's like his pilot light blew out once Mama was no longer around to love and mollify. I never realized before how much she'd been his purpose in life. I think he tried hard to keep going, hold out as long as he could, but a month after I graduated from college and he knew I was safely headed to graduate school, he was gone. Still in his fifties and in good physical shape from all the walking he did around the city in pursuit of stories. Just died in his sleep. Izzy, you would've loved him, and he would have thought you were a pistol."

We've bored Prince with all our talk talk talk that has nothing to do with him. He flings SpongeBob SquarePants at us out of nowhere in a flyby tantrum. Bob lands headfirst in the bowl of sliced melons, and as soon as I try to clean him off Prince shrieks like I'm torturing his pal. He swoops in to rescue the damp pillow, carries it off to the snuggle hideaway cave, where Prince coos at his friend to comfort him.

"Is there drama like this every day?" Izzy smiles, shakes her head.

"Oh, he's on good behavior because you're here, and he finds you intimidating. This is nothing!" I tell her about the time our mail carrier phoned the police because when she dropped my mail through the slot in the wall, Prince literally shouted, "Murder," at her—a term he probably picked up from the old *Columbo* reruns I enjoy watching. She could tell the voice belonged to a bird, but I wasn't at home, so no one answered when she rang the bell and called through the slot. She thought maybe the bird was calling for assistance for their person. Everyone got a kick out of that incident, the cops, the mail carrier when she learned everything was fine. Even Prince, who was treated like a minor celebrity and showered with attention. But not me. All of a sudden, I was a little girl again, hearing the crack of a breaking bannister and a stunned, sorrowful cry that seemed its own creature, rushing away from me into a crushing silence that is still with me.

Izzy and I go for a long walk along the Mississippi River, then take afternoon naps. In the evening we watch old film classics I've collected on DVD: *The Women* from 1939, where Norma Shearer and Joan Crawford are vicious rivals, and Rosalind Russell is the comic relief; *Laura* from 1944, featuring the luminous Gene Tierney and Clifton Webb as a brilliant villain; and *The Uninvited*, also from 1944, a movie I revisit every year. Mama introduced me to the film as it was one of her favorites. She would pop corn for us in a heavy saucepan—a rare treat—which made the viewing feel like a truly special event. Ruth Hussey and Ray Milland star as siblings who fall in love with an old house on a cliff overlooking the ocean which just happens to be haunted by the ghosts of two women. Gail Russell plays a girl the spirits fight over—one seeking to harm her, one to protect. When the dangerous ghost appears toward the end, I always made sure Ethel was facing away from the screen, and I'd watch the denouement peeking between the crisscrossed bars of my fingers. Tonight, I don't warn Izzy about the scare ending, and she grabs my arm at the critical moment, giving it a shake.

"Should we pause it?"

"No! This is great!"

Izzy sighs with deep satisfaction when the ghosts have finally been sorted.

"Have you ever seen a spirit?" she asks. I already know she sees them pretty frequently, though thankfully not in my condo.

I would like to tell her about the visit from my ancestor, but something stops me—a feeling that it might be disloyal. I tell her a different story. "Yes, back when I was a kid. I'd just become friends with a little girl named Sara; this was about a year after my mother died. Sara was kind and imaginative—we had so much fun making up skits we performed, just for ourselves. We were doing improv theater though we didn't realize it, of course. We'd laugh and laugh over the scenarios we invented. She would play the fussy person who was easily annoyed, and I'd play the prankster. One evening I was invited for a sleepover at her apartment, and Dad would've been fine with it, but for some reason I didn't want to go over there that night, though I'd stayed with her before and had a grand time. I ate Pop-Tarts for the first time at her place, which I thought were the best thing ever."

"Oh, gag! Though I loved them, too, back then."

"The night of the rejected invitation I slept for a few hours until Ethel's voice woke me. I thought I heard her talking to someone. I sat up in bed and immediately noticed Sara. She was watching me from the foot of the bed, looking desperately sad. 'What are you doing here?' I asked. 'I want to say goodbye. I'll miss you.' She held out her hand and I crawled toward her, but before I reached her, she was gone. I asked Ethel what was going on and she wouldn't answer." I pause, wishing I hadn't launched into this particular memory.

"This sounds like it's going somewhere bad." Izzy's voice is solemn.

"It is. All my father told me was that Sara had passed away. But he was suddenly very careful not to leave the newspapers lying around. I became suspicious. So, I rescued them from the garbage and learned that someone had broken into the back entrance of Sara's place without waking anyone, sneaked past the parents' room, and abducted Sara. She was a beautiful girl, with a sweet, upturned nose and huge brown eyes. I'm sure someone had been stalking the family. They never did find her, and the parents held out hope for years that she'd be returned to them. But secretly I believed that she was dead because of her visit. I never talked to anyone about it except for Ethel. I didn't think Dad could handle something like that."

"My God, that poor family! Wow. And what a burden for you to bear, that hidden knowledge."

Perhaps to lighten the mood Izzy goes on to tell me the story of her friend Patty, who has a squirrel living on her deck she swears is the reincarnation of her dead husband. "Apparently, he's taken over her back deck, treats it like his bachelor pad. Has a variety of lady squirrels who visit. They crack a few nuts, have some sex, and afterward he likes to cuddle." I'm laughing so hard Prince flutters over to check on me, curls in my lap.

"The reason she thinks the squirrel is her husband, Edmo, has to do with the way he lounges so casually, glaring at her through the window, daring her to evict him. And after he has sex, but before the spooning, she says he gives her this cocky, wise-guy grin. She says he 'oozes Edmo.'"

Thanks to my friend, another evening wraps up on a high note of laughter and we head off to bed. For once Prince doesn't complain when I get him settled in his fuzzy hideaway cave. Izzy and I have exhausted him.

When the lights are out and I'm alone in the dark, I send up prayers for my long-ago friend Sara and her family. I wonder if her parents are still alive, waiting for her to return. I can't imagine a worse situation. Then I think of my ancestor, the injured woman, how she preserves her wounds despite the constant pain, so they won't be forgotten. How she haunts herself.

Once Izzy is gone, headed back to Illinois, and I'm left alone with my thoughts and a codependent cockatoo, I feel crushed by the weight of the past, and guilty for speaking so openly about my mother and the ways she could be "difficult." Even that phrasing is a neat little dilution of reality—a conditioned reflex to choose my words carefully out of respect. What I feel guilt for is speaking so openly about the ways my mother could be dangerous. There was a great deal to admire about her strength, intelligence, pursuit of justice for the collective, and her occasional flashes of humor. There's so much that I love about her still. A question I rarely ask myself is: Do I miss my mother? I did as a child. She left a crater in our life so massive that it felt like Dad and I were living within a pinch of floor space surrounding a bottomless pit. But in all honesty, even then there was a pinhole of relief, a tiny opening in the pressure round my chest that released a minuscule yet continuous stream of anxiety from my young body. I couldn't bear that Mama was gone; it was unimaginable. Yet it was also difficult to bear the smothering weight of her.

Something in me does the equivalent of yanking the needle

off a record album. *No!* an inner voice scolds, *you can't continue to obsess about the past.* I spend the day distracting myself with work. I've been asked to blurb a couple of novels I haven't read yet, so I settle in to spend the hours immersed in someone else's story. The day passes in this pleasurable way, and I'm grateful I truly enjoy the book I'm reading; I can enthusiastically endorse it. Evening is soon upon us, and I check on Prince, who has been suspiciously quiet. He's curled up in his purple hideaway cave, sleeping. I think my inner wrangling has worn him out. I decide to follow his example and stretch out on the couch. I know I'm in my head too much, a by-product of anxiety, or maybe its instigator? I tell my mind to rest, just take a break and chill. I'm asleep as soon as I finish the thought.

It's night by the time I wake, though light from a full moon fills the room. I stand up, experiencing the confusion one does when a nap is too long. My legs wobble as they walk me into the bedroom where Ethel sits on the bed, her hands reaching out like she's giving a talk. On impulse I scoop her gently into my arms, the way I would handle a real baby, and carry her into the office. I keep her on my lap as I wake the computer, both of us facing the bright electric window. The cursor pulses on a blank text page in my Word program. My hand settles on her head, lovingly smooths her hair. I think Ethel has more to say that she's kept from me, so I title the new document "Mighty Ethel," and let her take over.

MIGHTY ETHEL

I was born on Jamaica Avenue in Hollis, Queens, inside the Ideal Toy Company's manufacturing plant. I felt like a precious secret because there were television monitors and guards patrolling the complex day and night to protect our design. I don't come from two parents like you, my girl, but it wasn't just machines that made me, put me together, dressed me. There were hands, too, and the hands carried histories, emotions, fears, and dreams. I have so many parents it's hard to know who I am. A doll is everyone's child, even if we're never chosen. But because your spirit called me and your father heard that call, I was born a second time on Blackhawk Street in Chicago. That's when I knew I was part of a family.

Don't go thinking that any of the magic of my aliveness is owing just to me. Maybe I've got something extra in my cells, who knows? All I know for sure is what power we have is given to us by those who love us and depend on us. You helped bring me to life because of how much you needed me. And isn't it good to be needed? I think so!

Maybe because you named me after your godmother, Ethel, I could hear her heart so clear. She saw something powerful and strong in you, which I know you'll scoff at. But she did. You always thought you were the weak one in the family, the one who didn't fight back so your mama had to fight for you, the one who imagined sticker burrs were tiny monsters. But it's a lie. Your mama wants you to know that. I can hear *her* heart, too, since she follows you around, never at rest. She's practically drowned herself in that French perfume, so you'll smell her presence. Even as a chubby-legged toddler you were already the family lion and protector. You kept watch over everyone's emotions, your whole body a fine-tuned instrument, wired to pick up discord and the barometric pressure of impending violence. You did this out of love, not fear. And your mama says she knows how well you kept her in your heart, no matter what she did or said, no matter how much she hurt you and made you doubt yourself. She wishes you didn't pick up that script she had running through her own mind, both of you torturing your-selves for no good reason. She says to change it up because it's nothing she would tell you now.

All the meanness is lies.

Your mother might be softer now, but dang, she's still bossy! She talks and talks at me ever since I woke up again. I'm filtering out the repetitions because I don't have patience for all that noise, but there's something she's saying now that's important. She says if ever you're lost, just return to your Dakhóta name, the one your grandmother gave you. That will tell you who you really are. That's your path. I'm a doll from Queens who won't begin to say this right, but let me try, to stop your mama from her wild gesturing: "Wanáȟča Wašté Wiŋ. Woman Whose Good Works Bring Flowers." That's you. It always was. But you've got to stop hiding from the world, and from your own powerful self. There's work to do!

Before I forget, I'm supposed to share with you what your godmother whispered in your ear right after you were born, still in shock from entering the world. She could *see*, you know, more than most, and she had a special feeling about you. What she said was: "Dear heart, you have pow-erful business here. You can make your story whatever you want."

The night she and your mother got drunk together making rum balls, she said something else that just kind of washed off your mom, who was pretty plastered by that point. Ethel knew you were over there in the corner, listen-ing, so she aimed it at you: "Don't let Time fool you, it's not dead in the ground. Don't ever think it's too late."

I didn't know what she meant until just recently—even a doll keeps learning. I know you'll figure it out yourself, so

I'll just say that the picture in my head is a map of the heart that runs past the body—love spilling on the dead as well as the unborn because once it gets going it can catch up to anyone.

Now I have a confession to make. I sound like I have all the answers when of course, I don't. I'm only passing on messages for the most part. When I was younger, it was different; I thought I could fix everything I didn't like. I was pretty high on myself compared to other dolls I saw who looked like they could only think as far as the sawdust or cotton wool that stuffed them and filled out their bodies. But then you grew up and I thought you didn't need me anymore. I spent so long in that trunk I just shut myself down the way you do your appliances, slept for what felt like a lifetime. Until that rowdy bird yanked me back into the world.

Your ancestors set this chapter in motion—they have a stake in everything that happens to you. I think they tapped me to get the ball rolling because you trusted me once. You're not the only one they're hoping to heal this time around, but a whole chain of you, carrying awful stories that get handed down from one generation to the next; harmful stories and mean thoughts that invade your mind, wreck your health, like you're all drinking poisoned water. So, they joined me up with your mama's doll—the dancing fool (I mean it kindly)—and the elder in our bunch, the one who witnessed massacres and fires. You spent so many years in this country's schools being trained out of what your ancestors would teach you if you knew how to listen, it might be hard for you to believe that a doll can have spirit. A loved doll. We become what we absorb. The three of us are old—a far cry from what we used to be—but our spirits are strong and determined, committed. We want nothing more than to rescue our girls and change your stories.

You're the writer, so you'll understand this better than me, but I learned that we can't heal the story by changing the plot, pretending the awful stuff didn't happen. Tragedy just breaks out somewhere else along the line. The story won't heal until the players do.

Ethel has finished talking and part of me is relieved. She's given me more to chew on than I'd expected. I think of all the ways the process of colonization got into our heads. How educational programs rewired our brains, so the default was to target ourselves, rather than our oppressors. The healing I've worked on for most of my life has, I realize now, been an extraction of the influence and judgments and values that infected generations of our children as much as smallpox and other diseases that indigenous people of this continent weren't prepared for. The more I reject toxic messages, the more room there is for ancestors to return and connect, guide me into a future where everything is once again alive, where everything is once again possible. Which sounds to me very much the goal of the Ghost Dance.

I've often wondered where I fit in our family lineage of leaders and activists. Me, the introvert hermit who lives in her imagination. Suddenly it's plain: I come from generations of storytellers. We are the chroniclers and interpreters, the speakers and translators, the ones who respect the power of language. I belong with them. I have my own words to craft and offer up to the present moment. Words can undo us or restore us to wholeness. I pray that mine will be medicine.

Now I understand my impulse to join an online class of the Dakhóta language. Each word we're taught opens up a world of stories that are very different from the ones I grew up reading. In two generations of one family, we lost the ability to think in words other than English. This loss reshaped our minds. English has its grand beauty that I will always admire, but it also has its agenda. Dakhóta is a missing piece for me in my quest to be whole. Snick. I hear it move into place.

I remember my grandmother, Cora, talking about puzzle pieces in her story, how she yearned to restore her beloved Jack so he could fit into her life. But he was the only one who could solve himself, which he never did. That thought clicks deep inside me and I have the sensation of being pulled in several directions at once, like I'm human taffy. I rise from the chair and stretch, wander into my bedroom. Restless. I begin to understand. Sudden, profound comprehension brings a kind of death—a frightening inner break that feels like falling.

When I'm able to breathe deeply, calmly, I look toward the window—my face drawn to the magnificent brightness of a supermoon, fully flowered and bursting with seeds of apricot light as it approaches perigee. This remarkable light from a being so far away, yet close enough to watch me stand in its beam, gives me the courage to open more fully than ever before. How can I be anything but rigorously honest with myself tonight, rooted by the back window of my bedroom, staring into the face of a moon that looks close enough to swallow me whole? I've spent decades attempting to heal what was broken in my life the day my mother died, which I used to think stood alone as an awful event beyond my comprehension, but now understand connects to a chain of misery and betrayal that came before. Though I tried a variety of methods and practices that no doubt helped me make some progress throughout the years, it feels like the warm light of this lush full moon, nourishing as honey, is the ultimate catalyst for transformation. *Mama's in that light,* I think, and the words bring a physical sensation, like I'm no longer a woman but a waterfall—love and forgiveness wash through me in a cleansing storm. I step out of my skin. Grief, anger, confusion, anxiety, shame, guilt—all of it sloughs off. There's someone else inside when I let that cover go.

I begin shaking my arms and legs in an exercise I learned in acting class back in high school, to accelerate the flinging away of everything that's weighed me down. I must look like a drenched dog shaking herself dry. No, this isn't wise—I'll only spatter the walls with toxic energetic sludge. I rush to the front of the apartment, stumble down a flight of stairs, burst through the main door so I can stand directly before the moon with no barrier between us. Her intense, devoted light pulls me straighter; I am infinitely taller tonight. I rub my neck, which has bothered me for decades; I'm so used to an aching pressure that bows me down. Now there is no tension or weight, not a single throb of pain. Maybe I was carrying more than shame and guilt, maybe it was Mama herself seated on my shoulders like we were about to play a game of chicken.

At this point, I am so intoxicated with how gloriously weightless I feel, unburdened enough to float, I don't care if anyone sees me here in the driveway of Crocus Hill, arms lifted as if I'm about to hug the moon. The night air smells faintly of lilacs from the tall bushes next door, which have just begun to bloom, laced with a hint of Chanel No. 5. I keep staring at the moon, hoping that what's happening to me this night is real and not just a beautiful dream. The next thing I know, a being slides away from me as if I've lost my shadow. The shade becomes corporeal, pinches my left arm—it's Mama, her hair in a flip that was popular back when I was a kid.

"I'm real," she says with a mischievous smile. And she adds my chosen name, Jesse. I observe her more peacefully than I'd expect, but I'm still so overwhelmed with the old love from childhood,

I have to look away. Mama and I brush shoulders as we stand together, staring at the soft, healing light. I feel another presence detach from me, and glide to my right. I sense the warmth of her before I turn and see my khúŋši, Cora. Her hair is long again, not the thin fluff I remember; she wears it in silver braids that glimmer in the light of the moon. She pats my shoulder the way you do when someone's done a good job, made you proud. Tears must be running down my face because I taste them. This remarkable moment fills me with gratitude. All astonishment is gone, because of course these women are here, they are always here. It isn't their fault if I didn't see them. As soon as I complete that thought, another part of me steps forward. It takes a long beat to recognize her as the visitor from my vision—for she is whole and beautiful, her flesh restored to what it was before the time of massacres. She's wearing a dark blue trade cloth dress decorated with elk teeth. My ancestor runs her thumb along my wrist in a simple gesture— intimate grace. I realize that of the four of us, I'm not the youngest, strange as that seems, having outlived my mother and this relative.

"Wačíŋyephiča Wiŋ," she tells me her name. Trusted Woman.

These women I come from, who also come from me, form a chain of clasped hands. I am held between my mother and grandmother, feel the soft pressure of their palms. Together we send light back to the moon—our distant relation who has wiped our tears. In the past my reason would have failed me, this intense experience sending me into denial or panic. But I'm healthier now, grounded. The four of us are a grove of trees. Our number feels significant, not arbitrary; I think of the power and stability of the four directions, four legs of a table, how we pin the world down from our different corners. It took all of us to make it here.

We thought we were victims, survivors, never knowing how strong we truly are. The supermoon is close enough to be heard:

"Pick up your power again and move forward in a good way." I didn't know light could speak.

I trust we all heard the message because suddenly I'm alone—my mother and ancestors have quietly moved on in a humble, heart-catching moment. No fuss for those who desire rest. I am neither relieved nor bereft. No matter where I go in what remains of my life, I'll carry them with me.

I conclude the book-length collection of stories I've produced in what feels like days, with a brief statement titled "Wisdom of the Dolls." Part of me believes this book has indeed come from my Ethel, and a Shirley Temple doll named Mae, and the ghost of a Dakhóta doll named Winona who left nothing behind but her loyal heart. Another part of me thinks it's my own creativity, forever mysterious and impossible to summon or control. Either way, I offered myself up to the process and typed what was given. The dolls have spoken. They tell me they did their best to heal the ones they love. But always they failed because even the medicine of love can't change what is broken. It's up to us to transform the story we're living. Though Ethel reminds me that an individual can't overturn a system all on her own, she must find allies to address the part prejudice plays in the undoing of our world.

The book is finished. I give the dolls the last word:

This narrative is a small branch of Story. We did the best we could with all we didn't know. We thought we were Things. We were always more than Things. Together, we have lived through many branches of Story. We did what we could to help. We all want happy endings. We are nudging everyone closer to Love. But when we fail, Time convinces us to try again. We flow with it in every direction. For inanimate beings stuffed with nothing but air or whatever came to hand, we know a lot about persistence and Love. In the end that's what we're really made of: Love Love Love Love Love.

We've learned that healing the present doesn't only clear waters flowing into the future, recovery also flows backward and alleviates the suffering of ancestors. So they can set down their tears and dark memories, their guilt and shame, their vengeance. And because Time is our relative, a flexible being that moves through every thought and memory, branching into a million rivers of possibility, healing even one of its streams will eventually heal the world.

Wrecked children inherit the power of the destroyed—a formidable energy. They create the ferocious allies they need either to survive or let go and embrace destruction. Mended children carry stronger medicine. Their magic unites the flow of Time with Love, our oldest waters. And so they bring us Home.

The End

Author's Note

This novel came as a wonderful surprise. I'd been working on another novel for a few years, then broke my arm near the shoulder and was recuperating when the impulse to change direction suddenly hit. Once I could type with both hands again, I launched into *A Council of Dolls,* completing it at the end of May 2021. While this book is a work of fiction and its characters a product of my imagination, some of the experiences depicted in these pages are inspired by stories my mother shared with me about what it was like growing up on the Standing Rock Sioux Reservation from the late 1880s (her mother's era) through the 1930s (the era of her own childhood). I hewed as closely as I could to the truth of these experiences in terms of historical and cultural detail, while allowing myself the latitude of fiction. For the sake of preserving authenticity when it comes to the historical record, I'd like to note choices I made where that record is unclear or where I allowed fiction to create its own design.

I was raised to identify first and foremost as a member of the Iháŋkthuŋwaŋna Dakhóta nation, though in later years learned our family is also Húŋkpapȟa Lakȟóta. The vocabulary my mother uses that comes from our original language reflects this dual heritage—including both Dakhóta and Lakȟóta terms. Therefore, I chose to use words from both dialects throughout the text to preserve this sense of a lived reality. My mother and her siblings grew up across the road from Sitting Bull's original grave and considered him their protector and confidante, always referring to him as "Lalá," a shortened version of the Lakȟóta word for grandfather: thuŋkášila. I found it impossible to change that detail though it would have been easier to use a single dialect.

From earliest memory I've been familiar with the history of the devastating Indian boarding school experience. Both grandparents on my mother's side of the family attended the Carlisle Indian Industrial School. While my grandmother was cognizant of the destructive nature of that educational system, she thrived during her years there, and decades after graduating continued to correspond with the family she lived with as part of the school's Outing Program. My grandfather's experience was wholly different—his time there was a catastrophic period, ruinous to his physical and emotional health. My depiction of the fictional characters' experiences at Carlisle is an attempt to reflect both truths.

I did extensive research on the history of the school in order to learn authentic details of student life. While instances of corporal punishment at Carlisle and the burning of student belongings soon after arrival are anecdotal rather than documented in the historical record, I chose to honor the testimony of those former students who claimed such experiences. No doubt school policies changed over time, accounting for different practices in the treatment of students across different eras. I took one liberty when it came to timing: a fictional character mentions the Carlisle football team's win over the Harvard Crimson in a match. This famous victory occured in 1911, a few years later than in the novel.

My mother also attended Indian boarding schools in her childhood; one was Catholic, located in South Dakota (which might have been Saint Joseph's), and the other was the Bismarck Indian School in North Dakota. I chose to combine the two institutions in the novel, placing the Catholic school in the Bismarck area.

For further reading on the Indian boarding school experience in this country, I recommend beginning with these books—*Boarding School Seasons: American Indian Families, 1900–1940*, by Brenda J. Child (University of Nebraska Press), and *Stringing Rosaries: The History, the Unforgivable, and the Healing of Northern Plains American Indian Boarding School Survivors*, by Denise K. Lajimodiere (North Dakota State University Press).

In the third section of the novel the narrator mentions that she was born near the Cannonball River in the vicinity of a massive burr oak known as the "Council Tree." In my original draft of the book the narrator was born near Battle Creek in what would become the state of South Dakota, where the true Council Oak is found. I transplanted the tree and moved it farther north for the sake of my story.

My grandmother was a month shy of three years old when our revered leader, Sitting Bull, was killed. Her father brought her to town with him when he went to investigate rumors of the terrible event. Some of the details surrounding Sitting Bull's death come from her memories of that day, but I also found a compelling description of the event in the text *We Are a People in This World*, authored by Conger Beasley, Jr. (University of Arkansas Press). Other elements of this historical moment came via the testimony of Little Soldier, a close friend of my family—details he shared with them, which were passed down to me. He is the only person in the novel who is not fictional. His warmly protective presence in the lives of my grandmother and her children made him a relative, someone my mother always refers to as "Grandpa Little Soldier." I wish to honor his generosity to our family by retaining his identity in the novel.

Finally, I wish to credit my cousin, tom kunesh, for unearthing an article written about my great-grandmother, Nellie Gates (daughter of Mahtó Núŋpa). The piece was published in *The Cambridge Chronicle* in 1899, nearly twenty years after the events they cover in a horrifically disrespectful manner, which includes the death of my great-great-grandfather. I refer to the article in the novel, sharing its actual title: "The Relapse of an Indian Princess Into Barbarity." Nellie Gates was a renowned beadwork artist, whose work is still honored for its beauty and power. My mother carries fond memories of her khúŋši's humility, kindness, and dignity, which demolish the racist caricature portrayed in the newspaper. Such outrageously prejudiced depictions of my ancestors and our people are one reason I became a writer. From childhood I felt an urgent need to speak my truth, which was long suppressed. Writing this book was a healing endeavor. May it support the healing of others.

Acknowledgments

I'm deeply grateful to ancestors whose presence and guidance I felt supporting me as I wrote this novel. I thank my mother, Susan Kelly Power, for proudly and generously sharing our history with me from earliest memory, and my father, Carleton Gilmore Power, for a foundation of love. I was fortunate to have parents with a profound reverence for literature, who encouraged my reading and writing.

Heartfelt gratitude goes to the most wonderful literary agent an author could hope for, Rachel Letofsky, and the brilliantly insightful editor Rachel Kahan, who knew what questions to ask to help me deepen my novel. I am so fortunate to work with you both, as well as your teams at Cooke McDermid and HarperCollins.

I'm grateful to the editorial staff of *The Missouri Review* for selecting my short story, "Naming Ceremony," as a runner-up in their 2020 Jeffrey E. Smith Prize in fiction, and for publishing the piece in their fine journal. I had no idea that early nod would lead to the development of a novel.

I offer deep appreciation to the many friends and family members who were early readers of this novel—your encouragement meant the world to me! In particular I'd like to acknowledge those who offered detailed notes and feedback: Dr. P. Jane Hafen, Barbara Kriete Landis, Maureen Aitken, and Louise LeBourgeois. Thank you for your warm support! And a special note of thanks to dear Alyssa Haywoode for mentioning that my short story, "Naming Ceremony," could become a novel.

I am forever indebted to the dear ones whose presence has been sustaining, invigorating. Thank you for being there in difficult, as well as joyful, times: LeAnne Howe, Nancy Linnerooth, Douglas & Jeanann Power, Marjorie Mbilinyi, Paula Anderson, Andrea Carlson, Irene Connelly, Elizabeth Fletcher, Elizabeth Diamond Gabriel, Susan Gooding, Tasha Harmon, and Shannon Scott.

During rough periods, especially these challenging years of the current pandemic, I was incredibly fortunate to have family members and friends step forward however they could assist, even sending supplies when I broke my arm. I offer warm appreciation for the generous help of Susan & Michael Howe, Annette D'Armata & Lourdes Perez, Elizabeth Jarret Andrew, Lisa Brooks, Sandy Brown, Ted Cushman, Gaylen Ducker, Kelly Dwyer, Louise Edington, Robert Enaudi, Heid E. Erdrich & John Burke, Kelli Jo Ford, Timothy Fox, James Johnson, Kathryn Ketrenos, Lou Kohlman, Kathryn Kysar, Cheri LeBeau, Mimi Hero & John LeBourgeois, Sheila O'Connor, Vivian Faith Prescott, Brad Pritchett, Siobhan Wolf Shaffer, Karen Straus, Cara Szeghy, and Arthur Tulee.

My mother, Maȟpíya Boǧá Wiŋ, raised me to know and honor the rich histories of our Iháŋktȟuŋwaŋna Dakhóta and Húŋkpapȟa Lakȟóta ancestry. I'm so thankful that our culture has survived, despite significant efforts to destroy it. I extend gratitude to all those working to preserve our languages, cultural heritage, history, and spiritual beliefs.

A special thank-you to cousins tom kunesh and Sallie M. Thurman, for sharing their research on our family so generously, and for others who contribute photographs, documents, and stories in the online community group Standing Rock Genealogy. I'm greatly indebted to Dawí (Huhá Máza) for invaluable help editing the Dakhóta and Lakȟóta language used in the book since I previously spelled these terms haphazardly, phonetically, rather than adhering to a single orthography. Any mistakes still found in the text are my own. I'm also deeply thankful for the more nuanced definitions he provided, which add layers to my understanding of our powerful language.

About the Author

MONA SUSAN POWER is the author of four books of fiction, including *The Grass Dancer*, which was awarded a PEN/Hemingway Prize. She's a graduate of Harvard Law School and the Iowa Writers' Workshop, and the recipient of an Iowa Arts Fellowship, James Michener Fellowship, Radcliffe Bunting Institute Fellowship, Princeton Hodder Fellowship, USA Artists Fellowship, McKnight Fellowship, and Native Arts & Cultures Foundation Fellowship. Her work has appeared in several publications including *The Best American Short Stories*, *The Atlantic Monthly*, *Granta*, *The Paris Review*, and *Ploughshares*. She's an enrolled member of the Standing Rock Sioux tribe (Iháŋktȟuŋwaŋna Dakhóta), and was born and raised in Chicago. She currently lives in Minnesota.